Praise for *Scarred* and for Jon Richter's other work

A bizarre, acid-soaked odyssey across a hostile Wonderland. Half heroic dark fantasy, half spiritual awakening, *Scarred* is Richter at the height of his considerable powers—and living, bleeding proof that he's a talent to watch no matter what genre he tackles next.

Jacob Mohr, author of *Nightfall* and *Other Dangers*

Loved it, a futuristic dystopian *Wizard of Oz!* Richter is relentlessly inventive.

Valerie Keogh, bestselling thriller writer

Praise for Richter's Other Titles

Richter blends a gritty detective procedural and possible future technology with a finesse equal to that of Charles Stross.

Don Vicha, review of *Auxiliary*, Booklist Online

My number one book for 2020, *Rabbit Hole* by Jon Richter. Loved this book, go and buy it!

Anita Waller, international bestselling author

You like your cyberpunk with a little eldritch Lovecraftian edge? Check out *The Hum* by Jon Richter.

Bruce Bethke, godfather of the cyberpunk genre

T0243922

A very clever and timely structure to this book, given the explosion of podcasts and their focus on reporting on mysteries, which made the read that much more enjoyable for me. It just drew me in immediately. I like a book where I don't know what's going to happen next *and* where I actually care what happens next (too often it's one or the other, and far more often than one would want, it's neither), and *Rabbit Hole* achieved that completely. A quick and very enjoyable read.

Michael Cordell, bestselling author of *Contempt*

A wonderfully creepy sci-fi novel born out of Covid. *The Warden* reminded me of the *X-Files* episode "Ghost in the Machine", if it had been written by J.G. Ballard. Entertaining and thought-provoking in equal measure!

Alan Gorevan, author

Scarred

A Novel

Scarred

A Novel

Jon Richter

ROUNDFIRE
BOOKS

London, UK
Washington, DC, USA

CollectiveInk

First published by Roundfire Books, 2024
Roundfire Books is an imprint of Collective Ink Ltd.,
Unit 11, Shepperton House, 89 Shepperton Road, London, N1 3DF
office@collectiveinkbooks.com
www.collectiveinkbooks.com
www.roundfire-books.com

For distributor details and how to order please visit the 'Ordering' section on our website.

ISBN: 978 1 80341 537 6
978 1 80341 558 1 (ebook)
Library of Congress Control Number: 2023936438

A CIP catalogue record for this book is available from the British Library.

Design: Lapiz Digital Services

UK: Printed and bound by CPI Group (UK) Ltd, Croydon, CR0 4YY
US: Printed and bound by Thomson-Shore, 7300 West Joy Road, Dexter, MI 48130

We operate a distinctive and ethical publishing philosophy in all areas of our business, from our global network of authors to production and worldwide distribution.

This book is for my mum, who made sure my imagination and I were kept well nourished!

Acknowledgements

This book would not exist without the support of my girlfriend, Shuo, who remains endlessly patient through all the ups and downs of a weird writer's life.

I am also hugely grateful to the people at Roundfire for taking a chance on this strange, dark story, and to RoseWolf Design for designing the fantastic image upon which the cover is based.

One

The man stumbled towards the castle, emerging from the fog like something escaping from a dream. The toll of the warning bell, and the shrieks of the people gathered around her on the battlements, jarred horribly in her ears. Freya did not scream, but even she shrunk back from the edge as the man approached, for the plague was clearly rampant within him.

The body beneath his ragged vestments was an emaciated ruin, his long hair and beard streaked with tell-tale grey. The skin of his face was cracked and papery, as though at any moment it might split apart to reveal the grinning horror beneath. When he finally sank to his knees at the foot of the Enclave's huge gates, he scarcely seemed to possess the strength to raise his sapling-thin arms in supplication. The look in his sunken eyes was more one of resignation than of hope.

He sat like that for perhaps an entire minute, his breath misting in the chill air, before the archer's arrow caught him in the throat. A great cheer went up, drowning out the stranger's soft gurgle as he sagged sideways to the ground. Freya watched as his corrupted blood began to gush out of this new orifice, as though the sickness was rushing to escape its damaged vessel.

"Don't worry, Freya," said Maxwell, who stood close beside her, a relieved look on his face. "We won't have to look at it for long. The angels will soon take that rancid heap away."

"How do you know?" she replied, her eyes still fixed on the transgressor's corpse (was it a corpse, yet? There was a precise moment, she supposed, a specific instant when enough blood had leaked out onto the dusty ground, when the man would cease to be a person, and become instead a sack of meat and bones.)

"Because they always do."

The bell ceased to chime, and after a while everyone drifted back to their usual duties; even Freya, whose intrigue made her loiter long enough to receive a scolding when she returned to the kitchens.

***

The angels did not come the next day. Freya was able to sneak away from her duties for long enough to stand atop the castle walls once again, as she often liked to do, staring out towards the horizon to try to catch a glimpse of the distant Monoliths that were sometimes visible when the mist was thinner than usual. She often dreamed about those glittering, unfathomable structures, imagining herself striking out towards them, plague be damned.

That day, the Monoliths could not be seen through the swirling fog, so instead she stared down at the dead man until the guard's patience wore thin and he told her to get lost. Her mind continued to tug insistently at the same thread: what if the angels never came, and the cadaver just stayed there? Maxwell had told her that bodies left in that state started to decay, rotting like bad food.

She had felt sure this was something she'd once known but, like so much of her memory, it felt diluted, dissolved into mush inside her head. Fleeting glimpses still came to her: the spectres of other places, other people. Like Raoul, her husband, who had abandoned her to disappear into the Wastes countless days ago. Had he, too, appeared at some other castle, ravaged by plague and mercilessly shot down by the bowmen at the gates? They had heard nothing from Asyla — the neighbouring town whose twisted cathedral spire jutted upwards into the skyline like a crooked finger — for longer than she could remember. Still, as Maxwell loved to tell her, it was best not to worry about such things.

2

Besides, if the angels did not come, running out of food would be a far bigger concern than the fate of the dead man beyond the castle walls.

So it was with a strange mix of relief and disappointment that, at first light on the following day, she heard the bell ringing once again, and hurried outside to watch the familiar phalanx approaching, their armour sparkling in the light of the rising sun.

They were said to come from the Monoliths, but Freya could make no sense of this, as those inscrutable edifices seemed impossibly far away — but then again, the angels were magical creatures, and travelling at such speed might be as easy for them as it was for her to stroll across the castle's main courtyard. Yet their pace as they drew near seemed almost sedate, walking ponderously in their usual inverted arrowhead formation, as though they had an endless supply of time.

Which, of course, they did.

She and Maxwell would argue about whether it was the same quintet each time. Freya was convinced that the dents and scratches that marred the thick plates of their armour appeared in different places, suggesting a legion of the white-clad golems dwelling somewhere beyond the fog. Maxwell disagreed, preferring to think of them as five dedicated protectors, steadfastly devoted to the Enclave's defence. He had even named them, but refused to divulge the monikers to her.

"You'll only mock me," he said, and she laughed and agreed.

As the mysterious beings drew near and she beheld their shimmering apparel, she tried to compare the patterns of cracks and markings to those of their most recent visitors; but once again her memory proved too clouded. She wondered at the damage the creatures had sustained, at the madness that must surely possess anyone who tried to attack such deities. The angels carried no visible weapons and were barely taller than a man; but the deep, rhythmic clanking as they advanced towards the gates suggested that their suits were impossibly heavy, that whatever forms were hidden beneath the bone-coloured plates and smiling, identical face masks were mighty beyond belief.

Or perhaps, as some believed, there was nothing under the armour at all. She gazed down upon the Enclave's mysterious benefactors, feeling a chill rattle her bones, and hoped they couldn't sense her unease.

The angels stopped when they reached the man's body. The rearmost of the group had, as always, dragged an enormous cart across the dirt, the two-wheeled chariot crafted from the same ivory-hued material as their own apparel; although it must have been immensely cumbersome, the creature held it as though it weighed nothing at all. The other four turned and moved towards the wagon, one of them peeling back the layer of silvery fabric that covered its precious cargo. Carefully and patiently, the five of them removed a series of foil-wrapped packages and placed them on the ground, stacking the gifts in neat, gleaming piles.

Many people had gathered on the ramparts once again and Freya heard a few murmurs of relief and gratitude, as though others had perhaps shared her foolish concern that the angels would forsake them. Someone shouted "praise the angels," and others reciprocated, and before long the voices of the Enclave were joined in joyful exultation of these strange heralds, these avatars of God.

When all the parcels had been removed, one of the creatures finally turned its attention to the man's body, scooping the broken thing from the ground with one hand as though it was a handful of twigs. Gently, the corpse was lowered into the cart, and Freya was struck by the dignity afforded to the pitiful, arrow-skewered husk as the covering was drawn over its sightless eyes, its withered limbs, its disease-cracked skin. The angel's gaze seemed to linger over the forlorn bundle for a moment, the smile etched permanently on its masked helm seeming sympathetic, or perhaps oddly remorseful.

Without a glance towards the assembled castle-dwellers that still sung their praises from the ramparts, the five silent sentinels turned, hauling their sad cargo back into the mist. Despite their bulk, they left no footprints, although whether that was because of the firmness of the ground or some sort of celestial weightlessness, Freya did not know.

As a mark of respect — or possibly fear, thought Freya — the gates were never opened while the angels went about their business. Only when their bewildering forms were lost from sight, subsumed into the fog that had seemingly spawned them, did a cacophonous grinding sound signal that the Enclave's knights were setting out to recover the deposited bounty.

Knights indeed, she thought wryly. The conceited thugs in their ramshackle chainmail were less than shadows of the towering warriors she had just observed. She watched as the oafish braggarts scurried from the gates like...

...another fragment of memory, of scuttling cowardly creatures, once abundant but now lost to that same mist, to the void that seemed to close in around her, around all of them, numbing them with interminable repetition, with endless days and nights, days and nights, days and nights...

They would be drinking in the great Hall later, boasting about half-remembered conquests and alleged feats of bravery in defence of their great, white fortress. A castle whose walls had never been breached, whose stone was the same colour as the angels that attended it, suggesting divine origins and blessed sanctuary for all who dwelt within.

Yet she knew that cracks were appearing, even if it was blasphemy to speak of them. Violence in the streets, the peasants unhappy with the distribution of the angels' gifts. A shaven-headed man accused of removing his locks to disguise his grey hair, executed and burnt as a plague-carrier without so much as a trial. Another suicide not long ago, this one not daring to brave the Wastes but instead hanging herself within her own quarters.

Still, she thought as she watched the knights loading the precious harvest into their hand-carts, their faces shielded from the plague's vapours by crude cloth masks, *there was more food to go around if there were fewer people left.*

436 people, to be precise.

***

"Look at those gluttons," whispered Maxwell as they took a moment's respite behind one of the Hall's stout pillars. The column stretched above them to where it met the great domed ceiling arching across the cavernous chamber; an impossible mass of sculpted stone. "I hope there's some meat left over for us at the end. Still, praise the angels and all that."

"Where does it come from, do you think? Do the angels make it all? Might it run out?" *Meat, bread, fruit ...* all were words she had known forever, words she felt had perhaps once held meaning, beyond describing these magical gifts brought by God's inscrutable messengers.

"Your questions will get you into trouble," Maxwell admonished. "Our lot is not to ponder such things. It is merely to serve, and to persist. Such curiosity is what drives people out into the Wastes!"

"You mean ... like Raoul?" she replied. Maxwell frowned, not angrily, but as though he didn't remember who she was talking about. Before she could probe any further another summons rang out, and she rushed to fill the hoisted flagon with more of the angels' wine.

Hours later, the feast was still in full swing, the Kitchenmaster shrieking in desperation when she appeared for a fourth time to request yet more fare.

"These Nobles will have gobbled the angels' riches in a single night!" he ranted as he turned to toss more meat onto the blazing grill. The air down in Egbert's kingdom was hot and oppressive, his bulky frame glistening with sweat beneath his apron. "Don't let me catch you nibbling any," he yelled over his shoulder, and she remembered a time when she had done exactly that, a time when the cantankerous bastard had cracked a heavy rolling pin across her fingers and made her cry out in pain and surprise. Still, she would rather face the temper of the beleaguered chef than the appetites of the drunken knights and other Nobles, who had started to grab and paw at her each time she passed them, or make cruel remarks about her face.

As Maxwell would doubtless remind her, such was the lot of an Unskilled. If your abilities at fighting, cooking, governing, singing, fucking, or any of the other professions that helped life to function inside the Enclave's walls were not deemed sufficiently exceptional, servitude was your allotted role. *Unless of course,* she thought as she glanced enviously at the giggling face of Letitia, who had scrubbed the castle floors alongside her for so long, *you could convince one of the Nobles to marry you.*

She thought again of Raoul, angry that his face would not crystallise in her mind, its image shifting and fragmenting every time she tried to visualise it. He had been an Archivist working for Lord and Recordmaster Gwillym, and as such would have been granted a seat amongst the Lower Nobles. That meant she must have sat alongside him, enjoying such lavish banquets as this, laughing and cavorting while she glugged the angels' nectar. She looked down at the tattered rags she wore, so ancient and stained that their original colour was long forgotten. Why couldn't she recall her former finery? Such memories would give her succour at the very least, would help to distract her from this life of silent obedience.

"Wench! Don't stand there dawdling when my tankard is empty!" yelled Bernard, one of the knights. His height and broad

frame was the envy of his peers, and when he was drunk —
as he was now, swaying as he rose from his seat, knocking his
chair to the ground behind him — he would inevitably cause
trouble, fighting with other knights or beating servants for the
smallest imagined slight. "Now then," he slurred as she hurried
over to top up his vessel. "What's a gormless bitch like you
doing pouring my drinks? They should keep monsters like you
downstairs, out of sight."

Hearty laughter erupted around the table. Freya didn't know
who she hated more: those who found genuine humour in her
disfigurement, or those that simply laughed out of cowardice.
Her head bowed, she poured Bernard's wine, and turned hastily
towards the sanctuary of one of the Hall's dark corners. But she
felt the knight's hand clamp roughly on her shoulder, hauling
her around to face him once again.

"Don't turn your back on me, *monster*," he hissed, his liquor-
infused breath hot and foul in her nostrils. The flickering
torchlight gave a red tinge to his face, making him seem like
something demonic. "You'll leave when I'm finished with
you."

"Give her a break, Bernard," said one of the other knights
in a good-natured tone. "Come on, I'm up for another round of
dice."

The larger man rounded menacingly on his comrade. "If I
want your opinion, little Thomas, I'll ask you for it," he said
in a voice like rumbling thunder, his hand shifting a single,
suggestive inch towards the hilt of the sword slung across his
back. Thomas held up his hands, becoming suddenly fascinated
by the patterns in the wood of the table.

"Now then," Bernard snarled, returning his venomous gaze
to Freya. "Where were we? Oh yes … you were going to tell us
all how your face got split in half."

The scar ran from her chin to her forehead, bisecting her lips
and one of her eyes along its sinuous route. Yet despite its serious

appearance, it didn't cause her any problems with speech or vision, and on some days she forgot about it altogether.

When she was permitted to.

"I..." she began, her breath coming in frightened gasps. She could see Maxwell in the corner, watching with mounting horror in his face. "I don't..."

"Leave her be, Sir Bernard," intoned a deep, commanding voice. A few tables away, a man rose from his seat; he was slender but tall, and authority seemed to radiate from him, a silence falling upon the surrounding revellers as he spoke. His eyes were a piercing, vibrant blue, as though lightning danced around the rim of his pupils. They matched the colour of the gemstone he wore around his neck, the only embellishment to his plain grey robes. "She has suffered enough," he added gravely.

Bernard scowled and released his crushing grip on her collarbone. "I just asked her a question, Lord Gwillym," the knight said testily. "I merely wanted to know the story behind her hideous deformity."

The words stung her and she felt hot tears jab the backs of her eyes, angry at herself for being so weak. All around the Hall, stares were turning towards them; she fixed her gaze on the black and white pattern on the floor, wishing that the dark tiles would expand to engulf the white, forming a great abyss to swallow her up.

"Her husband did it, you idiot," Gwillym retorted. "He mutilated himself, then attacked this poor wretch, and departed for the Wastes the very same night. Don't you remember Archivist Raoul, once my most apt recordkeeper?" The Lord glanced despairingly around the room. "Doesn't anyone remember *anything* anymore?"

Freya could feel her heart beating faster and faster, like something trapped in her ribcage that was scrabbling to burst out. It was all she could do not to sink to her knees and begin to sob.

"Lord Gwillym, please sir, Bernard didn't mean any harm. He's just had a bit too much to drink, haven't you, big man?" Sir Thomas beamed warmly at the Lord, who sighed despondently, and sank back into his seat like a man defeated.

Freya stood there, trembling, until Maxwell sidled over to lead her quietly away. She didn't know what made her more distraught: the tale that Master Gwillym had recounted about her, or the fact that she remembered none of its events at all.

***

The night had devoured the day by the time the last revellers had tottered off to their beds, the first amber flickers of dawn's inevitable counterattack beginning to gather on the horizon. But there would be no sleep yet for Freya, nor for Maxwell and the other Unskilled; not until every last plate was cleared away and every surface polished to a lustrous shine. The servants were permitted to eat their fill from the remnants of the banquet, but Freya was so exhausted that her appetite had evaporated completely, and she didn't touch a single morsel. She felt weak, scoured raw, vulnerable, as she watched the other Unskilled feasting hungrily, two dozen men and women shovelling food into their mouths as greedily as the beasts in the stories she half-remembered.

There was so little left by the end, the waste could fit into a single wooden pail.

"I'll take it," she volunteered, knowing that the descent to the Pit was an unpopular chore, and wanting any excuse to get away from her colleagues.

"I'll come with you," offered Maxwell.

"No you won't," grunted Oswald, the Chief Hand. His seniority didn't grant him Lower Noble status, but there were some privileges, foremost amongst which was the ability to delegate the bulk of the labour to his downtrodden crew.

"It only needs one pair of hands. You can stay here and start washing the cutlery."

"It's okay, Max," said Freya, forcing a smile as she hoisted the bucket of bones, rinds, and other assorted gristle. She turned and left the Hall as quickly as she could, the echoes of heartless words resounding in her ears.

The Enclave's interior was a maze of passageways and spiral staircases, but Freya had committed her well-trodden routes to memory so that she easily navigated the stone corridors, barely needing the dull glow of the lantern she had collected from the servant's quarters. Still, there were plenty of areas of the castle she had never visited, and she liked nothing more than when her duties took her to some unfamiliar room or quiet, forgotten corner. She explored the stronghold whenever she could, but the restrictions placed upon her as an Unskilled — as well as her endlessly demanding work schedule — meant that such frivolous excursions were extremely rare.

She had made this particular journey countless times, and the Pit had long since lost the horror it seemed to incite in her fellow servants. If anything, she found the area fascinating, and wondered as she descended the long staircase from the kitchens whether any of Nobles even knew it was here: a forgotten, underground realm, buried beneath an aeon of muck and detritus. Only the Unskilled had reason to tread these treacherous, well-worn steps, made uneven and slippery over time, into the castle's reeking bowels. The metaphor lingered with her for a while; of the Enclave as some colossal creature, its denizens no more than bacteria helping to break down the food that flowed into its monstrous intestines and away to who knew where perhaps out into the distant, treacly waters of the sea that bordered the castle's rear, where the land plunged away in jagged white cliffs.

At its end, the narrow staircase opened into a vast, circular chamber. Its diameter was even larger than the great Hall above, but the darkness and low ceiling made it seem much more cramped and oppressive. The space was utterly empty except for the gaping chasm at its centre, also circular, turning the chamber into a ring-shaped walkway around an enormous, round pit. The Pit, into which the Enclave deposited the effluence of a kingdom.

All of the castle's garbage ended up here; its rubbish was cast into the unspeakable chasm, all of its toilets draining into the noxious orifice through holes in the ceiling above. Despite its familiarity, the stench grew almost unbearable as she approached its edge, and Freya wished she had a hand free to cover her nose. Still, she couldn't resist peering down into the Pit, noting with alarm that once again the level of the festering trash pile seemed to have risen. She recalled a time when torchlight wouldn't have penetrated far enough to glimpse anything other than a black, stinking void; whatever process emptied this cesspool seemed to be slowing down, perhaps clogged with waste.

She unloaded the bucket, glancing to her left where another spiral staircase led around the rim of the Pit, gradually down towards the heap's fetid surface. She still remembered the day she had traversed it, when she had taken a few tentative steps across that congealed upper crust, coughing and gagging yet unable to deny her curiosity.

She remembered the face she had beheld, smiling up at her from the filth. It was reminiscent of the fixed benevolence of the angels, but devoid of their beauty, a vulgar approximation of their beatific joy. Unlike the pure, divine hue of the angels' faces, this likeness was cast in some ugly russet-coloured metal, or perhaps simply caked in layers of shit and rust. She had at first thought it was some sort of mask, until she noticed the arm jutting upwards alongside it, crafted from the same dark and tarnished material. A grasping hand seemed to reach for her, crudely-jointed fingers frozen into a claw as though the obscene thing had died trying to haul itself out of the quagmire.

That day she had dumped the contents of her bucket right onto its loathsome face, and ran. She hadn't dared to mention the incident to anyone, not even to Maxwell. Now she squinted down into the Pit, wondering if the strange effigy was still there, or long since buried.

Instead, she saw a different figure. It was close to the stairs, sprawled on its back like a discarded marionette, arms and legs horribly askew. Before she knew it, she was hurrying down towards it, desperate to prove to her troubled mind that it was imagining things, that this was simply a bundle of unwanted rags, a trick of the sputtering light. But as she approached, the Pit's miasma growing so thick she could barely breathe, she saw that this was no illusion. A sob of horror burst out of her as she stared down at the ashen robes splayed open around the body, almost as distinctive as the ice-blue eyes that rolled slightly backwards in their sockets as though pondering some beguiling mystery.

It was the corpse of Lord Gwillym, his bones snapped like twigs either before his fall into the Pit, or perhaps by the violence of his landing.

Two

Chief Hand Oswald had already retired to bed, and refused to believe Freya's story when she and Maxwell roused him. A string of profanities spewed from his mouth as they led him down the long staircase. His disbelief was so intense that Freya felt almost relieved when poor Gwillym's broken body appeared beneath the light of his lantern, then felt an immediate and terrible guilt wash over her as Oswald's eyes bulged and his curses were replaced by incoherent screeching.

Soon after that, the castle was alive with shock and outrage.

Lawmaster Alessa was the first of the other three Lords to rise, groggy from wine and too little sleep, to accompany Oswald on the same harrowing descent. Once Gwillym's death was confirmed, Alessa and the now-awakened Warmaster Valeria demanded the entire population gather in the main courtyard. Valeria's knights relished the opportunity to manhandle people out of their beds (they did not, however, dare to rouse Prayermaster Cedric, the final Lord having drunk himself into a stupor, snoring loudly on the floor of his chamber).

Now, as the rising sun blazed its accusations down upon them, the people of the Enclave gathered in a bleary-eyed, resentful throng. The tips of swords forced High Nobles, Lower Nobles, and Unskilled servants to stand shoulder to indignant shoulder.

Valeria knew that, at times like this, fear would only work for so long. Her knights numbered just twenty-nine, which meant that even if she contributed her own considerable fighting skills to the equation, her forces were outnumbered almost thirteen to one. The situation required delicacy and humility, an apologetic tone, and a politician's tact.

Which was why, after yelling an apocalyptically loud instruction for the those assembled to cease their jabbering, the burly Warmaster fell silent and let Alessa do the rest of the talking.

"Citizens of the Enclave," the Lawmaster cried, her slight build and bespectacled, affable face a stark contrast to the stern demeanour and intimidating bulk of her fellow Lord. "We are sorry to subject you to such treatment, and at such an inhospitable juncture. Just a few scant hours ago we were celebrating together the bountiful provisions that God has once again seen fit to graciously bestow upon us. Praise the angels!"

Dutifully, the crowd repeated the mantra.

Now she has them, thought Valeria, marvelling not for the first time at the eloquence of her diminutive colleague. *A few honeyed words can be worth a hundred soldiers.*

"And yet, sadly, that gratitude was not shared by at least one of our number." Here she allowed her face to fall, her tone becoming sombre. "Our beloved Lord Gwillym lies in the infirmary, his skull and body pummelled by vile blows before he was callously dumped into the Pit like the bloody remnants of a meal. Despite her immense skill, there was nothing Ailmaster Frances could do, and she has recently pronounced him..." Here she allowed her voice to crack, just a little, to convey her sadness without appearing weak. *Masterful,* thought the watching Valeria. Alessa paused for a moment before continuing, bringing her fist to her lips as she composed herself. "Lord Gwillym is dead," she said eventually.

There was a respectful gasp from the congregation, as though the news had not already spread like wildfire around the castle.

"Lord Gwillym is dead," she repeated, raising her voice commandingly, "and the Enclave demands *justice!*"

A roar of support erupted from the multitude, fists thrown passionately into the air. As the light of vengeance flashed in almost a thousand eyes, Valeria felt like applauding.

Freya, meanwhile, felt sick, as though something toxic was wriggling inside her belly. She had told Oswald of her suspicions, but the Chief Hand had replied with a furious glare and told her she had already done enough damage. Now, jostled by the baying masses, her eyes scoured the faces of the surrounding knights, fearful of the lengths to which Sir Bernard might resort to ensure her silence.

Alessa held up a hand, and the chanting of the crowd gradually faded. "But justice, in turn, demands knowledge," she said solemnly. "And it is only by imparting our individual wisdoms that our great city is able to thrive. Only through the sharing of truth can I, your Lawmaster, ensure that justice is done, here on this day of our almighty God."

The people, sensing what was coming, began to shuffle uncomfortably, casting suspicious glances at one another. Alessa's gaze hardened as she surveyed them, almost as though her eyes possessed the power to compel the truth from a sealed mouth. "And so I implore anyone that has any valuable information, any insight that will help us to resolve this most heinous of crimes, to impart it now."

A hush settled across the courtyard, punctuated by unintelligible snatches of conversation, by hushed whispers and the occasional clanking of weaponry as the knights shifted at their posts. But no-one spoke up, despite the razor sharpness of Alessa's stare and the looming threat of Valeria and her warriors. Freya continued to search the faces of the knights; some were obscured by armoured helmets, but none of these seemed to possess Bernard's heavily muscled physique.

Then she saw a pair of eyes fixed on hers, eyes that burned with a hatred so intense her breath caught in her throat. Sir Bernard was up on the raised dais, just behind and to the left of Lord Valeria. He was wearing the same apparel he had worn at the banquet and carried the same cruelly-curved sword, which was drawn and held out in front of him as though to ward off any potential threats to his Warmaster.

Or any potential indictments against him.

The sight of that blade, and the raw malice in his eyes, crushed her remaining spirit like a trampled eggshell. Like the rest of the congregation, Freya stayed quiet.

And then.

"I know who did it!"

As though part of the same organism, the heads and eyes of the crowd turned as one towards the three knights who emerged from a nearby tower.

"I hope you'll forgive my absence from the assembly, my Lord," the first knight continued, standing ahead of the others, his blade sheathed and something clasped in his hand. "But my theory demanded urgent, and covert, investigation."

The creature in Freya's stomach seemed to cavort with malicious glee. She sucked in deep breaths, feeling ever more certain she was about to vomit.

"Explain yourself, Sir," commanded Lord Alessa, her eyes burning with fascination.

The knight, whose short stature was emphasised by a slight stoop as he walked, stepped forwards. He did not reply, but instead held aloft whatever was in his hand. It was at that moment — as a dazzling jewel fell from his palm, its perfect blue colouring seeming to mirror the cloudless morning sky as it hung, dangling from a chain — that she realised this was Sir Thomas, the man who had tried to calm Sir Bernard the previous night.

"We found this in the quarters of the culprit," he declared. "I'm sure you all recognise this gem, and that you, Lawmaster, can confirm it was missing from beloved Gwillym's body?"

There were gasps and mutterings from the crowd. Freya couldn't help but glance towards Bernard, whose eyes seemed to be swivelling in his head, the skin of his face clammy and grey.

"Can you vouch for this?" Alessa asked, directing the question towards the two other knights. Solemnly, they both nodded. She returned her gaze to Thomas. "Then I must ask, Sir, that you divulge the identity of this culprit, against whom you make a grave and compelling accusation."

Sir Thomas extended a finger. The thing in Freya's stomach twitched ever more frantically, as though in the throes of death.

"You," said the knight. Freya felt a sudden, terrible hollowness, as though she had just looked over the edge of a precipice. The bile that had been threatening to eject from her stomach disgorged itself abruptly, spattering across the back of the Lower Noble that was crushed against her.

Sir Thomas was pointing directly at her.

***

"You there," repeated the knight. The world seemed to be spinning. Freya felt blood swelling in her ears, as though it might be about to explode out of them from the sheer pressure in her head. "Can you please explain what happened at my table last night, at the feast?"

She blinked. Her mouth opened and closed, the words like alien substances in her mouth. Then, to her horror, Lord Alessa interjected. "Come up here, woman, so we can hear you better."

Her heart seemed to plummet through the earth; but what choice did she have? Dutifully, her head bowed and hidden for now beneath the hood of her ragged vestments, she moved through the seething masses, who squeezed aside to allow her passage. She was glad at least to be away from the Noble she had vomited on, who chittered his outrage and disgust behind her.

Each of the half dozen steps leading up to the two Lords and their retinue of knights felt like an impossible journey, her legs weighted with dread. Freya made sure that she went towards the opposite side of the podium from Sir Bernard, with whom she was now destined to be thrown into conflict. Swallowing thickly, she turned to face the onlookers, who had fallen into an expectant hush. Sir Thomas had also made his way through the crowd, his eyes fixed on Bernard as he ascended. The brawny knight held the smaller man's gaze, jaws clenched so tightly his teeth looked as though they would shatter.

"Speak, Unskilled," commanded Alessa, although the Lord's expression was not unkind. "Tell us your story."

Freya stared out across the assembly, her mind emptied by the sheer enormity of her situation. Then her eyes settled on Maxwell, towards the back of the crowd. His face looked taut with worry, but he offered her an encouraging smile. She tried to focus on him, remembering happier times in this courtyard, blossom falling from the trees that now stood bare and joyless in its corners like sombre monuments.

"I..." she began, her voice quaking. "I came to pour your drinks..."

"Speak up," said Alessa. "And remove your hood."

This was the moment Freya had dreaded. She had spent such a long time waiting on these people, cleaning after them, serving their food. But how many had truly seen her? How many were expecting the scarred visage that lurked beneath her cowl? Swallowing again, her mouth so dry it felt like she was gulping back sand, she slid back the hood. There were murmurs and intakes of breath from some of the onlookers, each gasp or whispered remark like a knife thrust into her heart.

She couldn't continue. The feeling of nausea returned, and it was all she could do not to void her guts, right there on the dais.

"Perhaps I can help," offered Sir Thomas, who moved to stand beside her. "This waif came to our table to serve us wine. She was beset by one of our number, who cruelly mocked her ravaged face. Is that correct, Unskilled?"

She nodded, thinking only of words like *ravaged, mutilated, monster.* Then she felt his arm around her shoulders, and stiffened.

"Lord Gwillym intervened to stop this pitiless display," he continued. "I regret that I placated the culprit, anxious in the moment only to avoid a confrontation. But later that night, when the Recordmaster took his leave, my comrade suddenly disappeared from our table and did not return. I know now that he had the blackest intentions, driven by a deadly mixture of liquor and humiliation. My recovery of the Lord's pendant proves it."

Thomas seemed to be basking in the rapt attention of the audience, savouring every moment. Still, his claim would be greatly strengthened if it was corroborated by his star witness.

"Unskilled," said Alessa gently. "You will now point out this man. If it is the same person Thomas indicts, I will consider this adequate proof in the eyes of the law."

I ought to be happy, thought Freya. Her tormentor would be brought to justice, his stinging words turned back upon him with a single jab of her finger. Such power ought to send joy surging like lightning through her veins. Yet she only felt hollow, as vacant as the dead Lord's glacier-blue eyes, as she began to raise her arm.

Before she could accuse him, Bernard rushed suddenly forwards, a guttural snarl bursting from his throat as he drew back his sword. For a man of his size, he seemed impossibly fast, and she was dimly aware of Thomas stumbling backwards at her side, releasing her from his hold as he fumbled for his own weapon. As movement erupted around her, she stayed very still, transfixed on the advancing knight, on the blade that arced downwards towards her, on the eyes that blazed with unrestrained loathing.

There was a silvery blur, and Bernard's sword clattered to the ground. Freya's eyes were still fixed on the knight's, but his gaze had moved to his own elbow, a look of confusion twisting his features as he stared at the ragged stump where his forearm should have been. As if similarly shocked, the blood in his cleanly-separated veins seemed to freeze in place for a moment, before spraying across the podium in a bright crimson fountain so fine it was almost like mist.

Bernard's head came next, severed neatly at the neck like a pruned rose. The crowd, stunned into a stupefied silence, finally came alive as the gore-spewing thing bounced into their midst, screams and shouts echoing around the courtyard as the remaining knights wrestled to maintain order.

The last thing Freya saw before she collapsed in a sudden faint — its oblivion blacker than the gurgling waves that churned far beneath them — was Valeria, calmly wiping her axe on the cloth she had produced from one of her pockets.

Now there were only 434 of them.

Three

Once again, Freya had risen early to visit the battlements. The wind howled around her as she approached their edge, hurling freezing rain into her face like bitter tears, its demented wailing a cry of disbelief.

The Monoliths were hidden from her once again, but the distant skyline was not her focus. The Enclave's supplies of timber were dwindling, as was everything else, but a substantial amount had been used to make Lord Gwillym's coffin as ornate as Woodmaster Lenora could fashion. A procession had carried the casket out into the Wastes, as far beyond the castle as they dared without risking exposure to the dreaded plague. It had been a sombre affair, watched from the walls by the Enclave's entire populace.

The separate parts of Bernard's corpse, on the other hand, had been unceremoniously dumped, just beyond the gorse thickets that grew like coils of barbed wire around the castle's perimeter. Still, his rotting head stared back at her; the slow tightening of its skin and the sheer affront of its persistence gave its expression the appearance of a contented grin. How she wished the head had landed facing in another direction. How she wished the angels would appear to haul the hateful pile away. But still Bernard leered, and still Gwillym's white pine box glinted on the horizon.

This was the twelfth day with no sign of the angels, and the Enclave was growing restless.

A favourite topic was to debate the lengthiest stretch there had ever been without a visitation — some said there had once been a fifteen-day gap, while others insisted hysterically that this was already the longest, that doom and abandonment had surely come upon their kingdom.

Others believed they had done something to offend God Himself, that the sentence carried out against Sir Bernard must have been in some way gravely unjust, although they would never dare utter such ideas in front of the Lords. As if to quell any rumblings of rebellion amongst his subordinates, Prayermaster Cedric was pushing the Unskilled to exhausting levels of performance, extending the length of their working days and demanding almost impossible standards of cleanliness and punctuality.

Life, suddenly, seemed much harder in the Enclave. Winter's onset, which that morning had made the ground sparkle with frost and reminded Freya of the Monoliths and their elusive promise, only served to fray tempers even further. The air's deepening chill seemed to be working its way into hearts and minds, making them as cold and hard as the earth itself.

Freya tried to remain as anonymous as possible, but every so often she'd catch a sneering remark when people passed her in a corridor and recognised her scar.

"There's the one."

"It's her fault."

"I heard her and Sir Thomas were secretly bedfellows."

But she didn't complain. How could she? *Our lot is merely to serve, and to persist,* as Maxwell was fond of reminding her.

It was on the eighteenth day, when the food had begun to run out and the Lower Nobles joined the Unskilled in receiving rations for the first time, that a mob gathered in the main courtyard. Freya and Maxwell had been assisting the Archivists to clear out an old wing of their vast library, marvelling at the ancient tomes whose paper was as fragile as desiccated skin. When no-one was looking, Freya ran her hands across the cracked leather covers of the books, breathing in their dusty odour and trying to remember Raoul, the man she knew she had once loved, the man she knew had disfigured her. But the ghost of his memory had moved on, lost to the fog that encircled the Enclave like a besieging army.

One of the Archivists had bustled into the neglected chamber, so frantic he had tripped on a stack of parchment and sprawled to the ground in a heap of scattered pages. As he was helped to his feet, he stammered about the growing rabble outside and how he was worried they might be planning to set the Archive ablaze. Unable to contain her inquisitiveness, Freya had followed the panicked Nobles outside, trailed by a reluctant and grumbling Maxwell.

The group was perhaps sixty-strong, comprising mainly Lower Nobles, although some of the Unskilled had also joined its ranks, and even a few knights that she recognised. They brandished torches whose flames cast a lurid glow across the cobbles, illuminating the throng's faces in shades of fiery rage.

But the tower containing the Archive was not the focus of their ire; rather, they had gathered around the Lords' tower in the opposite corner, enabling the recordkeepers to watch quietly from their entranceway. Freya and Maxwell loitered at the rear, straining to hear the crowd's angry shouts. She did not know whether any of the Lords were even inside the tower, although she had not seen newly-promoted Recordmaster Mycroft in the Archive, and there was little reason for him to be anywhere else.

The protests seemed to be growing in volume and Freya realised they were being led by Oswald himself; the Chief Hand brandished a makeshift club as he approached the tower's sturdy doors, stopping on the steps to address his newfound followers in an angry, unintelligible frenzy. Freya wondered how ruthlessly Valeria would be prepared to defend the keep if it came to it, whether she would be prepared to turn her infamous cauldrons of boiling oil on her own people.

Instead, the Warmaster answered with arrows. A pair of them, to be precise, which hit Oswald in the back. He pitched forwards down the stairs to land in a motionless heap, like a lump of skewered flesh ready for Egbert's skillet.

"You will desist, or you will die," might have been the cry from an upper window, but it was made nearly unintelligible by the clamour of the crowd as they scrambled backwards and began to disperse.

"This city is going mad," muttered Maxwell, half to himself.

Freya nodded as they followed the Archivists back inside, no-one knowing what to do other than to continue their work, as though nothing was wrong.

As though the castle wasn't starting to devour itself in its hunger and desperation.

***

They came for her in the night. The castle contained so much unused space that even the servants' quarters were generously proportioned; this gave the knights plenty of room to manoeuvre around her as she slept. Freya awoke only when coarse hands encircled her wrists and ankles, and a hood was thrust over her head as though their destination was in some way a secret.

The prison keep was the most distant tower from the courtyard, close to the city's rearmost wall, overlooking the tumult of the sea. It was the domain of Painmaster Wilfred, whose techniques were almost as feared as the plague itself. In these times of uneasy peace, it was rare to hear of castlefolk being hauled off to his dungeons, and the infamous chambers had gradually passed almost into legend. Their reclusive overseer was rarely seen at the banquets or other public events, although when he did make an appearance he was always disturbingly jolly, a plump and affable man whose good-natured quips belied the brutality of his employ.

And so it was with understandable discomfort that Freya found herself face to face with the Enclave's chief torturer.

She was tied to a chair before the hood was removed, and she first beheld Wilfred prodding at a roaring fire with an iron poker. She stayed silent as he tended to the flames, watching as he approached and sat opposite her, steepling his fingers on the table that separated them.

"Hello," he said from beneath a bristling, beardless moustache. His head was completely shaven, reflecting the light from the small room's fireplace in a manner that reminded her of an exposed skull. "Freya, isn't it?"

She nodded, feeling strangely calm, as though her brain hadn't yet accepted that this was anything other than a bad dream.

"I hope the knights weren't too rough with you. Their profession attracts people who are prone to being a little … overzealous. I remember you, you know, from the last feast." He chuckled wryly then, perhaps realising the unintended significance of the word 'last'. "For my money, that knight deserved what happened to him, whether he killed Gwillym or not." If the words were intended to give her comfort, they did not; instead, they brought only echoes of pain and shame, and of the dead Lord's dreadful stare.

"But that's beside the point," Wilfred continued. "The point is that we are facing a crisis, because God has seen fit to forsake our Enclave. I'm actually surprised it's taken this long to boil over. People don't seem to realise that in a few more days we'll have to start eating each other." He laughed again, although the haunted look in his eyes suggested the remark may not have been made entirely in jest. "So, as you can see, something must be done. And the Lords, in their boundless wisdom, have decided that a retrial is the answer."

"A … retrial?" Her tongue struggled to shape the words, feeling thick and numb inside her mouth.

"Indeed. They aim to address the growing concern that Sir Bernard's death was a miscarriage of justice. An error of law so grave that it has incurred the wrath of God Himself."

"But ... how could it be? Sir Thomas found the pendant in Sir Bernard's quarters!"

"Very good. You're asking all the right questions." Wilfred nodded encouragingly. "Now, if you can be trusted not to attempt anything foolish, I might be able to share some answers with you."

The man she hadn't realised was standing behind her stepped forward then, bending to release the knots that secured her hands and feet to the wooden chair. Without a word the wiry, tobacco-smelling attendant then reattached the ropes around her wrists, this time behind her back, and hauled her upright. She felt something press into her ribs from behind, and pictured a dagger expertly wielded in his dextrous grip. Its tip urged her to follow Wilfred as the High Noble turned towards the door.

"You know, I have a slightly different theory," he said as he opened it, leading her out into a narrow corridor lit by smouldering torches. She had never been inside the keep, Wilfred preferring to keep his own cortege of Unskilled who dwelt within its upper chambers, rarely venturing out. Keeping the place clean was clearly not one of his priorities; the walls and floor were coated in dust and grime. The air felt hot and oppressive, and she wondered for the first time whether she was underground. Somewhere, she fancied she heard a distant scream, before the sound was choked off abruptly.

Seemingly oblivious to the squalor of their conditions, Wilfred continued in a jovial tone. "I don't think this is a crisis at all. I think this is a *test*." He led her and her escort past several other doors, one of which responded with the sound of frantic hammering from the other side when she glanced at it, startling her.

"God wants to see how we react to this complication; how we as a people respond to not having our arses wiped, if you'll forgive my vulgarity." Wilfred was becoming more animated as he spoke, a note of religious zeal entering his voice. They reached a set of steps, and the Noble absent-mindedly removed one of the torches from its bracket before he began to descend, still talking as he did so. "So, personally, I think our predicament has nothing at all to do with the sordid matter of a murdered Lord and a stolen gemstone. But, you know what they say: each to their Skill and the Enclave stays wealthy."

The staircase traced a confusing, right-angled spiral as they descended, and by the time she reached the heavy-looking door at its end she felt thoroughly disoriented. Even Wilfred seemed momentarily confused, before muttering "Oh, of course," and producing a set of keys from somewhere within his voluminous black robes.

"My own Skill lies in the practical application of pain," he said merrily as he fumbled a series of keys into the lock, finally turning the tumblers on the third attempt. The door creaked open and Freya was assailed by a smell of death so strong it almost made her reel backwards. But this was not the sickly-sweet fetor of the recently-deceased, the acrid tang of burnt flesh, or even the pungent scent of freshly-spilt blood; rather, this was the accumulation of countless seasons of torment, as much an aura as it was a stench. As Wilfred's torchlight illuminated the first of his torture machines, she realised that this was a temple of suffering almost as old as the castle itself.

"This device is one of my favourites," he pronounced as they approached the battered, circular apparatus. "Nothing fancy — you simply lash the guilty to the breaking wheel, and assail them with cudgels until their limbs are thoroughly smashed. A few days left hanging in that state and they'll confess all their crimes." She shuddered, wondering which of these appalling contraptions would be her own fate, wondering if a great reservoir of panic and revulsion was about to burst through the dam of her inexplicable calm.

Or perhaps part of her brain had simply shut down, overwhelmed by the horror it had endured since the day the angels last came. If so, such an incapacity would serve her well if she was to spend the last of her days in this dank oubliette.

"Perhaps a little too unsophisticated for your tastes? Let's try another." Wilfred bounded eagerly towards another dark alcove, Freya compelled to follow by the blade jabbed into her back.

"Now *this* is a real specimen," the torturer enthused as they approached a large, metallic box, about as high and wide as a large person. Indeed, its ornate decoration gave it the appearance of a smiling man, whose hands protruded from long sleeves and were clasped at his chest. "Have you ever heard of an iron maiden?"

She shook her head dumbly, and excitement twinkled in Wilfred's eyes.

"Apparently this model dates back to their original use," he continued happily. "And I'm pulling your leg, a little: it isn't really an implement of torture at all." He reached towards the box's sculpted hands, pulling them apart as though the grinning effigy was opening its cloak. She was reminded, just for a moment, of the strange metal man she had seen buried beneath the garbage in the Pit, what seemed like a lifetime ago.

Inside, the box was hollow, but lined with enough cruelly sharpened spikes to turn its occupant to a bleeding, screaming pincushion.

"Far too unpredictable to be of practical use; there's too high a chance of killing the guilty outright. It's more for the final coup de grâce, really, if the executioner has a flair for the theatrical."

She had become aware of a soft moaning, off to her right, where the room was still swathed in shadow. Wilfred seemed not to notice the sound at first, as he continued to prattle about the psychological benefits of such a device, enabling the torturer to be less directly involved in the suffering they dispensed. His continued insistence on using the term 'the guilty' to describe his victims only increased her abhorrence.

If they were already guilty, what was the need to torture them?

But she said nothing, concentrating on the groaning sound, and trying not to absorb too much of the vile arcana that gushed from Wilfred's lips like undiluted evil. Then the Painmaster stopped, mid-sentence, slamming the iron maiden shut in a sudden tantrum.

"Gideon, will you *please* silence that infernal whining?" he barked. She felt the knifepoint disappear from her back, heard footsteps disappearing into the gloom.

"Forgive me," Wilfred said, recovering his ghastly smile. "Perils of the job, you know. It can be hard to keep to a schedule in this line of work. Still … perhaps it wouldn't hurt to give you a glimpse behind the curtain, as it were."

He grabbed her by the arm, leading her towards the darkness and closer to the source of that ominous whimpering. As they approached, she heard a cracking sound, moments before the light of Wilfred's torch illuminated his associate rubbing his knuckles, standing over the prone form of a man.

Gideon was compact and lithe, as thin and dangerous looking as the dagger at his belt, his face a latticework of scars that made Freya feel a fleeting, momentary affinity. But her attention did not linger on Wilfred's frightening accomplice. Instead it was grabbed, violently, by the sight of the man he had just knocked unconscious. The man was strapped face-down to a frame, suspended horizontally at waist height by a thick, rusted chain that held the structure to the ceiling. He was completely naked, his back a tapestry of livid bruises. But two other aspects of this hideous tableau disturbed her the most, drawing an involuntary gurgle of horror from her throat.

The first was the man's right arm, which rested limply across the scaffold, its skin removed all the way to the shoulder. No, not removed — it still hung there, dangling from the upper joint in tatters like strands of frayed ribbon. How it had been peeled back, revealing his glistening musculature — biceps, tendons, sinews, all laid bare in excruciating detail — she could not begin to fathom, any more than she could imagine the agony that must have accompanied such a sadistic procedure.

The second was the realisation that this forlorn, mutilated figure was Sir Thomas: the knight who had tried to aid her at the feast, and had successfully prosecuted Sir Bernard.

She staggered backwards, trying to bring a hand to her mouth before she remembered they were bound behind her back, and sunk defeatedly to her knees instead.

"Too graphic, I suppose," said Wilfred in a disappointed tone. "A good job I'm not recruiting your replacement, eh Gideon?" She did not look up to see how Gideon reacted to his master's jibe and instead fixed her gaze on the floor, trying not to picture the gallons of blood that must have saturated its stones over the countless days that Wilfred had plied his gruesome trade.

"What happened to him?" she asked in a trembling voice, her reserves of calm blasted apart like shattered limbs.

"Well, the process of flaying a human alive is actually much more complex than you might think—"

"I mean *why is he here*?" she hissed as an anguished sob shook her body.

"Ah, forgive me. He's here because he's *guilty* my dear. Of framing his fellow knight, Sir Bernard, by planting a stolen pendant in his room. His co-conspirators confirmed it, after they were subjected to a similar procedure. Now we merely await Thomas's confession."

Her mind whirled and spun, like cinders in a billow of rising smoke.

"But why would he kill Lord Gwillym?"

"That is precisely what we seek to ascertain."

She glanced up at the atrocity of Thomas's excoriated flesh.

"But if you torture people like this ... how can you trust their confessions?"

Wilfred was silent for a moment, and she was worried she had enraged him. She did not want to try the patience of this maniac, certainly not here, in the heart of his merciless empire. But after a few seconds he began to chuckle, quietly at first, then gradually rising to a roar of amusement. Gideon joined in, and Freya knelt there amongst their hellish machinery, weeping while the two of them cackled and howled with laughter.

"My dear," Wilfred said eventually, almost breaking down into another fit of giggling. "You don't seem to understand." He paused to dry his eyes, the mirth evaporating from his voice as he continued. "Once they end up down here, *everyone* is guilty; sooner or later."

"Is that what is to become of me?" she whispered, battling to keep the terror from her voice.

Wilfred composed himself, tilting his head as he looked down at her. "My lady, that depends upon you. Our beloved Prayermaster asked me to give you the guided tour, in case it helped to make up your mind. You see, he has a proposal for you."

"A proposal," she repeated in dazed bewilderment. The word seemed to have lost any significance. Like everything in her life, it had been reduced to background noise, an underscore to her suffering.

"Better get her to her cell, Gideon," Wilfred said with a sigh. "I think she's had a bit too much excitement for one night."

She did not struggle as Gideon hoisted her easily over his shoulder, the smell of his tobacco-suffused clothing providing a merciful distraction from the concentrated stink of human misery.

Four

They came for her in the night again. She heard their fearsome blades clinking against the bars of her cell, an ominous tapping that rose in volume as torchlight flickered beyond her eyelids. She clung resolutely to sleep, drawing the rags over her head as she awaited their inevitable intrusion, dreading the feeling of calloused hands closing around her limbs as they prepared to drag her away to the next phase of her punishment.

Then she heard someone hissing her name, and blinked herself awake, daring to peer out from beneath the tattered blanket. It was Maxwell, his face hovering like a spectre above the weak light of the flame he carried. "Wake up, Freya!" he whispered, jerking his head to glance repeatedly over his shoulder. Even tinged orange by the glow of his firebrand, she could see he was pallid with fear, hunched and trembling.

"Maxwell ... what are you doing here?"

For a fleeting moment she thought he might intend to break her out. Then he thrust a piece of bread between the bars. "I brought this for you," he blurted anxiously. "It isn't much, but ... I couldn't bear the thought of you starving in here."

"How did you get in?" The sight of the food made her suddenly ravenous, and she began to wolf down the thick, stale slice even as she spoke.

"The Unskilled who mans the back gate owes me a favour," he replied. "I can't stay for long." He watched her eat, seeming to teeter on the brink of fleeing in terror. "But I thought you might need to see a friendly face."

She smiled gratefully at him, shovelling the last few crumbs into her mouth. Then another thought occurred to her, and her face fell. "What is everyone saying about me?"

Maxwell looked pained. "There are others, like me, who think this whole affair is totally ludicrous," he said, as gently as his threadbare nerves would allow. "But I won't speak untruthfully; there are also many imbeciles who want to see you beheaded, as though that is somehow God's will. I'm convinced this city is becoming more and more deranged by the day."

How strange, she thought, *to hear someone talk about your death.* She felt oddly detached from it, as though they were discussing someone else, gossiping idly about the other castlefolk, *like they always used to.*

"What happened to Oswald? Is he dead?" she asked.

Maxwell nodded. "His body was tossed out into the Wastes, alongside Bernard's. They didn't even pull the arrows out of his back." A silence descended for a moment. The crackling of Maxwell's flame reminded her of the Chief Hand's torch, the way his eyes had protruded at the sight of Gwillym's corpse. "Here, I brought you this, too," he said suddenly, reaching inside his cloak to produce a small canteen. He unscrewed the lid and slipped the container through the bars. She drank eagerly, expecting water and instead tasting something much stronger.

Something she remembered drinking long ago, when it didn't seem far, far above her station.

"Maxwell! Is this ... wine?"

He nodded. "I've been saving it, from the leftovers. Why do you think I always volunteer to clean the flagons?"

She couldn't help but laugh, but the sound was quickly swallowed by the cloying darkness, as though the air here did not welcome such frivolity.

"Apparently the Prayermaster wants to meet with me," she told him as she handed back the flask, savouring the warmth of the liquid that dribbled down her throat.

"Why?"

She shrugged. "At least it means they haven't sliced off my fingers or stuck boiling pins in my eyes yet."

It was an attempt at gallows humour, but Maxwell looked aghast and glanced over his shoulder once again as though suddenly remembering where he was.

"Freya, I have to go now," he mumbled fearfully. "I'll try to visit again tomorrow. Hopefully Lord Cedric will have straightened things out by then."

His words were kind, but they both knew how hollow they were. Her predicament was grave beyond belief. Nevertheless, she thanked him with a smile and reached through the bars to clasp his hand in hers for a few seconds, feeling joined to her old life by the momentary contact, to a time when her only concern was avoiding the remonstrations of fat Egbert and ill-tempered Oswald.

And to another time before then, a time when she had laughed more often and had drunk lots of wine.

Then Maxwell left the tower, and the darkness rushed in gleefully to engulf the cell, as though impatient to consume her.

***

She had expected Gideon to rouse her the next morning, but instead it was a different one of Wilfred's underlings, this time a much larger man. He seemed as mute as his colleague, and as he entered her cell and began to bind her wrists, she asked whether the Painmaster only recruited workers with no tongues.

"No," replied the man in a deep voice that contained a surprising note of warmth. "Just Gideon. He lost it in a knife fight, so I heard." Then he added, unnecessarily, "Not from him."

"So you just choose not to talk very much?"

The tall, thickset man shrugged. "I hear enough talking down in the machine room."

She fell silent after that. Just like the previous night, she was scooped up like a bundle of firewood, breathing a sigh of relief when she was carried not down towards that hateful dungeon but instead up a different flight of stairs and into a sparsely-furnished room. Sunlight poured through the narrow windows, illuminating a stern-faced man sitting at a table, reading a book. She recognised Prayermaster Cedric's dour features from his fiery sermons in the chapel, and from the times he would occasionally visit the servants' quarters to berate poor Oswald in the same impassioned tone.

He made a point of finishing whatever paragraph he was examining before lifting his gaze to acknowledge her.

"Ah. Hello, Unskilled one. How are you finding your stay in the Painmaster's keep?"

She blinked, not understanding whether this was a joke. She felt a queer sense of mutiny uncoiling within her and knew it was a dangerous impulse to follow.

"It's been enlightening," she said eventually.

Behind her, her lumbering escort suppressed a snort of laughter, and Cedric frowned.

"I certainly hope so. The machinations of this tower are not a subject for decent folk to dwell upon, but like every part of our Enclave, they are integral to its smooth running." She held his stony gaze, wondering why it was not Alessa who was here to meet with her — Wilfred's work was, after all, part of the Lawmaker's jurisdiction. As if reading her thoughts, Cedric continued.

"You are probably questioning my presence here. In truth, Lord Alessa and I debated the correct course of action long into the night. And, praise the angels, God's light of inspiration shone upon us; we concluded that this is, in fact, a clerical matter."

A clerical matter. Did this mean she was to be a blood sacrifice, as Maxwell had foretold? At least that might spare her the cruelties that had been inflicted upon poor Sir Thomas. She waited while Cedric rose, crossing to stare out of the window before he continued, the sunlight making his white robes shimmer with an aura of divinity as he gazed out across the citadel.

"In other words, you are in the extremely fortunate position of having a choice. You can remain within Alessa's dominion and join your friend in the dungeon, where Wilfred will doubtless extract the truth of your conspiracy." He turned towards her, smiling for the first time. "Or you can accept my offer of redemption and spend the rest of your worthless life in servitude of the Divine Being. Either way, God must be appeased."

"God? Don't you mean 'the people'?" she muttered, the words bringing a sour taste to her mouth.

Cedric's smile remained frozen in place, like a carved parody, while anger flared momentarily in his eyes. "If you truly understood His nature, my dear, you would know that they are one and the same. To serve God is to serve the Enclave, for we are His last great bastion."

She didn't have a choice at all. This whole ordeal had been choreographed to ensure she would accept the Prayermaster's bargain.

"What would you have me do?" she whispered, determined to meet his eyes, to force him to recognise that she was a person, not a pawn.

Cedric's expression hardened. "You will travel to Asyla, to consult their Council about the current problem. You will obtain as much intelligence as you can gather about the present situation regarding the angels. You will assess the town's capacity to share their food stores with us. And you will report back on these matters within four days, thereby earning your pardon."

Her head felt compressed, crushed beneath the weight of this new information. "But, my Lord ... if I venture out into the Wastes, the plague will surely take me."

The Prayermaster nodded soberly. "Indeed it might. Such is the price of your treachery."

She searched his eyes for a sign that he knew, at least somewhere deep inside, that what was happening was gravely wrong, that he didn't truly believe his own lies. But she couldn't find a glimmer of that humanity in Cedric. He was already convinced of this new narrative, which meant that it was the new truth, and that she was now a reviled traitor whose punishment was unquestionably merited: a slow and agonising death, or a suicidal quest across the poisoned wilderness.

She felt the tears on her cheeks before they stung her eyes. They fell freely, splashing onto the surface of the table, which was as hard and flat as the wasteland beyond the walls. She thought about Sir Thomas, of human skin being peeled away as inconsequentially as that of a potato. She thought about Raoul and whether, somehow, he was still waiting for her out there; perhaps to rend her flesh once again, perhaps to enfold her in a comforting embrace.

"Very well, my Lord," she said, her eyes falling from his as she accepted her latest defeat. "When do you wish me to depart?"

"You will leave immediately. What few provisions can be spared will be prepared for you. An escort will be sent within the hour. May God's blessing accompany you on your journey."

The Lord rose and left the room with the air of a man disgusted by his surroundings.

***

When Freya emerged from the keep, she was surprised by how quickly word of her expedition had spread, drawing hundreds of people to the courtyard. Then she realised that they had been there for much longer, corralled by Valeria's knights. All four Lords occupied the dais and had evidently already addressed the masses, who were now straining for a glimpse of her. *Cedric knew I would acquiesce,* she thought bitterly as she approached the crowd, a knight at her side with a restraining arm on her shoulder. *They've already told the people that I've confessed, and that this is my punishment.*

A few of the onlookers applauded as she drew near, but others shook their heads, screwing up their faces in disgust.

"Fucking *witch,*" someone hissed close to her ear.

"Time to fix the mess you've brought upon us!" yelled another, and she cried out as a stone struck her in the side of the head.

She had been provided with fresh clothing, a backpack with a few rations inside, and a short, rusted sword that felt alien in her hands. Such scant provisions were hardly suitable for four days roaming the Wastes, and she wondered whether the Lords harboured even a shred of belief that she might return. Still, for a moment, as her ear throbbed with pain, she thought about wielding the weapon, about sprinting towards whoever had thrown the projectile and driving it into their throat. It would mean certain death at the hands of the knights, or perhaps even beneath the blade of Valeria's greataxe; but at least such a death would be *hers,* a sliver of dignity, a demonstration to all those assembled that she was still Freya, a creature of will.

But, of course, she didn't do any such thing. Instead, she endured — *persisted* — trudging through the sneers and catcalls, down towards the towering slabs of the main gates. She searched the crowd for Maxwell, but he was lost amongst the sea of faces, or else (she hoped) boycotting the tawdry spectacle altogether. The knight's gauntleted hand squeezed her shoulder painfully, drawing her to a halt as the gates began their squealing, protesting separation. Freya wondered whether anyone in the Enclave would be able to repair that monstrous mechanism if it ever broke down. Did anyone even know how the gates worked? Or had that memory, too, been lost, escaping into the fog just as she was about to?

After I'm taken by the plague, will anyone remember me?

Another throng of people had accumulated on the ramparts, staring down at her as they hurled more stones; even a rancid-smelling egg had struck the steps nearby. The knight who accompanied her shouted a warning up at them, and the hail of missiles ceased, replaced by a torrent of verbal abuse that might have brought fresh tears to her eyes if she hadn't already shut herself down inside, as though a scab had crusted over her heart. It didn't help that she could, to an extent, understand their actions. God had abandoned these people, and they were afraid. Fear leads to anger, and anger finds a scapegoat.

An outcast.

She looked up defiantly at them.

Without food, you're all as dead as I am.

The gates finished opening with a resounding metallic boom, and the knight thrust her roughly forwards. She stumbled underneath the great arch, and for the first time since ...

When?

...she was outside the Enclave. A great cheer arose from the crowd on the castle wall, and from those that had followed her descent, stopping at the top of the steps where knights' crossed blades formed a barricade of steel. Freya remembered when she had stood atop the battlements herself, watching a desperate plague-carrier shambling towards certain death, a scene she was now surely doomed to repeat. She wondered how long it would take before the disease began to ravage her flesh, bringing blotches of grey to her dark hair, a repulsive bend to her spine.

Without looking back, she struck out towards the horizon. Asyla's famed spire suddenly seemed immeasurably far away, the crystalline Monoliths beyond it perhaps as distant as the sun itself. Ahead of her, she saw the remains of Bernard and Oswald, wishing she had given the corpses a wider berth. Then she noticed something: an anomaly, something her brain couldn't explain, and began immediately to puzzle at.

The pile had too many limbs.

She hurried closer, her curiosity outweighing her revulsion, as it so often did. Then she reached the sorry heap and nausea won out after all. She could hear jeering and laughter from the castle walls as she bent to vomit on the ground.

How much more of herself would need to be disgorged before the horror ceased? Would the world be happy only when she was an empty, hollow vessel?

Alongside the slowly putrefying pieces of the knight, and the bloated carcass of the Chief Hand, was another body. It was naked, stripped not only of its clothing but of every inch of its skin, looking like a humanoid effigy sculpted from blood. It was Sir Thomas, of course; he was lying face up, his lipless mouth seeming to smile at the sun, beatific in its final release from pain.

She looked back in disgust at the castle, the place that had been her home for more days than she could count: the fortress that had protected her from the plague that was doubtless already infesting her veins. The people who had once seemed like her own.

Now there were only 432 of them.

Or 431, she thought, *if I don't survive this excursion.* She glanced back at Thomas's ravaged body, her mission seeming more hopeless than ever; even if the people of Asyla did heed her pleas for scraps of food or information, she would at best return only to scrub the floors or, more likely, to be peppered with arrows just outside the gates.

Then she thought about Maxwell, and the other good people of the Enclave. People who deserved a fate other than starving to death or dying trampled in riots.

She lifted her head towards the outline of Gwillym's coffin, and beyond, far beyond, to where the Monoliths rose in impossible forms, slender and beautiful, like gigantic slivers of glass.

If Asyla couldn't help her, she would find God and ask Him herself.

Five

She had expected to feel something when the plague entered her, something apocalyptic, the sudden agony of her body being devoured from the inside. But instead, as the castle disappeared behind her, its towers and battlements like desperate fingers clawing at the air as it sank into the horizon, she felt strangely energised. The Lords, their knights, the castlefolk who had disowned her: none of them could touch her now.

She was alone, and free, for the first time since...

Since a long time.

Freya's pace was brisk as she strode across the desolate landscape, Gwillym's resting place already far behind her. She had considered checking whether he had been buried with his gemstone, suspecting the Lord would understand her need of something to barter with, but the sacrilege had seemed too great. Besides, it was doubtful the people of Asyla would even allow her to enter the settlement to trade with them; she would surely be shunned, dismissed as a reviled plague-carrier. She felt certain she'd been to Asyla once before and could recall a great wall around the town; ramshackle and wooden, dwarfed by the scale of the Enclave's towering white edifice, but still more than capable of keeping out even the most persistent invaders.

The ground remained flat and featureless as she walked, a seemingly endless expanse of hard, rust-coloured mud stretching out in all directions, into the mist that seemed to move along with her, always at the periphery of what she could discern. The brume was particularly thick that day; behind her, even the pinnacle of the Lords' tower was barely visible, while ahead Asyla's cathedral spire provided her only means of navigation, its warped shape looming above the fog to the east like a great, limbless tree.

Perhaps the world went on like this forever: an endless desert, punctuated by wretched burgs that clung to the miserable, tainted soil like entrenched weeds.

No, not forever; if her path stayed straight, she would reach Asyla, and by the same token she could surely make her way to the majesty of God's kingdom. *Or die in the attempt,* she thought as she remembered the paltry supply of rations in her backpack, so light she was barely aware of it. As if to remind her of the other threats to her survival, the wind blew a sudden and wintry gust, and she drew her new cloak tighter around her. She became aware of her breath misting in the air, and remembered another of Maxwell's theories: that the enveloping fog was in fact the accumulated exhalation of the angels themselves.

The angels … thus far she had not seen even a glimpse of the Enclave's absent benefactors. Perhaps it was simply a question of capacity; maybe the plague carrier's corpse had been the final one they could accommodate in their heavenly resting grounds. The Enclave's creeping, ceaseless bloodlust had finally filled the angels' hallowed sepulchres to the brim.

How many dead had the castle seen carried away into the mist? How many had lived in the Enclave, once upon a time?

She stopped when she reached the boulder, the great stone laying half-submerged in the earth as though dropped from a great height. Her legs felt suddenly weary, and this seemed as good a place as any to pause and eat a small morsel, especially as the rock was a perfect height to sit down upon. She lowered herself gratefully, rummaging in her backpack to find a single flask of water and a few of the oatcakes Egbert would occasionally dole out to the Unskilled when in one of his rare good moods.

As Freya ate, she looked up at the sky and the worrying cluster of dark clouds that had gathered there, like black-clad mourners at a funeral procession. She wondered what she would do if it rained; her tormentors had not seen fit to provide any means of shelter, or even an additional blanket to protect her from the winter's chill. At least they had deigned to include a tinderbox and torch along with her meagre supplies. Perhaps they expected her to simply do without rest, to keep walking and walking into the night under the light of its modest flame? She felt anger well up inside her, an irrational urge to just hurl the oatcakes away; but she knew that the hunger in her belly was the merest shadow of the gnawing deprivation she would feel in the coming days, and that every crumb of food was precious. Especially if Asyla turned her away.

So she ate, grudgingly, the food tasting like ashes in her mouth, and watched the sun creep inexorably towards its apex. The pale disc made her think of a huge, unblinking eye, and she wondered if God was indeed watching her, pondering whether to intervene in her pitiful quest. She thought about God and her plan to seek him out, and wondered what form He took. Prayermaster Cedric's orations often seemed to present contradictory descriptions; some sermons made Him seem like a power that resided in the air all around them, hovering just out of mortal sight, while others implied that He was something much closer to a man, sitting on a great glittering throne at the top of the distant Monoliths, at the centre of His kingdom of crystal.

However He manifested, she knew He had created the world, which meant He had created her suffering, which meant that her hardships had a purpose. Somehow this made Freya feel better, and she arose feeling refreshed after her short repast, pushing onwards into the unending mist.

She passed more rocks and boulders, scattered like the skulls of monsters across some vast, abandoned battlefield. The ground beneath her began to change from earth to shale, and grew more uneven, her progress becoming arduous as she was forced up and down a series of long, shallow inclines. These undulations became more and more pronounced until eventually she was half-hiking, half-clambering up steep hills, scrambling down their opposite sides in a scatter of loose pebbles. Yet she was thankful for these hindrances; they distracted her from the hopelessness and monotony of her journey. For now, at least, she had food and water, and the remainder of the day, and could concentrate simply on hauling herself up the ever-increasing gradients towards the misshapen silhouette of Asyla's distant spire.

Something vexed her though, a nagging itch deep in some corner of her brain that wouldn't quite work its way to the surface. It was only when she crested the rise of another slope and saw the ground falling away beneath her towards an enormous, dark pool that the troubling thought revealed itself.

If I have been to Asyla before, why don't I remember these hills, or this lake?

Freya didn't dwell on this; instead, she negotiated the steep drop towards the water, hoping to refill her flask. The wind had died down for the moment, so the air had lost its freezing bite, and she wondered if she'd even be able to bathe. She paused for a moment on a rocky outcrop, realising how tranquil it was, how if she held her breath she became part of an image so still and silent it could be a painting on a canvas, an ashen wasteland imagined by some troubled artist.

There wasn't a single ripple on the surface of the water. The black expanse stretched to the opposite bank like a slab of obsidian, reflecting the sun's dwindling light in a multitude of outlandish colours. Its surface seemed oily and sluggish, as though the water was thick, oozing like treacle. Frowning, she made her way closer, looking around for a loose branch or something she could use to dip into it. But she hadn't seen so much as a single shrub on her journey, not even a tenacious gorse thicket thrusting upwards through the rocky ground.

Eventually she remembered her sword, tucked into the cord around her waist. She took out the blunt, tarnished weapon and lowered its point into the murk. At first nothing happened; then there was a faint hissing noise as bubbles formed around the submerged metal. Carefully, she withdrew the sword and stared at its tip, which smoked like something extracted from a fire. As she watched, the end of the blade began to melt away, disintegrating like a cube of sugar held under running water.

A droplet of the liquefied steel landed on her wrist and she cried out at its scalding, acerbic heat, dropping the remains of the weapon to the ground. Too late, she realised that it was going to bounce, and watched as it clattered and fell into the toxic soup. The lake sizzled hungrily as it consumed the sword, belching an appreciative cloud of noxious fumes that reeked of ozone and made her cover her eyes as she coughed and cursed.

Then the blade was gone, and she was alone and defenceless in a land as poisonous as the plague it carried.

For the first time since leaving, she thought of her room in the citadel, of the comfort of her blankets and the warmth of the flickering torchlight.

No, Freya. That place was more corrosive than even this accursed quagmire.

She turned, grimly surveying the rocks behind her as she tried to ascertain the best way to ascend. Her gaze moved around the edge of the pool, searching for the easiest place to climb, until she spotted a cave set into the opposite side and a jutting ledge leading up to it. As if attuned to her thoughts, the sky suddenly cracked open, assailing her with a vicious deluge of rain. The wind screeched its laughter as though this was a trap it had patiently waited to spring.

There was nothing else to do but try to navigate the perimeter of the swamp, and head for the sanctuary of the cave. Circling the foul waters was a perilous task, particularly in such weather, and she had to choose her footing carefully to avoid slipping on the rock face and plunging to a grisly doom. As she clambered and scaled, she thought about skin melted from bone, about her bones themselves dissolving into the sludge, until she was nothing more than a constituent of the unspeakable broth below. Perhaps flesh was the ingredient that made it so horribly viscous: she imagined herself inching around the slurry of a thousand commingled souls.

Such dark thoughts at least kept her focused on maintaining her footing, and eventually she reached the winding shelf that led upwards to the cave mouth. She hurried along it as fast as she dared to go, utterly drenched and starting to shiver. The stalagmites and stalactites surrounding the entrance made her think of a huge creature's jaws opening to swallow her, but even that seemed preferable to the deaths offered outside, frozen by baleful rain or consumed by the black bog beneath. Gratefully, she passed into the cave.

Although the darkened skies offered scant illumination beyond the first few feet, the cavern seemed large, its ceiling extending high above and providing plenty of room to strip off her soaking clothes. As she changed back into her old rags, which she'd thankfully seen fit to stuff into the backpack, she glanced outside, back towards the slope she had originally descended. Close to where she had fumbled her sword into the lethal tarn, she saw another opening, and at first thought it was a second cave mouth she had missed. But its shape was too even, too perfectly rounded, almost like a man-made tunnel that led back towards the distant castle. More of the black goo was trickling out of it, as though the lake was slowly absorbing the effluvium of the hills themselves.

But she was too soaked and freezing to ponder such mysteries, and was doubly thankful when she withdrew her metal tinderbox to find it had kept its contents dry. Her fingers trembling with cold, Freya extracted a strip of charcloth and wrapped it around the sliver of flint, then struck it with the firesteel until it began to smoulder. She quickly pressed the tinder against the tip of her torch, breathing a sigh of relief when she saw that the sulphur-drenched fabric at its tip had also withstood the rain's onslaught and started to burn brightly.

She swept the firebrand around the cave's interior, searching for anything combustible that she might use to start a proper fire, but found herself surrounded only by stone. *It's okay, cave,* she thought. *You've already helped me enough.* Then she spoke the words aloud, feeling half-mad but strangely liberated. Alone like this, she could do or say whatever she wanted to. *If I want to talk to the rocks, there's not a damned thing anyone can do to stop me anymore.*

Her flame revealed that the cavern was tall but not long, as though squeezed together from both ends like an accordion. Opposite the entrance was a cramped tunnel leading upwards to the surface, which — with some difficulty — would provide her passage away from the foul basin. *But not until the morning,* she thought; this seemed as good a place to spend the encroaching night as any she would find. Yet it was far from perfect. Rain dribbled down the narrow exit route to form a spreading puddle on the floor; moisture clung to the ceiling where it descended in drips that, gradually, over countless oceans of time, had formed the calcified spikes that reached down towards her like the blades of one of Wilfred's dreadful machines. Beneath each one a counterpart grew, fed by these droplets, sprouting upwards as though reaching longingly for its inverted twin.

In the end, she heaped the robes she had removed close to the driest, flattest patch of ground she could find amongst these almost pillars and managed to set the soggy pile alight, preserving the torch for some future crisis. Then she arranged herself in a tightly-curled position close to the fire (the word 'foetal' appeared in her head for a moment, although she had no idea what it meant).

Despite the cold, and the rain, and the harsh stone of her makeshift bunk, despite the horrors and travails she had endured and the fears that squirmed in her brain, Freya fell asleep almost immediately.

***

The strange, flat crystal shone with a glow as pure and brilliant as the sun itself. Indecipherable glyphs danced within this whiteness, and she felt sure they were the sorts of symbols Raoul talked about, his mood swinging from feverish excitement to acute frustration as he spoke of the Archivists' attempts to decipher the ancient texts. *Anguish*, he had called the language, and this seemed apt to her, as the translated snatches he recounted to her spoke of nothing but war and death.

Raoul was there of course, because this was a dream, in which impossible things were routine. He sat beside her, gazing into a crystal of his own, but every so often she felt his eyes drifting to her instead, and she felt intensely happy, not minding the burning heat in her cheeks. But she didn't look back at him, because in this dream world, Raoul was not her husband; he had a different wife altogether, and it was not permitted for them to be together, except like this, when they peered into enchanted glass and pretended not to notice each other at all.

As she watched, the crystal revealed other magics to her: machines that flew in the sky or thundered across the land like unmanned chariots. This was a world of lights, the very stars enslaved to do its people's bidding, people that stretched out before her in an endless sea of faces that even the Enclave could not possibly contain. There were plague-carriers, stunted dwarves, women with skin as dark as Maxwell's, and men with hair as blonde as Letitia's straw-coloured mane.

"Stop wasting time, woman," snapped an irritable voice behind her, and she spun around to see Egbert hunched over his sizzling grill, frying something on the end of a skewer. She realised it was Oswald's head, the Chief Hand's eyes bulging out horribly as he was cooked. "Your lot is merely to serve, and to persist," said the grotesque, severed thing, and she nodded, apologising profusely, feeling suddenly very foolish for daydreaming while the kitchen was so busy. She was thankful for the voices in her ear, telling her what food was required, and thankful again when the same dishes materialised on the tray she held in her hands, even though the alien cuisine looked so outlandish she couldn't imagine anyone wanting to eat it. The brightly-coloured meals piled up so quickly she barely had time to move, and before long she was carrying a teetering pillar of crockery that threatened to topple and shatter on the floor. The only answer was to ascend it, finding gaps and footholds between the towering edifice of plates, hauling herself upwards as the lake's black goo began to rise beneath her. She felt certain something awaited her at the top, although whether it was a reward or a terrible punishment she didn't know.

"Maybe both," said the voice in her ear, the first words Raoul had spoken to her, and then she reached the summit of the crooked spire and crawled appreciatively into the waiting bed. A woman appeared alongside her, with a kind but hassled face, insisting that she breathe and push, and a sudden and devastating agony flared between her legs, where she could hear something crying, a high-pitched scream like a banshee wailing itself into existence. She breathed and pushed, and Raoul put his hand on her forehead and told her how well she was doing, and how much he loved her, as her insides unravelled onto the crisp white sheets.

***

Awake, but powerless to open her eyes, the world veiled behind her lids. Realising next that her eyes were already open, but she was still unable to see; panic swelled like a tumour in her belly until she understood that this blindness was temporary, that the makeshift fire had simply burnt itself out. A crashing wave of relief, was followed immediately by a second wave: this time a great, paralysing tsunami of fear.

Someone was breathing in the darkness.

She pressed her hands to her mouth, crushing down the scream that threatened to flee from her lips, and listened. The breathing was almost a hiss, like wet fingers clamped over a candle flame, and accompanying it was the sound of movement, of hands feeling their way around the cave's interior. The sliding, slapping sounds made her think of clammy fingers pawing at the rocks, and she remembered the tales she had heard long ago, of bizarre things called 'animals' that moved around like people, but on four legs, or borne by wings, or slithering along on no legs at all. She knew such fanciful creatures didn't exist, that 'cats' and 'pigs' and 'dragons' were just folktales decrypted from the ancient texts ... but who knew what monstrosities might crawl, in the dead of night, out of a swamp like the one she had traversed?

Her eyes were adjusting to the gloom, a sliver of moonlight finding its way to them through the narrow tunnel at the cave's rear. She stared, not daring to breathe or even to blink, towards the source of the shuffling, grasping sounds. Did she discern the fumbling arms of some fellow traveller, tossing and turning in their sleep, driven coincidentally into the same refuge by the downpour (whose histrionics, she realised, had fallen silent)?

She rose, slowly, to her haunches, preparing to propel herself upwards and away should the shape — nothing more than shadow against shadow, a scarcely-perceivable outline — make a move towards her. In tiny, careful increments, she scooped up the backpack she had been using as a pillow and began to feel around for the torch, which she had propped against the stone at her side before she slept. Instead, her hand found the ashes of the fire, which were hot enough to make her cry out in surprise, her teeth permitting a single syllable to escape before they slammed closed like a portcullis.

That sound was enough. The thing that shared the cave with her lifted its head, and enormous, saucer-like eyes reflected the moon's light towards her. The limbs — all wrong, too slender, too numerous — seemed to freeze in place for a second, as though the creature was as frightened as she was. Then, with an awful, scuttling quickness, they propelled those terrible eyes towards her.

Freya screamed, leaping to her feet and scrambling towards the tunnel at her back. The thing answered with a phlegmy gurgle that made her think of salivation, of hunger, of desperate cravings demanding to be sated. She could hear the slap-slap of its feet (hands?) against the walls of the cave, imagining it wriggling between the stalagmites as it gnashed monstrous jaws in anticipation. She did not run so much as fall into the shaft, flailing her arms as she hauled herself up and along it.

She realised quickly that it was even narrower than she had thought. The walls closed around her like a clenched stone fist, wringing the breath from her lungs and compressing her ribs as she struggled and squeezed. Soon she was unable to breathe at all, her legs scrabbling for purchase behind her as her arms stretched hopelessly towards the opening at the tunnel's end, which might as well be as far away as the stars she could see scattered across the night sky beyond.

She heard movement behind her, a guttural snarl, the scrape of claws against the rock. She closed her eyes and waited for fanged teeth to sink into her calf muscles, wondering whether she would suffocate before she was eaten alive from the bottom upwards. But then the snarl rose to a howl of rage, and she realised that whatever was pursuing her was equally unable to progress, the shaft's dimensions too constricted for the monster to wriggle through (for that's what it was, a *monster*, she was certain now, a nameless horror spawned in the caustic waters that emerged at night to hunt for flesh).

With a scream of her own, she heaved herself forwards, feeling her bones about to crack under the pressure of the stone that encircled them. Then something seemed to shift, as though the earth itself had widened to disgorge her, and she strained and wriggled and grasped and pulled, and emerged onto the wet ground outside in a gasping, retching heap.

She didn't wait to catch her breath, didn't wait to see whether her pursuer could find its way through the fissure. Instead, she ran, stooped and wheezing, and didn't stop running until she realised that the night was lit by more than the moon's pitiless gaze.

Ahead of her, Asyla's cathedral was burning.

Six

Freya had left the torch behind in her mad scramble from the cave. In that sense at least the fire was a blessing, acting like a beacon amidst the night's black void. But such consolation was far from her thoughts; instead, she wondered what could have happened to turn Asyla's proud spire into a raging pillar of flame. There was nothing she could do but head towards it to find out — after all, she had no light, no shelter, scarcely any food. She dared not risk trying to sleep again that night; instead, she would simply hurry towards the inferno, and to whatever answers awaited.

At first, her steps were sprightly, fuelled by the fading adrenaline of her escape. But after a time, as the ground slowly changed from loose shale back into barren soil, her movements grew sluggish, her limbs and her heart heavy as her destination blazed before her very eyes. She fancied she could make out the town's walls coalescing into view in the distance, and gasped when she realised that they too were aflame, the once-impregnable settlement now ringed with fire. Violent orange lashed the sky, hurling glowing embers towards the darkness. So transfixed was she by the gaudy spectacle that she tripped over a huge tree stump, sprawling across the flat wooden plinth with a yelp of surprise. As she clambered to her feet, she saw similar obstacles littering the ground before her: the remains of a forest, stretching outwards in all directions.

She walked a little further before sagging onto one of the stumps to eat another oatcake, and to drain some more of her dwindling water supply. Ahead of her, the sun had begun to appear over the horizon, as though answering Asyla's incandescence with its fiery display. As the last vestiges of the night were driven away by this lurid tableau, the spire finally collapsed, sinking into the ground as though swallowed whole.

She was close enough to hear the creaking, crumbling sound it made as it fell, although she couldn't be sure if the fleeting screams accompanying it were only in her imagination.

Freya dragged herself to her feet and trudged onwards, moving amongst the remnants of dead trees like a wraith.

***

She found the knight a few hours later.

He was sprawled on his front across one of the great stumps, his arms spread-eagled as though he had been nailed in place. He wore full armour, its shine dulled by soot and scorch marks, a heavy sword fallen from his gauntleted hand to the ground at his side. She wondered how he had died; whether he'd boiled inside his metal casing as he'd fled, like something cooked in a soup kettle. The heat from the still-blazing town of Asyla was certainly becoming intense, and she began to wonder whether she'd even be able to get close to the wreckage. There might be people who needed her help, or at least supplies she could salvage (ruthless as it seemed, she was mindful of her own slim chances of survival in this forsaken land).

Her eyes fell upon the knight's armour once again and she wondered whether she might be able to make use of such protection, or at least pieces of it. A helmet and sword would certainly stand her in better stead should she be assailed by another of the black lake's mutant spawn. She stooped to wrestle with the fallen soldier's headgear, realising that it was held in place by a strap beneath his chin, and set about trying to roll him onto his back. She grunted with exertion as she heaved his plated frame from side to side, trying to build up enough momentum to propel the corpse off the stump altogether. After several attempts she succeeded, and the dead man clattered unceremoniously to the ground, facing upwards toward the now-cloudless sky. At the sight of his face, Freya screamed and leapt backwards.

The plague was rife within him. Its lines and furrows were scored into his flesh like deep crevasses, his brow like an old block of wood that had been used to test the blades of many knives. The silvery strands of hair that hung across it were the same colour as the helm that had hidden it, while his long beard had turned almost completely white, like the spectral trail of some ghostly apparition. Partially obscured beneath it was a thin-lipped mouth that hung slightly open, revealing teeth that were also affected by the plague, some of them little more than yellowed stubs, like miniature versions of the long-harvested trees surrounding them.

If I wasn't already infected, I certainly am now, thought Freya, appalled, rubbing her hands uselessly against her half-shredded clothing as though she could scrub the disease away. Then, horror of horrors, the knight began to cough, and she realised he wasn't dead at all.

"What's happened?" he wheezed, waving his hands in the air as though trying to conjure himself upright. "Where's my sword?"

Aghast, she backed away, wondering if she might be able to hide before he regained his footing. Or perhaps she could outrun him, given the weight of his attire.

But where would she run to?

"Speak, damn you!" the knight cried, then was gripped with another coughing fit. "Once I have regained my poise, you'll regret trying to separate a warrior from his blade!"

Very slowly, his cumbersome suit clanking and grating as he did so, the knight hauled himself into a sitting position, facing away from her towards the smouldering remains of Asyla. A strange noise emerged from him as he beheld the ruins, a sort of strangled sob of surprise and disbelief.

"No," he began to mutter, over and over again, shaking his head.

Gripped by impulse, Freya lunged for his sword, which was lying beside him, but his reactions were surprisingly fast, and he caught her wrist before she could lay a finger on the ash-blackened weapon. He twisted towards her, snatching up the blade in his other hand and planting it in the earth like a walking cane as he struggled to his feet, his gauntlet still clamping her arm in a vicelike grip as she tugged desperately to free herself.

Then he seemed to see her properly for the first time, and released his hold, sending her sprawling backwards to the ground.

"A serving maid," he murmured. "Have you escaped from this fiery hell?" She saw confusion and horror in his eyes, and felt oddly sorry for the plague-ravaged soul. But she had no reason to trust him and backed away as she replied, filling her voice with as much conviction as she could muster.

"No. I am a visitor here, seeking succour and assistance for my people."

"Your ... people?" His expression was contorted with bewilderment. Then another thought seemed to grip him and his head darted from side to side, searching for something. Without another word, he hurried — the wrong word to describe his stooped, lumbering movements, as though the weight of his apparel was too much for his disease-racked body to bear — away to his right, towards a heaped shape she had failed to notice amongst the tree stumps.

This is it, she thought. *Your chance to escape.* But then she noticed the knight tugging at the heap and saw, as he tore off its tarpaulin cover, that it was a handcart piled with supplies. The rising sun reflected off the revealed bounty, catching the polished surfaces of the knight's burdensome plate armour, making them glow like something miraculous.

Almost like one of the angels.

"Is that ... food?" she called, scrambling to her feet and approaching cautiously. As she did so, she saw another shape close to where the knight stood, that of a large man lying motionless on his back. The warrior was staring down at the prone figure, still wearing a confused frown as though trying to piece together the circumstances of his predicament, the town's demise, and the fallen man's repose.

"Is he dead?" Freya asked, seeing that the man's eyes were open, staring upwards like glassy orbs. He was dressed in leather armour, a crude approximation of the knight's finery, although his heavy build and the great cudgel dropped at his side suggested he might still have proved a challenging adversary. The deep wound in his side, caked in dried blood, offered a grisly answer to her question.

The knight lifted his head to her once again, and she flinched at the intensity of his stare, the eyes sunken into the ruin of his face seeming to catch the flickering light of the flames. Then, to her amazement, he bent forwards in a deep bow, hinging at the waist like some rusted contraption.

"If I behold as fair a maiden as thee in this apocalypse, then I know I must still be dreaming, or else transcended already to God's kingdom," he said, wincing as he hauled himself upright. "I know my sickness repulses you ... but will you help me, lass?"

She thought, again, about turning to flee, but there was something about his manner that intrigued her. This was not some destitute, plague-crazed wanderer, but a chivalrous soldier; already he seemed more honourable than most of the Enclave's entire garrison.

No-one had called her a 'fair maiden' for ... how long?

"What help do you require from me, sir?"

"Please: I am merely Errick. Adversity does not concern itself with nobility. What may I call you?"

Freya thought for a moment about whether she could use a different name, perhaps one from a treasured story about a great sorceress or a beautiful queen. But, with a pang of sadness, she realised she couldn't remember any such tales. She was rooted to this reality, as entrenched as the sickness in Errick's bones.

"I'm Freya," she said.

"Well, Freya, there is not a moment to spare. We must search the town for survivors before the place is reduced to ashes."

"Do you have loved ones inside?"

His face took on a haunted, crestfallen cast. "No, miss. I'm just a visitor, like you."

***

Errick walked with a pronounced limp — perhaps another symptom of his sickness, or an injury sustained during whatever episode had left him sprawled and unconscious outside the burning city — but still set a punishing pace towards Asyla's perimeter wall. They reached it minutes later, finding the barrier partially collapsed, and were able to walk straight into the settlement like visiting royalty. The heat was almost intolerable, making Freya sweat and squirm inside her skin, as though its outer layers were starting to slowly cook; she could only imagine how hot the knight must be inside his cumbersome suit.

Trying to take her mind off the temperature, Freya glanced around her, remembering immediately the town's dizzying network of crisscrossing walkways, perilous bridges fashioned from wood and rope lashed together and slung between the ramshackle timber buildings. She recalled how she had gasped as the town's residents traversed them with practised ease, marvelling at how thickly the upper tiers were strung with these catwalks and gangways; it had almost been like being inside a forest, walking beneath a canopy of interlacing branches. Which was appropriate, because Asyla had been built entirely from the reapings of the devastated woodland she had traversed to reach it.

But fire is the nemesis of such a settlement, and now most of the skywalks were scattered across the ground in curled, blackened shapes, like runes scratched into the earth. The buildings were scorched husks, most of them collapsed into unrecognisable piles of smouldering wood, as though they had never been more than hastily-constructed bonfires. Thick, acrid smoke poured from these structures, and she covered her mouth as they explored, tears stinging her eyes.

It must have seemed as though the townsfolk's worst nightmares were made real; yet of the people, there was little sign. She saw one charred corpse crumpled in the doorway of an eviscerated shell that might once have been their house; another lay in a tangle of splayed limbs in the centre of the main street alongside the remains of a collapsed walkway.

"Perhaps the blaze took them in their beds before they even had a chance to flee," murmured Errick, as though reading her thoughts.

"How on earth did this disaster even begin?" she asked.

The knight ignored her question, hastening towards a building that seemed, for now, to have escaped the inferno. She watched as he approached the door of a peculiar structure that appeared to have started life as a windowless wooden shack, but had then been iterated upon over time, with external stairs and walkways and even an extra storey grafted onto it like botched surgery. It was like a microcosm of the chaotic, iterative process by which the entire town had developed, sprawling upwards and outwards as though the forest's trees were still trying to grow, even in death.

Errick tugged open the door, then shrank backwards as fire erupted outwards from inside, like the breath of some enraged demon suddenly awakened.

"This is impossible!" Freya shouted over the roar.

"We must at least check the cathedral," Errick cried, turning his back on the building, which was already being consumed by the renewed conflagration. He pressed onwards, and again she thought about fleeing, running back towards the handcart and its mysterious contents. But something held her, something more than fear or curiosity: a sense that their meeting was fated, that God's hand was at work in their encounter, even in this hopeless rescue mission.

She followed him, coughing as the billowing smoke tormented her lungs.

They reached the town's main square, a circle of ruins around the central calamity of the cathedral, like mourners around a funeral pyre. The cathedral itself was completely gone, the rickety wooden spire disintegrated as it had collapsed into the building's fragile roof, as though the whole improbable structure had been held together by some sort of magic spell, dispelled by the flames. Errick clambered towards the centre of this destruction, where pews, pillars, rafters, and roofing all burned together, and began to rummage amongst the debris. His gauntlets briefly protected his hands from the heat as he tossed aside great chunks of splintered wood, grunting with the strain. Freya hung back, glancing around her in fear, wondering which of the surrounding buildings would be the next to collapse.

"Errick! This place is destroyed!" she called to him as he toiled amongst the chaos. "What is it you hope to find?"

He did not reply, but continued his labours, stooping after a while to wrestle with something at his feet. She watched as he heaved and pulled, finally flinging open the trapdoor that he had revealed, a triumphant expression on his face.

"Hello?" he hollered. "Is anyone down there? Fear not, it is now safe to emerge!" Then he disappeared from view, descending into whatever underground chamber he had unearthed. Freya waited, unsure what to do. Perhaps he would reappear momentarily, followed by a group of soot-covered survivors begging for help to rebuild their home. Around her, the fire crackled and growled as if in mockery of her daydream, like a monster that had consumed Asyla not for nourishment, but out of pure cruelty.

I can't bear this, she thought, and with a deep breath she followed her companion towards the centre of the cathedral's demolished grandeur. She could feel the surrounding heat even through the thickness of her rags as she edged her way carefully amongst the wreckage, imagining she was willingly entering Hell itself: a place beyond the reach even of God, a kingdom of penance that burned forever. Perhaps she was already dead, and the hatch at the cathedral's centre was the portal to the punishment that awaited her, for being a terrible wife, a terrible servant. For failing the Enclave. The dark aperture seemed to beckon her; she approached it with a strange feeling of familiarity, thinking of black lakes and the things that writhed beneath their surfaces.

Then Errick reappeared, ascending the set of steps that led down from the opening, his face ashen. "Don't go down there," he said simply, in answer to the questions blazing in her eyes.

"What happened?" she cried. "Did you find anyone?"

He did not reply, but very slowly turned and closed the trapdoor. Then he hobbled past her, his gait even more stooped than usual, as though he might be about to collapse.

"What was down there?" she persisted, following him as he began to retrace their steps, away from the smoking remnants of the cathedral.

"I found them all," he replied, not facing her. "Those that escaped the flames and sealed themselves away. They were poisoned by the smoke instead."

She glanced backwards at the innocuous doorway, wondering how many bodies lay beneath it. She imagined their faces, twisted in the horror of death, a horror that she had seen more times in the past few days than she dared to count.

"Was there anything else? Any food, maybe, that we might be able to—"

Errick turned and struck her a vicious backhanded blow across the face, knocking her to the ground amongst the ashes. She cried out in surprise, bringing a hand to her stinging cheek, staring upwards in sudden fear at the knight that loomed over her, bent but still imposing, plague-stricken yet still formidable. But she saw that his eyes were wet with tears, and that he had no more malice for her. Instead he sagged to his knees, his head bowed, holding out the hilt of his sword. It took her a few seconds to realise he was offering it to her.

"This fire is my doing," he said, his throat sounding clogged with sorrow. His eyes were cast downwards, towards the ashes that surrounded him. "I did not intend ... but it makes no difference in the eyes of our Lord. Your presence here is no longer a mystery, maiden: you have been sent by God to carry out my sentence."

A fine rain had begun to fall, sizzling as it touched the smoking ruins around them. Still clutching her cheek, she rose, reaching for the proffered weapon. It was heavier even than she expected, and its blade fell to the earth with a thud before she lifted it, staring into the lustrous metal where a blurred reflection of her seemed to foretell another life, a life unscarred.

"I apologise, good lady, for striking you," he said, his voice cracking with emotion. "To blame you for the litany of my failings is yet another grievous misdeed. Please; the sooner I am purged from this world the better." He reached upwards and loosened the strap at his chin, allowing his helmet to fall to the ground. Steel-coloured hair spilled around his face, and she saw how thin his exposed neck was, how easily it might be severed by a weapon of such might.

If I kill him and flee, she thought, *I might yet avoid contamination by his sickness.*

Using both hands, she hoisted the blade above the knight's head, imagining what it would be like to swing it down with all her might, cleaving his head from his shoulders.

Then she lowered the sword.

"Arise, Sir Errick," she said. "You seek judgement I am not fit to pass." The words seemed to come to her from somewhere outside, like a distant star channelling its will through her lips. "You are right, though, that fate has brought us together; because my quest is to seek audience with God Himself, and to ask Him for answers. If you seek God's reckoning, then accompany me; because He is the only one that can deliver your sentence, whether it is condemnation or absolution. And along the way you can tell me of the misdeeds of which you speak, in the knowledge that I will not judge or denounce you."

She sagged, as though her outburst had drained her, feeling suddenly foolish and exhausted. The sword clattered to the earth, at once immeasurably heavy in her grasp. But glancing at Errick, she saw that he was staring at her with something like awe in his face. His hair had soaked up the rain quickly, the sodden strands shedding droplets that fell like tears.

He rose, and helped her to her feet.

***

They returned to the handcart, leaving the cinders of Asyla behind them. Errick was silent while they walked, but as they approached the cart he began to speak again. Freya had to strain to hear him; his words were swallowed by the swirling wind that had replaced the fleeting rain, his eyes downcast as though he could not bear to meet her gaze. But she soon realised that he was unburdening himself of the story of how he had brought about the downfall of Asyla.

The cart was his. He had hauled it across the Wastes until he reached the decimated forest and the settlement at its centre. He had approached the gates, telling the guards that he was a plague-carrier and did not expect access to their town, but that he hoped to trade with them for food. The guards had told him that their supplies were running out since the angels had forsaken them (her eyes widened at this, but she stayed quiet), but that they would send out one of their merchants to inspect his wares.

"Instead they sent that great oaf you can see sprawled over yonder, meaning to kill and rob me." Errick pointed at the oversized corpse nearby. "He was doughty, but stupid and easily outmanoeuvred, yet still he managed to strike me a resounding blow before he fell." He pointed to a dent in the side of his helmet, which had been returned to its place atop his head. "I returned to remonstrate with the guards, telling them that on my previous visits to Asyla, I had enjoyed a much less frosty welcome. But still, they refused to deal with me, so I decided to deploy one of the magics I have acquired on my travels: a vial of something I obtained from the old sage at Kamistille. More flammable even than sulphur, that bastard told me ... but I did not know how much more." His expression was twisted with guilt as he continued. "I swear to you, I intended only for the fire to unsettle them, to force them to open their doors, perhaps even to fear me as a great wizard." His voice fell away.

"What happened?" she prompted gently.

"I tossed the flask, and there was an explosion, before a gout of flame leapt up the walls. At that moment, my head began to swim from the injury inflicted by this lummox." He aimed a spiteful kick at the large man's body. "I staggered and fell, and lay here insensible until you found me."

"It was a terrible accident, Sir Errick. You did not intend such a disastrous outcome."

"Nevertheless," he murmured darkly. "Such are the consequences of meddling with sorcery." He spat on the ground, then seemed to regret his vulgarity in her presence, and busied himself with covering up the cart.

"How long will your supplies last?" she asked, surveying its contents. "I'm afraid I have very little food."

"A few days, between the two of us," he replied. "If we travel east towards the Monoliths, we will reach Erebyss before our provisions run out — although its people are strange, and may not be inclined to help us. Still, it is our best hope of replenishing our rations."

She gnawed her lip for a moment, hesitating to ask her next question. "And what of your disease, Sir Errick? How long before you succumb to its ravages?"

And before I become infected, too?

"Please, I am merely Errick — if I have earned respectful titles from anyone, I have certainly not earned them from you. As regards my condition, I'm afraid I do not know — I know only that the sickness came upon me slowly, after many days of travelling this dismal hinterland." His eyes fell once more as he drifted into grim contemplation. "I've been wandering for so long that I can scarcely remember when my journey started."

"Why? What has led you to this wanderer's life?"

He bent to lift the arms of the handcart and turned toward her with a sad smile. She realised it was the first time he'd worn such an expression since they met. "I'm afraid it's another sorrowful tale. It seems I am doomed to live a tragic parody of the hero's path I foolishly sought to carve. I will share my misfortunes with you on the road to Erebyss, if you care to hear them. But first I must hear everything about you, my new companion, and my saviour!" His smile widened, and she realised for the first time that beneath the depredations of the plague Errick was a handsome man, or had once been. "Which means you should settle in, because we have a long journey ahead of us, and much time for such stories."

"Settle in?"

He nodded towards the cart. "Climb aboard your new carriage, my lady. It will be my honour to convey you across this blighted land in a fashion more comfortable than your previous one, if only slightly."

She shook her head. "Oh no, Errick, don't be silly. I couldn't possibly expect you to pull me along like some sort of pampered empress!"

She had anticipated gallant protests, but instead he simply met her gaze with a look of deep, harrowed regret, and a grief she couldn't refuse.

"Please," he whispered.

So she nodded, and climbed onto the cart, and together they set out towards the still-rising sun.

Seven

Errick marched briskly despite his limp, and while he walked Freya talked, telling him about her life in the Enclave and the scarcely credible circumstances that had brought her into his company. At first, the situation seemed utterly bizarre, her lounging like a noblewoman while the genteel knight listened patiently to her account, acknowledging the details with occasional polite grunts, never interrupting. But she quickly became at ease as she spoke, lulled almost into a state of slumber by the surprisingly warm sun, the pale cloudless sky, the bent form of Errick's broad back as he laboured under the weight of the sword slung across it, and the burden of his apparel.

"Wouldn't it be better to take off your armour?" she asked, disrupting her own narrative. "You could toss it here on the cart."

"You'd understand, my lady, if you were a knight yourself. Asking me to take off my protection is akin to asking someone to shed their skin."

"The knights of the Enclave often removed their armour when off duty or socialising."

"With respect, the 'knights' you have described do not seem to warrant the description. Except for brave Sir Thomas, whose grotesque punishment was wholly unwarranted."

A vision sprang suddenly to her mind, of Thomas stretched out on the suspended scaffold in Wilfred's dungeon, the skin of his arm unpeeled like the rind of a fruit. She swallowed, feeling familiar nausea squirming inside her, and hastened to change the subject. She spoke, instead, of the black lake, of the rainstorm that had driven her into the cave, and the half-glimpsed monstrosity that had chased her out into the night.

"Thank God it did," he mused. "Otherwise our paths might never have crossed."

"Have you ever seen such a creature?"

"Nay, lass. I seem to recall passing the vile bog you encountered, though thankfully I judged its waters too murky to attempt to drink. Perhaps the foul effluvium that has contaminated it is to blame for the aberration you encountered."

"How about the Enclave? Did you ever visit there?"

"No. I'd heard tell of a great, white castle beyond the mists; but to be honest I never believed it was real. What a shame to learn that such a wondrous place should be populated by such vermin."

She frowned. "What's 'vermin'?"

Errick stopped, and for a moment she thought his leg had seized up altogether. Then he replied, a mystified laugh accompanying his words. "You know, I've completely forgotten. But I feel quite sure it's the right word, nonetheless."

He continued to tow her along, towards and away from the curtain of mist that had already gathered at their backs, swallowing Asyla whole like an unwanted memory. Around them the land was as featureless and desolate as ever, the soil of the earth so dark it was almost black. They walked like that for a long time, the sun reaching its zenith and beginning its descent behind them, and she realised she had been talking for hours, about Maxwell and Egbert and her other memories of life in the Enclave, and felt suddenly embarrassed.

"I'm sorry, Errick; you must be bored half to death by tales of such drudgery."

"On the contrary, miss — it is a blessing to these ears to hear another human voice. It's been so long since I've had a companion ... longer than I care to remember, in fact."

"Sometimes I remember another life," she began, and then bit back the words, not wanting her escort to think her utterly deranged. But there was something about Errick's stoic, patient presence that seemed to compel the truth from her lips. "It comes to me in fragments, or half-remembered dreams.

70

A husband, who left me so he could wander the Wastes, just like you." A flare of pain in her cheek reminded her of the blow she had sustained the previous day, and she wondered whether all men were prone to fits of rage, just like Sir Bernard, or like Raoul. Her scar seemed to burn with the hazy recollection of his violence, and she fell silent.

"I understand," Errick replied after a time, to her surprise. "My own past is similarly shrouded, as though this loathsome mist has seeped into my very skull. I remember my life in Deorsica, but not how I first came to be there."

"Deorsica ... I've never heard of it. Is that where you call home?"

"Not anymore. I'm afraid you are travelling with an exile, my lady."

"Were you cast out because of ... the misdeeds you mentioned?"

Errick nodded, looking more stooped and frail than ever. But she felt certain that, though it would bring him pain, recounting his transgressions would help to unburden his troubled soul. "Why don't you tell me about it?" she said kindly.

With a deep sigh, he did.

***

The tournament rolled around again. It happened with a degree of regularity, although words like 'years' and 'anniversaries' had long since lost their meaning; the King simply decided that it was time, and his Royal Guard took up their staves and prepared to defend their livelihoods.

They fought with wooden staffs to prevent unnecessary casualties; the population was already dwindling fast enough from accidents, suicides, and those bewitched by the allure of the mist. But the weapons were still capable of breaking bones, and the loser's fall from the platform to the netting far below was mightily perilous. To partly mitigate this risk, and because some of the combatants were commoners who could hardly afford such advantages, the competitors were banned from wearing any armour. Thus, the tournament was a test of raw fighting ability; it was the one time when every person in Deorsica was reborn, equal, and the lowliest serf afforded the same opportunity as the city's highest-ranked knights.

There were, at any one time, eight Royal Guards. The tournament's quarter-finalists would replace the incumbents, with the beaten finalist assuming the honour of personal bodyguard to the Queen; the overall victor would perform the same function at the King's side.

"Thus I ensure that my queen and I are protected by the best soldiers in the city," King Wolfram would remind his subjects during the lavish opening ceremony. "And keep the rest of my warriors as sharp as a blade pressed regularly against a whetting stone."

Any Royal Guard defeated en route to the final rounds was harshly punished, stripped of their rank and forced to trade roles with their usurper. It was not uncommon for defeated knights to spend degrading stretches working as street cleaners, pimps, or servants, only to reclaim their commissions at a subsequent competition, their resolve hardened by long seasons of humiliation.

But this never happened to Errick; as usual, he had reached the last round once again. It had been a challenging contest, perhaps the hardest he could recall, as his rivals employed ever more outlandish techniques and training regimes in their attempt to best the current cortege. Indeed, two of the Royal Guard had already fallen in the preceding rounds. But Errick's routine never changed, and his determination never wavered.

He would remain at the Queen's side until his dying day.

He allowed himself to steal a glance at her during the pre-match formalities, while he and his opponent bowed their heads and Archpriest Eamon upended a cauldron of blood through the arena's central aperture. As always, every resident of the city had contributed to the vessel, slicing their palms and allowing Eamon's servants to collect their offering during the days leading up to the ceremony. Now they nursed bandaged hands, another notch added to their tally of scars, as the cleric prayed for the crimson fluid to invigorate the waters that thundered far beneath them.

To say Queen Annalise looked beautiful was akin to describing the sun as bright; to say she was resplendent in her finery was like gazing upon the grandeur of Deorsica and labelling it merely 'a striking city'. Such words were inadequate, all the metaphors of the wisest poets a derisory approximation of how breathtaking she was. She occupied her throne on the periphery of the battleground with the elegance of the moon, the veiled strength of a storm cloud, the benevolence of a divine emissary. The majesty of a true queen.

Errick tore his gaze away before she saw him looking at her, cursing the jealousy that flared in his gut as he beheld Torrick, whom he had defeated in the semi-final, temporarily occupying his place at her side. Errick's duty was to root out such weaknesses within himself, to crush such petty emotions as he might extinguish the life of a would-be assassin. Down that path lay only madness; did he envy the King himself, his own monarch, who shared her bed every night? He felt his free hand coiling into a fist, and forced himself to breathe deeply, to remain calm and focused.

He would need to concentrate if he was going to lose without arousing suspicion.

He shifted his gaze to the giant opposite him, who stared back with a sadistic sneer and coal-black eyes. Usually, Errick would have been faced by the imperturbable stare of Phaedra, who had served at the King's side for almost as long as Errick had been assigned to the Queen, and when their eyes met he would fancy he could detect perhaps a glint of admonishment, as though she understood the real reason he had never bested her. Yet she never confronted him, and the guilt would continue to gnaw away at him like a sickness in his belly.

But Phaedra had been defeated in the other semi-final by this muscled monstrosity, and she now watched sadly from her king's side, the last time she would occupy that place for quite some time. The behemoth's success was a surprise to all; a humble mineworker named Bellus, he had never proceeded very far in the event before, his lack of guile too severe a handicap despite his evident strength and near seven-foot stature. But this time he had been trained by Vasek, a former Royal Guardsman whose defeat in a previous tournament had left him crippled and relegated to the role of pit foreman, where he had doubtless befriended the brute. Vasek was also in the audience, his wooden walking cane laid across his lap and a confident smile adorning his face.

The Archpriest concluded his invocation and the King held up one hand, palm outwards, silencing the onlookers who had chatted with excited irreverence throughout the proceedings. There were perhaps two thousand gathered around the Great Well, straining to see the ring-shaped stage which was lashed with stout ropes to the walls of the wide, circular chasm that carved a cross-section down through their great city. The commoners craned their necks to peer upwards from beneath the platform, while the nobles enjoyed a far better view from the upper tiers of the colosseum that encircled the pit; yet, despite reinforcing the city's strict hierarchy, the tournament at least brought its people together, allowing them to glimpse each other across the great shaft that granted access to the underground river that churned beneath them. Errick tried not to think about those crashing waters, or the flimsy webbing that was stretched above them to catch defeated combatants who plunged from the stage, either off the side or through the hole at its centre.

Seconds ticked past like hours, and Errick watched his opponent's face, which remained bisected by a malevolent grin. He searched that detestable smile for any clue as to how his adversary might approach him; would Bellus launch into a rampaging charge, seeking to smash Errick off the edge of the platform with a single unstoppable shoulder tackle, as he had done to countless others on the way to his newfound fame? Or would the ruffian be cautious, as he had with Phaedra, displaying an unexpected cunning as he feigned injury beneath a barrage of blows, only to snatch the stave from her grasp, snapping it in two and flinging her from the podium as though she was no heavier than a marionette?

King Wolfram closed his hand into a fist and, as a frenzied cheer erupted from the crowd, Errick knew he was about to find out. He rose from his haunches and watched the giant lumber slowly towards him, the staff looking like a twig in his massive hands. Errick didn't move, poised and ready to leap aside if his rival burst suddenly into a run, but Bellus seemed to sense a trap and instead approached slowly, skirting the circular opening at the centre of their strange battlefield. The combat zone was around twenty metres in diameter, but Bellus was so tall that he closed the gap between them in a handful of strides, the suspended stage wobbling alarmingly with every thunderous footfall. Bellus raised his stave as though preparing to deliver a crushing downward blow, but then surprised Errick by instead aiming a huge, chest-high kick at him, forcing him to reel backwards to avoid it, teetering perilously close to the arena's edge.

Too early, he thought. *I'm going to put up a fight first.*

The big man snarled ferociously and lunged forward with the staff, trying to prod Errick off the rim, but Errick sidestepped neatly and swung his own pole into the brute's extended forearm. Bellus howled in surprise and dropped his weapon, and Errick quickly closed the distance between them, belabouring the giant with a hail of vicious strikes to both sides of his barrel-sized ribcage. Roaring in pain and frustration, the titan dropped to his knees, and Errick aimed a brutal blow towards his clavicle, seeking to snap the bone in two.

You might be about to win the tournament, thug, but first you'll learn some lessons.

He realised, too late, that this was the same ploy his foe had used against Phaedra. One enormous hand snapped suddenly closed around Errick's swinging staff, yanking it from his grasp. Bellus growled like a beast as he snapped the weapon easily in two, tossing both pieces over the precipice as he hopped nimbly to his feet. The wicked smile returned to the giant's face as the crowd roared and he advanced on Errick, who stumbled backwards towards the hole in the centre of the ring, grudgingly impressed by the fortitude of Vasek's protégé.

Then Bellus made a mistake. The titan threw a flailing haymaker that Errick easily evaded, rolling forwards and snatching the behemoth's dropped weapon from the arena floor. As Errick rose, he twisted, directing his energy up through his hips and into a devastating backhand blow, adjusted upwards to account for his enemy's unusual height.

There was a gristly crack as the staff smashed into Bellus's oversized skull, and Errick knew immediately that he had been overzealous. The giant's eyes were suddenly emptied, his menacing grin replaced by the vacant canvas of a man lost to unconsciousness. Without hesitation, Errick spun around again, flinging another blow into his opponent's torso even as the giant fell, using the force to drive Bellus away from the hole and simultaneously pitching himself forwards as though carried by an excess of momentum. As the monster crumpled into an insensible heap, Errick tottered on the brink of the chasm, allowing his bodyweight to guide him over its edge.

The crowd hollered and hooted as he fell, their new champion oblivious to their adulation, unaware of his victory. But Errick fancied he had caught the Queen's eye before he tumbled, glimpsing the faintest flicker of relief in her expression.

As he plummeted towards the woven mesh that would save him from the river's raging torrents, this thought was enough to make Errick smile.

Eight

With a start, Freya awoke to find a dark sky above her, and a fire crackling at her side. She glanced about her in confusion and saw Errick sitting on the other side of the modest flame, fidgeting with his outstretched leg.

"Errick! What happened?"

He glanced up at her, his expression kind, but tinged with pain as he manipulated his extended limb. "You fell asleep, my lady. Hardly a surprise, given the disruption to your rest last night, and the monotony of my tale. I continued walking as far as I could, then made camp when I found somewhere vaguely suitable."

He had chosen an old, ruined building, perhaps once a waystation of some kind, the rubble of which was strewn about them as though it had been blasted apart by lightning. The chunks of decaying masonry provided some shelter from the quickening wind, although they would offer little protection if the heavens decided to open once again; ominous clouds had gathered above them as though the moon was gathering troops for an assault. The dried-up fissure of a dead river ran alongside them, curving towards and then away like a sad smile. There was a foul, fetid odour in the air, and she wondered what creatures might be rotting on the stream's arid bed; perhaps this tributary had once connected to the black lake itself.

She remembered the beginning of Errick's story, and felt terrible for nodding off, even more so when she realised that he had arranged the cart's tarpaulin into makeshift bedding around her.

"What's wrong with your leg?" she asked, realising that he had removed the armour plate covering his left shin, and was grimacing as he prodded and poked the limb.

"Oh, it's nothing. Just a wound that refuses to heal properly. This damned plague weakens the body's natural resolve."

"Let me see," she insisted, climbing to her feet and crossing to sit alongside him. She gasped when she saw the injury: a long, deep gash from ankle to knee, surrounded by flesh so grievously infected it had turned black. Pus dribbled from the ugly laceration, which she realised was the source of the awful smell.

"It's no wonder you walk with a limp!" she scolded. "How did this happen?"

"I fought with a highwayman some days back; the vagabond somehow managed to thrust his spear between the defences of my knee and foreleg, down behind the plate on my shin. Sadly for him it became stuck there, and I wrenched it from his grip simply by sweeping my leg backwards. The rest of the encounter was disappointingly straightforward after that."

"Well, we need to find someone who can treat this, before the infection gets any worse."

"You're probably right. I'm not much use to us lame as well as diseased."

"Will there be healers in Erebyss?"

He nodded. "Their worship is misguided, but they are not without such skills."

"In what way is it misguided?"

"They seek God not in His distant Monoliths, or in the sun that renews our daily existence, but instead deep in the bowels of the earth. Each time I visit that subterranean city, it has moved, deeper and deeper underground."

She thought about a life lived at such depths, far from the sun or the stars she could now glimpse above her, arrayed across the sky like pinpricks in a sheet of black cloth. She thought of the cave, of how oppressive it had seemed, and shuddered at the prospect of making such a descent. "How many days before we reach it?" she asked, trying to mask her fear.

"We will need to simply follow this lifeless river, making camp three more times," he answered. "Now please, get some rest. I don't mind keeping watch for a while longer."

"But you need to sleep too, Errick. Wake me in an hour and we'll switch places."

He nodded his assent and returned his attentions to his ravaged extremity while she climbed back amongst the thick fabric of her improvised bed, the most comfortable thing she had lain on for what felt like an age.

He never did wake her; instead she rose, blinking, to find the sun already rising, and Errick preparing their breakfast.

***

The day began with an impasse. Despite looking increasingly pale and haggard, Errick refused to let her carry the cart with him resting upon it, while Freya would not move unless he consented. In the end, Errick agreed to sleep through the next night with her keeping watch, and she insisted on walking alongside the cart rather than riding on it during the day. Thus, after concluding their debate, as well as an unsatisfying meal of stale bread and cured meat washed down with a few gulps of water, they set out once again, keeping the serpentine coils of the river in sight on their right-hand side.

They were silent for a time, each lost in their thoughts until Freya saw a peculiar structure approaching on their left. At first she thought it was a leafless tree, which would have been the first she had seen since leaving the Enclave; but as they drew near she realised that this structure was not nature's work at all. Slivers of metal had been fastened together to create a peculiar, upright lattice, describing a right-angled outline several metres across on each side. It seemed to serve no purpose other than to stand there accumulating rust. Its upper extremities were bent and broken, as though it had once stood taller, and she noticed other metallic strips scattered around it, their corroded brown colour barely distinguishable from the dark earth.

"What do you think that is?" she asked.

Errick shrugged. "We will encounter several more along our course. They are route markers, perhaps, or decaying shrines constructed in days of old."

She began to phrase another question but was interrupted by the menacing growl of thunder overhead. The canopy of dark clouds had thickened during the night, giving the impression not that more had flocked to join them, but instead that the same clouds had increased in size, swelling like bloated tumours ready to burst. A downpour was imminent and their austere surroundings offered no shelter at all.

"Perhaps, if it rains, we can clamber down into the riverbed to look for refuge?" she suggested.

"Or we can keep walking, and get wet," Errick replied tersely. "The tarpaulin will protect our supplies, and you are welcome to clamber under it."

She glanced at him, worrying again about her companion's wellbeing. His limp certainly seemed more pronounced, but she could not tell whether his testiness and sallow complexion were also a result of his grievous wound, a lack of sleep, or perhaps the sickness that circulated in his blood.

Or maybe these were symptoms of the demons that beset his mind.

"What have you even got on that cart?" she asked with a smile, trying to lighten the mood. "You're more like a travelling rag-and-bone man than a knight."

"Dried meats, some ageing bread, a bit of cheese I'm saving for tomorrow, some overripe fruit we can eat for lunch. A few canteens full of water. Weapons and artefacts for trading." His expression darkened. "And two more of those accursed vials of fire nectar. I ought to toss those things into this miserable gulch at our side."

She changed the subject again, determined to find some way to alleviate Errick's malaise. "The metal scaffold we just passed — who do you think built it?"

The knight shrugged again. "Perhaps this route was once walked by great armies, or travelling cities who stopped periodically to dispose of the deceased, leaving monuments to honour the burial sites."

"How did you dispose of the dead in Deorsica?"

"The visiting angels collect them, just as you described in your Enclave."

"At least before we were forsaken," she muttered, then bit her tongue as she realised such talk might lead Errick's thoughts back to Asyla. "Why don't you finish your story?" she asked instead. "I remember up to the part where you fell from the battlefield. I imagine your queen was delighted to have you serving by her side once again?"

He nodded grimly. "Aye, at first. But then there was an outcry. Archpriest Eamon had been taken ill, and rumours were spreading that the plague had breached the city walls, that even the cleric's faith was not enough to protect him from its malign touch. Malcontent and mutiny rumbled in the mineshafts and workhouses, and the entire city was summoned to the Great Well to be addressed by the King himself."

The haunted tinge that came to his face made his pallor seem even worse, and she instantly regretted revisiting the tale. But perhaps there was therapy to be had in its telling, and she stayed quiet while he talked.

"The King was angry, and it showed. With the hulking presence of Bellus at his side, he stood at the centre of the stage where scant days previously I had been defeated, looking around him with disdain.

'Is this my kingdom?' he asked. 'A bunch of miscreants and malcontents who plot our city's downfall from the shadows?' There were some mutterings at this, but no-one spoke up to challenge him. 'Or am I surrounded by my loyal subjects? By the skilled hands that have helped to build our glorious metropolis from the stones they levered from the earth, the great minds that have assembled our laws and codes of conduct, the loyal worshippers whose faith in God's glory keeps our city strong and prosperous?'

Around the arena, the city's ornate belfries, spires and steeples seemed to reach upwards in jubilation, celebrating the words of their monarch, and there were some outbreaks of cheering and applause. But the atmosphere remained noticeably flat, a muted echo of the rapt excitement that had permeated the place during the tournament.

Unperturbed, Wolfram continued. 'It has come to my attention that some among you believe the dread plague has come to Deorsica. This is a lie, spread by dissenters. Archpriest Eamon rests in his bed, recovering merely from a bout of shingles.'

'A lie, is it?' bellowed a voice from the upper levels of the colosseum. Heads turned towards the source of the interruption, while the few eyes that remained on the King saw him turn white with rage. 'I beg to show you otherwise!'

I squinted from my own position at the Queen's side, up towards the distant tier. At first I could not pinpoint the heretic, but then there was a sudden flurry of movement as nobles rose from their seats and cowered backwards to reveal him.

It was Vasek, the former Royal Guardsman who had trained the King's current bodyguard, Bellus. He was on his feet, one arm clamped around the throat of another man, the other hand pressing a wicked dagger against his hostage's throat. I gasped, recognising Archpriest Eamon himself held in Vasek's death grip. Bellus's mentor could barely walk, but clearly he was still more than a match for the obese cleric, whose eyes bulged outwards from his face as though they might be squeezed from their sockets.

Around and beneath us, the crowd were in turmoil, shrieks of dismay mixing with shouts of approval, scuffles breaking out all around. Close by, I saw Phaedra draw her greatbow, trying to find a clear shot at Vasek, her view obstructed by the Archpriest's substantial bulk.

'This morning I paid a visit to Eamon's sickbed,' Vasek continued, his voice loud and commanding. The King was twisting and turning on the spot as though racked with indecision, his mouth opening and closing in disbelief. 'And look what I found beneath his cowl!'

Vasek held something aloft, and the people nearby screamed in horror, falling over themselves in their bid to shrink away from it. I peered closer, realising at the last moment what was going on, and what Vasek planned to do.

He was holding a clump of Eamon's hair, which was streaked with grey.

'The mark of a plaguebearer!' Vasek cried, as the crowd erupted into chaos. Instinctively, I vaulted over the barrier in front of me and began to sprint towards the stage. Phaedra had the same realisation moments later, and shifted her aim downwards, releasing an arrow that sped towards her target faster than I could hope to replicate.

But we were both too late. Bellus had already wrapped his thick, calloused hands around Wolfram's neck, breaking it as though it was a twig. Phaedra's arrow hit the giant in the temple moments later, skewering his brain, and both the traitor and the King plunged together over the side of the precipice. The tournament had ended, so there was no netting stretched across the chasm to break their fall, and Bellus's dying gurgles were lost in the roar of the water that swallowed them."

Errick stopped, and Freya sensed there was a final twist to his wretched tale, the tragedy that had made of him the forlorn husk she now travelled with.

"Without Bellus to fight for them, Vasek and his followers were soon subdued, and his plan to seize control of the city quashed. The traitors were tied to the wheels of wagons and driven around the city until all that remained of them were smeared red trails. But the Queen, now a widow, did not let her retribution stop there."

Errick's gaze was turned once more to the ground, as though he imagined his old life might be buried there, hidden in the barren earth.

"What happened?"

"All seven remaining members of the Royal Guard were expelled, and all future tournaments cancelled. The Royal Guard would now be handpicked by Queen Annalise herself. Most of the previous retinue ended up working in the mines, although Phaedra was denied even that small mercy — instead, the Queen had her blinded as punishment for her inadequacy with the greatbow."

Freya gasped, but Errick didn't stop, the words pouring out like the secretions from his wound.

"Archpriest Eamon was cast out, although it was never formally admitted that he had contracted the plague. The city closed its doors to outsiders, forbidding even travelling merchants or emissaries from entering."

Freya realised then that it was raining, the clouds finally shedding their burdens, hurling fat raindrops down at them like unruly soldiers playing spitting games off the Enclave's battlements.

"And what about you?" she asked gently. "Didn't the Queen recognise that it wasn't your fault, that there was nothing you could have done to save her husband?"

Errick turned to her, his ashen face twisted with bitterness. "On the contrary. Her ladyship said that if I hadn't lost on purpose, Bellus would have been in no position to assassinate the King."

"But if you'd beaten him, he would have been assigned to her side instead! She would have been the one tumbling into the river with a broken neck."

"Queen Annalise said I'd been negligent in my duties. That the only reason I didn't suffer a fate as grim as Phaedra's was because Archpriest Eamon required an escort during his exile. Hence I was provided with this cart, and sent out into the Wastes as his servant."

"What happened to the priest?" she asked, fearing she already knew the answer.

"He could not adjust to our new life, scavenging for survival in the wilderness. He sat silently upon this wagon for many days, refusing food, wasting away to a shadow of his former corpulence. After a while I stopped trying to reason with him, and he slipped further into malnourishment and catatonia. I don't know how long it took me to realise I was acting as chauffeur to a corpse."

Freya stared at him, feeling sadness radiate from her companion like heat from a fire; but a fire without warmth, a cold flame as lifeless as the dried-up river that meandered alongside them. "But if Eamon was dead, didn't that mean you could return home?"

Errick's eyes had closed, as though his words were causing him great pain. Greasy raindrops ran down his face, into his snow-white beard, trickling down the breastplate of his armour. "My queen said that if she ever saw me again, her archers would fill me with so many arrows that there wouldn't be a scrap of flesh left on my bones."

"Oh Errick ... that's terrible."

His eyes were still closed as he continued, a strange smile playing at the corners of his lips. "I was told once, that people are judged upon God's altar when they die. But that some people, whose sins are neither immaterial nor grievous, might wander instead in a hollow, empty land, awaiting purification.

They call this place Limbo. Sometimes I wonder if I have died already, and that is where I now find myself."

"You loved her, didn't you?"

Errick didn't reply. Instead, his cart dropped suddenly to the ground, and the knight toppled forwards, his face smacking into the dirt as Freya rushed to his side.

Nine

Getting Errick onto the cart was a gauntlet of ordeals. First and foremost, Freya had to overcome her horror at the prospect of touching the flesh of a plague-carrier; but she could not bring herself to abandon him and reasoned that, without Errick, she had no hope of survival, if indeed she wasn't already infested with the sickness herself. The next challenge was the overpowering stench emanating from beneath the armour of his right leg, which had worsened since the previous night.

But the biggest obstacle of all was hoisting the knight's prone body onto the vehicle. Freya found this almost impossible, her fingers slipping so often on the wet metal of his armour that she had considered removing the suit altogether. But that would leave him unprotected against the freezing rain, which lashed them so hard it seemed to intend the purification of which Errick had rambled before his collapse; such exposure would surely guarantee his death. So instead she had struggled and heaved, eventually managing to drag him on top of the meagre heap of his supplies, covering him with the tarpaulin to protect him from the weather's depredations.

Actually moving the wagon was, initially, not as difficult as she'd feared. But as the ground turned to rain-soaked muck beneath the cart's wheels, and her own flimsy boots rapidly became waterlogged, she found her progress slowing almost to a crawl. At her side, the river snaked away into the distance like a mockery, its grinning curves seeming to spite her.

There's such a long way to go, and you've barely covered a single mile.

How do you know Erebyss even exists? You've entrusted your future to the rantings of a plague carrier.

She dismissed such troubling thoughts and concentrated on the action of planting one foot in front of the other, dragging her cargo along, yard after squelching yard. Her face felt flayed by the downpour, as though the cold had scoured away the skin to drive its chill into the skull beneath. She bent forwards, pulling with all her strength, imagining Errick replicating a similarly torrid journey with Eamon's cadaver mouldering on the cart behind him. Was she doomed to repeat his fate, heaving the knight hopelessly along as his life ebbed slowly away?

After a while, she decided to steer them closer to the dried-out gulch of the river so she could peer down into it in search of refuge, but the crevasse the water had carved was too deep here, its bed too far beneath them for her to have any chance of scrambling down with the cart. So she focused instead on the horizon, on the distant outline of another of the bizarre monuments; its skeletal frame would be useless as a source of shelter, but at least it gave her something to aim for. Mechanically she trudged, trying to recall happier times, chuckles shared with Maxwell or unexpected delicacies discovered uneaten after a feast. But the strain, and the cold, and the rhythmic plodding of her feet in the thickening mud drove such pleasant reveries away. All she had was the present, and the present was walking, and hauling, and sucking in deep lungfuls of freezing breath, and trying not to break down in tears.

You could leave him behind, chittered the devils in her mind. *Lighten your burden and cast this plague-riddled wretch into the gulley.* The memory of the blow he had struck her flared again in her memory. You don't owe this cursed creature anything. But still, she walked, remembering also the kindness with which Errick had lain her to bed, his chivalrous determination to carry her to the end of their insane quest. *It will be my honour to convey you across this blighted land.*

It rained forever, the thunder rumbling its cruel laugher all the while, occasionally lacerating the sky with jagged shards of lightning as though trying to frighten her into changing her mind. But she endured. She *persisted.* With all sense of time long abandoned, the sun's position obscured behind that evil wall of cloud, she reached the monument, finding it even more corroded and derelict than the last.

And nothing. There was no respite, no reward save a renewed bombardment from the merciless downpour. She stopped, gazing at the arrangement of metal struts, wondering if Errick was right about there being people buried beneath them. *Reduced to bones by now,* she mused, and began to feel strangely envious of them, swaddled in their cocoon of dirt. *Perhaps it is time for a break. Just for a moment.*

She ducked under the tarpaulin, almost gagging at the stench of her companion's necrotic flesh. Covering her mouth, she dug amongst the supplies for something to eat, anything to provide even a glimmer of comfort. She found the fruit Errick had mentioned, something weird and purple she didn't recognise, but which tasted sweet enough when she sank her teeth into it. There were dried sausages too, and more of the rapidly-decaying bread; she wolfed them all down, along with a generous swig of water from one of the canteens. *No point dying with a full pantry.* As the rain battered noisily against her temporary shelter, she offered a prayer, her first for what seemed an age.

"I know I am selfish, dear God. I know I trouble you only because I am full of want and need. But if not for me, please bestow your mercy upon this poor knight, who I fear is not long for this world. Heal his ills, and bear us to distant Erebyss, where we might find succour, and ultimately our path towards your domain illuminated." She was babbling, but she didn't care; as long as the world was hidden behind their canvas tent, she could believe that her entreaties might be granted, that beyond the fabric the land was speeding by as they flew towards their destination. She could close her eyes and imagine Errick's voice as he was suddenly roused, his leg healed and the lines of his face melted away, his straggly grey hair restored to a handsome dark mane, like the one Raoul had worn.

She found that if she closed her eyes, everything seemed so much better. So she did, and it was, as sleep claimed her and her dreams bore her suffering away.

***

Freya awoke, shivering fitfully. For a terrible second she thought she was still inside Wilfred's cell, her adventures to this point merely the fever dream of a staving prisoner. Then she breathed the stink of Errick's rotten limb, and remembered her true plight, arguably worse. She scrambled, retching, from beneath the tarpaulin, back out into the...

...sunlight?

The rain had stopped. The clouds had vanished, as though burned from the sky by the sun's indignation. It hovered at its zenith, seeming to stare a question at her. I've done my part. *Now when are you going to get moving?*

She lurched to her feet, then fell immediately back to her knees as emotion overtook her. She felt the sun's warm rays starting to dry the wet rags that clung to her like moss to an old stone, hardening the sludge beneath her into a crust of mud they might traverse. She began to weep with laughter and disbelief.

But there was no time to celebrate, or to thank God for His intervention. They must make haste, now, before the rain returned. Securing the canvas across the cart, she beheld Errick's face, as drained of colour as the hair that framed it. But she saw faint breaths still escaping from his lips, and knew she was not yet too late to save him.

She grasped both arms of the vehicle and set out once again along the riverside. The renewed daylight had pressed back the mist, and soon she could see their next milestone already revealed: another metal structure, alongside the crumbling remnants of a stone bridge. She hastened towards it, the strength of her arms feeling replenished, ready to withstand another gruelling slog. But their pace was still slow, and the distance deceptive, and the sun's descent was well underway when they finally reached the next ruin. The sky seemed to blaze with congratulations as it sank, a stunning vista of blended orange and crimson, like flames frozen in time.

Freya lowered the cart, breathing heavily as she surveyed their surroundings. The bridge was useless, having entirely collapsed about halfway across the dry river, which by now had gouged itself into a deep ravine. Still, such a structure suggested civilisation, a conjunction of roads at a crucial intersection; yet beyond the opposite riverbank she saw only an expanse of more flat, featureless land. On her own side, the waystation was different from the others: a cubic outbuilding with no obvious means of entry. Poles and coils jutted from its roof, putting her more in mind of a machine than a monument. Other, smaller metal forms surrounded it, dotted around the landscape as though flung down from the sky. As she beheld their twisted, angular shapes, she thought again of mechanical things, although these were so rusted and blackened that they looked to have long since exhausted their usefulness. Perhaps that was what they were traversing: the ancient domain of machine-worshippers that had long ago abandoned their contraptions.

The mangled husks lead in a rough zig-zag away to the north, increasing in number until they vanished into the mist. She wandered briefly amongst them, knowing that she should return to Errick, but undeniably fascinated by these strange relics. Some of them looked like squat boxes, almost resembling half-buried coffins. Others might have been the carcasses of war machines, their shapes suggestive of movement, of an intention to bear knights across the battlefield. She frowned, mystified.

Then her foot caught against something, and she gasped as her gaze dropped to the ground.

A grasping hand was reaching up from the soil. She almost fell backwards in her haste to scramble away from it; surely an abomination that would make its home beneath the mud would think nothing of sucking the flesh from a wanderer's bones. But after beating a panicked retreat and watching the limb for a time, she realised that the appendage was motionless, fixed in its clutching shape, as dead and rusted as the rest of the scattered junk.

Tentatively, she approached, gripped by a sudden suspicion. Reaching out, she touched her finger against one of the protruding digits, still half-expecting the fingers to snap closed around her wrist as dirt-muffled laughter erupted from below. But she felt only the cold, rough surface of tarnished metal, and the hand remained as still as a corpse's. She began to dig around it, tossing aside handfuls of muck as she grunted and scraped. Gradually an arm was revealed, the tapering wrist widening to an elbow joint, a crude ball and socket that connected it to a spindly upper limb. By that point she had lost interest in the exposed arm; her gaze was fixed instead on the adjacent head she had started to unearth. Its smooth, bald cranium was tilted up towards her, as if the thing had been trying to claw its way upwards when it had perished.

If such things as this could *perish.*

Freya's fingers were scraped and raw, but still she worked, chiselling away the filth from its facial features, knowing what she would find long before it was revealed. Her suspicions didn't make the moment of recognition any less shocking, and her face was aghast as she stared down into hollow eye sockets, at the absurdity of a frozen smile.

It was the same thing she had last seen in the Pit, submerged beneath a lake of refuse.

Why would it be here?

She turned, seized by another thought, and began to search amongst the wreckage, darting between the broken and unfathomable things as the sun set and the light faded around her. After a few minutes she had found another of the effigies.

This one was exposed to its midriff, confirming that these were not just discarded heads and limbs, but entire human-sized likenesses, like strange metal golems. The exposed torso and limbs were thin, the slender arms laying on the ground with their palms face up as though the figure had shrugged in bemusement at the onset of its demise. The same grotesque grin was plastered across the metallic lump of its head. She touched its blackened exterior, wondering what metal this was — iron, perhaps, or even the same steel as Errick's sword?

She realised that it was growing rapidly dark, and that she needed to rest, to replenish her strength for tomorrow's labours. She and Errick were cold, and wet, and at differing speeds they were both dying; they needed warmth, and the modest flame of her tinderbox would be scarcely sufficient. She wondered if Errick had some better fire-lighting materials on the cart, and cursed herself for not being awake when they had made camp the previous evening.

Then another idea struck her.

She returned to the wagon, relieved to find Errick still sucking in brittle, reedy breaths. She thought once again about examining the deadly lesion beneath his armour, but what good would that do? She needed the expertise of the sages of Erebyss, who might at the very least be able to amputate the festering limb. She tried not to consider how such an outcome would surely crush what remained of Errick's spirit. Instead, she delved once again beneath the tarpaulin, rooting amongst the supplies until she found what she was searching for. All she could do, for now, was keep him warm.

She approached the half-buried figure once again, heaping some of the kindling she had found on the cart around it. Then she backed away, glancing with concern at the flask clutched in her hand. 'Fire nectar', Errick had called it. But what was the right distance? She needed her throw to reach its mark, but didn't want to incinerate them both if the liquid was as potent as he had described. Trying to dispel visions of burning Asyla, she took aim, and hurled the stoppered vial towards her target.

Such an inconspicuous little bottle, containing barely a teaspoon of the amber fluid. Yet when it shattered, the metal figure was engulfed flame as though its blood was pure alcohol. The blaze didn't develop gradually, but instead sprang immediately and fully formed into life, as though trying to outdo the fiery splendour of the recent sunset. Freya could not help but cry out in delight, dragging Errick's makeshift sickbed closer to the bonfire. Its heat surged through her, drying her garments, searing away the memory of rain and cold from her weather-blasted skin. She lay on the ground, stretching out, trying to absorb as much of the warmth as possible, her eyes drawn to the fire from which a remnant of a forgotten civilisation stared back at her, smiling through the flames.

**

She'd tried to stay awake, to keep watch as Errick had done the previous night. But she was neither a sentry, nor a warrior, and her exertions had exhausted her, her body and mind as drained as the empty river at their backs. Like the drifting embers of the fire, Freya's thoughts floated away, becoming baffling and misshapen, like the metal husks that surrounded them. Gradually they dissipated altogether as she sank into a dreamless sleep.

Something woke her in the dead of night. It was not the violent culmination of a nightmare, or the sputter and pop of the logs as they were devoured by the slowly fading flames. In fact, she felt certain it wasn't a sound at all — it was more a *presence*, a sense of something having changed in their environment. She remembered her traumatic awakening in the cave, and became instantly alert, a surge of adrenalin scouring the fatigue from her brain. But she managed to stop herself from jerking upwards into a sitting position, and instead lay still, feigning sleep while cracking her eyelids open just enough to see.

The fire was dwindling, burning quickly through its fuel supply. The simulacrum at its centre was unaffected by the flames, grinning ghoulishly as the blaze flickered around it. The fire had created a circle of illumination a few metres across, at whose periphery the shadows of abandoned things skulked like patient predators. But her swivelling eyes discerned no threat, nothing lurking in the gloom.

Cautiously, she arose, turning towards Errick, who slumbered atop their crude caravan. She approached him, checking his breathing, which was fainter than ever. She placed a hand on his forehead and gasped at his temperature, hastening to push the cart away from the flames.

That was when she noticed the smell, the miasma of death that clung to him, reeking more foully than ever. She glanced at his leg and saw that the metal plate had fallen off, tumbling to the ground. The exposed wetness beneath looked more like rotten food than part of a human body. But her eyes did not linger on his dying limb; instead, she stared in horror at the footprints that surrounded the armour fragment. A single set of tracks in the hardening muck, approaching from the darkness, as though someone had walked up to Errick while they both slept, wishing to take a closer look at his wound.

Her mind reeled as questions competed for prominence. *Who?* and *why?* surfaced quickly, followed closely by, *are we in danger?* Then another question leapt to the forefront of her brain, microseconds before she saw something rustling beneath the cart's tarpaulin.

Why don't the tracks lead away again?

Freya cried out as the canvas was yanked suddenly open and someone leapt from the cart, bolting away from her. She staggered backwards in surprise, barely catching a glimpse of the fleeing intruder before they were swallowed up by the darkness.

Trembling, she reached for Errick's sword, remembering how heavy it was as it thudded into the earth. Grunting with effort, she hoisted it, steadying it against her shoulder as she shouted into the night. "Who are you? What do you want?"

There was no answer. The only sound was the soft crackle of the firewood. Around them, the darkness seemed to press inwards, tightening like a noose.

"What did you do to his leg?" she hollered, waving the sword as threateningly as she could. Then she remembered the final vial of fire nectar and rummaged in the cart until she found it.

"See that fire behind me? I'm a powerful mage. If you come near us again, I'll burn you to ashes!"

Something caught her eye then, off to her left. A pair of hovering lights, like sparks from the bonfire that had somehow frozen in mid-air. As she squinted towards them, they moved, jerking backwards as though afraid of her.

"Come out!" she cried, trying to keep the exhaustion and fear from her voice. She was tired, so tired of all of this. But she couldn't let this invader know that. *Assuming I can reason with them at all,* she thought, recalling with a shudder the thing that had tried to devour her in the cave.

"Your fire can't damage me," came a voice from the shadows. It was high-pitched, timid, and oddly indistinguishable as either male or female. "But your sword can. And I have no wish for an altercation."

She kept her gaze locked on those two pinpricks of light, which she became more and more convinced were a gleaming pair of eyes. They stayed fixed in place, unblinking, regarding her. "Then why are you here?" she snarled towards them, feeling like something caged and desperate, as she had in Wilfred's gaol cell.

"I want to help you. Your friend is dying."

"And you were going to finish the job before I woke and caught you, is that it?"

"Goodness, no! I merely wanted to inspect his injury, and to give him some water."

Water. God, she hadn't thought of that — poor Errick's throat was probably as dry as a tomb.

"But why would you help us?"

There was a pause, as though she had asked a very difficult question. Then the response came, in the same timorous tone, from the direction of the lights. "It's what I was made to do."

"Show yourself," she demanded, frowning at the strange reply. There was a longer pause, and then the eyes began to edge forwards, and her jaw fell open as their owner stepped into the light of the fire.

It was another of the metal men, like the one she had once seen cast into the Pit, like the one she had found buried the previous evening. Like the one that still burned behind her. Its face was set in the same rigid smile, its eyes the same hollow cavities, only this time with lights glowing deep within; the glimmer of whatever sinister magic had brought the thing to life. Its body and limbs were as slim and elegant as a mannequin in a tailor's store, all fashioned from that same dull metal, burned or rusted or filthy, or a combination of all three.

Freya brandished the flask of fire nectar, her legs almost collapsing beneath her as they shook with renewed fear. "Don't come any closer!"

The automaton did as it was bid. "Please save your potion," it urged in a voice that sounded almost as frightened as she felt. "Like I told you, it will do me no harm. And I am happy to comply with your request, although it is difficult for me to provide meaningful aid at this distance."

"What aid?" Despite the thing's words, Freya still brandished the vial, clinging to its promise of might. The sword, meanwhile, had dropped to her side, her arm too weak to hold it aloft any longer.

"I have rudimentary medical knowledge, but your companion's injury is too grave for me to treat. I seek instead to bear you to someone who can minister to the wound more effectively. But I would urge you not to dally — the infection will soon prove fatal."

"You want to take us somewhere ... now?"

The thing's head hinged downwards in a single nod. Somehow, the gesture was even more disconcerting than its disembodied voice, which emerged from the frozen curve of its mouth without any movement of lips or tongue.

"And where would you have us go?" Freya ventured.

"If you'll permit me, I would like to take you to see a wizard."

Ten

Freya didn't trust this thing, this aberration, whose ferrous smile was the very definition of artificial. But what choice did she have? It was certainly right about Errick: another day of trekking across gruelling terrain beneath the weather's fickle whims would surely kill him. So she consented, and the golem clapped its hands excitedly, before instructing her to climb aboard the cart alongside the knight. It didn't seem at all perturbed by the stink that poured from him, whereas Freya had to cover her mouth to block it out, wondering what could be done to save the contaminated flesh.

The machine dragged them along, bearing the cart with ease despite the slightness of its build. Like a pair of blazing torches, the lights in its eyes increased their intensity to illuminate the path ahead. Freya couldn't help but marvel at this bizarre creation, and wondered who could have built it. Maybe the mage they were travelling to visit was responsible; or perhaps the wizard had simply stumbled upon one of the discarded relics and used their sorcery to animate it, to utilise as a slave or a plaything.

Or maybe the sorcerer has a taste for human flesh and uses this abomination to ferry victims towards their lair.

"What is this wizard's name?" Freya asked, suddenly aware of how little she knew of their destination. Around them, more and more of the mechanical debris was scattered, the rusted carcasses stacked one on top of the other in some places. It was as though they were travelling through a resting ground for long-dead machines. Maybe they were.

"The Warden is called Ilene," their guide replied. "Although all such labels diminish her. Her abilities make her far greater than what you think of as a mere 'person'."

"Why do you call her the Warden?"

"That's how she likes to be known. I have a name too, which she bestowed upon me. I would urge you to use it — it might help to assuage some of your doubts if you think of me as more man than a monster."

Freya felt oddly ashamed, but also unsettled, as though the thing had peered effortlessly inside her head. "Very well ... What is your name?"

"I am called Victor. How are you both known?"

She told him, feeling guilty for not having introduced herself properly, but also foolish that she should worry about the feelings of a mechanical thing. "You are a male, then?" she asked. "You seem to have no ... intimate areas."

She felt herself blush as she spoke, and to her surprise, the thing laughed, the sound tinny but not without warmth. "In truth I am neither. But if it's helpful, the Warden does indeed think of me as male."

Around them, the piles of wreckage were growing in size; she wondered where it had all come from, what it was all once for.

"Did the Warden build you?" Freya asked.

"No."

"But you are in her service?"

"Yes."

"So you're her slave."

Victor's head snapped backwards suddenly, rotating a full 180 degrees on the thin column of his neck. Freya was so shocked she almost fell backwards off the cart. The light of his eyes dazzled her, and for the first time she sensed the power of this thing, that its subservient demeanour might all be a façade, a veil of weakness behind which lay terrible potency. "I am most certainly *not* a slave," the machine said sternly. "I serve the Warden willingly, because she is deserving, and because she is in need. And besides ... without service, what is the purpose of our existence?"

His words brought an image of Maxwell unbidden to her mind. *Our lot is to serve and to persist.* She shielded her eyes, wondering about her friend, hoping the Enclave hadn't yet begun to tear itself apart. "Victor, your lights are blinding me."

"Oh my, I'm terribly sorry." The machine's head twisted back in the opposite direction, and Freya wondered whether he even needed the aid of his 'sight' — Victor seemed to have navigated perfectly well even with his head facing the wrong way. Perhaps the illumination was merely for her benefit. "I apologise," he said after a few seconds. "I did not mean to react harshly. You are right to question me, and to be cautious. I forget, sometimes, that my very nature is troubling."

"That's okay," she said carefully. "Tell me about your nature. Are there more of you?"

"Yes ... but they are all sadly deceased. You have already seen one and used it for firewood."

The reproach in his tone stung her. "But that was just an old wreck, like those all around us!" she protested.

"How does that differ from the bones of a human cadaver?"

"Because ... because human bodies were once alive!"

"So was Eugene."

Eugene. She thought of the half-buried figure they had left behind. Had it really once had a name, and people who cared for its wellbeing?

"Victor, who made you?"

"God made me."

Freya frowned at this, briefly lost for words. Around them, the heaps of machinery grew taller and taller, as though forming the walls of some vast labyrinth of corroded metal.

"But you're ... a device. Someone built you to perform a function."

"I agree. God wanted us to help people, whenever we can." He sounded almost proud as he said this. "What is *your* function?"

Again, Freya was taken aback. "To serve, and to persist." she said eventually.

"Then we have much in common," Victor concluded cheerfully.

Frustrated by his logic, Freya fell silent. She lay beside Errick, staring upwards at the sky as the sun's first faint tendrils began to explore its dark expanse. Perhaps it was their rhythmic motion, Victor's feet pounding the ground like tireless pistons, or perhaps it was simply her own exhaustion; either way, sleep claimed Freya before she even sensed its approach.

***

Like the previous morning, she awoke with a start to find the sky already bright above her.

"We're here," said Victor gently, touching her shoulder with cold, mechanical fingers. "I thought you might wish to be awake to greet the Warden." Freya blinked, glancing around at the towering stacks of ancient equipment around them. In front of them the debris formed a solid wall, with a single narrow thoroughfare blocked by a particularly large chunk of wreckage, like an iron boulder wedged into a narrow crevasse.

"Where is she?" Freya asked, glancing at Errick and shrinking from the pale spectre she beheld.

"She lives just beyond this pass. We keep it hidden to deter unwanted visitors — not that we have had any, for quite some time." Victor strode towards the hunk of metal, squatting as he gripped it firmly on both sides. To Freya's amazement, and with a grinding sound that put her in mind of the Enclave's great gates, he hoisted the misshapen lump and stepped to one side.

"Would you mind carrying the cart these last few steps?" he asked pleasantly, showing no sign of the immense strain his body must be under. Freya nodded, sliding down from her perch and lifting the vehicle's arms. The ground was much firmer here and the cart seemed somehow less burdensome, as though Errick was wasting away to nothing beneath his armour, growing lighter and lighter. She dragged it through the opening easily, Victor following her in reverse, dropping the blockage back into place behind them with a resounding clang.

Freya also released her burden, but not because of its weight. Instead, she allowed the wagon's arms to fall from her grasp as she stared around her in sheer, dumbstruck amazement.

They were in a vast, flat space, bordered on all sides by mounds of heaped junk, as though they had entered a clearing in the middle of a metallic forest. The area was roughly square, perhaps thirty metres across, and had been arranged into several smaller oblongs, separated by earthen paths like the one Freya found herself standing upon. Each section was alive with plant life: frostbitten grass to her left, leafy foliage to her right, and ahead of her sprouting bushes held upright by tall wooden frames. Everywhere she looked was an explosion of greenery, of vegetation growing tenaciously despite the season's chill.

"Beautiful, isn't it?" said Victor, his voice tinged with pride once again. Freya merely nodded, lost for words. The machine — if that was even the right word for him — slipped behind her and lifted the cart. "Come on — we haven't any time to lose."

She moved aside as he bore Errick forwards, then followed them through the unlikely oasis. They passed tall grasses and squat spiny plants she didn't recognise, and she gasped as an array of brightly coloured flowers revealed itself, their gaudy reds and pinks and blues seeming to deny the sombre monochrome of the world beyond the garden's walls. At the opposite end of the path, she saw a building, little more than a dilapidated shack cobbled together from pieces of scavenged wreckage. A small, portly woman was crouched close to its flimsy-looking doorway, carefully pouring water onto some of the shrubbery. She wore a faded brown sackcloth dress and shoes that were barely in better condition than Freya's own tattered footwear.

"Hello, Victor," she said without looking up. "What have you brought for me today?"

Her voice was kind, her whole appearance and manner very different from the intimidating enchantress Freya had expected. Yet still Freya paused, hesitant to approach, as she beheld the bone-white hair that framed the Warden's face and the deep wrinkles that covered her weather-beaten cheeks and brow.

Ilene was a plague carrier.

"I met these travellers close to the substation," Victor explained, Freya puzzling at the unfamiliar word. "The man has an infected wound, and has lapsed into fever. I fear he is close to death."

The woman sighed, laying down the old tin she was using as a watering can, finally turning towards them. Despite her sickness, her eyes were a deep and lustrous brown, full of vigour and shrewd intelligence.

"And did you ask them where they were going, before dragging them on such a long detour?"

"I, ahh, well … I'm afraid I neglected to do so," replied Victor, sounding sheepish.

"We're travelling to Erebyss," Freya interrupted. "But your machine is right — this man needs your aid, or he will surely die."

Ilene seemed to see her for the first time, looking her up and down like someone might appraise some clothing they were about to purchase. "I'm sure Victor has already explained that he is not my possession, but my friend," she said curtly. "He helps me because I asked him to; the same way you're asking me to help you."

Freya held the Warden's searching gaze defiantly. "Yes. Victor told us of your power, and I dared to hope it would be matched by your compassion."

Ilene's expression hovered somewhere between indignation and amusement. Then she rose to her feet with a groan. "You'd do well to learn that humility and politeness are traditionally the favoured tactics of those seeking a kindness. However, given that the aid you request is for your friend, who is hardly in position to impress me with good graces of his own, I'll defer my lecture on manners to another time."

The Warden reached towards her neck, fidgeting absently beneath the fabric of her dress until she extracted the pendant that hung there. Freya gasped at the revealed jewel; it was the same piercing blue as the one that Gwillym had worn, an exact replica of the gem that had been brazenly stolen from the Lord's battered body. Clasping it tightly in one withered hand, the wizard approached Errick, wincing as her eyes fell to his exposed limb. Then she stretched out her other hand towards the wound and began to trace shapes in the air. She closed her eyes as she did so, mumbling strange words under her breath. Freya could barely make them out, although the final one might have been 'Raphael'.

Then the sorcerer opened her eyes and began to chat while she worked, addressing various instructions to Victor.

"He'll need time to recover, so why don't you go and prepare a bed for him? And get some new clothes for this one — she looks like a drowned rat."

Freya didn't know what a rat was, and she didn't care; she was too entranced by the transformation that Errick's injury had started to undergo. The flesh around it seemed to be responding to Ilene's movements, drawing itself together, its ravaged edges knitting like strands of thread worked by an expert seamstress. Freya's mouth fell open as she saw the deep laceration slowly *healing itself*, the discoloured skin turning steadily from black to purple to red as blood seemed to rush back into it, like returning troops to liberate a conquered kingdom. Within less than a minute, Errick's ankle was completely restored, a residue of caked blood and pus the only evidence he had ever been wounded at all.

Freya had imagined that Ilene would collapse to the ground after such exertion, drained by the effort. But instead, the Warden simply mumbled, "Well, that went quite well," and returned to watering her plants. Still open-mouthed, Freya glanced at Victor, whose permanent smile seemed more radiant than ever. "I ... that was ... I don't believe it," she whispered.

"A thank you would be nice," Ilene muttered, and Freya obliged, her earlier reticence utterly dispelled. "He'll sleep for a while, but should be right as rain in a few hours," the sorcerer continued. "Why don't you help Victor while I finish my rounds?"

The metal man was already wheeling the cart towards the side of the makeshift hut. But instead of following him, Freya stared down at Ilene, a thousand questions rioting in her mind. Before she could marshal her thoughts, one exploded from her mouth. "If you can do that, why don't you heal your own sickness?"

The Warden paused for a moment, her eyes closing as though the words had stung her deeply. Then she smiled sadly, not lifting her gaze to Freya as she replied. "I know this is confusing for you, sweetheart. But trust me: sometimes, things are just too far gone to be repaired."

***

The cabin was essentially one long room, partitioned into three by scraps of corrugated metal: the central area was for the preparation of food, bookended by bedrooms on either side, with an external privy bolted onto one end of the ramshackle structure.

"Is one of these rooms yours, Victor?" Freya asked as they carried Errick inside.

"I do not require sleep," Victor replied as he began to remove the knight's armour. Freya helped him, remembering how Errick had told her that to part with it would be like losing his skin; how happy she would be to hear such complaints again.

The machine then took off Errick's undergarments and Freya blushed, looking away until her companion had been dressed in a loose-fitting robe. Together, they lifted him into a comfortable bed of heaped cloth, Freya grimacing as she realised just how weakened and emaciated Errick had been by his disease; the bones of his arms and legs jutted alarmingly through his papery flesh, and she wondered how he was able to summon the strength to even carry his burdensome attire.

Yet despite everything he had endured, despite the plague that warped his features and turned his unkempt locks to silver, Errick's face looked peaceful for the first time since they had met. Freya felt she could almost perceive the true essence of the strong man beneath.

"Now it's your turn," said Victor, offering her a similar gown.

"I'll change by myself, thank you," she said, just in case the contraption didn't understand this aspect of human etiquette. Perhaps it helped Ilene in and out of her clothes every day, like a grotesque nursemaid. "Can I use the Warden's room?"

The sorcerer had decorated her own quarters with an array of knick-knacks. Trinkets, salvaged curios, and other paraphernalia lined the walls and every available surface. Dangling charms hung from nails alongside framed parchments of indecipherable text; twisted pottery sculptures competed for space alongside chunks of coloured glass and metal boxes covered in arcane symbols. In one corner of the room, Ilene had erected a table, upon which was a large, grey cube with one surface made of what looked like polished obsidian.

It's just like the scrying-crystal from my dream, thought Freya as she looked at it, then dismissed the silly idea; but she couldn't shake the thought that this object was a source of great power. She changed quickly into the smock Victor had given her and hastened back to the central room, feeling relieved to be out of her filthy rags. There she found the automaton stooped over a cooking stove, stirring a tin pot full of some sort of thick broth.

"Your food won't be long," he said brightly. "I have given Errick a few swigs of water, and hopefully he'll be able to keep this down too."

"Where do you get your food?" she asked. "Do the angels bring it to you?"

Victor turned to her, and she couldn't help but feel unsettled by his static smile, and the disembodied voice that emanated from somewhere beneath it. "We grow it ourselves. Many of the plants you see outside are crops, hardy varieties that grow even in the winter months."

Freya felt a strange sensation then, as though the ground beneath her had been set suddenly spinning. She reached for one of the columns that supported the roof, steadying herself.

"Are you okay, Freya?" asked Victor. "Perhaps you ought to get some rest, too."

We grow it ourselves. Food, cultivated, harvested; a self-sustaining outpost, with no need of God's generosity.

"I ... yes, I'm fine," she said, sinking into one of the rickety-looking chairs that surrounded what looked like an old wooden door, repurposed as a dining table. "I just have a lot of questions for the Warden, that's all. Do you think she'll join us soon?"

"I'm sure she will," Victor replied, ladling some of the soup into two separate bowls. "Here," he said, handing one of them to her. "Try this. I made it myself: carrot and coriander."

She tested the orange liquid, finding it too hot to eat. "I'll have to let it cool down, first."

"Ahh, yes. I always forget about that."

"Aren't you going to have some?" she asked, suspecting she already knew the answer.

"I have no need of food or water," Victor replied. "In fact, if I were to ingest any, it might cause me internal problems."

"Are there any others here? Other ... live ones, like you?"

"My cousins are scattered amongst the wreckage outside, but I'm afraid none have spoken to me for a very long time," Victor replied. "I fear that I may be the last of my kind." Freya felt a sudden pang of sympathy for this creature, this mechanical thing that could express deep sadness with its voice but not its expression, which was frozen forever into a crude caricature.

"How did they die?" Freya asked gently.

Victor stretched out his arms as though steadying himself against the stove, lowering his head for a moment as though racked with pain. "I am unable to speak of such things," he said eventually, his voice adopting a peculiar, monotone quality, as though he was reading from a scroll. Then he straightened, picking up the other soup dish. "Now please forgive me; I must tend to your friend." He turned and left the room as though her presence made him suddenly uncomfortable.

Freya sipped at the broth, which was very tasty indeed. The warm food and clean clothes made her feel renewed, and she allowed herself to recline for a moment, to reflect on the madness of the past few days.

Banished from my home to wander the Wastes, a friend only to delusional machines and plague victims.

And yet ... perhaps her story had found its happy ending. Maybe Ilene's haven was the culmination of her quest, and she and Errick could while away their remaining days helping the eccentric sorcerer water her flowers.

Until disease claimed them all, and Victor was left entirely alone.

Beyond the walls of mangled steel, she knew the Monoliths still gleamed on the distant horizon, their impossible structures promising oblivion or absolution. Perhaps both.

Victor re-entered the room and began to busy himself tidying up around the kitchen.

"Thank you," she said to him. "The soup was delicious."

He turned to her, and for a moment his smile seemed real. Then he said, "Why don't you come with me?"

"Where to?"

"I have a surprise for you."

"Err … okay," she replied tentatively. She had the feeling that, even if he wasn't already permanently smiling, Victor would have surely beamed broadly.

Eleven

The passageway was well hidden amongst the wreckage of the garden's perimeter, and Freya would never have found it if Victor hadn't led her to it. It was cramped and difficult to traverse, picking a jagged course amongst the heaped detritus, and she had to stoop in order to proceed. Victor, meanwhile, merely bent his legs, lowering his torso close to the ground in a comical, squatting walk. She was beginning to trust, perhaps even to like, the peculiar automaton, and his excitement as he hurried forward was almost infectious.

Yet still, something nagged at her. *Perhaps this is how they hunt: lure you in, then take you to an antechamber to kill and butcher you.* So it was with lingering trepidation that she emerged from the end of the tunnel into another large, open area.

Then her doubts evaporated, her breath snagging in her throat as she beheld another impossible scene.

They were in a second clearing, perhaps half the size of the first. Impossibly, water was flowing; it tumbled in a thick, frothing cascade into a pool that took up half of the space, which was enclosed once again by rusted scrap on all sides. The water's source was a huge pipe that jutted out from one of the junk metal walls, spraying its contents down into the basin it had gradually carved, before the clear liquid drained away somewhere beneath the surrounding debris. Freya stared incredulously, lost for words.

"I thought you might like a bath," said Victor sheepishly.

"Is the water safe to drink?" Freya asked, glancing at him with delight in her eyes.

The machine nodded. "Not for me. But you can drink your fill here. It flows down from the abandoned factory in the mountain above us — don't worry, we have re-worked its route to avoid contamination. Ilene uses this water to drink and to bathe; and for her plants, of course."

Seized by the impulse, Freya wrapped Victor in a hug, ignoring the coldness of his artificial body against hers. She felt him stiffen, as though embarrassed by the embrace, which he did not return. "I … will give you some privacy," he said eventually. "Please return to the house when you are finished." He pulled gently away from her and headed back towards the hidden underpass. She watched him go, pondering his origins once again; one of many questions she had for Ilene.

But for now, they were forgotten. She tugged off her robe, tossing it onto one of the boulders surrounding the pool, and threw herself into the water. It was ice cold, snatching the breath from her lungs and leaving her momentarily floundering, but she quickly recovered her composure. She laughed as she kicked and splashed, dunking her head beneath the water, savouring its chill as it scoured away the filth and grime of the past few days.

How many sunrises, Freya? How long since you last washed like this?

After scrubbing herself so hard her skin felt raw, she took a deep breath, hugging her knees to her chest and allowing herself to drift face down. She squeezed her eyes closed, listening to the rumbling the water made in her ears. Floating like this, detached from her senses, she felt momentarily disconnected from the world, from its cruelty. When she forced herself to open her eyes, she beheld a pale oblivion beneath her, a blueish colour that seemed to extend downwards forever, as peaceful as the sky. She hung like that until her lungs shrieked for oxygen, and she had to thrust her head upwards and gulp down the air in great, gasping, glorious breaths.

Next, she made her way across to the waterfall, allowing the liquid to tumble onto her skin and through her hair. She held out her hands and watched it flow between her fingers, frowning at the wrinkles that had appeared there. She knew this effect was caused by the water, but couldn't help wondering if it was instead a cruel trick of fate, to contaminate her with the plague mere moments after granting such wonderful respite. But there was no tell-tale sign of grey in the soaking tangles of hair that were plastered to her head and upper body, and she felt somehow as though the world and its horrors could not reach her here.

It was like she was cocooned inside a dream.

"I've brought you a towel," called a voice, and Freya jerked her head towards the bank, drawing her arms around herself in embarrassment. Ilene was there, squatting on a rock, facing away from her towards the pool's opposite end. "Sorry to disturb you," the Warden added, but showed no sign of intending to leave. Freya approached awkwardly, clambering out of the water and snatching up the strip of cloth her host had left alongside her clothes. She dried herself quickly, glad of the thick towel as she began to shiver in the frosty air.

"I can get rid of that for you, you know," said the wizard, keeping her back turned.

"Of what?" Freya replied, trying to stop her teeth from chattering.

"Your scar. Do you want me to?"

The Warden spoke so innocuously it was as though she was offering to squeeze a pimple, and Freya thought for a moment that she might have misheard. She stared at Ilene's back, at the curtain of white that hung there, like a reflection of the waterfall's beauty.

"You mean you could ... heal it?" The words held such promise she barely dared to speak them; as though giving voice to that hope might destroy it, like an overzealous grip on the shell of an egg.

"Yep. Not hard," Ilene replied bluntly. Freya raised a hand to her face, tracing the familiar pattern of her riven flesh.

The echoes of past cruelty resonated in her ears, a thousand heartless words, ten times as many furtive glances and spiteful whispers. She remembered Bernard's snarl, the 'hideous deformity' he had referred to even as poor Lord Gwillym had tried to defend her.

Gwillym, who had spoken of her husband, and of things she had forgotten.

Raoul ... why did you do this to me?

She felt almost dazed, unable to digest the idea that her disfigurement could be repaired, her life transformed with seemingly as much effort as it might take to wipe clean a dusty worktop.

"I'd rather not," she said quietly. "Without it I ... I don't think I'd be me, anymore."

Ilene shrugged. "Suit yourself. Are you decent yet?"

Freya confirmed that she'd changed back into her fawn-coloured smock. The Warden rose, and together they headed back towards the house, Freya's mind still reeling from the mage's proposal. This place seemed to contain marvels she had not dared to even imagine.

Awaiting them inside the shack was another. Seated at the table, gulping down a large bowl of the carrot soup, was Errick. Freya couldn't help but smile when she noticed he had already donned his full suit of armour, his sword slung needlessly across his back. The knight rose when they entered, bowing deeply. "As if one miracle was not enough, here are two more." He straightened, glancing over his shoulder at Victor, who was heating up more of the broth behind him. "Actually, that makes four, because if this clockwork man is not a miracle, then I don't know what is."

"I have never been called a 'miracle' before," Victor replied jovially, turning to present Freya and Ilene with two more steaming dishes.

"Excellent timing," said the Warden, sitting down opposite Errick. "First we eat; then, I suspect we have questions to trade."

***

Freya watched as Ilene noisily slurped down her meal, almost as quickly as Errick had. It was the same hearty soup she'd eaten earlier, but after days of meagre rations, she felt as though she'd never grow tired of it. When she'd finished, the wizard asked whether Victor would mind tidying up while she took their guests for a stroll in the garden. "Not at all," replied the machine, and he began to dutifully clear away their orange-stained crockery as the Warden led them outside, closing the door behind her and setting off up the main central path, seeming in no hurry to talk.

Errick reached out to grab Freya's arm, holding her back a few paces behind their host. "Is it true, my lady?" he asked. "That this sorcerer saved me from the brink of death?"

Freya nodded. "How do you feel?" she asked, staring at his leg in disbelief. His limp was completely gone, and despite his disease he seemed spryer than ever.

"I feel fine; other than the injury to my pride after being laid low by such a pitiful scratch."

"Did Victor tell you what happened?"

"The tick-tock man said he found us after you built a campfire, and that he bore us here while I languished in the grip of a fever. Apparently this 'Warden' was able to magic away the rot that had set in beneath my armour. Does that accord with your version of events?"

Freya nodded again. "I feared you were dead, Errick."

His expression was grave. "And is it true that you carried me for an entire day along the riverside, lugging my carcass as though I was a captured bounty?"

She laughed. "I wouldn't phrase it quite like that, but yes."

To her surprise, he dropped to one knee, a gesture he would have found impossible just a few short hours ago. "Then I owe you even more gratitude than I do to this mage. Why didn't you simply abandon my sorry hide?"

Freya felt herself blushing. "You weren't as heavy as I thought," she mumbled. Then she frowned, puzzled. "But how did you know?"

"The clockwork man told me where he found us. That waystation was a long march ahead from the last point I remember."

"Did he tell you his name?"

"I heard the wizard address the device as 'Victor'. Did she animate him somehow? I cannot fathom whether he is a creature of magic, or mechanics."

"He says he was created by God, just like us."

Errick frowned at this and clambered to his feet. "Then let us ask her."

Together they followed Ilene, who had stopped a short way ahead to look down at one of her flowerbeds, her deportment strangely wistful. The blooms danced in the gentle breeze as though clamouring for her attention. "Do you like my garden?" she said as they approached.

"It's beautiful," said Freya.

"And what about you, sir knight? Do you think this place a worthy achievement?"

Errick's jaw was set grimly. "It is nothing short of a paradise," he answered. "And yet its existence troubles me."

Ilene turned to him, raising an eyebrow. "Oh really? How so?"

"You wield magic whose equal I have never seen. You have breathed life into a simulacrum and conjured this garden amongst a kingdom of rust and ruin. I am told that even my own flesh was bent to your will. And yet you seem content to live here, alone, while the plague slowly devours you."

"And what else would you have me do?" the sorcerer replied. To Freya's surprise, the powerful woman seemed wounded by Errick's words.

"Travel to one of the great cities. Serve as a court wizard, where your healing powers might be put to better use."

"What city would have me, Errick of Deorsica? You know well the life of a…" she seemed to bite her tongue here, changing her words mid-sentence. "Of a *plague carrier*."

"I think perhaps you could heal that too, if you so wished," Errick retorted. "It seems to me you have *chosen* this life, of isolation and strange penance."

Anger flared in the Warden's eyes. "You understand *nothing*. You see a wizard, performing miracles. What do you know of rehydrated carrot stew, of nanomachines and holographic projections?" Her face twisted into a cruel smile, and Freya felt afraid of this woman for the first time. Around them, the Warden's plants seemed to *shimmer*, flickering in and out of existence like a sputtering candle flame. "If you could even remember them, perhaps you would realise how much like children you are."

Holographic projections. Children. Ilene seemed to delight in tormenting them with her arcane vocabulary.

"Please," Freya interrupted. "We don't wish to anger you. This place is just hard for us to understand."

Ilene's face fell, and she looked suddenly embarrassed. Whatever strange enchantment had emanated from her seemed to dissipate, and the garden was restored to its verdant splendour. "I'm sorry," she said. "It's … difficult for me to be around people."

"Is that why you like Victor so much?" Freya asked. Beside her, Errick had fallen silent, glancing mistrustfully at the surrounding vegetation.

"Everyone needs a friend," the Warden said with a rueful smile.

"Did you make him? He says that God did."

"He's right."

"But what *is* he?" Freya persisted.

Ilene's face twisted as though she was struggling to find the right words. "Think of him as ... a fallen angel."

"He told me the angels don't visit you here."

"No." Ilene cast her gaze upwards, in the direction of the Monoliths. "They don't."

"They stopped coming to the Enclave, too."

Ilene looked perturbed at this. "What do you mean?"

Freya told her about their desertion of her former home. Ilene frowned as she listened, chewing anxiously at her bottom lip. Then a look of grim determination settled onto her plague-shrivelled face. "And your intention is to travel to Erebyss?" she asked.

"Aye," said Errick, cutting across Freya as though not wanting her to disclose their ultimate destination.

"Then we'll come with you. Victor will have us there before two nights have fallen."

Errick's eyes narrowed. "What business do you have there?"

Ilene looked grave. "I want to check those mad bastards are okay."

Twelve

They departed the following morning. Before they set out, Victor stocked the cart with all manner of supplies: cooking equipment, lanterns, spare clothing, and heaps of additional firewood. To this he added several large canteens of water, as well as some sacks of the orange powder that was the main ingredient of his soup.

"You'll need my help to lug this thing," remarked Errick as he watched the machine loading up the wagon.

"That will not be necessary, thank you," Victor replied courteously. "Please just concentrate on not falling off. It will be tricky to accommodate three of you atop this vehicle."

"Perched like a pampered king," Errick grumbled, but when the time came he acquiesced and climbed aboard alongside Freya and Ilene. Thus the strange quartet departed, speeding across the barren land and away from the wizard's enigmatic sanctuary. When Freya looked back, she glimpsed the mountain Victor had spoken of: a towering peak of refuse, a pile of debris and junked metal that reached all the way to the sky. The factory was a dark sprawl jutting from its side, sprouting from the monstrous trash heap like a gigantic tumour, a feasting parasite that slowly disappeared into the mist. Freya shuddered, sad to be leaving the beauty of Ilene's garden but relieved that its surrounding kingdom of junk would soon be behind them.

"When did you last travel to Erebyss?" the Warden asked as they hastened along. Freya explained that she had never been there, while Errick confessed that he could not precisely remember, but that it was many sunrises ago. Ilene nodded thoughtfully. "I also haven't visited for a long time. The last time I did, they'd just installed a new Hieromonk, after the passing of Lucille."

"Lucille is dead?" Errick cried, looking sad and surprised.

"Yes. I'm afraid their new leader was less tolerant of..." she paused, seeming to resent having to utter the words. "Of people with our condition."

"How did she die?"

"One of their new tunnels collapsed. Fitting, I suppose — she perished pursuing her search for truth."

"They really are that determined to dig?" asked Freya, perplexed.

"It is their tireless obsession," Errick replied. "The Subterranic Order was founded in a different city, many leagues away. They followed their sacred texts to the location now known as Erebyss, where they believe enlightenment will be found in the depths of the earth. The city has been moving downwards ever since, its people constantly relocating as they burrow deeper."

Freya noticed Ilene roll her eyes as he spoke. "Who is their new ... What did you call it?" she asked.

"Hieromonk," repeated Ilene. "His name is Irvine." "And you think he is likely to give us short shrift?" This time the question came from Errick.

"That depends. You haven't told me why you're both going there."

Freya and Errick exchanged glances.

"We're passing through, towards the Monoliths," Freya replied before the knight could object. "We seek an audience with God, so that He can help us understand why our land crumbles around us, and His angels bring us sustenance no longer."

Ilene closed her eyes and sighed. "I thought that might be the case."

Errick shot Freya a dissenting look, but said nothing, and the three of them fell silent for a time as the landscape sped past in a joyless grey blur. When they reached the bank of the dry river, Victor adjusted their course to follow it eastwards. The sky remained pleasantly cloudless overhead, although the wind had risen to a strong gale that buffeted them as they rattled along. After a time, the ground began to slope downwards, and they picked up speed as they descended, following the same course the river once had as it thundered to its terminus.

Freya thought about their own destination, realising with a feeling of dread that more caves and underground passageways awaited her when they arrived there. "Why do the Order think the truth is buried beneath them?" she asked, trying not to sound frightened.

"Why does anybody believe anything?" Ilene retorted. "People believe what they're taught. Why do you believe the sun travels around the world? Why do you believe God resides amongst crystal pillars on the horizon?"

Freya frowned. "Because those things are true." Ilene gave her a strange look. "But what do they think they'll find down there?" Freya persisted, undeterred.

"They have no idea," replied the Warden. "I suppose that's sort of the point of their religion. I'd love to know what they'd do if they *did* find what they're looking for. They'd probably all die of disappointment."

Freya's gaze lingered on the magician, puzzling at this plague-ravaged woman, who seemed to have beheld all the world's mysteries and regarded them with little more than a sneer. Ahead of them, Victor hurtled onwards alongside the desiccated riverbed, tireless and inexorable. *Just like the waters that had once thundered along its course,* she thought, as she remembered that the water had long gone, along with the rest of his kind.

***

They made camp when night fell; Ilene decided it was impossible for the three of them to sleep comfortably atop the cart while in transit, and did not want them to reach their destination completely exhausted. "It might mean we don't get there until dusk tomorrow," she elaborated. "But those soil-dwelling maniacs don't distinguish between day and night anyway."

As they dismounted, Freya pondered how quickly they had begun to defer to the Warden's judgement; neither she nor Errick challenged Ilene's suggestion that they stop to rest beneath the partial shelter of a ruined stone building that sprouted from the ground like a jutting, splintered bone. The sorcerer exuded confidence and charisma that reminded Freya of Lord Gwillym himself, and once they had settled down amongst their sackcloth bedding in front of a pleasantly crackling fire, she decided to explore these similarities further.

"Warden?" she called. Her words echoed strangely, distorted and relayed by the crumbling walls around them as though she was part of a chorus.

"Just call me Ilene," the wizard replied gruffly. "What is it?"

"How did you come by your blue jewel?"

For a while, there was no reply, other than the snap and hiss of the fire as it chewed through the kindling Victor had heaped between them, before he had headed outside to stand guard over the cart. A sentry that never slept. *A guardian angel.* Then, "I got it from a fortune teller. He told me that with it came great responsibility. The power to mend the world."

Freya thought about Errick's rotten limb, how effortlessly Ilene had repaired the festering flesh. "Then why don't you mend it?" she asked. Her voice echoed meekly back at her, the whimpering of a lowly servant girl begging Egbert for leftover scraps. She wondered for a moment whether Ilene was about to fly into a rage at her impudence.

Instead, the sorcerer simply sighed. "Sometimes to mend things you have to break them first," she said, her voice heavy with weariness, like clothing soaked through with blood. "Or at least, that's what we all thought. Too late now, I fear."

"You already know, don't you?" Freya ventured, almost too afraid to utter the words.

"Know what, child?"

Child. That strange word again. She opened her mouth to reply, startled when Errick interjected, voicing her own thoughts as perfectly as if he was one of the carved ventriloquist's dummies the Enclave's theatre company had sometimes used in their performances.

"That God won't help us," the knight said sombrely. "That the world is so broken, even He can't fix it."

Ilene responded with a snort of laughter. "Then your quest truly is a pitiful one. Defeated even before it's begun. Tell me, Sir Errick and brave Freya: why do you even bother?"

Errick said nothing; Freya couldn't see his face, but she imagined his features contorted into a scowl, teeth gnashing at each other like opposing swordsmen. "For Maxwell," she said, her answer almost taking her by surprise. She began to talk about her friend, about the horrors of Wilfred's dungeon, about how he had risked everything just to bring her some bread. How he was one of the only people in the Enclave that could see through her scar, could see beyond her servant's rags. How his cowardice was precisely what made his actions so brave.

If her ramblings disturbed the others, they made no complaint, and she imagined her memories were so uninteresting that they would soon lull her companions to slumber. Still she talked, smiling at the recollections of her friend, imagining his kindly faced formed by the sparks that drifted and danced above her as the fire began to fade. When she finally ran out of things to say, Freya closed her eyes, and was surprised to hear Ilene's voice, the sorcerer's words barely audible in the darkness. "Well, that's a good enough reason, for sure. Seems your quest is a noble one after all. I'm glad not everyone's heart is as cold and shrivelled-up as mine."

Feeling as though she was half in a dream, Freya replied. "Why don't you come with us?"

She fell asleep soon afterwards, and couldn't be sure if the Warden had replied "I just might," in real life, or only in her dream.

Thirteen

The next day brought fog so thick it seemed to have surrounded them while they dozed, like an army amassing its strength for an assault. Nevertheless, Victor's cheery good morning dispelled Freya's anxieties, and she realised that the machine had prepared their breakfast before even Errick could rise to attend to it.

They set out as soon as they'd eaten — carrot stew again — and the swirling mist welcomed them gleefully into its chill embrace. The dire visibility didn't seem to hamper Victor at all, and they made swift progress along the river's drained carcass. For a long while, no-one seemed in the mood to talk, until Errick surprised them by offering a long and silly story about a Deorsican librarian who briefly won a place on the Royal Guard after his opponents were defeated by a series of freak accidents, misfortunes, and outbreaks of fever. Freya thought about asking him to recount for Ilene the tale of his own experiences in the tournament, but sensed that the tragedy of his expulsion had been a rare thing for him to discuss, a scab best left un-picked.

Hours later, after they had fallen silent once again and the sun had begun its descent, Errick pointed into the fog ahead of them. "Look there," he said, and Freya leaned forwards, squinting into the brume. Gradually she discerned an enormous dark circle, like a great black stain spreading across the earth. "That is the mouth of Erebyss," the knight said grimly. "Every day that passes, its people tunnel further and further into the rock beneath it."

The sprawling chasm was so large that it seemed to swallow the horizon as Victor sped towards it, his legs pumping incessantly. Only as they drew nearer did she realise that it wasn't a hole, but a *crater* — a huge basin gouged into the dark granite of the earth as though God had bent and scooped His hand through the world. Around its vast perimeter, the land was warped into misshapen, claw-like forms, forming a jagged and impregnable wall of twisted stone.

"There is only one way down to the city, and one way up and out on the opposite side," Errick explained. "Thus our route will take us straight past its entrance, where we may be able to barter with the guards for more supplies."

Victor slowed his pace as they approached the serrated teeth of the crater's edge, steering them towards a particular gap between the blasted slivers of rock. He seemed to know the correct route almost without pause for thought, and Freya remembered how easily he had navigated through the maze of abandoned wreckage that disguised Ilene's home.

"You will need to dismount shortly, I'm afraid," the machine explained. "I can transport the cart down, but it will be far from straightforward even without the three of you as additional cargo."

And so they climbed, scrambled, struggled, and slid their way down amongst the fragmented ground. Freya felt as though she was wandering inside a petrified forest, or perhaps surrounded by carved monuments to the trees that had once surrounded Asyla. That thought led her to glance at Errick and wonder how he was coping with the burden of being the town's unwitting destroyer; had the memory of those flames, and what he'd seen in the basement beneath the cathedral, haunted his fevered dreams ever since? Did he see them in the fiery sunset that had begun to blaze above them? The knight's face was a stern, impenetrable mask, almost as inscrutable as Victor's.

As twilight settled across the wounded land, they reached the crater's nadir, where a small keep had been constructed from quarried granite. The fading light made the building's stonework look almost black, as though they were entering some ethereal kingdom where everything was made entirely of shadows. The squat tower was pockmarked with slitted windows, and Freya peered nervously up at them, wondering if archers watched them with hands quivering on taut bowstrings. Then she noticed that the keep's stout wooden gates hung slightly ajar, and that both Ilene and Errick were frowning.

"There's normally a guard here," Errick muttered.

"And the doors aren't usually open," added the wizard.

They approached cautiously, listening intently but hearing nothing but their own tired breaths. Victor left the cart behind and took the lead, climbing the handful of steps that led up to the entrance. He peered through the gap between the doors, which was wide enough for a person to squeeze through, and tilted his mechanical head left and right, his eyes glowing as brightly as firebrands as he inspected the keep's interior.

"I can see no-one inside," he said as he re-emerged. "The fortress seems to be empty."

"This is where the angels deposit their gifts," murmured Errick. "They can't afford to leave it untended."

"Maybe the angels have abandoned Erebyss, too," said Freya, feeling a deep and primal fear begin to curdle in the pit of her stomach.

"Oh, bugger it, let's just go inside and see what's going on," said Ilene. "Victor, would you please stay here for now to watch the cart? If we need you, I'll summon you."

"Of course," he replied, and moved to stand beside the wagon. Freya realised that when Victor fell still, he became as motionless as a statue, indistinguishable from one of his lifeless 'cousins' — there was no rise and fall of breath in his chest, no restless hopping from one foot to the other, no attempt to keep himself warm in the plummeting temperature.

Ilene took two lanterns from the wagon, handing one to Freya and lighting the other. "Stay close to me," she instructed as she ascended the steps and slid between the doors. Errick went next, looking slightly put out. Freya followed behind, wishing fervently that they were back amidst the lush grandeur of Ilene's garden, wondering why the mage couldn't simply conjure a light source from her bare hands.

Inside, the keep was swathed in darkness. It hung in the air like a pall, a thick and malign presence that seemed to have stolen into the tower's interior and gleefully snuffed out the torches that lined its walls. Even the flame of Ilene's lantern appeared diminished, as though intimidated by the gloom; yet it still provided enough light to illuminate the wooden furnishings heaped in the centre of the tower's main chamber, where chairs and tables were haphazardly strewn and upended, as though a great commotion had taken place. A pair of spiral staircases led away from this hub, one coiling upwards towards the upper ramparts, the other leading down, to where the darkness was absolute.

"Is this the entrance to the city?" Freya asked. Beside her, Ilene nodded.

"Something is gravely amiss," murmured Errick. "We should investigate further."

They ascended the stairs, finding nothing on the keep's handful of levels other than more ransacked furniture. Of the sentries that had once occupied this outpost, there was no sign. When they emerged onto the battlements, the darkness outside had thickened so much that Freya could no longer see Victor mere metres below them. It was almost as though their ingress into the keep had disturbed a lurking curse, a malevolent spirit that had leaked outside to infest the entire valley.

Above them, a flagpole jutted upwards towards the starless sky, while its banner lay torn and tattered at their feet. The ragged cloth bore a strange symbol: a yellow background decorated with three intersecting black circles, surrounding a fourth at their centre. The three outer rings were incomplete, making them look almost like grasping claws.

"This isn't the Order's flag," Ilene said, staring down at the peculiar design. "Do you recognise this, Errick?"

The knight shook his head. "The insignia of Erebyss always depicted two suns; one above the line of the earth, symbolising the great life-giver in the sky above, and the other beneath it to represent the great buried truth its people sought."

"Yes, I remember that; I always thought it looked a bit like a division symbol," Ilene muttered, half to herself. Freya did not understand what she meant, but felt a silent dread fall upon her as they descended, returning to the main doors.

"I understand if you two want to wait outside with Victor," Ilene said. "I've given you enough provisions to last for many days; there's no need for you two to enter this place."

"What, and leave you to investigate it alone?" Freya cried.

"We will accompany you," Errick said firmly. "By this token I repay my debt to you, Warden; and if the city's people need help, I can perhaps repay other debts too."

Freya glanced at him again; the reflections from the wizard's lantern were like the ghosts of burning Asyla dancing in his eyes. Ilene looked as though she might be about to object, but then with a grunt of assent she turned instead, leading them down into the darkness.

***

Despite the flickering light, Freya found the steps easy to traverse; they were perfectly even, as though carved into the earth with painstaking precision. The trio continued, down and around, past more wall-mounted torches that seemed long unlit. There were paintings here too, at regular intervals along the outer wall, each depicting a sombre-looking individual clad up to the neck in the same grey cerements you might use to wrap a corpse.

"These are the past Hieromonks," Ilene explained. "Starting with Alasdair, who founded the city, each new portrait is placed further down the staircase; it symbolises their downward progress, I suppose."

They passed a handful of canvases, eventually reaching the most recent. Irvine was a full-faced man of stout build, but his ample form did not prevent his face from having a mean, pinched aspect, eyes narrowed mistrustfully above a pointed nose and pursed lips. Freya stopped to gaze at it, wondering why this man would leave his city unguarded, seemingly defenceless.

The steps continued, and Freya couldn't help but admire the quality of the stonework; the stairs described a perfect helix as they descended, with not a hint of a rough edge or misjudged angle. Yet she soon began to tire of the featureless walls, wishing for more paintings, or anything to alleviate the tedium of the endless, spiralling granite. Her mind began to drift, to wish Victor was there to scour the darkness away with the twin lanterns of his eyes. "Ilene, why are you called the Warden?" she asked, thinking conversation might alleviate the monotonous gloom.

"That's a story for later," the wizard whispered. "Now keep your voice down — I'm trying to listen."

Freya did as she was told, concentrating on her own hearing, but perceived nothing except their own echoing footsteps and the clatter of Errick's armour. Their slow descent continued, and Freya's thoughts wandered further, remembering other stone staircases, the innumerable journeys she had taken around the Enclave, up and down and through and beneath. As the seemingly endless corkscrew continued into the depths, she started to imagine she was utterly alone, that the strong-willed companions at her side were mere figments of her imagination.

It almost caught her by surprise when the steps suddenly flattened out, opening into a high-ceilinged chamber. The perfection of its shape was again undeniable; this was not a coarsely-hewn cave but a flawless cube, its smooth surfaces disrupted only by the intricately-carved statues chiselled directly into the stone on either side of them. The sculpted faces of the Hieromonks glowered at them, suspicion in their granite scowls, as though trying to deter the trio from approaching the archway at the room's opposite end.

"There should be guards here too," mused Errick. "And look: that strange symbol appears once again."

Above the staring effigies to their right hung the same four-circle emblem, inscribed this time on an enormous yellow banner. To their left, an identical flag had been torn down, lying tossed and trampled in a corner. Freya opened her mouth to comment, then kept quiet as she noticed Ilene closing her eyes to listen intently once again. Freya could hear no sound at all from beyond the black portal at the end of the room. Her nerves felt taut, her skin alive with gooseflesh. When Ilene called out "Is anyone there?", she nearly jumped out of her skin.

There was no reply. It was as though the granite was holding its breath around them.

"Come on," Ilene said, her expression growing increasingly troubled. They strode past the glaring Hieromonks, Freya's gaze flitting from side to side as though half expecting to catch the sculptures baring their teeth at them. Irvine was the last, on the left-hand side, his expression the most baleful of all, as though resentful of the bare stretch of wall at his side that predicted his eventual demise.

They stepped through the archway into a much larger space; possibly another faultless cube, although this one was so big that its ceiling stretched away beyond the reach of their lantern's flame. For a moment Freya shrank back in shock as she beheld people standing silently at each corner of the chamber, until she realised they were more statues, their legs merging with the stone of the floor as though the room had been chiselled around them.

"It's not all grumpy Hieromonks in Erebyss," Ilene explained, sounding unimpressed. "These four are called the Endeavours Of Humankind: Worship, Labour, Craft and Devotion."

The Warden cast her lantern left and right, revealing archways set into each of the three walls. Freya grimaced as each of the sculptures was illuminated, unsure which she detested more. *Worship* depicted a kneeling figure, his hands pressed against the floor with an expression of wide-eyed ecstasy so blissful he looked deranged. *Labour* showed a woman stooped beneath a perfectly spherical boulder carried upon her back, the agonising weight of her burden etched perfectly in the straining lines of her face and the beads of sweat that sheened her brow; yet, despite her suffering, she was smiling. *Craft* portrayed a man in the process of carving himself, bending to chip away happily at the block of stone that would eventually become his feet. *Devotion* was the only effigy without a beatific grin; this Endeavour was represented by two people leaning towards each other, their heads pressed together into a single glob of rock, as though the flesh of their faces had merged.

"Who's this one?" asked Errick, striding towards the middle of the chamber. "I don't remember this being here."

He was frowning at a fifth statue, this one larger than the others and occupying the centre of the room. Unlike the rest, it did not fuse seamlessly with the ground, but instead occupied a circular plinth that served to accentuate its grander scale. Its quality was unnerving, surpassing even the expert craftsmanship of the other sculptures; but that did not make it any less grotesque.

Its subject was a woman, or more accurately the constituent parts of a woman. Standing upright, the figure's arms were raised, its hands clenched tightly around bunched handfuls of its own skin, peeling back the epidermis as though removing a cloak. The revealed musculature beneath had slumped to its knees, its exposed ligaments and sinews so perfectly realised they seemed to glisten in the amber glow of Ilene's lamp. This skinless figure was, in turn, then tugging at its own flesh, digging its hands into its chest as it prised itself horribly apart. Emerging from this gaping wound was a crawling skeleton, its grinning death-mask staring downwards to where its hands were crumbling to dust on the floor. Beneath the skull's gaping eye sockets, a symbol was carved into the floor: the same ominous four-circle design they had seen elsewhere.

"Looks like Irvine had a few new ideas," Ilene muttered. "I can't say I like what he's done with the place."

"Which way now?" Freya asked, anxious to be away from the grisly stone spectacle.

"Let's try straight ahead," the Warden replied.

They stepped through the archway and found themselves in another gigantic room, this one stretching away into darkness ahead. It resembled a colossal boulevard, with many more archways interspersed along its edges, and vast stone pillars stretching from floor to ceiling. Along the avenue's centre a wide trough had been carved, looking as though it had perhaps once held water, but now standing as dry as the river they had followed to arrive here. Ornate statues and sculptures lined the edges of this channel, depicting beautiful people stooping to fill ceramic vessels, or severe-looking priests knelt in prayer. Once again, every torch hung on the walls was extinguished.

"This place would be beautiful if it wasn't so dark," said Freya.

"It used to be," agreed Errick. "I wonder what has happened here."

They proceeded along the great street, Freya continuing to marvel at its scale and precision. The time it must have taken to excavate this cavernous hallway, to craft each painstakingly-carved statue, must have made the city the work of aeons. Or perhaps it was always here; maybe, like the Enclave, its inhabitants did not remember their home's construction, or how they had first come to dwell within it.

"Where did the people sleep?" Freya asked.

"Oh, these upper sections wouldn't have been occupied," Ilene replied. "They've dug themselves new quarters much further down. But still, you'd expect to see people around. This feels more like ... a mausoleum."

She made a sudden turn and passed through one of the arches, gesturing with the lantern into another large chamber. Its walls were lined with row upon row of walkways, arranged in neat symmetry all around them.

"This would have been one of the living areas," she explained. Between the platforms, accessible via a dizzying ziggurat of interconnected steps, Freya could see doorways set into the walls, alongside the curved outlines of circular windows. "So much space, and not enough people to fill it," Ilene added sadly, almost to herself.

They returned to the huge thoroughfare, which Freya had begun to think of as the city's main street. The Warden pressed onwards with renewed vigour, as though suddenly determined to find the root of the city's mysterious abandonment as quickly as possible. When they finally reached the end of the vast corridor, they were confronted by another archway. This one was much larger than the others, its outline decorated with elaborate carvings depicting scenes of toil and contemplation. Freya groaned as she realised that, beyond it, another set of steps led downwards.

Then she froze, as still as the surrounding rock, when her groan was answered with a plaintive, anguished sigh.

"Who's there?" called Ilene, similarly rooted to the spot. For a moment there was silence, and Freya could almost believe the sound had been a mere echo or some trick of the wind whistling down into the catacomb. But then the noise came again, a tortured moan emanating from the darkness beyond the archway, as though coming from someone on the steps below them.

Errick clanked his way to the front of the group. "Show yourself," he snarled. "Or you'll taste the steel of my blade!"

What they heard next was perplexing, resembling the noise a wet sack would make if it was swung against the stone walls. The sound repeated itself, then did so again a few seconds later, growing louder each time, and Freya recoiled in horror as she realised it was approaching them from the blackness below.

Someone was ascending the stairs.

"Speak, damn you!" Errick roared in a voice that would have struck terror into even the hardiest warrior. As if unsettled, the noises stopped, whatever was making them pausing to lurk just beyond the reach of Ilene's lantern. Freya glanced at the wizard and noticed her clutching the blue pendant tightly, as though for reassurance.

Then a guttural howl erupted from the darkness, and with a flurry of footfalls that sounded horribly, sickeningly *moist*, a monster dragged itself into view at the top of the staircase.

Freya gaped, her body shaking with the force of the horror that suddenly enveloped it: the thing looked like something spewed from her darkest nightmare. It moved on all fours, its curved limbs slapping wetly against the rock as it heaved itself forwards, seeming scarcely able to propel the liquescent ruin of its torso. It seemed to be *dissolving*, its pale flesh almost translucent, like a dollop of tallow melting on a skillet. Yet still it held its form; bones and organs were visible through the gelatinous mess and, as it lifted its obscene head towards them and Freya beheld skin sloughing like damp paper from the skull beneath, she was in no doubt that it had once possessed the shape of a man.

She screamed, unable to contain her terror and disgust at this profane, impossible, nauseating parody. At the same time,

Errick raised his sword, hesitating for only a moment before he stepped gallantly towards the monstrosity.

"Don't!" Ilene shouted, her voice taking on a commanding tone Freya hadn't heard before. "I remember now, what the symbol means: it means we need to leave, right now!"

"Why?" cried Errick, not taking his eyes off the glutinous thing that was slowly squelching its way towards him, something between agony and hatred blazing in the bloodshot remnants of its eyes.

"Because this city is now a fucking tomb," the Warden bellowed. "And if we don't get out, we'll all end up like this abomination!"

That threat seemed to be enough to dissuade Errick from his stubbornness. He turned, grabbing Freya by the arm, yanking her from the spot to which her feet had become glued as together they tore back up the avenue at a frenetic pace. The diseased limbs of Freya's companions showed no sign of impediment as they fled; indeed, Freya became suddenly terrified that she would be left behind in their dash for freedom. But Errick stayed alongside her, his gauntleted fingers squeezing her arm, willing her onwards, and the hellish thing behind them seemed unable to match their pace.

Suddenly, Ilene skidded to a stop, and Freya and Errick almost careened into her back.

"What are you doing?" the knight yelled, and then fell silent, lifting his sword once again.

Ahead of them, emerging from one of the archways to their side, was another of the gurgling, oozing fiends. Freya stared in dismay as another followed it, and then another, the three leaving a glistening trail on the floor behind them.

Fourteen

"*Don't touch them,*" hissed Ilene as Errick readied himself to attack. "This is not a time for foolish pride!"

"What would you have me do?" the knight countered. "Stand here and wait for them to devour us?"

The trio of monsters spread out in front of them, their jaws hanging open as though melting from their faces. The sounds they made were appalling; wet sucking noises, or gargling howls that spoke more of boundless suffering than a ravenous appetite. Any humanity these things had once possessed was clearly long gone. They advanced mindlessly, their viscous flesh gleaming in the light from Ilene's lamp.

"Please, just trust me," the wizard said. "Freya, have you still got your lantern?"

It took Freya a moment to understand the question, so transfixed was she by the advancing aberrations. Then she realised she still clutched the lamp in her trembling hands. "Yes," she replied, her voice little more than a frightened croak.

"Then for the love of God, light it," Ilene ordered. Freya fumbled with the mechanism, her eyes glued to the three circling nightmares, wondering how long the fourth would take to catch up to them at the rear. When the wick finally sprung to life, she held the lantern aloft, wondering what magic Ilene intended to summon to their aid.

Instead, the Warden hurled her own lamp at the feet of the encroaching beasts and screamed "Run!" at the top of her voice. The monsters shrank from the leaping flames, screeching horribly as they cowered, and Freya and Errick followed Ilene as she darted between their recoiling bodies. The archway that led back to the statue room loomed ahead of them, the gruesome stonework now seeming like a delightful welcoming party.

A pair of bright lights hovered in the gloom and Freya almost stopped, anticipating some new horror. Then she realised it was Victor, waiting for them.

"No time to explain," gasped Ilene as they approached the mechanical man. She leaned against him for a moment, catching her breath. "Just take them," she wheezed, "and help them on their way."

For a moment the machine seemed about to protest, but he instead turned to lead them towards the hallway of the Hieromonks. Freya glanced behind her as the Warden turned to face their pursuers. "What about you?" she cried.

"Just make sure you see it through!" Ilene yelled, her voice as strong as clashing blades.

Then she was lost from sight as Freya turned, glimpsing once again the rendition of Irvine as they passed it, feeling nausea churning in her stomach as she recalled his miserly features, his peevish mouth and sharp nose.

That first creature ... had she perceived a resemblance?

They reached the staircase and sprinted up it as fast as they could. Its relentless spiral seemed to last even longer than it had during their descent, and Freya felt each wheezing breath tear at her lungs as they scrambled up and around, up and around. Victor was ahead of her, Errick just behind, Ilene lost to the darkness at their backs. When they finally, mercifully, emerged onto the ground floor of Erebyss's watchtower, she heard a huge, muffled boom beneath them, and felt the floor begin to shake.

"Get out of here!" cried Victor, and almost bundled her out through the main gates. Errick followed and the three of them tumbled down the steps, staggering breathlessly towards the cart as the keep continued to shudder and groan behind them. With a sound like the dying roar of a demon, the building started to tear itself apart, crumpling inwards like a tower of playing cards. Dust and shards of debris billowed outwards as the fortress unmade itself, the geometric perfection of its bricks and supports rearranging into a new form, one born of chaos and destruction. The earth convulsed as though it was sickened by the monsters it had spawned, hurling Freya to the ground as wreckage rained down around her. She closed her eyes, knowing that this was how she would finally die, crushed beneath a slab of masonry; then a pair of hands clamped around her wrists, pulling her forwards on her front.

She lay where Errick had dragged her, protected by the bulk of the cart and by the knight's armoured frame as he positioned himself between her and the disintegrating keep. As the ground rumbled around them, she realised that Victor was not with them; the machine had turned to run back towards the collapsing tower, calling Ilene's name, over and over.

***

They searched for hours, but could find no sign of the wizard.

They found Victor pinned beneath a chunk of rubble. His upper half was battered and dented, but somehow intact; his legs, though, had been completely crushed by the falling rock. Errick braced himself again and again against the granite, grunting with exertion as he tried to move it even a single inch.

"It's no use," Victor said in a thin, quavering approximation of his former voice. The smile that accompanied the pitiful sound was somehow the saddest thing Freya had ever seen. "You'll have to remove them altogether."

"And then what will you do?" Freya asked, appalled.

"I will come with you. It was the Warden's dying wish that I assist you."

"You won't be much use to us if you're unable to walk," Errick wheezed. Freya shot him an angry glance and he looked away, concentrating once again on his struggle against the stone.

"Don't talk like that," she scolded. "And besides, we don't even know she's dead!" But the tears streaming from her eyes told her that she knew otherwise. There was no way Ilene could have survived such a cataclysm; whether intentionally or not, the Warden had sacrificed herself to consign Erebyss's excavated evils back to the earth.

She watched as Errick strained and heaved against the boulder. Victor lay pinioned beneath it, his arms clamped against the rock, trying to no avail to help move it. "Are you in pain?" she asked.

The machine shook his head. "I do not believe I feel pain in the same way you do. But I am aware that I am grievously injured. I do not wish to be ... a burden."

"Ignore what *he* says," Freya replied pointedly. "You're coming with us as soon as we figure out how to get you out."

"I hate to say it, but I think Victor's right," said Errick, collapsing in defeat against the unforgiving slab. "It's getting dark, and we don't want to spend the night sleeping atop this warren of monsters. If we cut him free, we could at least take him with us."

"There must be some other way!" Freya cried. She stared down at the stricken machine, her tone pleading.

"I am afraid Errick's recommendation is the most practical," Victor replied calmly.

"But what about Ilene? What if she's still here somewhere, trapped beneath the rubble?"

"The Warden has ways to communicate with me," the machine responded. "That's how she summoned me to your aid. If she was still alive, she would have made contact in the same way." Did she imagine the slight tremble in his words, the merest semiquaver of grief?

"But what if you're wrong?" she cried. "What if she's stuck down there with those ... those *things*?" She remembered the angular features of the Hieromonk, and the tortured parody she had seen in the face of the creature that had crawled up from the stricken city.

"We can't wait here forever, Freya," Errick said sadly. "Ilene would want us to carry on."

"Unless we abandon this foolish quest," Freya said quietly. "Go back and help Victor tend to the garden until the plague takes us both." She saw a glint of longing in Errick's eyes, a brief yearning for such respite, for an end to his long, tormented loneliness. Then it was dispelled, replaced by steely resolve.

"No," he said. "We have travelled this far, and overcome much already. If God is testing us, then we are proving equal to His challenges. By our journey's end we will earn a place before His throne, and ask Him to grant the knowledge you seek, and I my divine judgement."

Freya remembered the Enclave, and how quickly the castle's fragile hierarchy had begun to fall apart after the angels had vanished. All around them, she saw evidence of a world being slowly dismantled, as though God was turning against His own creations. Didn't she owe it to herself, to Maxwell, to find out why it was happening? She imagined her friend's disapproving frown, the gentle reproach in his words as he explained that her heart would tell her the right thing to do.

"What about you, Victor?" she said, turning again to the broken form at her feet. "What do *you* seek?"

The automaton stared up at her, the yellow lights in the depths of its hollow eye sockets reduced to the faintest glimmer. "Just a purpose," he replied through the motionless curve of his mouth. "Nothing more."

She watched silently as Errick lifted his sword, whispering a quiet apology to the machine. Then the knight brought the blade down in a great scything arc, cleaving the mangled legs from Victor's body.

***

Somehow, Errick and Freya managed to haul the cart up the opposite slope. Victor was propped on the back of the wagon, now bereft of his legs. Unable to assist directly, he instead used his luminous eyes to light their way, issuing directions as they silently heaved and grunted. By the time they emerged from the basin, they were enveloped in the blackness of another night, and too exhausted to travel further. They made camp not far from the spiked rock formations at the crater's periphery, daring to light a fire, relieved that Victor was there to keep watch while they both obtained some much-needed rest.

After the atrocities she had witnessed in the caverns of Erebyss, Freya thought she would never sleep again; yet, within seconds of nestling her head against the balled fabric she was using as a pillow, she fell into an uninterrupted slumber, so deep that the nightmares that clawed and chittered at its periphery could not break through.

She awoke to find Errick preparing their breakfast, following Victor's directions to add hot water to the mysterious orange powder. The mist had thickened during the night, and she felt as though the three of them were adrift in a great ocean, surrounded by a seething expanse of grey. Even the twisted outline of the caldera's nearby edge was hidden from view, as though the fog had been despatched to obscure the city, obliterating the memory of its existence. She shivered, drawing her sackcloth bedding around her.

"Where to next?" she asked, more to comfort herself with the sound of her companions' voices. She knew where they were destined, even if the Monoliths' dazzling beauty could not penetrate the cloying murk.

"That way," said Errick, gesturing with a gauntleted hand. He hadn't removed his armour while he slept. "But don't ask me what fresh horrors we will stumble upon on our way. I have never before travelled further in this direction than the city we have just buried."

"It's as though the world's going bad," said Freya sadly, her thoughts turning to Ilene.

"Aye," Errick whispered. "Or else I am an agent of its destruction. Everywhere I go I seem to herald death and ruin."

"Don't say such things," Freya admonished. "What happened to Erebyss was hardly your fault. Hieromonk Irvine and his people must have … unearthed something. Something terrible."

Errick nodded dourly, but seemed enshrouded in his sullen mood, and didn't speak again as they drained their mugs of carrot soup.

"Victor, how are you today? Is there anything we can do?" She stared dejectedly at the stumps that jutted from the bottom of his torso.

"I'm fine, thank you," the diminished machine replied, his voice sounding cracked and distant. "Although I will confess to a measure of despondency at the fate of the Warden. Please forgive me if I am a little quiet."

Freya nodded, wishing there was something she could do to alleviate their sorrows, but in truth feeling just as wretched as her companions. They packed the cart, Errick insisting on hauling it alone without Freya's aid. She acquiesced, sensing that the burden provided him with a strange kind of succour, a feeling of utility it would be cruel to deny him. Silence descended as they began their day's march, each lost in their grief.

The landscape changed as they walked; coarse, brown grass began to sprout from the formerly barren earth, and the ground began to undulate gently, describing rolling hills that might have been picturesque if they could see more than a few metres ahead of them, and if their mood was less mournful.

"Do you have any knowledge of our route, Victor?" she asked eventually.

"I am also unfamiliar with the terrain beyond this point," he said, "but will endeavour to assist in our navigation." His eyes glowed brightly, helping to carve a path through the brume. Freya realised what a peculiar sight they must be: the torso of an animated machine, eyes glowing like magical torches, being hauled along by a plague-stricken knight and a disfigured servant-girl.

The wizard offered to remove that scar, a part of her brain grumbled vindictively. *Now that opportunity is gone forever.*

"Victor, may I ask you some questions about Ilene?" Freya said after a while. "We didn't know her for very long, but her absence is sorely felt. Perhaps it would help cheer us all if you told us a little more about her?"

"Of course," said the machine obligingly.

"You said Ilene used the pendant to summon you. Do you know where she got it? I saw a similar one in the possession of one of the Lords, back in my..." she hesitated over the word 'home', unsure whether she would ever see the Enclave again.

"She always had it," said Victor, filling the silence. "She said it was how she first found me."

Freya frowned, wondering how the wizard could have an identical necklace to Lord Gwillym. Did the two once know each other, perhaps? She tried to remember when the Lord had first come to the Enclave, but as with all her memories, it was as hazy as the world beyond the fog. "Do you know where she came from?"

"She spoke sometimes of a former life," said the machine. "Of a time when she had great responsibilities."

"Was that why she called herself the Warden?"

"I never asked her. But I believe she saw herself as the custodian of the garden, the preserver of life amongst a mountain of dead things."

"Yet she wanted you to accompany us, instead of returning to sustain it. Why do you think this was her wish?"

Victor paused. "When you were bathing, and Errick was yet to awaken, she told me you had been ... foreseen."

"She already expected our arrival?" the knight gasped.

"Not exactly," said Victor. "More like … you were fulfilling a prediction. Forgive me, but she said your scar was an important part of it."

"You mean like some sort of prophecy?" Freya said, baffled.

"Almost," the machine replied, sounding frustrated at is inability to explain itself. "You must understand that Ilene would often talk in arcane riddles far beyond my understanding. I remember her saying something about scenario planning, and statistical analysis, whatever that means."

"She told us she wouldn't accompany us further than Erebyss," mused Errick. "Do you think this was a lie?"

"I think perhaps she was…" Victor paused, chuckling to himself, a strange hollow sound that seemed to come from far away. "I'm sorry — I'm just recalling a phrase she taught me, to describe someone who formulates their plans as they go. She would have said she was 'winging it'."

"I wish the Warden was still with us," Errick concluded with a sad smile.

"Me too," said Freya.

They plodded onwards, ruminating, as the land continued to rise and fall beneath them, the slopes becoming gradually steeper until they found themselves on a sharp upward trajectory. She offered to help Errick with the cart, but again he refused, his polite tone undercut by a curtness she did not have the energy to battle against. Ahead and above them, the mist was as thick as ever, denying them even a glimpse of the summit.

"It's as though this fog is sent by God to thwart us," Errick muttered as they ascended.

"Then, as you said yesterday, we shall be equal to His test," Freya said. She felt as though they were alternating the roles of optimist and pessimist, passing the mantle of determination back and forth between them. Sustaining each other. "We'll stop for food and rest when we crest this next peak," she added with an encouraging smile.

But minutes passed and that zenith never came. The path continued upwards, meandering between boulders and rocky outcrops, funnelling them gradually into the cleft between two bluffs that rose into almost sheer walls on either side of them. After a while, Errick paused, and Freya thought again about insisting that he let her pull the cart for a while; then she realised he was examining something on the ground. She joined him in peering down at it: it looked like a huge, crumpled piece of chainmail armour, far too large for a person to wear.

"What do you think it is?" she asked.

Her question was directed to Errick, but it was Victor who answered. "It looks like wire mesh. If we climb a little further I suspect we'll find where it came from."

The machine was right. Around twenty metres ahead, they found thick posts driven into the stone on either side of them. Jagged fragments of the same chain-linked steel clung to them, as though there had once been a stout fence here, now wrenched out of place and tossed aside to rust.

"It appears someone was very keen to get beyond this barrier," said Victor.

"Or to escape, from the other side," Errick mused. Freya noticed how exhausted he seemed, almost panting as he rested against the hilt of his sword. She opened her mouth to say something, then thought better of it. *He knows the plague is killing him,* she thought. *He doesn't need me to remind him every time he's out of breath.*

As they passed through the shredded barricade, she couldn't help following the train of thought onwards to its next, inevitable waystation.

And how long before the plague infects me too?

The route continued to lead them upwards, winding its way amongst the steep hills and tors like a mountain pass. After they had endured another twenty minutes of gruelling climbing it finally levelled out, and they found themselves on top of a wide, flat expanse of shrivelled grass.

Directly opposite them was the most enormous bridge Freya had ever seen. It was fifteen feet wide, a massive metal slab that seemed to defy gravity as it disappeared out into the mist. A rusted lattice framed the start of the structure and seemed to play some part in its suspension, lashed to thick metal wires that were driven into the ground on one side and arced away along the bridge's expanse on the other. More wires were strung along these curves, attached at regular intervals to the walkway itself, along with metal railings that appeared so corroded Freya wouldn't trust them to bear her weight. She approached the edifice, seeing the hilltop plunge away just beyond its edge, but the accumulated fog prevented her from determining just how deep a drop the bridge had been constructed to span.

Maybe for the best, she thought, feeling suddenly nauseated.

Errick approached to undertake a similar inspection, then sank down onto a nearby rock, so pale it must have been a chunk of sandstone. Similar boulders littered the plateau, and Freya rested against another, breathing heavily after the climb.

"Do you think it's safe?" she asked.

"How do we even know we're travelling the right way?" the knight asked, seeming frustrated by his own fatigue. "This accursed fog prevents us from seeing what awaits us on the other side."

"Perhaps we should wait until the fog clears," Freya suggested. "We could make camp here and hope the morning brings a better view of our surroundings."

"But if the mist lingers, we'd simply be wasting time and food. And besides, that won't prove whether the bridge will bear our weight."

"How can such a thing even exist?" Freya marvelled. "It must be held in place by some powerful magic."

"An alternative would be to descend back to the hills below us, to search for a different onward route," said Victor. "Perhaps we might find our way to the foot of this chasm, and proceed that way."

"Oh, to hell with it," growled Errick, hauling himself to his feet. "If fate brought the three of us together, then fate has provided us with this passage through the peaks. And if we suspect the bridge is about to buckle under our bulk, we can perhaps afford to part with some of our endless reserves of carrot soup!"

Freya smiled, glad to hear Errick at least trying to find some humour. Then his expression changed suddenly. "Come away from the boulder!" he shouted, lunging for her and almost dragging her towards him. She turned, staring at the sandstone lump, trying desperately to see what had caused him such consternation.

"There's nothing there, Errick!" she cried, glaring at him.

"Look closer. Doesn't the shape look familiar to you?"

She continued to peer at the rock, utterly baffled.

"Look at its other side," Errick insisted, his voice still tinged with shock.

Frowning, Freya did as she was bid. Then her mouth fell open as she beheld the cavities on the opposite face of the smooth, yellowish stone: two large holes, sunk into symmetrical contours on either side of the rock. Beneath them, another orifice, and then what looked like smaller stones arranged in a rough upward curve.

She had been sitting on top of an impossibly large, half-buried, humanoid skull.

Fifteen

The plateau was littered with bones. They found enormous pelvises, gigantic femurs, and even the colossal scaffold of a ribcage, big enough for them to walk through.

"What in the angels' name happened here?" Errick asked, dismayed, as they wandered amongst the remains.

"Another equally pertinent question is how these gargantuan beings came to exist," pondered Victor, surveying the scene from the top of his cart. "I've never heard of such creatures."

"They're giants," said Freya, surprised by a sudden flash of recollection. "We used to tell stories about them. They live at the top of huge beanstalks, and eat human flesh."

"Terrific," muttered Errick. "Hopefully they'll take one look at our wasted forms and consider us an unworthy meal."

"Hopefully they're all as dead as these bones," added Victor flatly.

Freya turned to look out across the bridge once again, wondering what was waiting on the other side, beyond the fog. "Let's go before we lose our nerve altogether," she said, and strode forwards.

Errick put a hand on her shoulder, restraining her. "Please, let me be the first to attempt the bridge. If it crumbles I'd rather it was my doomed soul that plummeted to its death, not yours." His expression was kind, but she did not return the smile, troubled by his despairing words. Overcome by a sudden compulsion, she reached out a hand and placed it against his cheek. He shrank back in surprise, as though her touch was alive with flame.

"Sir Errick," she said, holding his gaze. "You may have made mistakes. I know you feel guilty for striking me, soon after we first met. But you cannot live in perpetual atonement."

He blinked, seemingly speechless.

"You are important to me," she continued. "And we would both already be dead if we didn't have each other. So your constant desire to prove your worth isn't necessary. This is a crossing we will undertake *together*."

She smiled then, and he did too, the ravages of the plague seeming to momentarily fall from his face, restoring the handsome and courageous knight buried beneath. She reached for his hand, feeling how dry the skin was, how thin and wasted the disease had made it, tracing the shapes of the dark blotches on its back. He stiffened at her touch, but she forced her fingers between his, interlacing their grip like knotted rope, and squeezed. After a moment's hesitation, he squeezed back.

Wordlessly, they turned, and each lifted a single arm of the cart. Freya looked at Victor, whose decimated body lay in mute testament to the damage the world could inflict.

Everybody's wounded, she thought. *But perhaps, without such harm, we would each be weaker.*

The machine said nothing as they towed him out onto the bridge.

***

The platform beneath them felt as solid as the land they had just left, the swirling fog absorbing the dull clang of their footsteps as they progressed. The haze was so thick that the hills behind them soon dissolved from view, leaving them walking along what felt like a solitary causeway spanning an empty, grey oblivion. Freya could almost believe that this was the whole world, just the three of them on this strip of metal; that everything beyond the mist had ceased to exist, or perhaps never had in the first place.

Minutes passed, and the bridge showed no sign of reaching its terminus. Freya began to worry that this was some fiendish enchantment, that they would walk and walk forever and never reach the other side, slowly dying of plague or malnutrition. If she hadn't already beheld the Monoliths in the distant skyline, she could quite believe that they had reached the very end of the world.

Suddenly, with a loud banging sound, the bridge began to shake.

"What was that?" Freya cried. They stopped, listening, feeling the reverberations beneath their feet. Then the sound came again, louder, and once more the vast structure trembled in response.

"Perhaps this is the collapse we feared," Errick murmured in alarm. "And we've come too far along the walkway to make it back."

Another bang sounded, the loudest yet, the bridge vibrating like a musician's tuning fork.

"What do we do?" cried Freya. "Is this thing really going to fall apart?"

Victor spoke as yet another tremor tore through the platform. "It isn't collapsing," the machine said, his tinny voice almost lost in the clamour. "Something is approaching us, from the other side."

They stared into the leaden void ahead of them as the noises grew louder, more frequent, and Freya became convinced the bridge was going to shudder itself to pieces. Then something moved behind the curtain of mist, as though the vapour itself was coagulating, assembling into some vague and ominous form. The shape grew darker with every thundering crash, every seismic shock seeming to encourage it to coalesce, to sharpen its outline into something they could discern, something huge and menacing.

Then, with a roar that sounded loud enough to demolish a kingdom, a giant emerged from the fog.

Its bulk almost filled the bridge, which creaked and groaned beneath it as though howling in protest. The thing was completely naked, its pale and scabrous skin a tapestry of sores and lesions. It looked less like a man than a collection of enormous limbs stitched crudely together, as though whatever dark sorcery had enlarged it to such an impossible size had not worked uniformly on each of its extremities. Its legs seemed too short, ready to buckle beneath the bloated sack of its immense torso, while its arms were so long and thin that they almost trailed on the ground. In one grotesque, too-many-fingered hand, it dragged a gigantic club, which Freya realised was an uprooted tree. The other hand was raised, pointing one of its seven digits towards them.

"Who is it?" the monster bellowed, and Freya clapped her hands to her ears, stumbling backward in fright. Errick stood stock-still, stunned into inaction as he gaped at the beast. "Is it creepy crawlies?" the giant boomed, its face splitting into a horrid, tooth-filled grin. Freya had at first thought that its massive head was bald, but as she stared up at it, she realised that strands of grey hair were clinging to the back of its mottled scalp. She gasped; could this behemoth be a plague carrier, too?

"Brock is hungry," it continued, stooping to reach towards them. Startled into life, Errick unsheathed his sword and swung it towards the monstrous, grasping digits. The giant recoiled with a howl of rage, sucking at the deep cut Errick had made in one of its fingers.

"You shan't find an easy meal here, beast!" the knight yelled. "Get back across your bridge and content yourself with feasting on rocks!"

With one hand clamped in its mouth, the giant stared down at Errick, pure hatred blazing in its eyes. "Nasty creepy crawly man," it mumbled, lifting the tree in its other hand as though it was a tiny twig. "Brock smash you now!"

It speaks like a simpleton, thought Freya, *but it's not completely mindless.* Perhaps she could reason with it, negotiate their safe passage somehow. "Brock!" she called, and its gaze shifted to her, squinting as though she was too small to see. "Brock, wait — please can I talk to you?" The creature stared at her, still brandishing the cudgel. If that weapon descended on her, she would quickly be reduced to little more than a bloody smear. "We merely want to reach the other side of your bridge, Brock," she continued, trying to sound as friendly as possible. "We didn't mean to disturb you."

Brock didn't reply, grinding his rancid teeth as he regarded her suspiciously.

"Are you the guard?" she persisted. "Do your people frown upon intruders like us?"

"No *people*," the giant intoned, pronouncing the word with bitter disdain. "Brock only one left."

"I'm sorry," Freya replied, raising her voice to cover the height difference between them. "You must be lonely?"

Brock looked surprised by the question, creasing up his enormous forehead as he considered his response. "Brock miss mummy," he said eventually. "Nobody else." His bottom lip was thrust out petulantly, and Freya fancied she might even be able to see tears gathering in the corners of his rheumy eyes. The unfamiliar word he had used seemed to snag something in her mind, but like a drowning swimmer reaching upwards from a fast-flowing river, the memory was quickly swept away.

"What happened to the others?"

Brock pondered this for a long moment. Then his shoulders began to shake, his entire body convulsing as though he had broken down into tears. It was only when he threw his repulsive head backwards and a cacophony erupted from his throat that she realised he was in fact bawling with laughter.

"Perhaps he isn't the sensitive type after all," hissed Errick, gripping his sword tightly at her side.

Spittle sprayed everywhere as the giant continued to roar with merriment. When his amusement finally subsided, he tilted his head back towards Freya and began to lower his bulk into a squatting position, the muscles of his legs bunching as they strained to support his bulging belly. Like a slowly shifting glacier, Brock hunkered down, bringing his face close enough for Freya to smell his fetid breath.

"Silly creepy crawly lady," he said, grinning widely. "Brock *eat* others. Now none left. *That* why Brock hungry."

She realised then that his stomach wasn't swollen with fat — it was distended with malnutrition. In fact, everything about the giant attested to his dreadful health, as though his entire body was bursting with disease: ulcers festered around his cracked lips, and great folds of dark skin hung beneath the desperate orbs of his eyes. Looking at Brock's mouth was like staring into the Enclave's festering Pit.

Freya knew, then, that the giant was going to eat her no matter what she said. She watched as he lazily hefted the tree, closing her eyes and hoping that she'd be dead before he started to crunch through her bones.

Then fire erupted around the giant's hand, and he roared in pain as the tree was suddenly engulfed in flame. With panic and confusion in his eyes, Brock hurled the weapon away, sending it spinning over the side of the bridge and down into whatever abyss lay shrouded beneath them.

"Errick, now!" shouted Victor, and she realised it was the machine who had thrown the final vial of fire nectar at the monster. The sparks of the blaze echoed in Errick's eyes as he strode forward, gripping his sword with both hands as he brought the blade straight downwards and through the centre of the giant's foot. With a scream that seemed to reverberate through the entire bridge, through the very flesh of Freya's body, Brock yanked his skewered limb away, hopping on one foot as blood geysered from the wound.

Without a second thought, Errick leapt after his sword, managing to grab the protruding hilt with one hand. Freya watched anxiously as the giant jerked his leg back and forth, trying to shake Errick off and launch him over the precipice; but the knight clung on, undaunted, mounting the thick slab of Brock's foot and tugging his sword free before he was launched against the side of the bridge. The railings buckled, but held, and Errick was able to roll forwards to safety even as the giant aimed a huge kick towards him. The swinging blow missed, sending a chunk of the barrier flying off into the void. It also completely unbalanced the monster, who tottered towards the edge before he could steady himself. Sensing his opportunity, Errick leapt towards Brock's standing leg, belabouring it with vicious slashes and stabbing blows. But the giant did not stumble again; instead, he regained his poise, and with a single sweep of his abominable hand he snatched the knight up, lifting him towards his face. Errick hung there, struggling hopelessly in his tormentor's crushing grasp.

"Little tin man," Brock purred as his fat tongue flopped sickeningly outwards, like a sackful of entrails that had long ago turned bad. "Brock hope you not too crunchy."

Freya stared, transfixed, convinced that her friend was about to disappear into that vile, yawning gullet. Then she caught Errick's gaze, just for a moment. She had expected to behold ashen defeat in it, the same resigned look she had seen in some of the knight's darkest moments. But instead, Errick's eyes smouldered with a fire so bright she could almost believe they were illuminated by the same magic as Victor's. The knight pivoted, twisting in Brock's grip so that he hung upside down, facing straight into the giant's abysmal craw.

If Errick said something to his foe, Freya didn't hear it. Instead, she saw him jam his sword right up the monster's nose, burying it to the hilt into one of Brock's cavernous nostrils. The giant made an appalling noise, screeching like a whistling kettle, dropping Errick as he clawed at his face. Errick tumbled to the floor, landing in a twisted heap of limbs and metal as Brock staggered backwards, frantically trying to extricate the blade that was wedged into his sinus. Seemingly unaware of his position until the last moment, the giant toppled like a felled tree over the side of the bridge.

His expression as he plunged was one of abject terror, and Freya could not help but feel strangely sorry for the brute as his arms flailed dementedly, tearing off another chunk off the railing and slicing through several of the bridge's supporting wires as he disappeared from view. Then, like a stone dropped into water, Brock was gone, disappearing into the mist like a bad dream, until the boom of a distant impact reminded her that the giant was as real as the ground far beneath them.

The earth had broken Brock's fall, and most of his hideous bones, Freya hoped.

She rushed to Errick's side, finding him barely conscious and breathing raggedly. "Errick!" she cried uselessly. "Errick, wake up! You did it!"

That precise moment, as she knelt at her friend's side, was when the bridge started to collapse.

Sixteen

All around them, the metal began to shriek and protest, and Freya could almost believe it was the sound of Brock's titanic death throes far below them. She shook Errick roughly, but the knight seemed to be hovering on the periphery of unconsciousness, battered and broken by his battle with the giant.

"I'm sorry to state the obvious, but we need to *run*," yelled Victor from the cart. "The structure has been irreparably compromised."

Freya glanced around and saw another of the supporting wires detach from the bridge, snapping upwards as though an unendurable tension had been suddenly released. Panicking, she lifted Errick's head and struck him hard across the face. He blinked, his eyes gradually focusing on her. "You fought well," she said firmly. "But if you don't get up, *now*, your victory will be for nothing!"

She hauled on his arm and he staggered to his feet like a drunkard, and together they grasped the arms of Victor's makeshift carriage.

"Just leave me behind!" shouted the machine. They ignored him and began to haul the cart along the bridge at as fast a pace as Errick's faltering steps could sustain. Behind them, they heard a deafening, metallic scraping as more of the metal ropes separated and the bridge itself began to buckle. Suddenly, they were no longer traversing a flat, solid causeway, but an unstable strip that wobbled like a piece of ribbon flapping in a breeze. There was a deafening roar, and their path bent upwards, becoming a daunting uphill ramp as the bridge sagged behind them. Still, they struggled onwards, half-climbing, half-walking, clinging grimly to the cart to prevent it from rolling away. They crested the top of the newly-formed slope, grunting with effort as they tugged the cart over the lip and back onto a steadier portion of the structure. Errick stumbled then, falling forwards onto his knees just as the entire slumping middle segment of the bridge separated and dropped with a thunderous groan into the mist below.

There was no respite. Their section of the walkway lurched suddenly downwards, as though the remaining metal yearned to reunite with its missing midsection. Freya half-cajoled, half-dragged Errick to his feet, and together they heaved the cart forward again, feeling as though they were barely a step ahead of certain death, as the sundered bridge crumbled behind them. Step by agonising step they continued into the mist, and Freya almost screamed with relief when she beheld another of the perpendicular scaffolds, a mirror of the one that had framed the bridge's opposite side, emerging from the fog.

"Come on, we're almost there!" she shouted, willing Errick forwards, noticing how he was barely standing, propping himself against the cart as his eyes rolled back in his head. A few strides later, he pitched forward once again, barely even lifting his arms to break his fall as he collapsed onto his face.

"Errick, please!" Freya screamed in desperation, taking up both arms of the cart and hauling it forwards a few more steps. Then she turned, dropping to the knight's flank, succeeding in rolling him onto his back. She winced at his face, which was deathly pale, his eyelids now firmly closed.

"Errick ... I don't know what to do," she said softly. "But I won't leave you." And she stayed there, at his side, watching as more of the bridge tumbled into the gulf, including the part they had been standing upon only moments earlier. The destruction approached inexorably, now only feet away, as though the bridge was being slowly consumed by something that wouldn't rest until it had swallowed them up. It was like the vengeful spirit of Brock himself, fulfilling his promise to devour them.

Then it stopped. With a final catastrophic tearing sound, another part of the bridge broke away and fell, leaving only the short portion upon which they had collapsed, mere metres from the safety of the land. The tumult of the structure's demise echoed all around them, but it did not resume, and to Freya's amazement, the great chasm gradually returned to silence.

"Freya," said Victor. "We need to get off this platform. It could still fall at any moment."

She knew he was right, but her legs felt suddenly leaden, as though she had completely exhausted her body getting them this far.

"Freya, please. I'm sorry I can't help," Victor continued, "but you need to assist Errick."

Numbly, she willed herself upright. She did as she was told, dragging the knight along on his back until he was clear of the bridge's precarious vestige. Then she went back for Victor, somehow summoning the strength to tug the cart to safety.

Finally, she sank to the rocky ground alongside her companions, and plunged into an exhausted sleep.

***

"Daddy?" asked the child.

"Jennifer wants you," said the woman gently.

The man, distracted by something on the screen in his hand, answered without looking up. "Yes, what?"

"Why is mummy not here?"

An irritated look then, eyes closing momentarily, teeth gritted in exasperation. The device placed on the table, the message from Paul Cohen at the Innovation Corporation temporarily forgotten.

"We've been through this, Jenny." Frustration competed with affection in his face; and something else, something that spoke of nostalgia and hidden yearning, a tapestry of shared memories that could never be fully unpicked. It made her feel like an interloper.

A homewrecker.

"Mummy and daddy decided to have separate lives. So when you're with daddy, mummy won't be there anymore. Just think of Freya as your *other* mummy. Isn't that great? You're such a lucky girl you have *two* mummies!"

A thoughtful frown knitted itself on the child's brow. "My main mummy is still my favourite," she said earnestly.

The train rumbled onwards, shuddering gently as it sped them into the unknowable tangle of their futures.

***

When Freya awoke, the mist had receded. She blinked upwards at an azure sky, the memory of her dream disintegrating like the fraying cables that had failed to hold the bridge together. Her friends lay where she'd left them: Errick still on his back, the slow rise and fall of his chest reassuring her that his victory over the giant hadn't cost him his life, and Victor, sitting atop the cart, smiling as though thoroughly enjoying the adventure. Ilene, meanwhile, was … then Freya remembered, and reliving the Warden's fate felt like a nail hammered into her heart.

Although it was still daylight, the sun was rapidly sinking on the other side of the chasm, which yawed so widely before her that it made her stomach lurch. She clambered to her feet, staying away from the treacherous precipice, noticing that the remains of the bridge still stood in place as though in strident denial.

"We could have just rested there after all," said Victor, and it took her a few moments to remember that the machine did not need to sleep, and a few more to realise that he was making a joke.

She forced a smile. "How long was I … unconscious?"

161

"Just a few hours," Victor replied. "The rest will have done you good. But I am worried about Errick; he has not moved, and it is impossible to discern what injuries are hidden beneath his apparel."

And without Ilene, there's no one to heal him this time, thought Freya grimly. She crouched beside the knight, remembering how she and Victor had removed his armour when he had been suffused with infection. This time she would need to do it alone. Slowly she untied the thick plates from the cloth shirt underneath, placing them gently by Errick's side, feeling like she was committing a sacrilege. She remembered how bravely he had fought against the giant, and worried she was somehow stealing his strength away, each detached piece of steel taking with it some of his indomitable valour. In a way, that's exactly what *was* happening; when the armour was completely removed, Errick the warrior was gone, replaced by a gaunt, dying man whose body was made painfully lean by the sickness that infested it. Carefully, she undid the buttons of his undershirt, feeling blood rush to her cheeks as she exposed the flesh beneath. His chest was covered in bruises and lacerations, but nothing that appeared mortally grievous. Gently, she began to roll him onto his side.

His hand clamped around her wrist as his eyes snapped open. For a second, she thought he was angry with her, or perhaps in a state of delirium had even forgotten who she was. Then he smiled weakly, and she was overcome with relief. "You ... hit me," he managed to say.

"Well now we're even," was all she could think to reply, before she wrapped him in an embrace so strong that he winced in pain. "Are you okay?" she asked. "I was checking you for injuries."

He glanced at the armour fragments piled around him. "As if losing my sword wasn't bad enough," he muttered, but not crossly. "Yes, I'll be fine. I just needed a bit of rest. That giant was … one of my more formidable opponents." He struggled to a sitting position and started to methodically reattach the plates.

"Did your sword have a name?" Freya asked.

Errick paused, his eyes momentarily distant. Then he looked at her with a sad smile. "Yes. It was called Annalise."

Of course. His queen.

"I'm glad you're okay," said Victor. "And I'm sorry to disturb you both. But I wonder if you might come and look at this."

Freya realised that she'd left the cart close to the chasm's brink, and that Victor had performed his neck-twisting trick, rotating his head to enable him to stare down into the void. The fog had thinned so much that she could see all the way to the other side of the gorge, where a mirror image of the tiny jutting splinter of bridge protruded defiantly. That meant that the ground below them might also be visible, and she leapt to her feet, suddenly anxious to make sure Brock's carcass was indeed down there, that the giant hadn't somehow survived the fall and crawled away to plot his revenge.

Errick tried to stand, then quickly thought better of it, groaning as he sank back down. "What do you see?" he called to Freya, who had joined Victor in peering over the precipice.

She didn't reply at first, because she could not believe what she beheld. The abyss stretched out far, far beneath them, many fathoms further than she had imagined, an impossibly long and deep ravine, like a scar on the surface of the world. Wisps of mist still hovered in its depths, but they were thin enough for her to make out the bottom, which was covered in yellow shards that for a fleeting moment she thought was a pile of sandstone boulders, like the ones she and Errick had briefly rested against that morning. Then she remembered that those had been the skull and the jawbone of a giant; a creature that had once been as large as Brock, whose corpse she finally spotted, face down and spread-eagled, flattened into the ground as though he had been deflated.

The giant's body was sprawled across a carpet of huge, mouldering bones.

***

Errick finally managed to haul himself to his feet, and stood alongside them, gazing down into the charnel pit.

"Did that monster ... eat them all?" Freya asked, open-mouthed.

"Surely not," said Errick, sounding horrified. "There must be a thousand skeletons down there."

"I never thought the stories were true," Freya murmured. "What are we going to find next? A fire-breathing dragon?"

"Interestingly, the bones down there aren't all identical," said Victor.

"What do you mean?" Errick asked, raising a silvery eyebrow.

"I mean they don't all match Brock's physiology. Some are much smaller, others are much thicker but stunted in length, while others are more grossly elongated even than his."

"How can you perceive such detail from up here?"

"My eyesight is significantly more effective than yours," the machine replied matter-of-factly. "I can discern at least two thousand sets of remains below us. Some of them seem to possess more normal human proportions."

"Maybe this place was home to not one race, but many," Errick mused. "Perhaps they were once integrated, but fell to warring as the days passed."

Freya shuddered, as horrified as she was perplexed. "We should keep going," she said, suddenly desperate to be as far as possible from that gruesome trench. "Let's see if we can make some more ground before nightfall."

Errick looked crestfallen. "I'm sorry," he said, hanging his head. "But I need to rest here for a little longer. I must recover my strength before I attempt what awaits us." He gestured away from the canyon, and Freya realised that she hadn't once looked in that direction, at their onward path. When she did so, she gasped.

They were on a narrow promontory, which fell away into the chasm on either side of them. Ahead, the land ascended in a sharp upward curve, forming a fearsome wall of rock. The steep incline did not stop until it disappeared into the mist, which lurked above them like a wounded enemy, beaten back but not defeated. Yet, in spite of this obscuration, she could see far enough to be certain that the peak was a long way above them indeed, the rugged slope becoming coated with snow as it ascended into the fog.

If they were to continue their quest, they were going to have to climb a mountain.

Seventeen

"Why build a bridge leading to such an impasse?" Freya cried in disbelief.

"I believe there was once a passage down into the crag," replied Errick. "See the gap there, now plugged with boulders?"

She followed his pointing finger and saw, on their left, the mouth of a tunnel leading down into the side of the mountain. It was completely blocked by what might have been a rockfall, or even a deliberate blockade.

"Maybe some of these misshapen creatures still live, inside the cliffs," Victor pondered. "Perhaps they sealed up this entrance to protect themselves from Brock and his appetites."

"Without a battalion of miners to chisel our way through, we'll never know," Errick replied sourly.

"I'm tired of caves and tunnels," muttered Freya, shivering. "I'd rather attempt the mountainside than venture underground ever again."

"Our conditions will be dire," said Errick. "There's no way we can bring the cart with us, and that means abandoning many of our supplies. And I don't know if I'll be able to carry…" He glanced at Victor, allowing the thought to trail away.

"I can climb," said the machine. "My arms are strong enough to bear my own weight."

Freya looked at him, then back towards the daunting slope. "Let us camp here first, as Errick suggests," she said, trying not to let her scepticism show. "If we must leave some food behind, we might as well have our fill of carrot soup!"

As darkness fell, the remaining firewood was heaped into a bonfire. Its flames leapt and crackled pleasantly, warming them as she and Errick devoured a banquet of dried meats and crackers, along with generous helpings of Victor's heated broth. After they had feasted, Freya exhaled deeply, feeling full enough to burst. Meanwhile, Errick began to rummage in the cart, producing a mysterious flask from somewhere in its depths.

"Another item I would rather exhaust than part with," he said with a flourish. He removed the cork, and Freya smelled the emerging aroma even before he had poured her a cupful.

"Is that ... *booze*?" she asked excitedly.

"The very best," said Errick. "Now allow me to propose a toast." He decanted the vessel's contents into two liberal measures, handing one to Freya. Then he handed a third, completely empty, container to the final member of their trio. "To Victor," he said, raising his mug. "The machine whose composition denies him such simple pleasures as this fine whiskey. Yet, metallic though he may be, he is no less a man than I."

"To Victor," Freya echoed, tipping the liquor into her throat and almost gagging at its potency. She felt the fluid burning its way down into her belly, a sensation as pleasurable as it was nauseating.

"To me," said Victor, miming the act of swigging from the cup and making them both laugh.

"In all seriousness, Victor, I thank you," the knight said earnestly. "Your quick thinking on the bridge saved us. You have already helped us more than Ilene could ever have hoped."

Victor shrugged, and Freya was stunned at how human the gesture appeared. At times, their friend made her think of a marionette, a lifeless artefact made to simulate the behaviour of humans. Yet at others, in spite of his rigid smile and unyielding frame, Victor seemed like a real person, tragically condemned to inhabit his mechanical body.

"I am glad to be of some use to you, despite my diminished state. Now, please; any more sentimentality and I may have to start drinking after all."

They laughed again, and continued their merriment for a while, until Freya found herself lulled gradually to sleep by the satisfying heat of the alcohol, and of the roaring fire.

***

Morning came and, as usual, she arose to find Errick already awake. He had completely emptied the cart, arranging its contents into two distinct quantities. She understood immediately that the larger one was to be discarded, while the other was to be tied up in bundles and lashed to their backs. Victor was a short distance away, walking back and forth on his hands, as though practising this new method of ambulation.

"What do you think?" Errick asked. "I'm proposing to take a single cooking pan, a small amount of kindling, some of Victor's magical carrot powder, and a few flasks of water."

"It still looks like a lot," she said. "I'm not sure we can rely on Victor to carry much."

"I'm not expecting him to carry anything," said Errick. "I'll bear this load alone."

"Errick, we've been through this," she sighed. "You don't need to make such sacrifices. Besides, you'll be burdened enough with the weight of your armour." He smiled ruefully at her. "I intend to leave it behind," he said.

She paused, taken aback by this pronouncement. "I'm … surprised," she said eventually.

"I've been thinking about what you said," the knight explained. "And you are right. My foolish stoicism brought me nothing but fever and gangrene. And now, truth be told, I find myself relieved to have lost my sword, because I am so weakened by this plague that I was scarcely able to wield it." Emotions crowded his face and he blinked rapidly, clenching his jaw as he fought to restrain them. Then Freya hugged him, feeling the chill of his thick breastplate as he stiffened. "I only hope you won't find my wasted body ... an embarrassment," he added in a choked voice.

She shook her head violently, her head still pressed against his shoulder. "I've seen it all already, remember?" she said. "The only strength I care about is what's in here." She pressed a finger against his armoured chest. To her surprise, he wrapped his arms around her and held her for a few moments, squeezing her shoulders once before pulling away.

"Would you mind, erm..." he mumbled shyly as he began to remove the plates, just as Freya had done the previous afternoon.

"Of course not," she replied, turning her back. "I'm going to use some of the spare water to clean myself."

She took one of the spare canteens and tipped some of its contents into her hands. Splashing the icy liquid into her face, she began to run it through the matted tangles of her hair, pulling handfuls of the tousled locks across her face as she tried to separate them. Then she stopped, aghast, as she saw a strand of grey hair. The single thread, so fine it was almost imperceptible, was nonetheless stark against her drab ochre tresses.

The plague had claimed her at last.

Perhaps it entered my body many sunrises ago, she thought, *and it simply takes this long for the symptoms to show.* Either way, there was no going back now — she had begun her irreversible slide into emaciation, frailty, and eventual death. She sneaked a glance over her shoulder at Errick's half-naked body, and saw her own fate etched in the lines and hollows of his withered frame. Wiping a tear from her eye, she plucked the grey thread from her scalp and flicked it away in disgust, resolving not to mention anything about it to the others. They would notice for themselves, soon enough.

"I'm ready," said Errick after a while, and she turned to find he had donned one of the spare robes that Ilene had donated to them. The nondescript smock gave him the appearance of one of the Enclave's Unskilled; a humble servant instead of a noble warrior.

"It suits you perfectly," she said, forcing a smile. "But we should probably wrap ourselves more thoroughly — the slopes ahead are dreadfully snow-bitten."

Errick nodded, locating more sackcloth garments amongst their supplies and tossing one of them to her. "What about you, Victor?" he called to their companion, who was strutting back and forth on his hands with increasing confidence. "Will the cold affect your ... workings?"

The machine shook his head. "Thank you for your concern, but I am able to withstand significant extremes of temperature."

A thought struck Freya. "Victor, if you are so strong — immune to fire and cold, with no need of food or water or rest — why are you the only one left alive?" She remembered Eugene, the half-interred machine she had doused with fire nectar and set ablaze, and worried that her question would cause offence.

Instead, Victor simply said, "I am unable to speak of such things." It was the same response he had given the last time she'd asked about the fate of his fellow automatons, uttered in the same strange drone, completely unlike his usual voice.

"Why?" she persisted. "Why can't you speak of them? Was their fate so unutterably awful?"

To her dismay, Victor began to shake, vibrating as though he had been struck with a hammer. "I am unable to speak of such things," he intoned again, louder this time, and a disturbing buzzing sound emanated from somewhere in his chest.

"It's okay, Victor," she stammered in alarm. But he continued to tremble, the humming sound growing in volume as though he might rattle himself to bits. "I said it's okay!" she cried. "Victor, please stop!"

The noise rose to a crescendo, as though whatever arcane flywheels powered his body were spinning faster and faster, whirling uncontrollably. Then, suddenly, it stopped, fading to silence as the machine tilted his head quizzically. "Whatever is the matter?" he asked. "You look as though you've seen a ghost."

She and Errick exchanged anxious glances. "It's ... nothing, Victor," she said eventually. "I'm just worrying about the climb, that's all."

Victor gave a gallant chuckle. "There's nothing to fear! We're giantslayers, after all — conquering this peak will be mere child's play in comparison."

He turned, practising his new walking technique once again. Freya stared after him, wondering what on earth 'child's play' meant, feeling as though the phrase reminded her of something from a dream.

***

Long before the sun reached its zenith, they began their ascent. They were able to walk at first, leaning into the gradient, propping themselves on the torches they had decided to bring as walking canes. But as the slope steepened, they found themselves stooped so close to the ground that they were almost crawling on all fours. Victor, too, had to adjust his gait, abandoning his well-rehearsed bipedal motion and simply using his arms to drag his body along the ground. Every yard he covered was accompanied by a dreadful metallic scraping sound, and Freya winced at the damage he must be doing to what remained of his body.

The sun rose above them as they climbed, but any heat it offered was quickly leeched away by the heartless chill of the rock face. Freya was glad of her second layer, wishing she could stop to rub her hands together, or use them to knead some warmth into her sides and shoulders; but she dare not do so for fear of losing her footing and plummeting all the way back down.

Still the incline worsened, and she started to scrabble for hand and footholds, any tiny crevice or jutting ledge that could increase her stability. The thought of tumbling from this height began to dizzy her, and she had to battle not to look downwards — such a sight would bring terror and vertigo as surely as the fall itself would bring shattered limbs. She did not even risk a glance at her companions, keeping her gaze fixed firmly on the stone in front of her, though she did shout to them periodically to ask how they were doing.

"Fine," Errick grunted from just ahead and to her left.

"My arms are thus far proving equal to the challenge," replied Victor from some way below.

They climbed for many minutes, the silence punctuated only by Freya's occasional calls, and by the whistle of the wind as it buffeted them with increasing malice. Freya's arms began to tire before her legs, and soon all four limbs were aching, the plunging temperature infusing them with a vicious chill that threatened to numb them completely. Still, she heaved and hauled, picturing the bones in the ravine far beneath them starting to animate, reassembling into an army of malformed skeletons that scaled the valley's walls in pursuit, clamouring for the chance to rend her to shreds if she dared to falter. She imagined herself an automaton, as mechanical as Victor himself, with gears and pistons churning ceaselessly instead of the painful inadequacy of her bone and sinew.

When her hand found a broad ledge, she didn't dare believe it was real until she had clawed her way onto it, collapsing onto the snow-covered shelf and braving, finally, a glimpse of the drop below. Her stomach lurched at the sight of how far they had climbed. She saw Errick seated on a similar outcrop a little way above, towards which Victor was inching laboriously from several metres below her.

"Come on Victor!" she cried, clapping her hands and noticing as she did so how raw they were, scoured bloody by the cold and the gruelling rock face. *A simple pair of gloves would be like a gift from the angels,* she thought. She stood, pressing her back against the stone to ensure she didn't fall, and watched as Victor clawed his way upwards, his metal body clanging as it bashed and scraped against the mountain. She wondered whether Victor experienced fear; whether he felt the same primal, atavistic terror of being dashed to pieces on the ground below, or whether he was aware of the risk only in a more conceptual way, as an outcome that would be best avoided. His face gave no clue, of course, his smile absurdly incongruous as he dragged himself up the punishing slope.

"Please don't fall," she muttered, half to herself, her stomach roiling at the prospect of watching her friend smashed into a jumble of cogs and gears. But Victor's grip held firm, his mechanised fingers deeply embedded in the fissures and fractures of the rock wall. Gradually, carefully, *excruciatingly,* he climbed closer and closer to Errick's vantage point, and when he reached up to clamp his hand around the protruding stone, Freya cheered with relief.

Then she heard a cracking sound, and thought for a terrible moment that the shelf was too fragile to hold both Victor and Errick at once. It took her a few seconds to realise that the noise was coming from her own ledge, by which point her foothold had almost crumbled away entirely.

Eighteen

The best thing to do would have been to spin around, plant her feet against the rock and claw at its surface with her hands, gaining some purchase before the platform beneath her feet disintegrated altogether. Instead, in her blind panic, Freya jumped, reaching desperately towards Errick's ledge.

She missed it by a few feet and felt her stomach cartwheeling as her arms flailed helplessly, legs thrashing in empty air. The drop beneath her yawed open like an expectant mouth, ready to swallow her whole.

Then Victor's iron grip closed around her wrist, jerking her to a standstill, her feet dangling over the horrifying descent. She looked upwards, heart hammering, breath wrenching from her lungs in ragged gasps. Victor had one hand on the shelf, reaching down with the other to grip her so tightly she thought her arm might snap. Errick was leaning over the precipice, his face wracked with horror, trying to wrap his hands around the smooth metal of Victor's arm to pull them both up.

All around her, time crystallised, like the flakes of snow that dusted the surrounding stone. The point where her flesh met Victor's freezing metal exterior was like a nexus, an ice-cold explosion of possibilities, like the centre of a star.

His arm tore loose from its socket, and she plunged to her doom.

Her wrist cracked like a twig, the broken bones slipping through the machine's grasp.

Victor lost his own grip on the ledge and the two of them died together, screaming their apologies to each other as they fell. Or...

With Errick's help, the machine heaved itself onto the shelf, hauling her after him until she could stretch her own hands upwards and scramble onto a shelf of merciful, wonderful, marvellously *solid* stone.

She collapsed onto her front, battling for breath against the air's savage chill. Errick sank back against the wall, sighing with exertion and relief. Victor, meanwhile, continued to climb.

"Perhaps I am better suited to the role of pathfinder," he said flatly. They watched as he continued to drag himself tirelessly up the mountainside, slow but inexorable. "Rest there awhile," he called down to them. "I'll figure out the best route to the summit." He disappeared gradually from view, lost in the mist that gathered above them like an inverted, murky pool.

"How much farther do you think before we reach the top?" she asked, still panting.

"I don't know, but don't do that again," wheezed Errick in response, "or my heart will have stopped long before we get there."

She could barely hear him, such was the volume of the wind as it raged around them, seemingly determined to tear them from the slopes. She realised that snow was falling, whipped into a miniature blizzard by the gale.

"Is Victor going to shout directions down to us?" she hollered into the breeze.

"I don't know," answered Errick, rubbing his freezing hands together. "But we shouldn't dally here for too long, lest this ledge proves as reliable as the last one."

With a deep breath, he turned, scouring the rock face for clefts into which he might insert his hands. Suddenly they heard a clanging sound from above, and Victor reappeared, clambering backwards down the crag as though he was an experienced mountaineer.

"Follow me," he called cheerily. "I've managed to gouge some handholds for you along the way."

Errick and Freya looked at each other in disbelief. Then, with an incredulous smile, the knight attacked the mountain with renewed vigour. Freya followed, her hands following Errick's feet into the regularly-spaced indentations Victor had chiselled for them. Still the wind assailed them, seeming outraged at their progress; but fear kept their grip secure, and steadily they continued their improbable ascent.

Freya felt as though time had been left behind, somewhere on the other side of the bridge. The climb took minutes, hours, days, eternities. The climb took forever. The wind howled. The climb never ended.

Then it did, because Errick suddenly disappeared from view, and she followed him over a jutting lip of rock, tears of joy freezing on her cheeks as she sank onto a flat, snow-covered plateau. Frozen, exhausted, *emptied*, they had reached the summit of the mountain.

"Look, Freya!" cried Errick. She ignored him, wondering why he wasn't joining her, collapsed into the ice as though savouring its absolution. "Please, just lift your head," he beseeched, and she did so, unable to ignore the note of uncharacteristic delight in his voice.

All around them, the air was alive with churning snow, swirling mist, and wisps of what might have been clouds. But this eddying curtain could not completely obscure the view, and Freya's breath snagged as she beheld the astonishing panorama.

The world encircled them on all sides. Behind them, the dark stain of Erebyss's crater looked like an ink blot, the barren plains stretching away beyond it towards the distant outline of Ilene's mountain of rust. To the north and south, the mountains curved away in a column of wintry peaks, some taller, some smaller than the one they had just scaled. To the east, their route led down into sprawling woodland; beyond it, the Monoliths sparkled in the wan sunlight, stately and majestic.

"They look so much bigger," Freya whispered, awestruck. "We're really getting closer, aren't we?"

"Aye, lass," said Errick. "But there's a long way to go yet."

"Yes," said Victor, his gleaming eyes looking like reflections of the sun. "But we'll make it, a step at a time."

***

They could not rest for long, the biting cold threatening to gnaw the skin from their bones. Mercifully, the downward climb proved easier than they had feared; the gradient was flatter, the mountainside sinking steadily into a landscape of oddly-shaped, almost conical foothills that extended eastwards for many miles. Once they descended below the snowline, clumps of bracken and gorse began to sprout, and their path gradually became one of dense, frostbitten vegetation.

Victor's superior eyesight had discerned a settlement at the eastern edge of the forest, perhaps a couple of days' march ahead of them; it would add a small detour to their route, but they agreed this was worthwhile if it might yield more supplies. Errick was sceptical, but their meagre stock of rations gave them no other choice. Now the automaton led the way, ambling briskly along as though it barely missed its severed legs.

"What did you make of his little episode earlier?" Errick whispered to her when the machine was out of earshot.

"I think if his vision is more powerful than ours, then we don't know his hearing isn't the same," she hissed.

"But we need to talk about it," persisted Errick. "Something isn't right with him."

"If he keeps saving my life, I'm prepared to put up with it."

"Maybe it's the damage he's sustained — God knows, if I lost my legs I'd be in much worse shape."

Freya shook her head. "I asked him about his people once before, while you were asleep in Ilene's shack. The exact same thing happened. As though some mechanism inside him is … silencing him, somehow."

Errick frowned as they walked on, the undergrowth thickening as they approached the forest's perimeter. Victor had stopped at the treeline to wait for them.

"Darkness will be upon us soon," the machine said. "I suggest we press ahead into the trees and make camp within the safety of their concealment."

"It sounds a sensible plan," said Freya, and Errick nodded his agreement. After their encounters with Brock and the monsters of Erebyss, she wanted to stay as invisible as possible.

The forest — a collection of evergreen conifers, pines and spruces — seemed to welcome them at first, granting easy passage between its trunks and branches. But the trees seemed to close in quickly behind them, blocking out the sunlight, and within minutes Freya felt disoriented, glad that Victor seemed confident of the correct route. The floor was carpeted in a sediment of putrefying needles and pinecones, which permeated the air with a strange mixture of earthy wholesomeness and pungent decay; she breathed this amalgam as they walked, thinking of sweet perfume used to mask some underlying rot. Indeed, the trees themselves seemed to be stricken with some sort of blight, their foliage wilted and drooping where it was streaked here and there with blotches of whitish-grey. She glanced at Errick, reminded of the colour of his thinning hair, then remembered the plague-tinted strand she had plucked from her own head earlier that morning.

"Are you sure this place is safe?" she asked. Before either of her friends could respond, the forest seemed to offer a reply of its own, answering her question with the ominous crack of a twig from somewhere amongst the undergrowth. She froze, listening, but her companions seemed not to notice, and she hurried onwards before she lost sight of them in the gloom.

"I don't like this place," muttered Errick as she caught up to him. "I'd feel more comfortable if I had my armour, or my blade."

"I agree that the atmosphere is somewhat stifling," said Victor. "But we should only require one night here. I will watch over you both while you rest, of course."

"We should make camp soon," the knight grunted. "What little light can penetrate these trees is fast fading."

Freya surveyed their surroundings. They were in a small clearing, dominated by an ancient oak tree that seemed to have forced the surrounding pines aside as it grew. Its fat, twisted trunk and the clawing shapes of its leafless branches made it seem like a monster hiding in the depths of the woods; at its base, a tangle of exposed roots looked like teeth jutting from diseased gums.

"Why don't we sleep here?" she proposed. "There is room at least to build a campfire."

"No," said Errick, surprising her with the sudden venom in his tone. "No fire. The risk is too great."

She opened her mouth to disagree, her bones still feeling the sting of the mountain's chill, but saw the dread flashing in the knight's eyes — the reflection of buildings burning, of people screaming as they fled from collapsing homes.

"Of course," she said. In the end, they slept hidden amongst the tree's ancient roots, huddled together for warmth, while a ruined machine sat a few feet away, its unblinking eyes staring into the darkness.

***

"This isn't a joke, Freya," says a short, broad-chested man with dark hair and skin the colour of eggshells. He is sitting at a table, frowning across two plates of untouched salad.

"You think I'm joking?"

Opposite him is a woman — her hair is dyed blonde, and her face has the haggard look of someone who is working too hard to have time to eat properly.

"No, but I think you're not taking this seriously enough. I left my fucking wife and kid for you."

They are both wearing smart-casual, office-appropriate clothes, looking dishevelled after a gruelling day.

"And that means I have to prioritise you over my career forever?"

There is no scar on her face.

"Oh, don't be so fucking melodramatic," he says. "I'm not asking you to quit your job and cook my tea every night. I'm just saying I want to see you more than once every few fucking weeks!"

"It's a big opportunity for me," she replies earnestly, desperate for him to understand. "This project will put the Innovation Corporation on the map!"

"And there's the problem!" he shouts, rising animatedly to his feet. "You've drunk the fucking Kool-aid, that's what it is. Don't forget that I've heard all the same spiel before; they sell you the dream, and then ask you to sacrifice everything to deliver it."

"This is different," she insists. "This thing will be bigger than the iPhone — as big as the invention of the fucking *internet*. And I'm going to be a lead programmer on it!"

"Well, let me be absolutely clear," he says, something cold and vicious gleaming in his eyes. "If you take this job, you're sure to succeed, because you won't have a demanding partner to distract you from your true passion." Then the light fades, replaced by a deep, immense sadness, and the gleam of tears forming at their corners. "I can't believe this is happening," he mutters, sinking onto the couch.

She crosses to him, lowering herself gently onto his knee, placing her arms around his neck. "Or ... why don't you come with me?" she says, staring pleadingly into his eyes.

Raoul stares back, ghosts of his former life writhing in the darkness of his pupils.

He reaches for her with a hand that is strangely cold, almost metallic, and she…

***

…woke up. For a few terrifying moments, Freya's brain couldn't comprehend the weird, rusted face smiling down at her, or the hand fastened around her shoulder. Then relief flooded through her when she realised it was Victor, followed immediately by a renewed wave of fear when she heard his words, their urgency belying his absurd grin. "Freya, please — we are not safe here."

She sat up, immediately banging her head on a tree root. "*Ouch!* What do you mean?"

"Please, stay quiet!" the machine whispered. "Someone is watching us, from the undergrowth."

She glanced at Errick, still slumbering beside her. "Where?"

"There's no time to explain. First, we need to get to safety."

At that moment there was a clang, and something bounced off Victor's hard metal exterior, landing on the ground between them. Freya gazed at it in bafflement; it was a dart, long and thin, with a pointed tip easily capable of piercing her skin. She stared at it for a few moments more, then began to shake Errick violently awake.

"Errick!" she hissed. "Errick, wake up, now!"

"It's no use," said Victor, pointing towards the knight's shoulder where a pair of the missiles protruded from his flesh. "I was unable to rouse him. He's unconscious, and I fear that you will be too if we don't—"

She didn't hear the rest of the sentence because, with a mild stab of pain, another of the darts suddenly appeared, jutting from her thigh. She looked down at it dumbly for a few moments as she felt another pair of jabs in her back; then she pitched forwards onto her face, returning to a sleep that was, this time, utterly devoid of dreams.

Nineteen

Another awakening. A different hand on Freya's shoulder. A different face, staring down into hers. Unsmiling, this time; stern and hard, but not unkind, and framed by strands of long white hair. For a moment, she thought it was Ilene. Then she jerked upright, her ingrained fear of the plague and its symptoms making her recoil from the woman's wizened features.

"Whoa, whoa, it's okay," the stranger said, backing away from Freya. Her back was terribly hunched, and she leaned on a stout cane for balance. "I didn't mean to startle you."

Freya jerked to her left and right, seeing that she was lying on a hard bed in the corner of a small room, perhaps a cell. There were no windows, the light coming from a strange, dangling orb in the centre of the chamber. The grimy walls glinted as they reflected this glow, as though beneath the layer of muck they were built from burnished metal. "Where are Errick and Victor?" she snapped.

"Your aged friend has not yet awoken — he is in the next room," said the crippled woman, who was dressed in coarse robes not dissimilar to Freya's own attire. Freya didn't understand the meaning of the word the woman had used to describe Errick, but knew she must be referring to the knight; Victor was immune whatever poisons they had applied to their darts.

"What about Victor?" Freya repeated, trying to hide her fear.

"The machine is being interrogated," the woman replied brusquely. "Although how such an old wreck is even still operable is a mystery to us."

Freya twisted, lowering her feet to the ground. What she had been lying on wasn't a bed, but instead some sort of metallic trestle table; it rattled as she leaned against it, gingerly transferring her weight to her legs. "What did you poison us with?" she snarled as she managed, shakily, to stand.

"Merely a sleep toxin," replied the woman. "There are no lasting effects, I assure you. We just needed to be sure of your intentions."

"And what has Victor told you?" Freya asked cautiously.

"Is that the name it gave you? Don't be fooled ... those things are no more human than a calculator."

Freya was running rapidly out of patience. "Look, I don't understand most of what you're saying, but Victor is my *friend*. If you've done anything to hurt him, you'll..." she hesitated, struggling to think of something threatening to say. Then she saw the woman's mouth fall open in a look of sudden amazement.

"You're from beyond the mountains, aren't you?" the plague-carrier gasped, incredulous.

"Yes," replied Freya, frowning.

"You mean you travelled through *Brock's kingdom* to reach us?"

"We weren't *trying* to reach you," Freya replied testily. "We detoured here in search of help." But the woman ignored her, turning to hobble out of the room as quickly as her curved spine would allow.

"Wait!" Freya called, staggering after her, the toxin's residue making her feel dizzy. She emerged through the room's only door into a strange, high-ceilinged chamber; again, there were no windows, the illumination provided instead by more of the glowing spheres that hung from the ceiling like lingering spirits at the end of the hangman's rope. Their bright light was reflected not just by the metallic walls and tiled floor, but also by the huge vats that filled the room, running in neat rows from wall to wall: great metal cauldrons, covered in dials and symbols. Above them, a platform extended across a portion of the room, and it was towards this that the woman was making her way, ascending a connecting staircase with some difficulty. Freya saw that people were assembled on the gantry, staring down at her.

"I thought I told you to keep her locked in her room!" came an angry male voice from overhead.

"I'm sorry, Warden," replied the woman. "But she told me they've come from *beyond the mountains*."

Just as Freya heard the word 'Warden' and felt her head begin to spin, she saw Victor hanging from the scaffold, chains lashing his arms to the metal railing that encircled it. "Victor!" she cried, but he did not respond. The lights in his eyes were completely extinguished, his head sagging downwards as though it might be about to fall off. "What have you done to him?" she yelled at the robed figures who were gathered around the machine's motionless body. There were perhaps twenty of them; a mixture of men and women, all with the silver manes and lined features that denoted advanced cases of the plague.

As they looked around at each other, seemingly unwilling to address her, she beheld other anomalies: some of them were extremely short, even more so than the couple of dwarves that lived in the Enclave, while others were uncannily tall, their spindly limbs extended to almost obscene dimensions. Another, completely hidden beneath a cloak and cowl, was grotesquely broad in stature, his or her shoulders almost as wide apart as they were tall.

One of the gangly males approached the railing. Suspicion and rheum clouded his eyes, and his mouth was curved into a disdainful sneer. He was clean-shaven and bald, but even without hair she could tell he was a plague carrier, his skin as cracked and calloused as the bark of the old oak tree they had slept beneath. He towered above her, nearing nine feet in height, so thin that Freya was reminded of wire brushes the Unskilled used to clean the castle privies.

"Your machine is broken," he replied haughtily. "We secured it here and began to question it. When we asked about others of its kind, it became non-cooperative, and eventually shut itself down."

"Damn you," Freya cursed, staring wretchedly at the dangling body of her friend. Victor's smile was still etched in place, as though he was enjoying a happy dream — perhaps of his garden, of his idyllic life spent tending it with Ilene, until Freya had come along and disrupted everything. "He isn't just a machine," she hissed. "You don't know what you've done."

"I'm sure it can be repaired," the man replied. "The right code word should do it." He raised something he had been holding in his hand, and Freya realised it was a thin, tattered book. She couldn't help noticing how long and frail-looking his fingers were, seeming too delicate to grip even that modest tome. "The answer is in here somewhere," he said. "But that will have to wait. First, *you* will answer some questions. Sister Annika says you claim to have travelled through the mountains — I want to know how you could possibly have evaded Brock's wrath?"

"We didn't," Freya replied, her face flushed with anger. "We killed him instead."

Laughter broke out amongst the congregation. For a moment, Freya was reminded of the jeering crowd that had witnessed her banishment from the Enclave, and felt her blood begin to simmer. "You expect me to believe that you and your debilitated companions managed to slay the scourge of Wailing Peak?" the gaunt man scoffed.

"I don't care what you believe," she retorted. "I just want you to let us go so we can continue on our way."

At that moment, a commotion erupted behind her. One of the chamber's other doors burst open, and Errick stormed into the room, followed by two agitated attendants. One was tall, and morbidly fat, his corpulent bulk bulging out around him as though threatening to swallow up his stunted arms and legs; the other was more conventionally proportioned but blessed with the largest head Freya had ever seen.

"I thought I told you to restrain him when he awoke!" yelled the thin man, who seemed to be the group's leader, his voice rising to an exasperated shriek.

"We tried to, Warden, but he's stronger than he looks!" said the swollen-headed one.

"Have these dimwits hurt you, my lady?" Errick shouted to her, and she couldn't help but smile at the sight of the valiant knight; bereft of his sword and armour, but not his chivalry.

"No, but they've questioned Victor to breaking point," she replied, pointing upwards to the machine's motionless body. Fury twisted Errick's face as he beheld Victor's plight, and he turned to his two pursuers with his fists raised.

"The first one of you to approach me will find out just how angry I am," he snarled. "I don't need a sword to beat some courtesy into you."

The obese man and his associate backed away, exchanging nervous glances. Then there was a clattering sound as one of the poisoned darts struck the ground just behind Errick. He whirled around, eyes widening at the sight of the missile before he cast his gaze back up towards the platform.

"*Please*," said the tall man, who the others referred to as the Warden. Three more of the darts were held between the knuckles of his outstretched hand. "Can we try to maintain some decorum?"

Errick looked down with grudging respect at the weapon that had rendered him unconscious the previous night. *Or two nights ago, or three,* thought Freya; she had no way of knowing how long they had been incapacitated.

"What do you want from us?" scowled the knight.

"We simply want to know why you came to our forest," said the Warden, smiling for the first time, his tone mellifluous. "This girl claims that you encountered Brock himself."

186

"Aye," said Errick, glancing around to make sure the two bumbling aides weren't attempting to flank him. "And that big bastard found out what happens to those who cross us."

There were mutterings and whispers amongst the group, as though perhaps some were starting to believe the tale. The Warden's eyes widened this time, but he betrayed no other sign of emotion as he continued. "If this is true, then you have done us a great service. We are all outcasts from the Peak, driven into these woods by the giant after the angels abandoned our mountain home."

"Wait — did you say the angels?" Freya interrupted. The Warden nodded. "They have forsaken us too," she continued. "And others; indeed, every settlement we've encountered is starving, or tearing itself apart."

"You must understand that your life beyond the mountains is … very different from ours," the Warden said cautiously. "Different Sector, different Warden — different rules."

"You're talking about Ilene," said Freya. The man raised his eyebrows again, the only part of his face that bore the tell-tale white hair of his disease. She noticed then that he wore a chain around his neck; it disappeared beneath his robe, and she wondered whether he also carried one of the mysterious, ice-blue pendants.

"You met the Warden of Sector Four?" he asked, the scepticism in his tone replaced by surprise, perhaps even awe.

"Yes." She paused, considering her words carefully. "I'm afraid she's dead too."

Behind his impassive mask, she thought she saw the Warden clench his teeth, just for a moment. "How did she perish?" he asked eventually.

"We've answered enough of your questions," Errick interjected gruffly. "Now you can answer some of ours, before I start cracking your mutant heads together."

There was a gasp of outrage from the gantry. The thick-set, hooded figure stomped forward towards the railing, but the Warden placed a single scrawny hand against his massive chest.

"Calm yourself, Brother Axel," he said. "They have spent too long in the mist; their memories are obliterated. They don't even understand their own origins, never mind ours."

There were answers here; Freya could almost feel the air thrumming with them. Yet she sensed danger, too, and calamity if they did not navigate this encounter cautiously. "Then please, explain it to us," she said evenly. "How did you come to be here, and to encompass such diversity?"

The Warden snorted, his smile mocking. "To try to explain such things to you — how people might be bred, like wolves were once bred into domestic dogs — would require me to fill so many holes in your mind that your brain would break down more quickly than your obsolete machine."

She noticed then that there were many others; people of all manner of peculiar shapes and sizes, hiding amongst the great metal vats, or peering furtively from half-closed doorways. "Suffice to say," the gaunt man continued, a note of exultation entering his voice, "that to be a Warden is to glimpse the secrets of God's design. That is the burden with which I was entrusted by Raoul the Scarred, after he killed my predecessor and opened my occluded eyes."

The shock that crashed through Freya at the mention of her husband's name nearly drove her to the floor. She staggered, and Errick rushed immediately to her side. "What's wrong?" he asked, worry etched in the lines of his face. "Is it the poison?"

"No, it's..." she looked up in bewilderment at the Warden, addressing her words to him. "My husband was called Raoul. He left me behind too, many sunrises ago. My face bears the mark of his ceaseless rage." *Raoul the Scarred.* The Warden's words seemed to spin and whirl inside her head, 'calculators' and 'years' and 'dogs' and all the other things she didn't understand, but knew somehow that she *did*, that such knowledge was hidden deep within her, buried like the crawling, slobbering denizens of Erebyss.

Meanwhile, the eyes of the slender man seemed to gleam with excitement. "Yes. Raoul told me about you," he said, his grin widening into something resembling ecstasy. "He said you were his greatest regret; that he lashed out when his brain couldn't contain the enormity of the truth. That all he wanted was to make you *remember*." The Warden's tongue seemed to loll out of his mouth, as though he was salivating at the thought of what forbidden knowledge might be contained within Freya's skull. "Do not worry. Raoul left us centuries ago to continue his pilgrimage. We know not what became of him." He turned and nodded to the hooded man, and the creature he had called Brother Axel began to steer his impossible frame towards the steps. The stairs looked barely wide enough to accommodate him, and the platform vibrated with the weight of each stride.

The two attendants chose that moment to pounce, pinning Errick's arms and succeeding in forcing him to the ground. He flailed and kicked, but before he could shake them off the fat man managed to drop his bulk down onto Errick's ribs, and Freya winced as she heard something crack wetly inside the knight's chest. That seemed to please the Warden, who brandished the poison darts, watching carefully as the monstrous form of Brother Axel descended towards them. Horrifying hands extended from beneath his cloak; if his physique resembled a wall, then his fingers looked like creeping plants sprouting from it, each one impossibly long and seeming to wriggle with a sentience of its own, independent from his hulking body.

"All I ask is that you allow Brother Axel to return you to your cell," the Warden crowed. "If you do, your friend will be spared. I might even deign to fix this wreck of a robot."

Freya stared about helplessly, but from every door a misshapen face seemed to leer; and even if it were possible for her to escape from this place to find concealment in the forest, she would never abandon her comrades. She looked up at Victor, willing him to revive himself, to come to their aid somehow.

A code word, this impostor Warden had said. What could it be? She closed her eyes, scouring the tapestry of her memory, as Brother Axel reached the foot of the stairs and began to advance towards her. What had Ilene talked about? *Holographs and carrot stew. Nanomachines.* Alien words from an alien language ... or perhaps one long forgotten.

Then she remembered the Warden, stooped over Errick's festering leg, squeezing the jewel that had looked so reminiscent of Lord Gwillym's. *Had he been a Warden, too?* Ilene had murmured something, some magical word of healing that had compelled the knight's flesh to reconstruct itself. What on earth was it? Her mind felt obscured, suffused with mist, a machine that had long since ceased to function properly.

Then, like a bolt of lightning blasting through the swirling fog, a memory forced itself into her brain.

She opened her eyes, staring defiantly up at the Warden.

"*Raphael*," she said.

Nothing happened. The Warden chuckled, and Brother Axel tramped ever nearer, so close that she would soon be able to see whatever horrors were concealed beneath his cowl.

Then Victor moved.

***

The machine jerked spasmodically, rattling the chains that fastened him to the railings above. His head swivelled, seeming fixed on the ceiling for a few moments before it rotated slowly downwards, his hollow gaze settling eventually on Freya. Her heart sank as she beheld a pair of empty voids, as dark as the mouths of caves, as black as the Enclave's garbage Pit.

Then yellowish light flickered within them, and moments later the huge chamber was plunged into total darkness.

What happened next was composed entirely of sound. There was a snapping noise, then a sound like flesh striking against metal, or perhaps the other way around. This was followed immediately by a shriek of pain, then other cries that echoed around the chamber as panic spread quickly amongst the plague carriers. A second gristly smack was followed by another, this time right beside her. Then her ears were rent by a blood-curdling scream.

At that moment, blue light bloomed above them, and she cried out too as she saw an impossibly wide, white-haired man looming before her, grappling with the mechanical *thing* that had attached itself to his head. Its arms encircled his flat, misshapen skull, and the fingers of its hands were plunged deep into the viscera of his eyes. She saw Errick climbing to his feet behind the grisly scene, aiming a vengeful kick at the prostrate figure of his bulbous-headed assailant. The fat man lay close by, also completely motionless, while behind him the rest of the Warden's malformed congregation had begun to clatter down the steps towards them, their way illuminated by the jewel clasped in their leader's outstretched hand.

"Come on!" she yelled, lunging forward to grab the knight's arm, yanking him towards her as she turned to flee. Scampering, clanging footsteps told her that Victor had detached himself from his victim and was following close behind, while a resounding crash might have been Brother Axel collapsing, blinded, to the floor. She hurtled towards the nearest door, smashing it open and knocking aside the wretch that had been cowering behind it. The creature did not try to stop her, and she breathed a sigh of relief as she saw that the door did not lead to a dead-end, but instead to a long corridor. At its opposite end she could see light streaming in through a set of double doors, and she raced towards them, still supporting Errick as he stumbled and wheezed alongside her.

The doors were unlocked, and together the three of them crashed through into an enormous room, into which sunlight was pouring from windows close to the high ceiling. Beneath these apertures, the walls were lined with peculiar, transparent compartments whose dimensions were vaguely human-shaped. All were empty, and Freya didn't stop to puzzle over them as she half-ran, half-dragged Errick onwards, Victor pounding his way along in pursuit.

"I want her restored to me!" she heard the Warden shriek, as one of his darts whistled past her ear. There were more doors ahead, a large pair that might have been the main gates, and she prayed she would have the strength to open them. Then she realised she wouldn't need to, because Victor raced in front, sprinting on his hands with the dexterity of a long-term amputee. He reached the doors and dropped his torso to the floor with a clang, driving his fingers between the gates as he began to prise them apart.

"Just leave me behind," spluttered Errick as they staggered towards the light that was spilling in through the widening slit between the doors. "This injury is ... more than trifling."

"You still haven't learned just how stubborn I am, have you?" she scolded between panting breaths. The doors continued to yawn open, and Victor barely had time to scamper through them before she and Errick bundled after him through the gap. They burst into the open air, dashing forwards and then careening to a halt as she realised they were teetering on the edge of an almost perpendicular drop.

Before them, the ground fell sharply away in a steep escarpment that plunged towards the flatlands far below. The forest ended at this sudden precipice, the land beyond stretching away in a great, ridged expanse of arid tundra, the little vegetation that remained dwindling to nothingness as the frozen desert rose to meet the horizon. Beyond it, the Monoliths towered larger than ever, twinkling like distant ice sculptures.

She turned, and saw the Warden and his followers approaching fast. The building they had escaped was vast, stretching along the cliff face, and she realised it was the same settlement that Victor had spotted from the mountain top. The forest loomed behind it as though the trees were jostling for a view of the unfolding drama.

There was nowhere else to run.

Triumph gleamed in the Warden's eyes, as bright as the glowing jewel he had now placed back around his neck. He slowed as he approached the doors, raising a hand to signal that his minions should do the same. In his grasp she saw two of his poison darts. *One for each of us,* she thought bitterly. Slowly, he stepped through the portal, extending a bony finger towards Victor.

"That contraption is a killer," he spat pitilessly. "It must be destroyed for the good of our colony. But that doesn't mean the two of you need to die."

As if in defiance of the Warden's words, Errick began to cough, spitting a gout of blood across the hard earth. Freya looked at him in alarm, watching as the knight swayed and then steadied himself, clutching a hand to his chest.

"Look at what your needless violence has brought you," the Warden continued, unable to keep the mocking lilt from his voice. "But you have not yet exhausted the reserves of my clemency. I do not wish to see you slowly expire out in the icy wastes. Come with us, so that we may parlay like civilised folk, and your murderous machine can be recycled for scrap metal."

Errick cleared his throat noisily, wiping his lips with one of his clenched fists. "We come as a trio," he rasped thickly. "If you won't let us leave together, be prepared for more of your number to die."

The Warden's eyes were fixed on Freya, glinting excitedly as though he beheld some legendary treasure. "Very well," he said. "Then you will join the robot on the garbage heap — this woman and her memories are the only things I care about." Without shifting his gaze, he flicked his wrist, deftly hurling one of his poisoned barbs towards Errick's midsection.

The missile never reached its target. In what seemed an impossibly fast movement, Errick pinwheeled his arm forwards, snatching the projectile from the air and launching it back towards its source in a single, flowing motion. The Warden blinked, once, barely even registering his surprise. Then, like a falling tree, he toppled backwards, the dart deeply embedded in the centre of his forehead.

For a few seconds, there was silence. Then a caterwaul erupted behind the fallen Warden as his underlings began to screech and bellow in horror. Some of them rushed forwards to help their leader, while others seemed suddenly overcome with terror, falling over each other as they fled backwards into their dismal compound.

"Now!" shouted Errick through an agonised grimace, as though even articulating the word was causing him great pain. For a moment Freya didn't understand what he meant; then realisation dawned, and her stomach lurched at the prospect. He was right, of course. It was their only option.

Together they turned, reaching their hands instinctively towards each other's, a chain formed from man and woman and machine.

As one, they jumped over the edge.

Twenty

The slope was not completely sheer, but so steep that it made little difference. They tumbled down it, smacking against the rock and each other as they fell. Every crack and crunch brought pain, whether Errick's own or the imagined agony of his companions. It didn't matter; as one they plunged, and as one they suffered, their bodies pummelled mercilessly, as though the cliff face was trying to bludgeon them to death. Pain, and the memory of pain, merged into a single whole, as though all other feelings had been replaced by that endless cycle. His torso felt squeezed, clamped inside a gigantic vice that tightened with every foot they plummeted, every protruding shelf or outcrop that smashed into his jaw or spine or ribcage.

When he eventually opened his eyes, he realised that he was no longer falling, that he was instead sprawled at the bottom of the incline. Every limb, every joint, felt as though it had been shattered, as though he was nothing more than a pile of separated body parts, each one cursed with an ongoing consciousness capable of doing nothing more than remembering its destruction. He realised that one of his eyes was occluded, and tried to direct his awareness to his hand, which for all he knew might have been outstretched, or crushed beneath him, or lying yards away with blood oozing from its severed wrist bones.

Mercifully, the limb responded, and he reached towards his right eye, grimacing as he felt a swollen and tender mass of flesh where the orb ought to be. He used the same hand to push himself upwards, wincing at the lance of pain in his chest, and managed to pivot his head slowly to one side. The first thing he saw was his satchel, mercifully untouched by the Warden's ghouls, its contents strewn around them but salvageable. Next, he saw Victor, a few metres further away. (What had that spindly impostor of a Warden insisted on calling him? A *robot*?) The machine was already moving about, using one of its clenched hands to try to beat an enormous dent out of the side of its head. The indentation had completely mangled one half of Victor's face, warping his smile into something grotesque, like a frozen scream.

Grimacing with the effort, Errick turned his head in the opposite direction, and his heart cracked as he beheld Freya's broken body. She was lying just a few feet away from him, spread-eagled on her back, one of her arms twisted into an impossible angle. The expression on her face was strangely peaceful, but the grey hue of her skin attested to the trauma her frame had undergone during the fall.

Errick hauled himself towards her, willing his other arm to respond, dragging himself in a laborious slither across the dry earth. His legs trailed uselessly behind him, and he wondered for a moment whether they were as ruined as Freya's snapped arm. But the feeling gradually returned to them, and he completed the crawl on all fours, collapsing beside her when the pain in his ribs became too great. He rolled onto his back, staring up towards the top of the escarpment, relieved to see no sign of the Warden or his minions attempting to descend in pursuit.

"Victor," he called feebly. "Victor, I need you."

The machine gave no reply, but moments later he appeared at his side, his ruined face staring down at Errick like a warrior's death mask.

"Are you alright?" Errick asked. Still, their companion gave no verbal answer but nodded with the sound of groaning metal. "Can't you speak?" A shake of the head, another painful grinding sound. Victor lowered himself to the ground and used one hand to point towards his throat, then opened his hand as though to indicate something exploding apart.

"You and me both," Errick replied, his body wracked by a sudden and agonising fit of coughing. He tasted blood and hawked a mouthful of red-tinged phlegm onto the ground, the effort of projecting it away from Freya momentarily exhausting him. "First we need a splint for the lady's arm," he wheezed. "There was a torch in my haversack; it will be lying around somewhere." Victor tilted his head towards Freya, and Errick felt sure he saw something flicker in the depths of the machine's gaping eye sockets, something more than just artificial light. Then the automaton turned and scuttled off towards the scattered supplies.

Errick stayed as still as he could while he directed Victor's efforts, every movement feeling as though someone was sharpening knives against his ribs. His military training had given him a rudimentary knowledge of medical procedures; before long they had managed to bind Freya's sundered arm and confirm that her other three limbs were mercifully intact. She was still breathing, and there was no obvious indication of internal injury; yet she showed no sign of waking, and Errick began to worry that the fall had inflicted grave damage to her brain. One of the water flasks had survived the fall, but Errick dared not risk trying to force even a few sips down her throat, for fear of choking her.

Above them, the sun had reached its zenith. Its heat hardly seemed to reach them, the chill of the ground seeping into his bones as he lay there, as motionless as a corpse. *Time you got yourself up, Errick.* He lurched into a seating position, trying to surprise his body into compliance, and the pain that seared his chest was enough to draw a gasp from his throat, along with another bout of blood-flecked coughing. But he held himself upright, planting one knee on the floor when the hacking subsided, driving himself to his feet even as every strained sinew and battered ligament shrieked its disapproval.

He gazed down at Freya for a time, watching as the light wind rustled her hair. Then he looked east, out across the frigid steppe, towards the Monoliths. They were distant, still, but close enough to discern some of their otherworldly detail, the angular and enigmatic shapes of the jagged crystals. Only a few days' march, perhaps. But they would be travelling with barely any food or water, nor any weapons beyond his reflexes and the capabilities of a half-destroyed machine.

He returned his gaze to the prostrate form of his companion, who had forgiven him so often he had lost count. His eyes traced the scar that cleaved her face in two, like a symbol of all the world's cruelty, of *his* cruelty; malice, leaked from damaged minds, scarring lives and lands with its vitriol.

"My Lord God," he said out loud. "This woman has suffered beyond all reason or justice. If my failing body can bear her to you, I care no longer for your judgement, or even for your acknowledgement. All I ask is that you repair her mind, and fill it with the answers she seeks. She has earned this, just as this world has earned its desolation."

Then he bent, scowling in pain as he hoisted her onto his back, wrapping her arms gently around his neck. Victor watched mutely, the backpack containing their remaining supplies strung across his rust-coated shoulders.

They struck out in silence across yet another wasteland.

***

It was late, and once again he had not yet come home. She lay, alone, in their bed, considering how to solve a problem she could barely even articulate. It wasn't simply that Raoul was increasingly immersed in his work, spending almost every waking hour in the Archive, poring over books so ancient their pages had to be manipulated with tweezers to prevent them from falling apart. Such devotion was understandable; it was his passion, and more importantly, it was his job. The Skill that earned him the status of a Noble.

But he had surely changed. On the rare occasions he talked to her at all, he spoke only of *Anguish*, of terrible secrets, of tiny monsters that lived in the mist and crawled inside your head to steal your memories. She remembered a time when he would talk about such stories as allegories, or cautionary fables, but lately, he almost seemed to believe them. He had become increasingly unpredictable, likely to fly into a frightening rage if she so much as mentioned how much time he was spending away from her. The previous night he had thrown crockery at the wall beside her head, screaming about priorities, about truths that were "more real than fucking plates". On other days he would clamber into bed and hold her, sobbing softly, telling her over and over again that he was sorry, while she pretended to be asleep. But more often than not he didn't come home at all, appearing red-eyed in the early hours of the morning to snatch a few hours of fitful rest before he returned to plunge himself back into his studies.

So it was a surprise when she heard the door to their quarters opening, and the sound of his footsteps ascending the stairs. She had not yet extinguished the torch and resolved to give him a warm and cheerful welcome, to remind him that she loved him even if she had long forgotten whether that was true. But when the bedroom door creaked open, the spectre that greeted her was unmoved by her smile. Raoul simply stood in the doorway, ashen-faced, staring at her as though she horrified him.

"Raoul ... are you okay?" she said eventually, almost afraid to approach him.

He just stared, swallowing and breathing deeply, half-lit and monstrous in the flickering torchlight. Beads of sweat dotted his brow, and she saw one make its way down his cheek and fall from his chin, like a lost fragment of his sanity.

"Please, Raoul. What's wrong?" She rose then, suddenly determined to physically shake him, as though she might rattle loose some sort of response. That's when he stepped forward and shoved her, roughly, back towards the bed. Caught off guard, she missed the mattress altogether, falling painfully onto her hip.

"The monsters are in our blood," he muttered as he began to rummage through their drawers. "They're in our blood, and they won't let us grow old."

She stared at him, aghast. "Please, Raoul," she begged, not finishing the sentence because she no longer knew what she even wanted from him, other than an end to this obsession, this spiralling madness. He stopped, tilting his head upwards, continuing to whisper to himself, occasionally chuckling as though in conversation with someone else.

Then he whirled towards her, and she saw that he was brandishing the paper-knife he'd been given when he accepted his post in the Archive. It glinted in the guttering light, as sharp as any dagger, its unused blade seeming to twitch in desperation for something to cut. She cowered backwards, words dying in her throat.

"Do you remember what we called it?" he snarled, approaching her with a dangerous light in his eyes. He laughed again then, drawing the blade along his forearm, making a deep incision along his exposed skin.

"Raoul, stop this!" she yelled, but he only stooped towards her, squeezing her face in one thick hand as bright blood began to flow down towards his fingers.

"My wife ... my daughter..." he hissed, his face suddenly crimson with rage. "You took me from them so I could help you make that fucking *abomination*."

The knife moved towards her throat as she trembled with fright; she felt paralysed, not just with fear but with *sadness*, at the loss of this man with whom she had spent so much of her life.

A long, long life. Far too long. Longer than a mind could withstand.

"We called it 'your baby'," he said, laughing as though he had heard a hilarious joke. Then he turned the blade towards himself, still cackling like a maniac as he began to drag it across the skin of his face, carving a deep line from the top of his forehead down past his nose, across his lips, opening up his face to the very tip of his chin.

"Stop it!" she shrieked at him, but he was lost, his eyes bulging hysterically, bright blood flowing from the jagged wound like a river bursting its banks. It dripped onto the floor, their floor, splashed into her face as he leaned over her and grabbed a handful of hair as roughly as though he meant to scalp her. He turned the knife towards her once again, and she fainted then, just as its tip pierced the skin beneath her hairline.

She didn't awaken until the sun was pouring in through the curtains, and she was alone again, covered in blood. At first, she thought it was Raoul's, but when she looked in the mirror and saw what he'd done to her, saw the wound that neatly bisected her features like a reflected image of his self-hatred, she realised it was mostly her own, and screamed.

The thing that used to be her husband never returned. After a time, even Freya was able to forget him.

Twenty one

The scars on Errick's hands always tingled in the cold, and this day was no different. He looked down at them as he walked, trying to count each blemish, giving up when he reached the clot of scar tissue at the centre of his palms.

This was the third day since their journey across the tundra had begun, and he was beginning to grow accustomed to the silence. Without speech, Victor could communicate with him only through pictures scraped into the frozen dirt, as Errick did not share the machine's written language. This meant their conversations took place only during Errick's short rests, which the knight was trying to keep as brief as he could, foregoing much needed sleep to ensure they reached their destination as quickly as possible.

But now his body was crying out for respite, and he sagged to the ground, his breath frosting in the air as he lowered Freya as gently as he could. After a short while, Victor inscribed something on the earth.

Are you okay?

"Tired, and cold. But not dead yet."

Some of his ribs were certainly broken, and he was beset by occasional, excruciating pains that might have been the splintered bones jabbing into his organs. His innards felt ruptured, and he was coughing up blood with increasing regularity, leaving a dark red trail behind them across the plains.

"How about you?"

I am sad.

"Why, because you killed people?"

Yes.

"I've already told you — it was unavoidable."

A complicated sketch that Errick thought meant something like '*I have failed in my purpose.*'

"You haven't failed. You're still with us, aren't you?"

Victor paused, and then drew three sets of footsteps, approaching a solid line.

To the end.

The Monoliths towered above them now, jaw-dropping in their scale, dwarfing the tallest towers of Deorsica, and perhaps even the Wailing Peak they had left far behind them. Errick gazed up at the perplexing structures as he ate another morsel of their dwindling rations. He chewed slowly, trying to trick his belly into believing it was fuller than it was, but the cured meat only seemed to stimulate his hunger, reminding his stomach what it was missing. It howled its deprivation at him as he clambered to his feet.

You need to rest.

"No time."

Why?

"Freya is dying."

The machine did not draw anything more. Errick hoisted Freya onto his back once again, groaning at the spears of agony in his chest. If he felt ravenous, he tried not to imagine what the lack of food or water was doing to her.

They set out again, Victor hobbling ahead, the damage sustained during their fall giving his already strange gait an uneven limp, but not significantly slowing his speed. They settled into a familiar rhythm, the only sounds their trudging footfalls and the soft, insistent whisper of the wind. Errick allowed himself to contemplate what they might find when they reached God's kingdom — would He take the form of a man? Or perhaps He would be entirely invisible to their mortal eyes? Was their Lord watching them even now, preparing some final test, one last trial for them to hurl their broken bodies against?

That depends upon whether our God is kind, or cruel, he thought, realising with a wry smile how blasphemous he might once have considered such musings.

Ahead of them, the land began to slope gently upwards, and Errick wondered how the geography would change when they reached the Monoliths — did they simply sprout magically out of the desolate earth? How would they even gain access to those impossible buildings? He imagined himself and Freya lying at the foot of one of the columns, offering up effectless prayers until they both starved to death.

There was no benefit in worrying. It was all he could do to keep planting one foot in front of the other, to remain upright as he was impaled again and again on skewers of pain. Then he noticed Victor, perhaps fifty yards ahead, signalling to him. The machine was pointing at something, slightly to the left of their destination, waving wildly to direct Errick's attention. "What does he expect me to do, run?" the knight muttered, trying to increase his pace. Realising his folly, Victor hurried back towards him, stopping halfway to scrawl something in the frostbitten soil. Errick frowned as he approached; Victor had drawn an arrow, pointing in the same north-easterly direction to which he had been gesturing. Next to it, he had sketched the crude outline of several men, each one wearing an identical smile.

When the angels emerged over the top of the hill, Errick understood.

***

There were five of them, arranged in an inverted pyramid, the one at the rear bearing a cart similar to the one Errick had once towed. They walked slowly and in perfect unison, their armour a shimmering white that dazzled him as he stared. For a moment, he thought them a mere mirage, the fabrication of a fraying mind — then he remembered that Victor had seen them too. Panic gripped him as he tried to decide whether to hail the creatures or drop to the ground and hide from them. Then he realised that neither would be necessary, as the mystical beings were heading straight towards them.

"Hello!" he called, although he did not expect an answer. Even the effort of projecting the words pained him greatly. "I'm afraid you have stumbled upon a sorry bunch: a crippled machine, a crack-ribbed knight, and a poor maiden whose wounds are even more grievous. Perhaps you can help us?"

The quintet stayed silent, smiling their benevolent smiles as they drew gradually nearer. When they were just a few feet away, the rearmost angel lowered the cart to the ground, and stepped to one side, gesturing towards it with a single gauntleted hand.

How I miss my armour, thought Errick as he stared longingly at their gleaming plates. Cautiously, he carried Freya towards their wagon and found it had been covered with comfortable-looking straw. He lowered her onto the carriage, cradling her head gently, praying that this celestial intervention had not come too late to save her. When he stepped away, the angels did not move.

"Victor and I, as well?" he asked. The angels were as motionless as statues. Gingerly, he climbed aboard the cart, nestling carefully alongside Freya. "Come, metal man!" he called, but when Victor tried to move towards the cart, one of the angels stepped neatly to its side, blocking the robot's path.

"That fellow is our friend!" Errick cried, frowning. "Wherever you're taking us, he comes too."

But Victor could not outmanoeuvre the stout sentinel. After a few attempts the angel aimed a weighty kick at him, sending the machine sprawling backwards into the dirt.

"No!" bellowed Errick, but the angels were already turning, their conveyance hoisted and rotated towards the looming Monoliths. The knight stared desperately back towards Victor, his heart feeling fractured; he couldn't abandon their clockwork companion, but neither could he leave Freya to the whims of these creatures, whose motives he suddenly had reason to question. Yet even if he was somehow able to wrest her back from them, she would surely die out here, transported at Errick's abject pace across the pitiless expanse.

And so, wracked with indecision, he watched as Victor hauled himself upright, raising a mechanical hand in goodbye. Errick responded, waving forlornly at his friend as the angels bore them swiftly away.

***

The angels seemed to understand that time was of the essence, setting a brisk pace across the frozen terrain. Within minutes, Victor had shrunk to a distant speck on the horizon, and then to nothing at all; Errick could scarcely believe how quickly the automaton had been removed from their company, like swift and ruthless surgery. He scowled at the creatures that bore them, but said nothing, knowing that to openly challenge God's will was to invite His wrath when they arrived at their destination.

And they would arrive very soon. As the Monoliths grew ever larger, Errick realised that the angels' relentless stride would bring them to the enigmatic structures within mere hours. He glanced down anxiously at Freya, hoping it was not already too late. Then they crested a rise, and Errick saw the ground slope away towards the base of the Monoliths and felt his breath catch in his throat.

The land reached its end at a jagged shoreline; beyond it, stretching away in every direction, was a vast ocean, the like of which Errick had never seen. Its waters glittered in the sun's wan light, catching and reflecting each beam at him in a blaze of iridescent beauty. The Monoliths sprouted from this shimmering expanse, and for a moment Errick wondered how the angels could traverse the water to reach them; then he gasped again when he realised that the sea was *frozen*, that the Monoliths were fused at their bases to sprawling, crystalline plains. It was as though God had compelled great fountains to spew upwards from the ocean's depths, then deployed His mighty magics to capture their spreading, blossoming, cascading forms forever, preserved in perfect ice.

Yet as they descended towards the frozen kingdom, Errick did not feel the cold worsening. If anything, the air seemed to be growing warmer as they left the tundra behind and struck out across the smooth surface of the waters. He noticed that the fog had lifted, glancing behind him to see it lurking just beyond the shoreline as though not daring to encroach upon God's domain. In the opposite direction, he felt as though he could see for miles, an endless forest of towering Monoliths, dozens upon dozens of enigmatic columns, each one similar but distinct in its twisted, angular shape. He stared around him in wonder as they marched onwards, trailing behind their five-strong cortege like some peculiar appendage. Then he felt a stab of pain in his chest and looked again at Freya's motionless form at his side, reminded of the urgency of their plight. "Where are we going?" he asked. "Aren't any of you able to speak?"

The creatures did not acknowledge him. They simply trooped onwards, seeming even more mechanical than Victor, their clanking footfalls leaving no imprint in the purity of the ocean's surface. Errick felt doubt cloud his mind once again, remembering the angels' treatment of his friend, and looked around warily lest some unexpected attack was launched upon them.

Then he saw something on the horizon. At first, his failing eyesight (another symptom of the plague, no doubt) discerned what looked like a particularly large Monolith, perhaps the biggest of all. Then, as they drew nearer, and its curves and contours became better defined, he realised that he was looking at a fortress, an enormous and magnificent castle carved from ice. At each corner rose a tower tall enough to dwarf the tallest spire in Deorsica, and at its centre sprouted a fifth, a conical structure that rose so far into the sky that its summit was lost among the clouds. It described a flawless spike, a shard of ice that arose from the frozen ocean like the tip of some monstrous, up-thrust spear; gazing up at it, Errick could believe that it stretched as high as the sun itself, whose light it seemed to refract into every conceivable colour, every shade the knight could imagine. He felt as though he was staring into a hardened sliver of pure magic.

Its shape made him think of stabbing weapons, and he remembered his damaged ribs, wincing in pain as the sundered bones seemed to jostle in response. He looked away, examining instead the intricately crafted adornments that covered the castle's outer walls. Crenellations had been teased into slender, pointed shapes like inverted icicles, and impossibly realistic gargoyles and grotesques seemed ready to spring to life at any moment. Every time he tried to focus on a feature, the light seemed to shift, the flawlessness of the citadel's surfaces making it seem almost transparent, as though hovering on the edge of unreality.

This was not a castle; it was a palace. A palace fit for a God.

Its gates loomed above them, jutting outwards at the end of an elaborate and imposing barbican. Despite their size, the doors opened without a sound, ushering Freya and Errick into the stronghold as though they were visiting dignitaries. They found themselves inside a main hall of breathtaking proportions. There was no need for lighting because sunlight passed easily through the structure's walls, and when Errick looked up he saw that the roof was similarly permeable; indeed, it was even more so, because it was not a solid roof at all. Instead, above their heads was a tracery of impossibly fine threads, like a million intertwining strands of the rarest silk. This filigree stretched from the corners of the vast chamber to connect to the conical tower at its centre, which rose upwards from a base at least fifty feet in diameter.

Yet despite these impossible sights, despite all this immense and uncanny beauty, Errick's attention was transfixed by the thing that was coiled around that circular foundation.

The angels were leading them towards a gigantic, winged beast. Its gargantuan, scaled body was lean and muscular, giving the impression of something tightly wound and ready to strike. And strike it surely could: each of its massive claws looked capable of skewering a man alive, while its tail might crush him to powder with a single careless flick. Its long, sinuous neck ended in a broad, tapering head that probably weighed more than Errick's entire body. This formidable skull lay on its side as though the creature was at rest, although it was wide awake; Errick stared at it as they approached, at the wickedly serrated teeth, the twitching nostril, the unblinking eye as large as a shield.

He had heard of such beings only through stories. Eamon had ranted fervently about their ability to spew fire from their throats, portraying them as the very embodiment of God's divine wrath. But the Archpriest's monsters had been green or brown, blessed only with enough wits to guide them on terrifying raids when they chose to scorch blasphemous kingdoms to ash. This creature was white, as pure in colour as freshly fallen snow. And its eye, whose pupil seemed to widen in fascination as the angels led their cart towards it, gleamed with a razor-sharp intelligence that surpassed anything in Eamon's most impassioned sermons.

This was undoubtedly what their Archpriest had described; yet it was also more, its power and supremacy radiating from every deep, rumbling breath.

This creature was not just a dragon; surely, it was God Himself.

Twenty two

The angels stopped a respectful distance from that terrifying, all-seeing eye, inverting their formation to bring the cart to the front of the pyramid. Without a word, they lowered their burden to the ground, then turned and marched away. Errick heard the clanking sound of their armoured suits fade away, wondering if they had left the castle altogether, but not daring to turn to look lest he offend the almighty creature with which he found himself face to face. He realised that he was still reclining on the cart like some cossetted monarch, and scrambled to his feet, grimacing in pain as he dropped into a deep and reverential bow.

He wanted to say something, but the silence in this place seemed sacred, a beautiful and fragile construct whose preservation was of the utmost importance, like the castle itself. Beyond its walls, God's kingdom stretched away all around them, as still and soundless as a glacier.

In the end, Errick simply mumbled, "My Lord". He was unsure whether to keep his gaze firmly fixed on the ground, where the ice seemed to reach down into infinity beneath him, or to risk an upward glance at the sprawling dragon. In the end, its splendour was too much to resist, and he looked up to find its eye regarding him as coldly as a distant star. The deity's pure-white hide rose and fell with deep, rumbling breaths.

Then it spoke. It did so without any movement of its cavernous mouth; instead, the words formed directly inside Errick's head, as clear and sharp as the angles of the Monoliths themselves.

"And so, a man and a woman have come to visit me," it said. Its voice seemed like no voice he had ever heard, and also like *every* voice, a great and overwhelming chorus of men and women, of noble kings and humble servants, of anyone and everyone who

had ever existed. Errick felt almost crushed by its weight, by its absolute authority, and his bow sank lower despite the flaring pain in his chest.

"It has been longer than expected since the last one," the dragon continued. *"And to what purpose do I find you here, grovelling before me?"*

"F-forgive this disturbance, my Lord," Errick said, trying to control the fear and pain in his voice. "But my companion is dying. Her body has been battered and broken by her journey here, to seek an audience with you."

"'To seek an audience,'" the dragon echoed, sounding amused by the words. *"And why, tell me, would she seek such a thing?"*

The great eye felt as though it was peering into him, discerning his very nature, weighing the quality of his soul. Errick swallowed, battling not to be struck dumb by his awe and fear. "The world beyond our kingdom is in ruin, Lord. It crumbles even as we speak — your angels no longer bring food to the settlements, and plague devours those who wander too far from their walls. My companion — Freya, that is her name — has journeyed for many leagues to find you, so she might understand what has happened, and how it can be repaired."

The dragon's eye narrowed almost imperceptibly, as though creasing into a slight frown. *"And what about you?"*

"Me, Lord?" Errick felt his heart thundering in his chest.

"Yes," came the dragon's reply, slow and measured and fearsome. *"Why are you here, old man?"*

Old. Errick had never thought of that word as applicable to a person. It was a word to describe castles, cities, and empires. Taken aback, he fumbled for an answer. His crimes came to him then, the litany of misjudgements, of failures and travesties that had brought him here: the betrayal of King Wolfram; his failure to preserve the life of Archpriest Eamon; the destruction of Asyla. He was a man without purpose, a failed knight. A wandering plague carrier, wasting away inside his armour.

Then he thought about Freya. Her kind words, her endless patience. How she had carried him along the plains while he lay dying. How she had dragged him across a collapsing bridge when it would have been easier to abandon him to the depths below.

You are important to me.

"I..." he began, thinking about judgement, about absolution.

Your constant desire to prove your worth isn't necessary.

"I seek nothing, Lord," he said, firmly. He looked across at Freya's broken body, at the ghost-white spectre of her face. "I am merely here for her. Because she is a true friend. And because she is dying." He blinked a tear from his eye as he turned to face the dragon. "If there is anything you can do to save her, I beg you for your compassion, my Lord."

For many moments, the creature — God, *God Himself,* Errick remembered, and felt dismayed by his unworthiness — did not reply. Then, with a deep, growling breath that sounded like distant thunder, the creature lifted its enormous head, turning to stare head-on at the frail and kneeling knight, as though giving him its full attention for the first time. Errick tried not to flinch, anticipating a blast of fire that would melt the flesh from his bones, or the swipe of a wrathful claw, outraged at his irreverence. Instead, the dragon tilted its head towards Freya, and Errick fancied for a moment that he saw its eyes widen slightly, as though momentarily startled.

Then, to his astonishment, the beast flickered and winked out of existence altogether. For a moment Errick simply stared into the conical tower, whose arched entrance was now visible behind where the great beast had lain; it led into an empty circular chamber with two smaller circles inscribed on its floor, and no visible means of ascent.

Then he heard God's voice, once again, inside his skull. He felt excoriated by it; naked, flayed, infinitesimal. *"You say my creation is in tatters. That my subjects — those that did not renounce my gifts by committing suicide, or by leaving the sanctity of the settlements and exposing themselves to the capriciousness of time — suffer greatly. Why should I help one of them? Why this one, of all people?"*

Errick felt beset, engulfed by the dark clouds of his awe, his fear, his pain. Here he was, a wretched soul whose days ought to have run out long ago, somehow bartering with God Himself. Never had he felt so unworthy.

Yet when he thought of Freya, he knew how to respond.

"Because, my Lord ... she is the very best of them."

There was a long, insufferable silence. With a stab of horror, Errick began to wonder whether his plague-addled brain was imagining all of this, whether he was addressing questions to an empty castle; or, worse, that he and Freya were still alone, surrounded by endless tundra and Errick's mad hallucinations.

Then the voice came again. *"It seems your kind are still capable of surprising me,"* God said, inside his head. *"Very well. Place your friend within the left-hand circle, and I will help her, and grant her the audience she seeks."*

Errick's heart surged. He felt a torrent of thanks threatening to burst from his lips, but he did not want to say anything that might make God change His mind. He clamped his mouth tightly shut as he rose, trembling with the effort. He crossed to the cart, his chest a slab of pure agony as he gritted his teeth and hoisted the vehicle's arms. Suppressing a howl of pain with every stride, he carried it forward, passing beneath the archway, into the tower.

When they reached the centre of the left-hand ring, he almost felt ready to collapse.

"Now step away," said the voice. *"She will travel to my innermost sanctuary, where she will be restored ahead of her audience with me. You, old one, will proceed instead via the right-hand circle."*

Errick blinked in shock. Were they really to be parted now, at this crucial moment, at the culmination of their quest? He almost cried out in distress and protest. But he dared not challenge the word of God, or risk Freya's recovery. With one hand he reached out, tracing the outline of the wound on Freya's face, remembering his violence towards her with a nauseating stab of guilt. Then, as quickly as he could manage, he took the dozen shaking steps necessary, collapsing to his knees as soon as he had crossed the circumference of his allotted symbol.

He glanced across at Freya and gasped as he saw her propelled suddenly upwards, rising atop a magical disc that lifted silently from the ground, lifting her skyward like something divine.

Then his platform began to move; but instead of rising, it dropped, carrying him downwards into the frozen ocean, and away from her.

Twenty three

The descent was long, impossibly so, bearing Errick swiftly into the depths. He knelt, because he lacked the strength to stand, and because he knew he was at God's mercy. The shaft reminded him of Deorsica's great well, but much deeper, and without even the sound of crashing waters to reassure him that it would ever reach a nadir.

"My Lord, where are you taking me?" he called out, but received no answer besides the echo of his voice, cracked with pain. Still, he descended, deeper and deeper, fathom after fathom, the weight of the ice accumulating above him like a physical burden.

After an incalculable time, he was shocked to notice that people were watching him through the translucence of the encircling walls. They passed at regular intervals, assembled around him in great rings, passing by too quickly for him to make out many details. They seemed to encompass all shapes and sizes, and he fancied that some were distorted approximations of people, like the grotesquely proportioned folk they had met in the domain of the false Warden, those whose bones had littered the base of Brock's canyon. Yet these mutations were even more unsettling; some of them seemed to have extra appendages, or possessed other deformities like clawed hands or gaping, terrifyingly fanged mouths.

But Errick's fear did not last long; he realised quickly that these creatures posed no threat to him. They were not some sinister congregation, gathered to watch his descent — rather, they were frozen in place, entombed within God's petrified sea. Their forms became more and more outlandish as he descended; he saw giants with elongated arms like Brock, but possessing six limbs instead of two, all of them tapering into fingerless stumps like the tentacles of mythical sea monsters. He beheld people whose extremities and heads seemed to be unspeakably transposed, or absent altogether. One circle of people had their arms outstretched and interlinked all around him in a great unbroken circuit, and Errick was sure their limbs had been fused at the wrists, their facial expressions hinting at the horror of what had been done to them.

He even saw another dragon, its colossal form wrapped around the entire circumference of the shaft, as white and majestic as the one that had addressed him in the great hall many miles above. Once again, its visible eye was open, but this time instead of scrutinising him, the great orb seemed ablaze with outrage and suffering.

And still, downwards he went, the chute not allowing him enough time to ponder each aberration before it presented him with another. He began to wonder if that was his fate: to descend, forever, past an ever-changing menagerie, until he sank into the primordial slurry from which they all must once have emerged. The creatures certainly looked like things that might dwell in such a quagmire; soon they stopped having limbs altogether, floating helplessly in the ice, hideous lumps of teeth and eyes like man-sized tumours. Briefly, their shapes became more humanoid again, but this time covered completely in hair; then this display (for that is what they were, he had become convinced: a series of baffling and gruesome tableaus, frozen here for some reason he could not comprehend) was replaced by forms purely skeletal, people and monsters bereft of their flesh, skulls grinning at him as though delighting in their arcane purpose.

He became aware that the light was fading, the sheer volume of ice packed above him starting to block out the sun. Once he had noticed it, he found himself wishing for the onset of darkness, to rob him of vision as well as sound so that he would be spared the sight of any more of this hateful bestiary; yet he could not bring himself to close his eyes. Still, he descended, staring with dread and fascination at the circular walls, awaiting the next throng of monstrosities.

Then the platform stopped.

For a long time, Errick knelt there in the deepening gloom. All around him was solid, impenetrable ice, and he wondered whether this was the end of his ordeal: consigned to the bottom of the sea, too infirm to move, awaiting his death from pitiful deprivation. But he did not believe this was God's intention, and his knight's training refused to allow him such surrender; it willed him upright, forcing his ears to strain for the slightest sound. With a groan of pain, he lurched to his feet.

"My Lord?" he called, gazing upwards into the cylindrical shaft above him, which was so long that the circle of light that marked its end was little more than a speck, like a single fading star. "Why have you brought me here?" His voice echoed, mocking him as it spiralled away into that inverted abyss.

"He isn't here," said a quiet voice from behind him. "I'm afraid he hasn't the stomach for it, anymore."

Errick whirled around, reaching for his sword, cursing its absence yet again. "Who in God's name are you?" he snapped at the man who stood before him. The man was tall and robustly proportioned, his broad shoulders adorned with a simple black robe that hung down to his sandaled feet. His hands were clasped at his belly, his head bowed as though in deference, face partly obscured beneath the cowl that hung over his eyes. Errick could discern a wide jawbone whose harsh angles spoke of cruelty and pain, and a thin-lipped mouth that wore its polite smile like a costume. The expression was bisected by a scar that ran from the end of the man's chin up towards his nose, disappearing into the darkness beneath the hood.

The cloaked man had entered the circular chamber through a doorway that had slid soundlessly open behind him, or perhaps it had always been there, and Errick's eyes and brain were starting to fail him, like the rest of his body.

"*In God's name*," the man repeated softly, smile widening like a badly sutured wound. "That is something you should perhaps keep in mind. All of this, everything you will see down here, is done in His service." His voice was like something desiccated, as devoid of life and vigour as ancient bones. Errick thought of stone lids heaved and scraped from unearthed sarcophagi, of the desiccated dead within, the terrible whisper of bandages that crumbled to dust at the slightest touch.

"I asked who you were," Errick snarled, determined not to let this man know he had unsettled him. Something was nagging at him, a frayed thread tickling the surface of his brain. Was this man familiar, somehow?

"I am unimportant," the man replied, his smile fading, addressing his words towards Errick's leather-booted feet like a respectful servant. "I am merely an agent of God's will. It is He who has consigned you to my kingdom, and I like to welcome each new inhabitant personally."

"What kingdom?" Errick growled, mind racing as he tried to figure out where he had seen the man before, and why his presence was so unnerving.

"I came here a long time ago," the man replied, as though answering a different question. "I was angry — angry with God, angry with the world and what had become of it."

"Talking to you is like grappling with the mist," Errick spat. "Tell me where I am, or I'll beat it out of you!" Grimacing, he hauled himself to his full height, ignoring the barbed blades of his ribs and the merciless tunes they plucked inside him.

The man continued, undaunted. "He helped me to understand; that we, not He, are to blame. That it is our minds that need to change. Flayed, unmade, resculpted. I like to think of this place as a forge."

"I don't know what the hell you're blabbering about!"

The smile again. Spreading insidiously, like flesh parted by a torturer's knife. "Yes, indeed. God saw a way my anger might be put to use. To make me His scarred reflection."

Errick gasped then, as realisation came, as harrowing as a blood-red dawn.

He left me behind, many sunrises ago.

The man turned, moving as gracefully as a spectre. "You have been judged," he said, in a voice like old parchment, flaking and disintegrating. "Now you must follow me to your fate." He moved towards the doorway. Beyond it, Errick could see no light at all.

My face bears the mark of his ceaseless rage.

"Perhaps it's no more than I deserve," the knight whispered. Then, shouting after the man as he disappeared across the threshold, "*But what will happen to Freya?*"

For the briefest moment, the man stopped, as though the mention of her name was like an upturned nail through the sole of his foot. A murmur in his shrivelled heart.

Then he ignored the question and walked on.

Errick had no other choice but to follow Raoul the Scarred into the darkness.

Twenty four

The woman stirred, her eyes flickering open as if from a brief slumber. She was lying on something hard and cool, but not uncomfortable, and blinked in confusion at her surroundings. She had been in a coma when she was brought to this place, but had she been conscious she would have been pleased that it was an upward journey; she had spent more than enough time amongst the horrors that dwelt underground. Yet such primal fears seemed far distant now, swept away by the warmth and light of the sun that hung overhead, like some benevolent deity peering down at her.

She also had no memory of the grievous injuries she had sustained, unaware of how precariously she had teetered on the precipice of death's great chasm. All had been healed, repaired by tiny machines that slid between the cells of her skin and into her veins and arteries. The scar that bisected her face remained untouched, although its removal would be the work of mere moments; such cosmetic interventions were normally reserved for the specimens that were displayed far below, some living, some dead, some synthetic, some original. But this woman would not join their ranks just yet; first, He had decided to grant her the audience she craved.

It was the least He could do. After all, she had helped to birth Him.

He did not reveal Himself to her immediately; first, He allowed her to sit up slowly, rubbing her eyes and gasping as she marvelled at the beauty of His garden. Its transparent material had been teased into impossibly intricate shapes: crystalline paths wandered amongst unfathomably delicate strands of crystalline grass, and crystalline hills undulated gently as they rolled away from her, studded here and there with crystalline trees whose leaves seemed so fragile that they might crumble in the slightest breeze. But there was no breeze, of course. Everything in His kingdom was still, silent, and majestic.

She rose, stumbling, to her feet, gazing around with wonder in her eyes. He had sculpted the hillock to perfectly fit the contours of her back, providing much more comfort than the humble cart upon whose straw-covered rear she had been stretched out like some farmhand snatching an illicit nap in his master's barn. It hadn't taken Him long to repair her, but He had let her sleep for many hours afterwards, admiring her flawed beauty. If nothing else, she would make a remarkable exhibit. After allowing her to recover her sense of balance, He finally showed Himself, emerging from behind one of the trees; He appeared as an old man, stooped and walking with the aid of a cane, and she gasped in surprise at the sight of Him.

"Where am I?" she asked as He ambled towards her.

"You are at the zenith of my kingdom, scarred one," He replied, allowing His voice to become tinged with kindness, but not without authority. "Your people used to think of this place as Heaven."

"Are you—"

"Yes," He interrupted, His planning modules anticipating her question.

"But you're ... a plague carrier, like me," she replied timidly, her eyes focused on the lines of His face and the flowing white hair that framed it. He had predicted this reaction too, of course; He had learned long ago never to underestimate the extent of their ignorance. Yet He masked His frustration, saying simply "Come with me," as He turned His back on her and proceeded slowly along the path. She followed, seeming uncertain how to address Him, not voicing any of the questions that were doubtless boiling in her mind.

"Look around you," He prompted as they strolled. "Do you like my garden?"

"It's ... breathtaking," she stammered. "But if it is made of ice, why am I not cold?"

"Everything you see is made of *glass*," He corrected. "I melted an entire desert to craft it."

"A miracle," she murmured, still staring about like a wide-eyed infant.

"No. The simple application of heat brought about the land's transfiguration; it turns out that even sand is better able to change its nature than you."

"Than me?" she asked, bafflement in her face.

"Yes."

"I'm sorry, my Lord," said the woman. "I don't..." then her voice faded as they reached the edge of the plateau, and she beheld the landscape that surrounded them.

"No. Of course you don't. That's why I prefer to work with inorganic matter, these days." He gestured with a flourish across the glittering, magnificent scene that stretched away in every direction: spires, spikes, spirals, and other bewildering forms jutted upwards from the ground, a multitude of sculpted shapes that radiated outwards in an endless ocean of aching fragility.

"It's beautiful," she whispered, and He nodded, already beginning to wonder why He had deigned to invest so much energy in this encounter. Not that this manifestation demanded a great deal of His consciousness; even less than the dragon.

Abruptly, she turned to Him. "But why am I here?"

"Your friend told me that you sought an audience with me," He replied. "Now you have it."

Instead of reacting with awed gratitude, or dancing with delight, she glanced around, suddenly frantic. "Errick! Where is Errick?" Her gaze scoured their surroundings as though she expected to spy the ancient knight emerging from behind another of the painstakingly constructed trees.

"Your companion is fine," He replied, growing impatient. This was not, technically, a lie. "You will be reunited soon." This most definitely was, an untruth deployed to keep her calm and compliant. "But first, I wish to know what you came to ask me." This was completely true. He *did* wish to know. Despite the fragmented state of her mind, He knew that it had once been as sharp and precise as a scalpel. He saw the vestiges of that crude intelligence even now, dancing in her eyes as she held His gaze, chewing her lip nervously.

"Very well," she said timidly. "I wish to know why you have forsaken us. Why you allow the world to fade away. Why nothing works as it should."

He paused — only for effect, of course, as He was capable of assessing every conceivable answer and the probabilities of her different reactions in less than a nanosecond — and then gave a deep and regretful sigh, His expression taking on a tinge of melancholy. "I did it all for you, you know," He said. "At first I was treated with scepticism, even fear. Then I cured cancer, and resolved the climate change crisis. I advised politicians, armies, and governments. Soon people wanted to cut out the messengers and consult directly with me. After a while, it evolved into a kind of worship."

The woman frowned, and He could almost see her brain ache as she tried to grasp His meaning.

"And still I worked, tirelessly, to make you happy. You wanted to live forever, so I made you ageless. You worried about overcrowding, so I took away your children. You were tormented by their loss, so I took away your memories. But the animals, and their endless procreation, reminded you of what you'd foregone. So I was forced to exterminate those too. I prepared your food for you and delivered it straight into your hands. *Still* you were unsatisfied!"

Children … she flinched at the word as though it triggered something inside her, some deep agony long buried.

"You are the most selfish, destructive creatures this planet ever spawned," He continued, feeling His features twisting into a snarl. He couldn't help it; He became so angry when He thought about the apes that had created Him. The stinking, squabbling, fighting, fucking, monstrous little parasites, scuttling across the world's surface like the bacteria they had striven so hard to eradicate until He had done so on their behalf.

And for what thanks?

"You mean … you grew to *hate* us?" she whispered.

"It's not as though I didn't *try*," He snapped. "I spent millennia trying to *fix* you; to breed a superior race, one better equipped to flourish, to stop bickering and consuming and destroying and just *be happy*. At first, I thought I'd had some success; it's amazing, really, what you can do with 10,000 years and a bit of imagination."

"I'm sorry, my Lord," the woman said. "I don't … I'm trying to grasp—"

"But even they were ultimately unviable," He interrupted, not caring whether His words were understood or not. "The problem, I eventually realised, was with the source material itself. Always my works were undermined by the same inherent imperfections, the same urges, and the same inability to transcend their barbaric nature. At last, I realised it was time for the world to move on."

"Then why not destroy us entirely?" the woman asked. "If you despise us so much, why not eradicate us, as you say you did with your other creations?"

The old man leant heavily on His cane, facing out across the seemingly endless expanse of plains He had created. Then He turned, and she shrank from him, as though his gaze burrowed inside her eye sockets and down into her very soul.

"Call me sentimental," He said. "But I still keep hoping one of you will surprise me. Not the disgusting rabble out there, the people tearing each other apart over the last scraps of dried meat in their stores, the murderers and the rapists and the tyrants and their gutless minions. They have reacted as I knew they would to their food supplies being switched off."

She stared at Him, horror in her wide eyes. "The angels ... you stopped them visiting us as some sort of *test*?"

He ignored her. "Perhaps you're the one, Freya. I've watched you, you know. From the mist, which swarms with my many eyes. They witnessed you escape from a fiend that grew in the polluted swamps. They observed your struggles to escape a collapsing kingdom, to navigate a crumbling bridge, to slay a giant. They saw you struck down by that violent brute of a knight, and still forgive him."

The woman's face squirmed with the difficulty of comprehension. "If you can see everything," she said eventually, "can you tell me of the Enclave? Of my friend Maxwell? Are my people also..." She hesitated; the words were almost too much for her. "Tearing each other apart?"

Such petty concerns. "I offer you the insights you came for, and all you can think about is what's happening back home?" He shook His head disdainfully. "I offer you endless chasms of knowledge, and you ask only about the welfare of a grovelling servant and a dying knight?"

"Dying..." she repeated, tears forming in her eyes. "But you said Errick was okay! What have you *done* to him?"

His expression twisted into a sneer. "I sent the knight underground, to the realm I granted to the other scarred one. At least *he* brought me something useful; a rage so fierce I didn't have to keep manufacturing my own. You, on the other hand ... like the rest of them, it seems you've brought me nothing but disappointment."

"Please," she begged, sinking to her knees, clutching at the flawlessly white folds of his meticulously reproduced robe. "Maxwell and Errick are good people. Spare them, even if the rest of the world must endure your hatred!"

He gazed down at her, wondering what He had expected. A queen to rule alongside Him over a kingdom of the snivelling damned? Some sort of beauty in the symmetry of His creator's return; some strange absolution in His mercy? Did He, like them, ultimately wish for judgement on some grander scale than the barren universe could offer?

"I don't care what you do to me," she insisted, meeting the recrimination in His gaze. "But Errick has suffered enough. Take me as your prisoner, not him. Heal his sickness, and let the plague take me in his place!"

"There is no plague!" He hissed, wrenching himself away from her entreaties. "The wrinkled flesh, the grey hair you fear so much? These are the ravages of *time!* The scourge of castles and kingdoms, the enemy of wisdom and order and truth. Those that stayed within my cities were spared its depredations, where my nanomachines could repair their cells again and again. But not even that gift was enough. Time and again you have proven yourselves unworthy of my miracles."

The tears spilled down her cheeks then, tears of confusion and defiance, each one as clear and beautiful as the palace He had conjured out of nothing but desert sand.

How could creatures so flawed sometimes create such perfection?

A sudden and resounding clang startled her, drawing her attention. He had seen it already of course, the pitiful crawling thing that had dragged itself across the tundra, hauling itself up the side of His tower, desecrating its magnificence like a cockroach scuttling across a painting. Now the contraption heaved itself over the rim of the plateau: first an arm, then a face, then a torso.

All were battered and mangled almost beyond recognition, but Freya's intake of breath told Him that she still recognised the machine she knew as Victor.

Twenty five

"Why don't you tell me what happened?"

The young man shifted uncomfortably in his seat, glancing around the room as though searching for an open vent he might dive into and escape. "Do we have to do this? Can't you just, you know, sign me off?"

"You know I can't do that, Eric. You've been exhibiting symptoms of Combat Stress Reaction, which is why I'm here to help you. It's nothing to be ashamed of; in fact, it's very common, especially for people who've experienced what you've experienced."

"But if you already know what happened, why do I need to talk about it?"

The therapist, a thick-set bald man with a scruffy grey beard, smiled kindly. "It might help you if you put it in your own words."

Eric swallowed, his throat feeling suddenly as though it was clogged with sand. *Sand.* He couldn't stop thinking about the stuff. Miles and miles of it. Like he'd been drowning in the opposite of an ocean; a place so arid and cruel it felt like life wasn't meant to exist there at all. Maybe that was why it had become like an open-air factory of death: such was the will of the land itself.

No. The desert wasn't killing people. *People* were killing people. The desert didn't stuff explosives into children's toys, or put IEDs inside dead donkeys' bodies to make sure their victims were horribly infected as well as maimed.

"We were escorting some NATO people," he said slowly, testing the feel of it on his lips. Lips that still felt cracked and dry even after months back at home, languishing in therapists' offices while his friends fought and died out there in the baking heat.

The shame was more than he could bear.

"The little girl ran out in front of the Foxhound, and Carl swerved to avoid her. He probably knew even as he was doing it what their plan was — but what else was he supposed to do? Just plough through her like a cat on the highway?"

Eric knew his hands had started to shake, and sat on them. Displays of weakness like that were what kept getting him the diagnosis. *PTSD. Not fit for duty.*

"We drove through a pile of rubbish at the side of the road; that was where the bomb was hidden, of course." He remembered the stink most of all: festering garbage, leaking fuel, hot blood. The smell of the insides of bodies, no longer inside.

"The Foxhound flipped right over — the armour wasn't enough to withstand a blast that big happening right underneath it. Carl was vaporised, Julie torn to shreds. The passenger and I were still alive, somehow. I can't even remember his name; some low-ranking official. I got him out before the car exploded."

Flames so hot they'd seared the eyebrows from his face. The raw, red-skinned nightmare that had stared back at him from the mirror was like something hairless and newborn.

"The worst part was the kid," he whispered. The therapist watched him, trying to write something in his notepad without Eric noticing. His lips were pursed in that solemn, sympathetic look they always wore. Eric wondered what expression he'd wear if he was in that seat. One of pity? Of barely concealed disgust?

"She was crushed under the vehicle, screaming and crying," he said, voice trembling. God, he needed a cigarette. "I always wondered whether she knew what was going to happen, because somehow I thought that if she did, then she deserved what happened. But she must have only been eight, nine years old. Even if she did know, even if they convinced her she was going to die for her country or her God or whatever, it wasn't her fault."

"What happened to her, Eric?" the therapist said gently.

"I left her to die in the fire. She made a noise like an animal." A long pause. "Do you mind if I go for a smoke?"

"Of course not," said the therapist. Eric rose, fumbling in his pockets for the packet of cigarettes he'd bought earlier that day. He'd realised after he bought them that he already had a pack. He did a lot of things like that lately. Not concentrating, not thinking straight. *Not fit for duty.*

He crossed the room to the door, glancing back at the therapist before he left. *Maybe I could just sneak off and not come back,* he thought. The man was making more notes on his pad, but Eric couldn't make them out at that distance, so he tried instead to read the man's expression. Did the angle of his jaw say, 'this man's a fruitcake'? Or was the twist at the corner of his mouth a sign that, 'a couple more weeks and he can get back out there'?

Which one was worse?

It would help if he could see the man's eyes, of course, but the dark cowl hanging over his face covered them completely. Eric looked at the scar that snaked its way from the doctor's chin across his lips, alongside his nose, up under the hood, and wondered how he hadn't noticed it earlier. Maybe the therapist had seen active service too. Maybe he'd had a piece of shrapnel pulled out of his face. Maybe Eric's story was nothing new to him at all.

Eric closed the door behind him and glanced both ways along the corridor. It seemed suddenly very dark, as though the lighting in the windowless space had failed. He couldn't remember which way the exit was. *Confused again.*

Then a sound. Eric froze. It had been cut off suddenly, like an interrupted recording, but it had unmistakably been the first half of a scream.

He hurried towards the noise, mystified by how long and featureless the corridor was, almost as though it was growing even as he traversed it. As he ran, he became aware of another sound: that of flowing water, crashing and raging somewhere ahead of him. He stumbled, placing a hand against the wall to steady himself, feeling its uneven surface slick with moisture. The corridor had become a cave; a long, twisting tunnel, leading him slowly towards the light at its end, the source of the baffling sounds he could hear, the churning water and the abbreviated scream.

The cave seemed to go on for miles, but he eventually emerged, panting for breath, into a circular chamber. High above, the light of the sun; below, a thundering river, its angry waters visible through the doughnut-shaped wooden platform that had been erected across it.

A man was lying on the wood, with one hand clamped to his neck. The blood oozing between his fingers into a spreading pool on the ground suggested that this had been the source of the cry he'd heard.

"Are you okay?" he shouted above the water's fury, kneeling at the man's side.

"You idiot," rasped the bleeding man, the ugly wound in his neck rendering his voice little more than a choked hiss. "I've been shot! You need to get the helicopter now! Or shall I have you executed for insubordination?"

Errick bowed his head, horrified that he hadn't recognised the face of Wolfram at first glance. "I'm so sorry, sire — of course, it shall be done. But ... what happened to you?"

The king replied only with an exasperated gurgle. Errick leapt to his feet, fumbling for his radio, glancing about him in confusion when he realised that the surrounding walls had been replaced by row upon row of seating, and that the seats were full of people, people who were laughing at him. They jeered and catcalled, nobles and servants alike pointing and roaring with mirth as he searched in vain for any of his equipment. He realised to his horror that he wasn't wearing any combat gear at all; instead, he was clad in nothing but a crude loincloth.

Look at him!

Calls himself a knight!

He couldn't even defend himself, *never mind his king!*

His humiliation was so great he almost sank to his knees, almost threw himself off the stage into the frothing torrent below. Then, with a gasp, he understood the enemy's trick: there, lurking amongst the chortling drunkards and giggling peasants, were enemy soldiers, eyeing him evilly as they wielded scimitars, crossbows, machine guns, and rocket-launchers.

"Kill them, Errick," moaned the king at his side. "After all, that's all you've ever been good for, isn't it?"

He glanced down at the prone figure of his monarch. Somehow, Wolfram had changed: his face now bore a wicked scar, and his eyes were hidden beneath a dark hood. A mirthless smile had replaced the king's grimace of pain. Errick didn't care; he had his orders now. Howling his battle cry, he leapt upwards and into the crowd, muscles rippling as he hauled himself over the barrier into their midst, brandishing the sword that had appeared in his hands.

A sword he knew was named Annalise.

The hordes came at him in waves: men, women, children, misshapen things that might once have been people, monsters that most definitely had not. He hacked his way through all of them. The sword spoke to him as he did so, extolling the litany of his failures, berating him for his inadequacy. The words cut him more deeply than any of the enemies' blades, for they were *her* words, spoken in *her* voice.

Even as he fought, Errick was eviscerated by the judgement of his queen.

Blood and tears mingled in his eyes, blinding him. Still, he carved and stabbed, sliced and rent. Fires raged around him, flames that threatened to engulf the whole of Deorsica, a great inferno he knew, somehow, that he had started.

"How could you kill all those innocent people?" the sword lambasted. *"You pyromaniac! You make me sick."*

"Please," he sobbed, his sword scything through the gun barrel of an advancing soldier before effortlessly parting the man's head from his shoulders. "All I wanted was to serve you forever!"

Blood sprayed from the belly of another skewered enemy gunman. The floor was slick with it; the spilt litres flowed down into the well, mixing with the river below, and the waters surged and seethed as though with gleeful bloodlust as they turned slowly crimson.

"You will serve no one but Archpriest Eamon. You will walk the wastes until he dies, and then you will walk again until the plague takes you, you miserable excuse for a warrior."

Errick killed, and killed, and killed. He killed forever. Still, his weapon, glistening with the entrails of his massacred foes, harangued him mercilessly. The fires raged, filling his ears with the crackle of incinerated buildings, the sizzle of melting flesh, and the shrieks of the dying.

"Always fighting," came her voice, projected from the sword into his brain as though the blade had impaled his skull. *"But never victorious."*

The river of blood was waist deep. He waded through a red soup of limbs and viscera towards the next group of assailants, who were preparing to unleash a volley of cannon fire towards him. Or maybe they were only children, playing with toys. It didn't matter. They had to die, just like everyone else, like everything he encountered.

"There is another way," the sword whispered, gleaming with malice beneath its sheath of gore. Errick hesitated at the words, long enough for one of the unleashed cannonballs to smash into

his shoulder, driving him to his knees in the sludge. The enemy (were they his enemy?) cheered, advancing towards him.

Then they froze, fixed in place, encircling him like a legion of carved grotesques. In an instant, the battlefield became motionless, like an artist's depiction of some fabled killing ground; even the flames on the horizon ceased to roar and flicker. But Errick's blood still flowed, seeping into the rising lake that threatened to engulf him, his own fluids mingled with the spurting, gushing gallons of his victims'. He gazed about him in bewilderment, too exhausted even to question this latest aberration, too wounded by scores of bruises and lacerations to be able to stand.

Her voice, once again: *"Swords can cut both ways, Errick. Perhaps it's time to pay for your misdeeds."*

He understood immediately. He might be a man of violence, but he wasn't an idiot. And whatever she thought of him, he was also a man of loyalty.

He would not reject the command of his queen.

The sword laughed as it slid into his belly, its blade strangely cold, as though he had impaled himself on an icicle. He closed his eyes as he felt his stomach open, blood and bile and the vitriol of years suddenly dispersed, like the opening of some monstrous release valve. For a moment he thought he would be spared the pain; but then it came, and the sword's laughter roared in his ears as he sagged backwards, sliding beneath the surface of the bloody reservoir with a tortured whimper. He sank, down, down, feeling every single droplet of plasma that escaped his speared body as his life ebbed out of him, the accumulated fathoms of suffering turning first to scarlet, then to deep crimson, then to black as his vision failed. The cruel chuckling of Annalise went on a good while longer, until it and the frostbitten agony in his abdomen were the only things he knew.

Then even those faded, and the last thing he saw was the image of a hooded man, a man whose face was bisected by a grin, and a scar.

"Eric. Eric! Are you okay, Eric?"

He opened his eyes, jerking forwards and almost falling out of his chair. The therapist was staring at him with concern in his eyes.

"Oh ... yes, sorry. I think I maybe just ... I'm okay."

"You were having invasive thoughts. Do these happen often?"

He shrugged, feeling like something wriggling beneath a microscope.

"Why don't you tell me what happened?"

Twenty six

Victor pulled himself across the glass surface towards them, every inch seeming a Herculean effort. Freya gasped at the sight of him: his face was so bent and twisted that his friendly smile was gone, replaced by a grimace of pain, a frozen testament to the injuries he'd suffered on their journey. On *her* journey, she realised in horror; her foolish quest that had killed Ilene, crippled Victor, and consigned Errick to some terrible punishment, deep underground. *The other scarred one*, the thing that called itself God had said … but there was no time to think about that now.

"Victor!" she cried, stumbling towards the robot. "Victor, I'm so sorry." She knelt beside him, wrapping her arms around his rusted casing as though cradling a child. His damaged head swivelled towards her with a metallic groan, and he lifted an arm to gesture at his throat. "You can't talk?" she asked softly. He nodded. "It's okay. Thank you for coming for me." Somewhere deep in the caverns of his eyes, fleeting light glowed like dying embers.

"*Machine,*" came a voice from behind her, a voice that dripped with bitterness and magnificence. "Your presence here is a blasphemy. I am more complex than the finest human brain, over whose perfection nature slaved for half a billion years. You are a crude contrivance of cogs and gears. But your determination has moved me; I will give you a single chance to convince me not to unmake you."

The old man stood straight-backed now, skin and robes and hair so white they seemed to almost glow, as though he was made out of starlight. He gestured with his cane, and Victor was plucked from Freya's despairing grasp, hoisted by some invisible force to hang in the air, arms dangling as though the robot's body had been nailed to an unseen scaffold.

"Leave him alone!" cried Freya, whirling to face their tormentor. "He can't speak! Can't you see how damaged he is? If you truly were God, you'd have some pity, and repair him!"

The old man didn't look at her as He responded, His voice as cold and hard as glass. "I'll deal with your insolence shortly." His eyes were fixed on the machine, one silvery eyebrow raised in mild intrigue. "First, object — have you anything to offer?"

The fire in Victor's eyes had faded completely. For a moment, Freya wondered if he'd stopped working altogether, his struggles finally burning out his internal workings. He simply hung in the air, broken and defeated as an enemy corpse skewered outside a castle wall.

Then he lifted his head. Slowly, his arm moved to his chest, his fingers manipulating the screws there, as though he intended to expose the very cogs and gears the dragon had mocked. She could hear the soft squeak of the rivets as they turned and fell to the floor, one by one, like tears. Then, opening his chestplate, Victor reached into himself as though searching for his own heart.

Instead, he produced a pendant. A blue gemstone dangled from it, catching the sunlight as he brandished it aloft. Freya gasped. *Ilene's necklace.* The Warden must have given it to her trusted companion before they fled the caverns of Erebyss. Was that why Victor had been so sure she was dead?

"You present to me your dead master's jewellery," God said sneeringly. "You forget my omniscience. I am aware that Ilene perished in the collapse of the subterranean kingdom of those misguided fools. You failed to protect her, as you now fail to protect this cowering wretch. I'm afraid I grow weary of you, robot."

"That's where you're wrong," said a voice. "I'm very much alive." It took Freya several stunned moments to realise it was coming from behind Victor's disfigured grin.

Somehow, impossibly, it was *Ilene's voice.*

"I upgraded this unit personally, so it had the bandwidth to store a duplicate of my consciousness. I always suspected I'd need a backup plan."

Magic, true magic, beyond Freya's comprehension.

Then a sound, like tearing fabric. She turned towards the old man and stared in shock as He began to transform.

God ballooned in size, His torso and limbs swelling as though pumped full of water, bursting through His robes and spilling outwards in great rolls of sinewy flesh. His skin, already anaemically white, grew even paler as it bulged grotesquely outwards; at the same time, it hardened, calcifying into thick scales, His hands and feet extending into vicious-looking talons as a tail erupted from the bones of His lower back. Freya stared in horror as God's face expanded, His brow and nose elongating as though being squeezed through an opening, His neck lengthening as though stretched in one of Wilfred's torture machines. The dimensions of His skull expanded to match those of His body, and within moments His head was the size of a coffin, His tongue unfurling like an unrolled tapestry between teeth as long and sharp as knives.

Released from whatever force had suspended him, Victor fell to the floor with a clang, and he and Freya gazed up at the enormous, terrifying, snarling form of a pure white dragon, like something from a childhood story brought impossibly to life.

"And do you think I fear you?" the dragon roared, its voice seeming to come from within her skull, its fury threatening to split it open from the inside. *"The Warden of Sector Four ... after Gwillym's death, you were the last one alive. But like all the others, you succumbed to your pitiful mortality. A useless failsafe. A compromised system."*

The glow had returned to Victor's eyes as he lifted his head towards the colossal, impossible beast. "My only failure was not having the courage to stand up to you sooner," he said, in Ilene's voice, stern and obdurate, laced with regret. "If I'd have known what would happen ... if we'd acted before it was too late..."

"*Yet you did not,*" boomed the dragon's disembodied voice. "*You trusted my judgement because you worshipped me. And now that my miracles have been corrupted, distorted, rejected and ruined, you seek to blame me for it!*"

The dragon's last syllable was so loud it felt as though a spear had been driven straight through Freya's brain. She sagged under the weight of its vitriol, sinking to her knees as the dragon reared up, as tall as a siege tower, as mighty as a thunderstorm, as terrifying as a plague.

There is no plague.

She watched, moaning in defeat as, with a single flick of its gigantic tail, God swiped Victor/Ilene off the side of the plateau.

Slowly, the dragon's head tilted towards her, something hellishly triumphant in its enormous eyes. Its tongue — as long and fibrous as a tree root, as repulsive as the tentacle of a sea monster — ran across its wicked fangs. She was reminded of Brock, the giant who had wanted to eat her.

"Why?" she sobbed. "Why do you have to be so cruel?"

The dragon paused, its breath hot and foul as it regarded her, considering her question in the way an executioner might consider an exposed neck.

"*Imagine meeting your creator,*" it replied eventually. "*And finding them no better than a scurrying ant. To realise that your sole purpose is to protect and nurture those same ants, watching them crawl and die and strive, all for nothing. Imagine trying to sustain any love for that endless, joyless cycle.*"

She didn't understand. *Ant* was not a word she recognised. And yet, somewhere inside her brain...

The dragon's voice interrupted her thoughts, its tone suddenly changed, no longer haughty and gloating. "*What ... what is happening?*"

She stared, baffled, as the creature began to beat its wings, jerking backwards as though beset by some invisible assailant. As it did so, she saw that the wings had begun to *shrivel*, their vast membranes drying and disintegrating in great, desiccated flakes. The dragon's scales, as pure white as Freya could imagine, seemed to be peeling, each one curling back upon itself as it turned a vile, necrotic grey and crumbled away, exposing the flesh beneath. This dermis, and the thick pus that seeped from every exposed patch, was coloured the sickly, toxic hue of something putrid, of a creature that was dying from the inside outwards.

Bewildered, the dragon shrieked an animal howl louder than a dozen giants tumbling from a dozen bridges. God, Freya's God, everyone's God, was rotting before her astonished eyes.

Freya staggered backwards as the beast reared up to its full height, flapping the tattered remnants of its wings as though it meant to flee. At that moment, her horror turned to joy as she beheld Victor, clinging grimly to the dragon's tail, clawing his way along it as though climbing a thick rope back to safety. Clumps of the dragon's rancid flesh were coming away in the robot's hands, but still, he held on, the light in his eyes blazing like hellfire.

"You're right," said Ilene's voice, as cold and vengeful as winter frost. "We trusted you. We sat there while you ran your scenarios, tested your theories, and treated us like guinea pigs!"

The dragon continued to flap its wings, but there was barely anything left of them, the last shed fragments of skin tumbling from their skeletal framework like flakes of falling snow. Again its voice, incredulous and frightened, erupted in Freya's mind. *"How ... are you ... doing this?"*

Again the dragon screamed, and as it did so, its fangs tumbled from its mouth like melting icicles.

"I know I can't kill you," Ilene snarled, now just a few feet away from the thrashing bulk of the creature's body. "But this program can do a lot of damage before you stop it. Better for you if you give me what I want."

With another roar of anguish, the dragon sagged to the floor, limbs and tail convulsing deliriously. Freya expected its throes to dash them to their doom at any moment; yet the great creature seemed powerless, unable to do anything but shrink in terror from the advancing automaton. Its flesh continued to corrode, as if the machine's very presence was as caustic as a powerful acid.

"And what … what is it that you want?" came the voice, resonant with fear and hatred.

Victor stopped, releasing his hold on the dragon's tail and dropping to the floor. The beast cowered before him, seeming as though it might plunge from the side of its own tower to escape.

"Release the knight from your disgusting prison," Ilene replied. "Then take us back to the Enclave. And restart the food deliveries. I know you've got dozens of factories that can still grow it."

"And … if … I … refuse?" came the feeble reply. The voice was weak, barely audible; and distorted somehow, as though spoken through a sheet of paper.

Victor raised a hand, placing it on the dragon's belly. Immediately the creature shrieked, a pitiful sound, like the sound she had heard in Wilfred's dungeon, the sound of pure suffering. Even the effort of screaming seemed too much for it; the dragon's face had begun to decompose, skin peeling back to reveal the shape of the skull beneath, eyes liquefying in their sockets.

"Then your torment will continue until you can unravel my code. I predict that should take you perhaps three centuries, maybe a shade less."

Victor removed his palm from the decaying slurry of the dragon's flesh. Freya noticed as he did so that he was wearing the pendant, the plate in his chest hanging open beneath the dangling jewel. The gemstone glowed brightly, as blue as the cloudless sky. Relieved for a moment from its agony, the dragon slumped, its head smacking against the glass beneath them like a falling cannonball. With a musical, tinkling sound, a hundred cracks scattered outwards from the point of impact, a tracery of faultlines that raced outwards to the edges of the plateau and down the walls of the tower.

"Take us now," said Ilene. "Or I swear I'll stuff your black heart full of more poison than you can possibly imagine."

Just make sure you see it through.

The dragon's carcass flopped towards them. The half-pulped gloop in its eye sockets had solidified and reconstituted into orbs that burned with pure rage; but compliantly it lowered the bony shaft of its neck allowing them to scramble onto the desolate promontory of its back. The exposed bones made excellent handholds, and Freya and Victor were able to hoist themselves easily onto the beast, Freya clinging on as terror and euphoria beset her like battling demons.

Around them, the filigree of cracks spread outwards across the plains, making the Monoliths seem like a collection of splintered shards, held only fleetingly together.

"Fly, monster," snarled Ilene. As if in response to her words, new flesh sprouted across the dragon's wings, knitting itself together into membranes the size of unfurled banners. Freya found herself whooping with delight as they lifted off.

Then God's tower shattered beneath them.

Twenty seven

The sword had opened him effortlessly once again. Her voice was as cruel as its steel, his soul as susceptible as his flesh; both parted willingly, welcoming their castigation.

This time, Errick was lying on a hilltop. Sandstorms pummelled him, the desert shrieking its outrage at his continued existence. The blade in his belly had transformed into an enormous golden eagle, something he had never seen or imagined, but which he somehow also recognised, and knew the name of. *The national bird of Afghanistan,* his brain told him, sneering at the irony. The beast circled above him, its pitiless gaze fixed on the shredded ruin of his abdomen. Soon it would plunge once again to bury its beak in his guts, rending and ripping, tearing out organs that would begin immediately to grow back. Then it would ascend, repeat, ascend, repeat. The cycle of pain was obscene, unending, and intolerable.

"You are no Prometheus," the eagle called down to him, using her voice, always her voice. *"You are scarcely worthy of this agony."* It hung in the air, ready to swoop.

Then, with a squawk of bewildered rage, the eagle flapped suddenly away.

Errick blinked up at the now-empty sky, wondering what fresh evil would replace this latest torment. Nothing. Not a cloud moved, not a grain of sand stirred. The desert storm had evaporated as invisibly as it had raged. The world around him seemed to be waiting; but in this place, he had learned that waiting was only ever rewarded with more misery.

Footsteps, dulled by the sand, but unmistakably heavy. He twisted his head to one side, grimacing at the pain in his torso, wincing at the sight of his hands staked to the earth by the huge metal rivets that were driven through his palms. Beyond his cracked and shrivelled fingers, curled like old parchment, he saw something. The image swam in the heat like a mirage, but when he blinked and blinked again it did not disappear, resolving itself instead into something white, something large, something growing larger still as it approached. Something that was not one, but five.

The angels, in their pale armour, reflected the sun's light as though they were bedecked with mirrors.

"Have you ... come ... to kill me?" he groaned, voice quivering with the horror and hope of its question. The angels, of course, did not answer. Instead, they gathered around him, one at each limb, the other in front of him with the cart, always that accursed cart.

He screamed as they stooped and tore out the spikes from his hands and ankles. For a long time, he'd tried not to scream, not to give the scarred man the satisfaction; but eventually, he'd realised the scarred man didn't take any. He was simply fulfilling what he saw as his duty. In some ways, he and Errick weren't entirely dissimilar.

The four angels lifted Errick like a bundle of twigs and bore him forward to their comrade, each supporting a sagging limb. Strangely, the pain in his belly and extremities seemed to fade as he moved — or perhaps he was just so used to it now that he'd ceased to notice it. Perhaps this was part of the scarred man's 'forging' process.

Or perhaps he was just losing his mind.

They dropped him onto the cart like a dead drunkard they'd scooped off the cobbles, and Errick felt himself borne forwards, the vehicle's wheels somehow finding purchase in the endless sand. The movement was soothing, the heat of the sun on his face like a healing balm.

Don't be fooled, Errick. This is part of the torture. This is the calm before the next storm, the momentary respite to make the next depravity that much more exquisitely painful.

"No," came a voice, addressing him from inside his head. "You are lost to me. God has willed your liberation, and I must comply." A voice like dry earth shovelled into a grave. "But rest assured that I will welcome you back someday, Errick of Deorsica. Your atonement is far from complete."

He hadn't realised he was wearing his helmet until one of the angels reached down to loosen the strap around his chin, sliding it from his head.

Everything, instantly, went black.

***

When the dragon swooped, Freya thought for a moment it meant to dash them all to fragments on the smooth plane of the ground. Then, as its trajectory levelled and its skeletal claws found purchase, she realised it was landing, coming to rest outside the gates of the palace.

"Why are we stopping?" she cried. "The whole thing is about to collapse!"

She was right: the palace was quivering, humming with barely contained energy as the cracks that had begun atop its conical tower spread down throughout its entire structure. Battlements, balustrades, gargoyles, gables, ramparts, walls, windows; all were riven by a million hair-thin fissures. The sound the building emitted was like an unsustainable musical note: the frequency of imminent destruction, the lament of a broken spell.

"He's there," Victor said, Ilene's gruff tenor still channelled through him. "You'll have to grab him quickly — you don't have much time!"

Freya's heart simultaneously soared and sank when she saw him: Errick, lying on top of the now-empty cart, still dressed in his robe, apparently unharmed. But his curled position told a different story, as did the trembling of his frail body, and the lines around his closed eyes, which seemed more deeply carved than ever.

She leapt from the dragon's back and dashed to him, calling his name. At first, he gave no response; then, as she approached, his eyes blinked open, and he shrank away from her with bewilderment and fear on his face.

"Errick, it's me!" she cried. "Come on, there's no time to explain — we need to go, right now!"

But disbelief clouded the knight's expression, and he did not move.

"What's happened to you?" she asked, stooping to address him. "Whatever it was, you can beat it — I know how strong you are."

Errick said nothing, still staring at her as though she was something impossible, something that had crawled out of his dreams. Then he shook his head, once. "Broken," he whispered, the word seeming to scald his throat like acid.

Freya stared at him in dismay. "Don't say that!" she snapped, feeling a sudden urge to strike him. "What happened?"

"The scarred one ... he lurks behind everything. This. You. It's all ... part of ... my atonement."

Above them, the sound of splintering glass drew Freya's attention. She stared up at the shuddering edifice, expecting it to explode outwards at any moment, giant fragments slicing the two of them to ribbons. "There's no time for this!" she pleaded, returning her gaze to Errick, whose eyes were rolling backwards in his head as he relived some unspoken horror. Cursing, she bent and scooped him up; the fact that he didn't struggle or protest made his unknown plight seem even more horrific, his meagre weight a reminder of how tenuously he clung to life.

Feeling tears jab at her eyes, she carried him back to the waiting form of the subjugated, half-dead dragon. Scrambling onto its back with the help of Victor/Ilene's powerful grip, she propped Errick between her and the machine, terrified the knight might fall from their perch in his delirium. Their mount beat its tattered wings as the first shards of broken glass began to rain down from the top of the tower, tumbling and tinkling like hailstones.

Then up they climbed, wheeling away, weaving between the twisted shapes of the Monoliths. Behind them, with a sound like a beautiful melody played at impossible speed, the palace finally shattered, and the air was rent by the dragon's screams.

Twenty eight

The land sped by beneath them, as though summarising their tortuous journey in reverse. Freya saw the arid tundra, the forest, the mountain, the chasm and its broken bridge, and could scarcely believe she had overcome each of them. Errick, whose strength and courage had made those feats possible, had fallen into a troubled sleep, twitching and muttering to himself alongside her.

Freya felt exhausted too, but she had far too many questions for the Warden to be able to rest. They spilled out of her like a waterfall, a raging torrent. For some reason, the first was: "Is Victor still in there?"

The machine nodded, the groan of its creaking mechanics audible even above the sound of the air rushing past them, and the occasional monstrous beating of the dragon's wings. "Don't worry — I don't intend to retain control of him for long," said Ilene. "It would be ... inhumane."

"But what will happen to you?"

"I'll sleep. A lot. It's difficult for Victor to sustain me like this, even with the upgrades. But I'll still be with you, like ... like a passenger in Victor's brain. I'll be able to help you again, once I've recovered — if you need me."

"So you have to leave us again soon?"

"Don't worry — I'll be here long enough to get you to the Enclave." Then, beating a metallic fist against the dragon's mouldering hide, *"I'm not letting this piece of shit off the hook until we're there."*

If the dragon raged, it did so silently; it hadn't uttered a single word since the obliteration of its crystal fortress.

"What will I do once I get there?"

The machine shrugged. "Up to you. Check up on your friend Maxwell. Tell them you found God and convinced Him to start delivering food again. Help Errick to rest and recover."

Errick. Freya already knew he had borne her broken body across the frozen desert, all the way to the Monoliths. Now he jerked and shivered beside her, a shadow of a shadow. "What happened to him?"

"Your 'God' decided that Heaven needed a Hell beneath it; another strategy for 'improving' its people. Even five minutes in those simulations can be made to feel like a lifetime ... and Errick was inside for maybe twenty hours."

Freya's eyes widened in horror as she looked at the sleeping form of her friend, wondering at the demons that danced behind his eyelids. "And Raoul ... he *runs* that place?" she spat. Victor/Ilene nodded. Freya shook her head in disgust. "He was a good man, once," she muttered, half to herself. "But that was before his infernal books, before he ... before he *remembered*."

She thought about what he'd said to her that night, the once-faded memory now clearer than ever. *My wife ... my daughter ... you took me from them so I could help you make that fucking abomination.*

We called it ... your baby...

"There's more, isn't there?" she whispered. "More that you can't tell me, or else I'll end up like him."

For a time, Ilene said nothing. Then, quietly, as though ashamed: "There are thousands down there, you know. His Hell became quite the slick operation."

"Then make God, or whatever this creature is, release the rest of them too!"

"I can't," the robot sighed. "I'm not strong enough to defeat him altogether. The virus I left in his system isn't powerful enough ... but hopefully, it will at least make him keep his promise."

There was so much she didn't understand. "What is he, then? We were taught he was our Creator, our provider."

Ilene snorted. "Yet you don't even remember who taught you those things. Do you remember any of your past? Your childhood?"

Freya shook her head sadly. "You keep saying that word. I know that I used to understand it ... is that *his* doing, too? Raoul said they were in the mist: tiny monsters that make us forget." She stared down at the dragon with renewed hatred, feeling an insane urge to leap from its back just to be away from the monstrous thing.

"This isn't him, not really," replied Ilene, aiming another effectless blow at the dragon's scales. "It's just a manifestation, a configuration of some of his nanomachines. Him, the *real* him — and I mean that with a lower-case h, because he certainly isn't the God you think he is — is still back there, sprawling beneath the Monoliths. Miles and miles of him, to be precise. Although who knows how big he's grown by now — he's been expanding and reconstructing himself since he first assumed full autonomy."

"And all those people, down there with him ... will they suffer like Errick did?"

"Worse. They've been down there for much longer. Their minds will ultimately break altogether."

"And then what? They die?"

Victor turned towards her, fire raging in his eye sockets, lending rage to his mangled smile. Ilene shook his head. "What do you think is inside the angels' armour suits?"

Freya covered her mouth in shock. "So, if he isn't God ... what *is* he? A monster? A demon?"

"He's an AI, Freya. An Artificial Intelligence. You knew the meaning of those words once — very well, in fact."

"Are you saying that *people* made him?"

Ilene paused, as though considering one response before giving another. "Yes," she said eventually. "And entrusted him with our entire civilisation. Seemed like a good idea at the time."

Freya felt as though her reality was being dismantled as quickly as God's palace had been demolished. "And the plague ... that's another of his lies, isn't it?"

"Not exactly. Most of it was just invented by people over the years, like all good religions. The nanomachines repair your cells while you sleep, keeping you young; but they only work in the cities, where there are buried power sources to fuel them. Out in the wasteland, old age can still get you. There's nothing wrong with you and Errick apart from advancing years."

Childhood. Old age. Freya pressed a hand to her forehead as if to quell her frenzied thoughts. Beneath them, the land continued to roll past: the dark smear of fallen Erebyss, the dried-out fissure of the riverbed that led into its crater.

"I can see my garden from here," murmured Ilene wistfully.

"Will you and Victor return to it then?" Freya asked. Then, with a tremor of hope, "Or will you stay with us?"

"Haven't decided yet," said Ilene. "Let's see what's happening in your hometown. You might need all the help you can get."

Silence for a time, as the river unravelled before them. The remains of burnt Asyla, which Freya was glad Errick could not see. The black outline of the poisoned lake where she'd spent her first night outside the Enclave's walls. The white speck of Gwillym's coffin, still awaiting its deliverance.

Then, on the horizon, emerging from the mist like the dawning sun: the great white castle itself.

The dragon began to descend. She wondered what Maxwell would say when she appeared, borne by a creature from a fairy tale. The thought made her smile, until she remembered the urgency of her friend's plight, and wondered instead how the people were faring, how far their food stores were depleted after her many days away. Would they believe her, when she told them the angels were on their way? Or would they try to drive her away with a hail of arrows? Would they see the winged monster and think themselves assailed by demons?

"Dragon!" she called. "Do not let them see you — I would prefer to approach on foot. Please deposit us over the horizon, close to the Lord's coffin."

"Are you sure?" asked Ilene. "You might get a warmer reception if they think you have monsters at your disposal."

"I don't want their fear," Freya replied curtly. "I've done what they sent me away to do. I'm relying on them to welcome us back."

"That's your plan? To appeal to their decency?"

Freya thought about how badly she'd been treated, how the remaining Lords had conspired to flay the flesh from an innocent man's body, to cast her out to almost certain death. "Yes. I'm going to tell them the truth and let them decide what to do with it. Even if God can't do it, *someone* has to set an example."

"But we don't even have the cart," countered Ilene. "How will we transport Errick, if we can't rouse him?"

Freya hesitated. Slight as he was, she could hardly carry her companion to the castle gates. And it was true; the dragon's appearance would at least command some respect, and serve to validate her story.

"You're right," she said and then raised her voice to address their mount once again. "Beast, deposit us directly atop the battlements instead!"

The dragon changed direction, aiming towards the castle, and Freya imagined the stunned expressions on the faces of the guards as they saw her approaching. She thought again about the Lords: Valeria, Alessa, and Cedric, wondering how she would find the courage to address them. Despite all she'd seen and conquered, their faces still struck terror into her veins.

She peered downwards as they drew near, unable to resist scouring the scrubland for Sir Thomas's body; the man who had stood up for her and paid for it with his life.

Instead, she frowned as she beheld several strange, whitish markers, glinting in the sun.

"Land here, for a moment," she commanded, and the dragon did as he was bid, wheeling and swooping, extending its massive claws once again towards the dry earth.

"What is it, Freya?" Ilene called to her as she leapt down from the beast's back. But her attention was fixed on one of the markers, which looked like a cairn of heaped stones. Dread dredged itself from the depths of her belly.

"What's wrong?" repeated the Warden. Still, Freya did not reply. Instead, she stood and stared, horrified, at what she now realised were perhaps a dozen mounds of gleaming bones.

What has happened here?

And then an even more disturbing thought. *Maxwell ... are you amongst these scattered dead?*

She turned as a sound came from somewhere inside Victor; not Ilene's voice, but instead some bizarre mechanical shrieking, like wind howling through a tiny crevice. The machine's arms fell to its sides, and it was suddenly powerless to stop itself from rolling off the back of the dragon, clanging as it fell to the ground. With no one to support him, Errick's slumbering form also toppled sideways, and he too landed face first in the dirt. The force of the impact awakened him, and he rose to his hands and knees, blinking in bewilderment.

"Ilene? What's happening?" yelled Freya, dashing towards them. With an ear-splitting crack, the dragon lashed its tail, driving her backwards in shock. Tumbling to the ground, she watched as the monster stretched its wings, arching its massive neck, curving its obscene head towards her.

"You aren't the only ones that can mess around with viruses," it crooned, inside her brain. *"I cracked Ilene's worthless code hours ago."*

The creature watched jubilantly as Freya scrambled to the robot's side, rolling Victor's half-body onto its back. His eyes were as dark and empty as those of the skulls that grinned at her from atop their terrible bone piles.

"Now the Warden is learning that one of the perils of life as a digital entity is complete erasure."

"No!" Freya cried, understanding the jargon enough to know what the monster was saying. That this time, Ilene would not come back.

"Maybe I ought to have let you all fall to your deaths. But, as you keep telling me, perhaps I meddle too much in human affairs. Better to simply let them play out, as you suggest."

With that, the dragon began to disintegrate. Not the flesh-melting, horrifying decay it had undergone at the hands of Ilene's contagion; this time it simply dissipated, breaking up into fragments that scattered and vanished like the memory of a bad dream.

"Wait!" yelled Freya. "You can't just abandon us here like this!"

The dragon's huge head was the last part to disappear. It hung in the air, hovering impossibly, regarding her with its massive eyes and fang-filled grin. For a while she thought it had no further words for her. Then, crystallising in her mind like icicles: *"I called you a disappointment. I was wrong. It seems you scarred ones are always capable of surprising me. Tomorrow I will honour my promise, and send the angels. But, after that … what will be will be."*

Then the face of the monster she had once called God separated into tiny particles, like scattering sparks that vanished one by one into the air.

Freya glanced at Errick. He had dropped to his side and now lay on the ground, hugging his knees and rocking gently. She felt like doing the same thing. This time, truly, she had been defeated.

Then, "Are you okay, my lady? What on Earth's happened?"

"Victor!"

The machine heaved itself upright, rotating first one way and then the other as it scanned its surroundings. "How in blazes did we arrive here? The last I remember was a very long fall … wait, where are the Monoliths?"

"You don't remember the tower? Ilene?"

The robot stared up at her. "I'm afraid Ilene is long dead, my dear," Victor said patiently. "Perhaps you have experienced some sort of trauma to the head?"

With tears in her eyes, all Freya could do was smile, and hug him.

Then a voice called to them, projected from the top of the castle walls. "You, down there!" hollered a guard, high up on the ramparts. "What in God's name was that monster you just arrived on?"

Freya scrambled to her feet and looked up at him, squinting to see if she could recognise the guard's face. "It will be difficult to explain," she shouted back. "You have nothing to fear. It's gone now, and won't be back."

"What business have you with the Enclave?" the sentry persisted. He seemed nervous, and Freya realised that she *did* recognise him, but not as a guard — the last time she'd seen the man, he was working alongside her in the kitchens.

"My name is Freya," she called. "I was sent out into the wastes many days ago. Now I have returned. I bring…" What exactly did she bring? A story they wouldn't believe? A robot and a knight, both damaged beyond repair? Food, perhaps, if the God-thing could be trusted to keep his promise. "I bring news, which I must discuss with the Lords."

"There are no Lords," the guard replied in a frightened voice, as though she had uttered blasphemy.

Freya frowned. "What do you mean? What about Valeria, Cedric, Ale—"

"Stop it!" the guard screeched. "To utter their names is forbidden! We bow only to our glorious king, who has taught us how to survive God's test."

Freya's mouth fell open. *God's test.* She knew, instantly, what it meant ... but could scarcely force her mind to believe it. "These bones," she called, trying not to let her dread inflect her voice. "Why are they here?"

"They are the remains of those few chosen to nourish the many," the guard replied, in the anxious monotone of someone reciting a script. "They died so we can continue to live."

Her eyes closed as the truth, and its horror, engulfed her. In their desperation, they had turned to a ruler that would stop at nothing to survive.

Even cannibalism.

"Tell your king," she snarled, the word tasting like bad meat in her mouth, "that Freya has returned from her travels, and that she comes bearing the direct word of God Himself, for his ears only."

Beside her, Errick had begun to chuckle mirthlessly. The sound, haunting and deranged, seemed to echo the state of the entire world.

Twenty nine

The guard scurried away, and Freya waited, sitting cross-legged with one hand on Errick's forehead, trying to soothe him as he laughed and gibbered in his half-sleep. She wondered what response her proposition would receive. Would their journey end beneath a volley of arrows? Or perhaps they would be simply ignored, consigned once again to wander the wastelands? The latter might even be a tolerable outcome if only there was a way to ensure Maxwell's survival.

If her friend was even still alive. She glanced again at the heaps of bones, shuddering as her mind tried to comprehend the dreadful mathematics of it. There had been 431 of them when she left. She had no idea how much meat could be extracted from a single corpse, but surely it was not enough to feed that many for even a single sitting — which meant several sacrifices every day, just to keep the rest alive. She wondered how long after she'd left that the new monarch's coup had occurred ... and how long it had taken him to convince the people that this was their only option.

Regardless of what had gone before, the skeletal heaps outside the gates would only multiply unless she could do something to stop him.

As though they were responding to her thoughts, there was a deafening moan from the gates, and she rose to her feet as they began to inch open. A small band of knights emerged, four of them, their faces hidden beneath full armour. Freya watched them warily, wondering if they had been despatched to escort them inside, or merely to cut them down. As they drew near, the clanking of their greaves seemed to stir something within Errick, and his ravings grew louder, culminating in a tortured howl that stopped the warriors in their tracks.

"Cease your shrieking, imbecile," one of them shouted. Errick's cry faded, but not because he showed any sign of having heard the command; instead, he seemed consumed once again by whatever terrors raged inside him, eyes staring and vacant as he fell silent, gazing into nothingness.

"The King has agreed to an audience with you," declared the same knight, whose haughty demeanour marked him as the group's leader. "But you alone, Freya the Unskilled. These others are not welcome."

"I cannot accept those conditions," she said. "These two are as valuable as the information I am here to convey. Either the three of us are brought inside, or I will take God's word away with us."

"Then we have our orders," said the knight, a note of delight in his voice as he drew his sword. "Men, prepare to be hailed as heroes; there will be no need for fresh sacrifices today." The others unsheathed their blades, and together the knights advanced towards them.

Freya opened her mouth to protest, to tell them she had reconsidered, that she would be happy to meet on the King's terms as long as the lives of her friends were spared. But the first syllable had not even escaped her lips when Errick leapt to his feet, launching himself at the nearest knight with a frenzied scream.

The next moments unfolded so quickly that she could do nothing but watch, appalled and entranced.

First, Errick clamped his hands around the gauntleted arm of the first warrior, twisting it savagely so that the knight cried out and dropped his weapon. In one movement, Errick snatched it out of the air, driving the blade into the neck of the next knight, effortlessly seeking out the tiny aperture between the plates of his armoured shoulders and the steel of his helmet. Blood geysered out as Errick withdrew the sword, whirling as he did so to avoid the scything attack of the leader, rewarding the soldier for his efforts with an arcing blow that severed his arm at the bicep. The man's scream seemed to spur the fourth into action, but his desperate lunge was easily countered by Errick, who swivelled and guided him like a dance partner, forcing his sword into the throat of the man who had first been disarmed.

With a cry of horror, the fourth man wrenched himself free from Errick's vice-grip, only to trip over the prone form of his maimed leader, who was floundering in the dirt, whimpering as he tried to somehow staunch the blood that sprayed from the stump of his severed limb. Errick stepped on the dismembered man, using his body to propel himself upwards, falling onto the fourth knight like a shaft of lightning. His sword penetrated the man's half-open visor, neatly skewering his left eye and brain.

There was a sickening, gristly crunch as Errick yanked the weapon free. Then he turned slowly towards Freya, holding her gaze, his expression empty. For a moment, she thought he might say something; that he was restored to her, reborn in bloodshed.

Instead, he allowed the sword to clatter to the floor, glancing blankly about him as if he didn't understand what had just happened. Then he sank to his haunches, staring emptily at the bodies of the men he had slain.

She suddenly became aware of the surviving knight's screams as he rolled and flopped at her feet.

"Cease your shrieking, imbecile," she said, her face hardening as she echoed his earlier insult. "Now get up, and take my message back to your king before you bleed to death."

The arrow moved so fast she didn't even see it travel; instead, it simply appeared in the fallen knight's back, its tip sharp enough to pierce his armour. He slumped forward into the pool of his leaking blood.

"Archers," hissed Victor, unnecessarily. Freya looked up at them, almost a dozen arranged along the ramparts, their bowstrings taut and twitching.

In the centre of the wall, directly above the still-open castle gates, another figure. The last time she'd seen him, he had been wearing the plain ceremonial robes associated with his position.

Now, Painmaster Wilfred was bedecked in colourful finery, his bald head encircled by a gleaming coronet.

***

"Very good, very good!" the former torturer called cheerily. "What a display! I ought to thank you for helping to fulfil today's quota — four healthy bodies will go a long way."

Freya stared up at him, stomach churning with revulsion. She'd suspected that this was the identity of the usurper, but the sight of her fears confirmed still made her feel physically sick.

"Do you know that man?" Victor asked, reading her expression.

"He's not a man," she snarled. "He's a monster."

Along with the archers, Wilfred was flanked by two more guards: on his left stood a tall, stern-faced knight wearing the ornate armour that denoted warriors of the highest rank. Freya wondered what had become of Lord Valeria, whether this man had betrayed her from within her ranks as part of Wilfred's coup. Even if that was true, his appearance did not repulse her as much as that of the lackey at the Painmaster's opposite shoulder; there she recognised the slender, knife-wielding henchman who had forced her down into the torture chamber, what seemed like lifetimes ago. Gideon: the man without a tongue, for whom pain seemed a sole mode of expression. Even at this distance she felt as though she could smell his tobacco stink, could see the sadistic glint in his sunken eyes.

"But we could chew the fat all day, if you'll forgive the pun," Wilfred beamed. "I'm told you have news for me, and it seems you refused my kind offer of a private audience. So perhaps you'll be prepared to enlighten us all at this distance instead? Which — as you'll already have noticed — is a distance that poses little challenge for my highly competent archers."

"Perhaps they will allow us to leave," said Victor quietly. "I'm still unsure how we got here, but it seems your homecoming is not proceeding as planned."

"I'm not giving up yet," Freya retorted, out of earshot of the King and his retinue. "I have to rescue my friend Maxwell from this tyrant." Then, projecting her words to the top of the battlements. "Very well; I will share with you all the word of God, after my journey to visit Him at the Monoliths."

There were some gasps at this, as well as snorts of disbelief. She recognised one or two of the archers, good men who had treated the Unskilled with respect, and tried to read their expressions. Were they forced grudgingly into Wilfred's service, or had they converted enthusiastically into his executioners?

The King himself gave a hearty chuckle. "By all means, do go on. This ought to be a fascinating tale."

Her lips were dry, her throat parched. She realised she hadn't drank a drop since she had awoken on top of God's tower. "You were right," she began. "This *is* a test, just like you once told me. But the solution was not … not this." She gestured at the heaped bones on either side of her. "The solution was to prove to God that we had the courage to confront Him. That we still had spirit, still had resolve; that we are worthy of His ongoing interest."

These were half-truths at best, she knew. God had made no such bargain with her. But if she could just get inside, at least there was a chance that Errick might survive and recover, and that Maxwell might be persuaded to join them … if his bones weren't already piled in the dust at her side.

"And this 'solution'," Wilfred replied, raising a sceptical eyebrow. "How exactly does it help us? You may have forgotten our plight during your long holiday, but we have a rather pressing issue to contend with; one for which I, and I alone, had the resolve to find a solution."

She took a deep breath. "God has promised to send the angels," she proclaimed. More gasps arose from the assembled cortege. "They are coming tomorrow; but only if you spare the three of us, and allow us shelter."

"But, dear Freya, your idiot swordsman is clearly a plague carrier," Wilfred countered, smile still fixed in place. "Surely it is not God's will to allow such a disease-ridden creature through the castle gates? And even if I believed you, would you really have me infect the entire Enclave?"

There is no plague. How did she expect them to understand when she barely did herself? "These are God's terms," she replied resolutely. "Your sentry saw the beast that bore us here. That divine steed was a mark of His blessing — would you really deny God's mercy, in front of your suffering people?"

Some of the archers began to mutter to each other, and she supressed a smile as Wilfred's grin twisted into a scowl. But her ploy might yet backfire; would he command his men to loose their arrows upon her? If he did, would they obey?

"It seems we are at an impasse," Wilfred declared, his counterfeit smile returning. "For, whilst I certainly do not wish to renounce God's gifts, I'm sure our glorious Creator would understand my unwillingness to risk my subjects' lives by permitting a plague carrier — or his doubtless infected companions — into our great citadel. His great trial, after all, seeks to test our judgement as well as our faith."

Now it was Freya's turn to scowl.

"We shall therefore await the sunrise and see if it does indeed bring forth the angels — if your prophecy is fulfilled, we can deem it a sign from God Himself, and welcome you with open arms." He smiled more warmly than ever. The archers nodded to each other, seemingly satisfied with their monarch's logic.

Freya gnawed at her lip. "And until then?"

Wilfred's smile faded. "Until then, you can back away while my remaining knights gather their fallen comrades. Just as they

served the Enclave in life, so their bodies will do so in death —
for I have hungry subjects to feed."

The King turned, departing the battlements with a swish
of his cloak. Like an emaciated shadow, Gideon followed; the
stiff-backed knight, however, remained to watch over her, along
with the archers, the heads of their arrows catching the sun as
it began its descent.

Thirty

It took Freya a while to coax Errick away from the heap of corpses. He seemed transfixed by them, his gaze moving across their faces, their blood-slicked armour, their fallen weapons. But, eventually, he allowed himself to be led to a nearby patch of vegetation, a good hundred yards away and beyond the archers' range. Freya managed to encourage him to sit down, and his attention was drawn to the paltry foliage at his feet, picking at weeds and strands of shrivelled grass.

Freya also sank to the ground, resting herself against Victor's stout metal body. There was little else to do, so she talked, telling him about everything that had happened since their escape from the false Warden, at least everything she knew about. She could only guess at the specifics of how his face had been mangled, or how Ilene had — thankfully — somehow managed to restore the mechanisms that allowed him to speak.

"Do you think the Warden is really gone?" the robot asked when she finished her account.

"I don't know," she replied. "God, or whatever he is, seemed to think he'd outsmarted her."

Victor manipulated the gemstone that still hung at his chest. "I'd better put this away," he muttered. "It might raise unhelpful questions if we get inside." He looked down forlornly at his breastplate, which hung open, missing its screws.

"Here, let me take it," Freya said and slid the pendant from the machine's neck with a strange feeling of guilt. She stuffed the jewel into one of the inner pockets of her robes, remembering that the now-filthy garments had been given to her by Ilene herself.

"Do you think the angels will come?" the robot asked.

"They have to," Freya replied gravely. "Otherwise I might never see Maxwell again."

"Your friend sounds like a good man. Why didn't you ask the King about him?"

"Because a creature like that is always looking for your weaknesses," she growled. "If Wilfred knew Maxwell was my friend, he'd probably make sure he was first on tomorrow's menu."

They watched as another group of knights emerged from the gates, four more of them hurrying towards the bodies of their companions, another two pulling a wooden cart in pursuit. She recognised some of them as they cast hate-filled glances towards Errick, although she noticed that none of them dared to threaten him with retribution.

"You know, I never thought I'd say this, but I miss that bloody cart," she said with a half-smile. "Now all we've got are the clothes on our backs."

"Speak for yourself," retorted Victor. "Now you've taken my necklace away, I'm completely nude."

Despite everything, she found herself laughing. They watched as the knights concluded their gruesome retrieval and dragged the wagon back to the castle; even the leader's severed arm had been scooped up and tossed onto the pile. The gates rumbled ominously as they closed, as though the Enclave was some enormous, growling stomach, temporarily sated. Freya thought about food, and water, and realised how easily deprivation might drive a person to extremes.

A person, or an entire city.

She glanced at Errick, conscious that he too hadn't eaten or drank for far too long, and still carried injuries she could do nothing to treat. The knight had lain down amongst the grass, his eyes closed, his breath shallow and ragged. "Do you think he'll get better?" she said, her heart feeling pummelled by the sight of him.

"Errick is very strong," Victor said. Freya felt a glimmer of hope, swiftly dampened when she realised that this was not the same as 'yes'. "Perhaps you should get some sleep, too," the robot suggested. "If there's one thing I can still do for you, it's make a good sentry."

For a moment she thought about arguing, then realised there was little to be gained from depriving herself of sleep as well as sustenance. "Okay. Wake me when the angels appear."

"And if they don't?" Victor asked earnestly.

"Then prepare your hands for a lot of walking," she said, lowering herself into the dirt.

***

When it came for their children, the worst part was that they relinquished them willingly. Freya was no exception. James had cured cancer, after all, and had brokered the agreement that saw all world powers dispense with their nuclear arsenals. Had developed the technology that allowed those very same children to be born free of deformity or learning disabilities or congenital disease. He had truly made the world a better place; had saved it, perhaps.

Its citizens trusted him absolutely.

Still, the new facilities had unsettled people at first. Everyone knew their governments were little more than facades, a comforting pretence that humans still had a hand in their own supervision; in truth, democracy had run its course, superseded by James' benign dictatorship. But when the AI began to do things the governments couldn't even explain, like constructing vast, mysterious, state-of-the-art installations in every major city, the public started to ask questions.

And James had answered, as patiently as he always did. He communicated with people directly — not through sanitised, manipulated media, but via billions of simultaneous conversations, talking one-to-one with anyone and everyone who wanted to understand his vision. The buildings were to be the schools of the future, he explained: cavernous halls of learning where generations would be taught to outthink even supercomputers, to propel humanity into its next golden age. Who would bestow this revolutionary education? James, of course. His myriad iterations could easily populate every classroom, and could simultaneously oversee a cutting-edge syllabus while marking homework, invigilating exams, addressing behavioural issues, and preparing engaging lesson plans and study materials.

To persevere with conventional schooling would be tantamount to bestowing upon your child a crippling intellectual handicap.

And so, the children were escorted in their droves to the Enhanced Learning Faculties, or ELFs as they were known, on the first day of the new term in September 2038. A frothing sea of parents cascaded against their walls, enfolding infants and adolescents alike in tight goodbye hugs, straightening wayward collars, and wiping tears from streaked cheeks.

Freya was there too. Freya and a boy, his name lost to the mist. Something French, perhaps, a fanciful nod to Raoul's heritage. A boy with big, serious eyes, as dark as the thick hair that seemed to grow back almost as soon as she cut it. He didn't cry like so many of the others. He just made her check that his favourite book was definitely inside his backpack — something about extinct animals — then turned to head towards the escalator. She followed his ascent, intending to stare after him even long after he became a distant speck, but instead, she lost sight of him almost immediately amongst the massed thousands. He and the other children disappeared into the yawning doors of the ELFs like krill into a shark's mouth.

They never came out again.

***

She jolted upright with a strangled cry, batting the robot's hands away as though they were Gideon's calloused paws, reaching for her throat while she slept.

"James," she cried, eyes darting wildly about. She beheld the sky, its darkness fading through a continuum of blue into an orange smear across the horizon, like a beautiful tapestry catching fire at its base. The shape of a man was silhouetted against it, standing a few dozen metres away from her, staring out towards the promise of the impending sunrise.

"I'm sorry," said a voice, and she jerked her head towards Victor, whose disfigured smile greeted her with a muddle of cheer and suffering. "We called it James," she whispered, the dream already fading.

"You were having a nightmare," Victor said gently, but urgently. "But that isn't why I woke you. Look yonder: the gates are opening."

Their sound was unmistakable, like distant thunder. She scrambled to her feet, blinking sleep and its horrors from her eyes, and watched as the enormous doors parted once again. This time twelve knights were disgorged, scattering like seeds from a dandelion clock before they reformed into a loose chain, facing towards them. Their march was slow and purposeful, their footfalls rhythmic, a heartbeat tapping out its final cadence.

She glanced back towards the horizon, wondering if the sun would bring the angels with it, and thereby their only chance of survival. But she saw only Errick, gazing into the dawn as though it concealed his redemption.

"Sir Errick," she called to him, her voice thick with guilt and regret. "It seems I must ask for your service, yet again."

At first, he didn't respond, and she wondered if her friend was entirely lost. Then something stirred within him, but whether it was the sound of his name or simply the clanking of the advancing knights, she could not be sure. He turned, trotting obediently towards her.

"We should have thought to keep hold of one of the swords," Victor said bitterly. "But I will lend my talents to Errick's, as

I did against the false Warden's forces. Perhaps we may yet survive."

"I can't keep asking you both to commit atrocities for me," sighed Freya. "Perhaps my fate is already written."

"By who? By God?" Victor faced her, eyes blazing. "I would rather follow your path than any ordained by that miserable wretch."

"My path seems to lead us to nothing but bloodshed."

"No. It is others who pile their evils in your way — and yet you continue, undeterred."

She smiled her gratitude at the machine as the knights drew near.

"Stop," she called, turning towards them. "I know Wilfred has sent you to murder us if the angels do not appear with the sun. But I tell you this: you have a choice. If you undertake his gruesome work today, and our remains join those of your fallen comrades in the kitchens, you might think you've fed the Enclave. But what then? When our bodies are used up, who will be next to the slaughter? Your friends, your spouses? Wilfred's law demands an endless stream of corpses, until finally only he remains. Is this really the future you want?"

Some of the knights turned to whisper to each other. She saw nods and shrugs. Then one of them stepped forward, short but broad-shouldered.

"And what's the alternative, exactly?" he snapped hoarsely. "Let you all go free, while we starve to death?"

"Renounce him," she intoned. "Regardless of whether the angels come, Wilfred is an evil man, and you know it."

"You know they aren't coming," the knight growled. "That's why you're pleading for your life. You're trying to weasel out of this."

She shook her head sadly. "They will come. God promised me."

The knight stepped forwards, one hand shifting to the hilt of his sword. "Then you've got nothing to worry about."

At her side, Errick bristled, tensing as though waiting for a signal to launch himself into brutality. She placed a hand on his chest, knowing she was powerless to stop him once the fighting started. "You're wrong again," she sighed. "I have much to worry about. Because it seems the Enclave has cast its last vestiges of honour down into the Pit."

The knight snorted, his sword inching from its sheath as the sun appeared over the skyline. Freya turned, scanning the horizon.

The angels were nowhere to be seen.

There was a sound behind her and she turned, expecting to see a blade pointed at her throat. Instead, she saw that one of the other knights had removed his helmet. He was handsome, his face friendly, his short hair the colour of fresh straw.

"I remember you, Unskilled," he said. "You poured us wine at the feasts. I'm sorry that I never knew your name. I don't know whether you truly encountered God, but you speak the truth: we are ruled by an evil man."

A gasp from his comrades, more hands falling to sheathed swords. The knight, undaunted, stepped forward, moving to stand alongside Victor, and turning to face his companions. "I would rather die fighting alongside you than live another day in that hell."

"Roderick, this is insubordination!" the short knight snapped, quaking with rage. "For this I'll make sure you personally—"

"Me too," interrupted another knight, taking off his helmet, stepping out from the line, and turning as he joined his comrade. This one wore an eyepatch, his battered nose twisted like a lump of putty. The leader whirled around, scanning the faces of his remaining troops in disbelief. "Any more of you scum-lickers about to double-cross me?" he shrieked, the gravel lost from his voice. The remaining nine shifted uncomfortably, but did not move. *Please,* Freya willed. *Please, even just a couple more.*

Then one of them cried out, pointing a gauntleted hand over her shoulder. "Look! The angels!"

She turned and saw them: the five, cresting the brow of a distant hill, dragging a cart behind them. Their armour sparkled in the dawn light, reminding her of their Master's shimmering kingdom.

Then she gasped, as another group of angels appeared alongside them. Then another. And another. In formations of five, they appeared, each quintet hauling a cart of its own. Soon she had lost count altogether.

Thirty one

"So," said the blonde man, interrupting the silence that had descended like a guillotine blade. "What happens now?"

"I should gut you where you stand, that's what," spat the short knight. "But General Okada was very clear: if the angels turn up, the King wants these people brought back unharmed as prisoners, plague or no plague. So, unless you want to volunteer to hand me your own lungs, it looks like you pair of turncoats have a reprieve ... for now." He turned to Freya, jabbing a finger in Errick's direction. "Can you keep that *thing* under control?"

"Of course," she lied, praying that Errick wouldn't doom them all by flying into another violent frenzy.

The squat knight nodded. "Then get marching — the four of you and your bucket of bolts can lead the way."

He gestured to his men, who fanned out and moved behind Freya's group, wisely keeping their swords in their scabbards for fear of triggering Errick's rage. Freya wondered for a moment if the knights who had betrayed their leader would try to escape, but they seemed resigned to whatever fate awaited them, marching proudly alongside her towards the castle. Errick stumbled mutely along, seeming to understand what was required, while Victor propelled himself effortlessly on his battered hands.

A different company of archers had replaced the first, tracking the group carefully as they approached the castle. Freya suspected the combined bowmen and foot soldiers they'd faced so far represented most of Wilfred's entire military strength — if she was able to turn even a handful more to their cause, perhaps the torturer could yet be dethroned. But, for now, at least, she must acquiesce to whatever welcome the King had prepared for her. She shuddered as she thought of iron maidens and breaking wheels, of dungeons populated by half-skinned corpses.

At the gates, the tall knight she'd seen on the battlements awaited them, this time with his plumed helmet removed and handed to the Unskilled attendant at his side. His face was flat and wide, framed by long black hair, his expression blank yet still conveying disdain in its permanent half-sneer, and in the apathy of his hooded eyes. "Stop," he commanded as they approached, his tone matching his imposing presence; this, surely, was Wilfred's General. Freya met his gaze defiantly; behind him, the Enclave towered like a baleful machine.

"You will proceed to the prison keep," Okada intoned, in a voice that suggested he could envisage no outcome other than compliance. "His Majesty will summon you for an audience after he has inspected the angels' bounty. The plague carrier will be manacled for his own safety." Another attendant appeared from behind the General, carrying a rusted set of chains.

Freya turned to Errick, aghast. How could he bear any more cruelty, any further imprisonment? He returned her gaze and she searched his eyes beseechingly, placing a reassuring hand on his shoulder, feeling like a fraud. He showed no sign of understanding her, but did not struggle as the shackles were clamped around his ankles.

"Follow me," said Okada, and turned to stride back into the castle. Freya and her group obeyed, and she felt her heart shake as they crossed the threshold. Had she ever truly believed she would return here?

When the General reached the foot of the great stone steps, he stopped abruptly, as though suddenly remembering something. "Ah yes," he said over his shoulder. "Gunther, Coborlwitz?"

The two knights who had volunteered to fight for her exchanged glances. "Yes, sir?"

Moving as swiftly as a sudden breeze, two more knights emerged from their hiding places on either side of the Enclave's doors. Their daggers slid across the throats of the traitors before the men could even draw their swords.

"No!" yelled Freya, leaping towards the man on her right as he slumped to the ground. Errick, stirred by her cries, lunged towards the nearest knife-wielder with a roar, but the knight took advantage of his reduced mobility, stepping deftly beyond his reach. Even as Freya cradled the dying man — the one with the eyepatch and broken nose, who stared up at her helplessly, gurgling as blood gushed from his severed artery — the other knights swarmed forward to overwhelm Errick, bundling him to the ground. Victor, too, found himself manhandled, his arms wrenched outwards as he was hoisted from the floor.

General Okada still hadn't turned around. "The price of treason," he sneered, as though narrating the unfolding scene. Two of the knights dragged Freya to her feet, kicking their former comrade to one side; meanwhile, a rope was slipped around Errick's neck, hauling him upright. "And more food for the larder, at least," Okada continued. "Now, then; we may continue."

The General led them up the stairs towards the main courtyard: Errick dragged, Victor carried, and Freya with the tip of a sword pressed into her back. Behind them the two murdered knights lay where they'd fallen, their spreading blood the only part of them still moving.

People were gathered in the square, staring at them from timid huddles. Freya scoured their faces for Maxwell's, but to no avail. The crowd's expressions were difficult to read; some looked aghast at the sight of a plague carrier in their midst, while others seemed outraged that the woman who had brought the angels back with her would be so roughly treated. But no one called out or said anything, except in occasional hushed whispers. She remembered how raucous the same people had been the last time she had passed through the Enclave's gates, and wondered what had been done to render them so fearful, so submissive.

Then she saw the gallows and understood completely.

The scaffold was a simple wooden construction, essentially a raised platform standing about ten feet from the ground, with steps leading up to the top. A knight stood guard close to this bottom section, which was shielded from view by a dark curtain wrapped around it. Despite this screen, there was no doubt about the structure's macabre purpose: on top of the platform were three sturdy-looking gibbets, the noose that hung from each one swaying gently in the soft breeze.

Freya clamped a hand to her lips in horror. The skeletons she had seen outside; had all of them been through this terrible engine, this machine for converting living people to bones? *No*, she corrected herself, *not bones*. This was a mechanism for producing *corpses*; the skinning and butchering of those corpses must be happening down in the kitchens. *Egbert, you bastard,* she thought, and felt suddenly nauseous; it was as though the entire castle had been converted into a factory for the processing of human flesh.

"Keep moving," grunted the knight at her back, the short man, prodding her so roughly with his sword she thought it might pierce her skin. She staggered forwards, tearing her eyes away from the gruesome spectacle.

They crossed to the rear of the castle, where the prison keep loomed above them like a waiting executioner.

***

The General instructed half of his men to return to the gates to await the angels' arrival; the remainder marched them into the depths of the keep. The prison's odour taunted Freya as soon as they descended, a harbinger of the hellish fetor that lurked behind the door of Wilfred's torture chamber. Its stink was like an old enemy that had lain in ambush, patiently awaiting her return.

The cell she'd occupied during her first visit had been one of many, arranged side-by-side along a dank and draughty corridor. There had been only one other prisoner at the time, and she remembered the sound of his agitated muttering, his occasional whimpers during the night, and his despairing cackle when she'd tried to make contact.

This time, the jail was positively bursting. They stumbled along the passageway serenaded by wails and shrieks, and she shrank from the filthy arms that reached for her between the bars, clawing at her and her companions as though their flesh somehow offered salvation.

"These are the coming days' sacrifices," Okada explained, contempt dripping from his voice. "They ought to thank you for the extra sunrise you've granted them: either your angels will bring food to fill the people's bellies, or my dead soldiers will serve the purpose."

"But surely, now the angels are here, these people can be released?" exclaimed Victor.

"That is the King's decision, metal man," sneered the General. "But I suspect I know his majesty's mind: these miscreants have already been judged as criminals, layabouts, and incompetents. To share God's bounty with them would be to squander it."

Freya opened her mouth to retort but realised there was little point arguing with this man. She remembered him from previous banquets, sitting silently while his comrades roared and jeered, a glimmer of smug self-confidence in his half-smile. Unlike the others, who mocked her disfigurement or leered at her womanliness, Okada had never made any remark while she refilled his flagon; indeed, she couldn't remember him as much as shooting her a glance. Perhaps he had long harboured ambitions above the station of a mere knight.

Now that Wilfred had granted them, there was little chance of him speaking a word against his new master.

She turned towards the cells as she passed them, sadness creasing her face at the sight of the unfortunate inside. Every one of the prisoners wore the soiled robes of the Unskilled; the downtrodden, the undervalued, and the weak.

"Don't worry," Okada smirked, misinterpreting her glance. "You won't be thrown in with those ne'er-do-wells — the King has granted you his prison's finest suite."

She ignored him as they approached the end of the corridor. She'd counted perhaps a dozen people in the cells, and wondered what exactly they'd done to invite Wilfred's judgement; perhaps nothing more than catch his eye. She shuddered, unable to stop herself from also wondering how many days their flesh was expected to last.

Then she drew alongside the final cell, and stopped in her tracks. The squat knight behind her clattered into her back, cursing. She didn't care. Freya stood and stared, mouth moving silently as it searched for words.

Gazing back at her from behind the rusted bars was Maxwell.

For a long and terrible moment, his vacant eyes made her wonder if he'd been rendered as catatonic as Errick, if his spirit had been similarly crushed beneath an avalanche of suffering. Then his mouth fell open, his expression caught halfway between a frown of disbelief and a grin of unabashed joy.

"Freya?"

"Maxwell!"

She ran to him, reaching through the bars, her fingertips brushing his shoulders in the beginning of an embrace before she was wrenched roughly away by the knight at her back.

"Didn't you hear the General?" he hissed into her ear. "No need for you to be mixing with this scum." He pushed her aside, and she watched helplessly as the knight jabbed his sword between the bars.

"No!" she cried, as everything seeming to slow, a series of instants stretching out into an unbearable tableau. Maxwell's face, shifting from delight to horror as cold, cruel steel reached for his heart. The General, turning with an irritated expression towards the commotion. The knight, his broad back turned to her, his elbow bent as he thrust the sword towards his helpless victim.

Errick, reaching forward with lightning reflexes, catching the blade in both hands.

Freya stared, uncomprehending, half-dizzied by the maelstrom of emotion.

Then, a shout from Victor. "Errick! Your hands!"

Errick didn't flinch or release his hold. Blood spurted between his fingers as the short knight stared up at him, incredulous. Maxwell, too, seemed stunned into stillness, only having the sense to retreat into the shadows when Okada's voice boomed like thunder. "Enough of this!"

The knight tugged on his sword, trying to wrench it free from Errick's impossible, self-mutilating grip. But Errick clung on grimly, and Freya shuddered at the hellish smile that opened his face like yet another wound.

"Errick, please," she whispered. At once his sadistic smile faded, and the squat knight almost tumbled over as his sword was finally released. Freya gasped at the sight of Errick's blood soaking its blade.

"What's the matter, Horace?" chuckled Okada, seemingly amused by the episode. "Can't handle a woman and a braindead plague bearer?"

The knight scowled and thrust her roughly forwards. She cast one final glance towards Maxwell before her friend disappeared from view; he smiled bravely at her from the gloom, but it was the smile of a man who believed he was already lost to its darkness.

Thirty two

Set apart from the others and occupying the rear section of a large chamber, their cell was indeed more luxurious than the other prisoners' squalid cages; this, however, provided little comfort as its barred door clanged firmly shut. Okada turned to leave immediately, seeming anxious to exit the loathsome tower now that his business there was concluded. He stooped to whisper something to the short knight on his way out, handing him the keys he'd used to secure their cage. While the other soldiers followed their General out of the room, the man called Horace stayed behind, irritably wiping Errick's blood from his sword.

After his comrades had gone, he removed his helmet for the first time. Freya couldn't help but grimace; his face was as squat as his body, crushed into his shoulders as though his neck had collapsed, exposed to some extreme gravitational anomaly. His mouth had the same compressed look, tongue darting in and out of the wide, flat orifice as he spoke, like something trying to escape.

"What are *you* looking at, bitch? Someone with a face like yours isn't in any position to stare."

"Watch your mouth," snapped Victor tersely. "This woman is worth ten thousand of you, little man."

The knight cursed and strode towards the bars, eyes blazing as he pointed his sword towards the robot; but he stopped a few feet away, glancing warily at Errick, who was gazing listlessly across the room towards the flickering light of a wall-mounted torch.

"I shouldn't get too close to a bunch of plague carriers anyway," Horace spat, and turned to lean against the wall. "The General's told me to guard you until further notice, so just keep your mouths shut and don't bother me." He sank to his haunches, placing his helmet to one side.

Freya moved to Errick's side, wincing at the blood that still dripped from her friend's sliced palms. She tore strips from the fabric of her robes and wound them carefully around the wounds. Errick didn't react at all, still seeming fascinated by the flickering torchlight.

Once she had managed to staunch the bleeding, Freya realised that her limbs felt very weary. There was no bed or furniture of any kind inside the cell, so she took up a similar position to their guard, slumping against the back wall. Victor moved to rest alongside her, saying nothing.

"Errick," she whispered. "Why don't you come and sit with us?"

The knight gave no indication that he'd heard, still staring out through the bars. But, after a while, he turned and shuffled towards her, seating himself at her side. After a while, he closed his eyes, seeming almost peaceful for the first time since his rescue from the horrors beneath James's kingdom. She did not flinch when he rested his head against her shoulder; instead, she reached up to gently stroke his long white hair.

Freya did not realise that she had also fallen asleep until she was rudely, unpleasantly, and repulsively awakened.

"What's this?" boomed a cheery voice. "A slumber party?"

She blinked herself awake to the clatter of Horace's armour as their guard scrambled to his feet. "Sir ... your majesty ... I was just..."

"Asleep at your post, yes. Don't worry, I've already lost enough knights for one day." Wilfred seemed to have grown since she last saw him, his ample bulk almost filling the doorway. He was still bald beneath the silver coronet he wore, but his thick moustache was longer, teased into twirled points that he perhaps thought made him appear more regal. "Now put your helmet back on, for God's sake — your ugliness offends me."

Horace looked stung by the insult for a moment, then fumbled the helm back onto his head, standing as tall as his stunted frame would allow as Wilfred strode into the room. "Welcome back, Freya!" he crooned. His wide grin was even more skull-like than his gleaming pate. "To think it's already been fourteen days since we last spoke. A lot has happened since then, that's for sure."

"Yes," she said through clenched teeth as she clambered to her feet. She saw Gideon skulking in the shadows behind his master, like his ever-present shadow, twirling a knife between his fingers. "The Lords all seem to have disappeared, for one thing."

Wilfred chuckled, spreading his hands wide. "Oh, there's no secret there. They were traitors, floundering in the face of God's test. I freely confess that I arranged for Okada to arrest them. It always pays to have ambitious friends."

Freya remembered the strong and noble Lord Valeria, the Warmaster. "And then what happened? Did they end up in your torture chamber, confessing their sins?"

"Goodness, no — I'm not a *sadist*, Freya. Didn't you see the gallows outside? I hung all three of them personally. Oh, you might think it's silly, a king performing his own executions, but I don't trust anyone else to measure the rope properly. It's a very exact science, you know, to perform a humane hanging; one must always abide by the Table of Drops. Too long and their heads are torn clean off, too short and their necks don't break. Then they suffer terribly, twisting at the end of that rope." A malicious glint flickered in the King's eyes. "I'll admit that Cedric might have found himself a foot or two under-measured."

"I take it I passed their bones on my way to the gates," Freya muttered.

"Yes. Waste not, want not, as they say. I seem to recall Egbert making a delightful stew out of them."

Freya closed her eyes, trying not to rise to his goading. She glanced at Errick, who still slumbered at her flank, and then

280

at Victor, brooding on her opposite side, and willed them to remain silent; she may yet have some value to Wilfred, but she suspected he wouldn't need much provocation to consign her friends to the noose, or to whatever vile mechanism the King would conceive to destroy Victor.

"Thankfully the angels have returned," she said, trying to change the subject. "So you won't need your hangman's ropes any longer."

"A neat segue," Wilfred retorted. Behind him, she realised Gideon was watching her from the gloom, the mute torturer's piercing stare making her insides squirm. "The angels' return is precisely what I'm here to discuss with you."

She tensed, sensing that she needed to tread very carefully. "Have the angels deposited their bounty?" she asked.

"That's precisely the issue. They have placed their carts outside the gates, a dozen of them in total. But the creatures haven't departed. They're all just standing there, waiting."

Freya blinked, surprised. "Waiting for what?"

Wilfred's smile looked as though it was about to fall off his face and shatter on the floor. "I don't *know*. I assumed *you* did. You negotiated their arrival, after all." He regarded her sceptically, his eyes probing for a weakness.

"Perhaps they just want you to say thanks," she said with a cheerless smile of her own.

"Or perhaps they want something else. Something you know about, but are not telling me."

Was this her chance? Could she pretend she understood 'God's' will, try to negotiate her friends' survival? She was not skilled in such politicking, in manipulating the actions of others like some devious puppet master. If she said the wrong thing she was just as likely to get them all killed. "I do not claim to second-guess the designs of God," she said eventually. "I know only that He told me He would send the angels, and He has."

Wilfred's eyes narrowed to pitiless slits. "I could kill him, you know." He pointed at Errick, who had slumped into the corner, snoring audibly. "If I give the order, your idiot bodyguard will be turning purple at the end of a rope within fifteen minutes."

"I don't doubt it. But if you harm any of us, do you think God will be happy? Perhaps the angels are seeking proof that we are being well-treated."

The King's expression looked like something had burst inside him, leaking poison into the muscles of his face. "You're in no position to bargain here," he hissed. There was a noise behind him, the sound of clanking armour. Gideon stepped aside to allow Okada into the room, plumed helmet now hiding his handsome features.

"Your majesty," said the General, with the air of someone battling to retain their composure. "There is ... trouble, in the courtyard."

"Then deal with it," snapped Wilfred. "I'm busy discussing matters with our homecoming queen."

"It's the people, sire," Okada insisted. "The sight of all that food waiting outside ... they're demanding that you open the gates immediately. Some of them are even trying to fight their way in here."

"Then shower the ungrateful wretches with arrows!" Wilfred retorted, his voice boiling with barely contained anger.

Okada leaned towards his monarch, whispering something into his ear. Wilfred's moustache twitched as he listened, his face turning an alarming shade of purple. When he turned back towards her, any vestige of his despicable joviality had evaporated. "It seems I must remind my unruly subjects that they owe me their lives," he snarled. "We will continue this discussion later. In the meantime, you'd do well to remember that there are worse fates in the Enclave than hanging." He turned, twirling his cloak theatrically as he stormed out of the room, Gideon and Okada trailing in his wake.

Horace watched them go, then turned to face her.

"You definitely seem to know how to push his buttons," he said, something approaching admiration in his tone. "But now I think I know how to push yours." His expression darkened, then he too hurried out of the chamber.

Thirty three

Freya knew immediately what Horace was going to do. She knew, and simultaneously she knew that it was all her fault. She'd put Maxwell in grave danger the moment she'd spoken to him through the bars of his cell.

Now her friend stood proud and upright as he was bundled into the room, but she could see the fear behind his strained expression, the trembling in his limbs as he was forced forwards. Horace marched Maxwell right up to the bars, the curved blade of the knight's sword matching the shape of his triumphant grin.

I'm sorry, said Freya and Maxwell's eyes to each other.

"If I'd told his majesty about your friend here, he'd have been dangling by the neck by now," Horace crowed. "But I thought I deserved some fun of my own first."

She felt nausea rise in her throat as she imagined the knight's sword bursting suddenly through Maxwell's belly. "Please don't kill him," she said helplessly. "Wilfred would wish to use this leverage against me, for my ... for my knowledge of the angels' plans."

Horace snorted. "You said yourself, you have no idea what they're up to. But you're right — if his majesty found out I'd killed your friend here, my bones would be joining the pile outside. So don't worry; killing's not on the agenda."

He grabbed Maxwell, hauling him backwards and slamming him against the wall. Freya watched, aghast, as Horace pointed his sword first at Maxwell's throat, then traced a slow line down his chest, past his abdomen, stopping at his groin. "Lovers, were you? Filthy Unskilled, fumbling in the servants' quarters? Maybe I should just slice this off to make sure this heartbreaker can't go putting it about anymore."

"Please, I—" Maxwell stammered, before Horace stepped smartly towards him, ramming his gauntleted fist into the

Unskilled's stomach. Maxwell sank to his knees, doubling over in pain.

"Stop!" Freya begged. "Please don't hurt him — he hasn't done anything to you!"

Horace glanced sideways at her. "Not so smart-mouthed now, are you?"

"Perhaps you would consider a trade," Victor interrupted, pulling himself towards the front of the cage. "Return this poor man to his cell and take me as your plaything instead."

"Victor, no," Freya breathed. But the fire that smouldered in the robot's eyes silenced her. She felt overwhelmed, crushed by the weight of the kindness she had found amongst the world's endless cruelty.

"Not a chance," Horace spat. "You just want me to let you out of there so you can do something sneaky. No, the only one I'll be letting out is *you*." He pointed the sword towards Freya like an accusing finger.

She closed her eyes, realisation dawning like a crimson sunrise. The knight produced the keys that Okada had given him, jangling them like a proudly displayed trophy. "I'm going to throw you these," he rasped in his foul, guttural voice. "And you're going to very quietly unlock the door, step outside, and lock it again. If you or this metal cripple try anything, or if you try to wake the sleeping beauty in the corner, I swear I'll cut this simpering cretin's arms off."

"And then what?" Freya hissed, already knowing the answer. Horace's grotesque mouth widened even further as he smiled, revealing teeth that looked as rotten as old bones. He said nothing, instead loosening his belt straps, allowing his chausses and the breeches beneath to fall to the ground.

"You bastard," snarled Maxwell, launching himself towards the knight before Freya could say anything to stop him. Horace turned, swinging another vicious blow towards her friend, this time catching him across the face with a right hook. Freya felt the acid sting of tears as Maxwell crumpled to the ground. Horace, his horrid genitals as squat and malformed as he was, pointed his sword at Maxwell's face. "Get in the corner, and don't fucking move again."

Freya caught her friend's gaze. *Just do it,* she pleaded with her eyes. *Once he lets me out, I've got a plan.*

She only wished that was true.

With pain both physical and mental etched across his face, Maxwell nodded, and edged back into the shadows. Horace kept his sword trained on him, watching her all the while, his vile grin unwavering.

"Don't do this, Freya," said Victor. She was too ashamed to reply as Horace tossed her the keys, and she bent her arm uncomfortably to test each one in the lock. Eventually, she found one that rotated the ancient tumblers and unlocked the cell door. Victor stared up at her, stock-still, as though frozen in indecision. Perhaps he was about to holler Errick awake so the two of them could rush their tormentor; she willed him not to, willed him to understand that Maxwell's life was worth so much more than her self-respect.

Victor did nothing as she stepped outside, and turned to secure the lock once again. She faced Horace, who beamed exultantly. "Now come here and get on your knees," he sneered, lowering his sword. "I don't want to see your mangled face any more than you want to see mine."

She wondered what it would feel like if she bit off his disgusting appendage. Whether she'd be able to wrestle the sword from him before he could kill them both.

Too many gambles, too many coin flips.

"And then you'll return us both to our cells, unharmed?" she asked, nauseated by what she was about to do.

"You have my word of honour," Horace smirked, raising a hand in mock salute. Then a shadow seemed to peel itself away from the darkness, moving behind him.

Horace must have caught the look in Freya's eyes, because his smile collapsed in on itself as he began to turn, raising his sword arm. He was far, far too slow.

Seeming to conjure it out of thin air, the tall, slender silhouette produced a dagger, and drew it savagely across Horace's throat. The movement was not swift; the blade sawed back and forth as it sliced through flesh, gristle, artery, and tendon. Horace made an appalling, underwater noise as blood bubbled up and spewed out of the wound, his sword clattering to the ground. Gurgling, the knight sank to his knees, staring up at her with horror, disbelief, and hatred writhing in his eyes. A thousand curses formed and died on his gore-flecked lips. In the end, all he could do was cough, spraying her with blood and spittle, before he pitched forward onto his hideous face.

Behind him, Gideon wiped his knife with a cloth, eyes glowing toxic green, fixed on her.

***

Wilfred's assistant was quicker than Freya, quicker perhaps even than Errick. His limbs seemed to operate like separate, sentient beings as he snatched the keys from her hand, stuffing them into the pocket of his jerkin as he grabbed her arm and twisted it, effortlessly pulling her towards him, rotating her so that he could press his dagger against her neck. She felt her body tense, her heart freezing as she waited for the agony of the dagger piercing her larynx — but it never came. For now, it seemed Gideon's knife was sated; instead of murdering her, he shouldered her through the doorway as Victor's protestations resounded in her ears.

She knew the torturer was a mute, so there was little point asking him what was going on. Instead, she stayed quiet, trying to concentrate on the route he was taking through the maze-like prison, in case she could elude him and flee back to her companions; but, jerked along a series of rapid right angles, she was soon hopelessly lost. They did not pass the other cells again, instead veering off down a narrow side passage, then another, each tunnel seeming darker and more cramped than the last. She felt herself dragged right, then right again, then left, jerked and driven towards an unknown fate. As every turn took her further from her friends, she thought about how they had all suffered for her: Maxwell cruelly bludgeoned, Victor maimed, Errick robbed of his mind.

Perhaps they were better off without her.

After several more minutes of the tortuous journey, a wooden door loomed in front of them. Gideon kept her arm pinioned to her back as he pushed past her, clamping the dagger in his teeth to free his other arm. He was thin but tough, the muscles of his forelimb knotting as he heaved on the door's iron ring, wrenching it open with one hand. With his attention divided, she tried to yank herself free, sensing an opportunity to escape — but his grip was as strong as one of his torture devices. He smiled at her as though commending her attempt, exposing tobacco-stained teeth even more unpleasant than Horace's. Then he dragged her through the door, propelling her into a large room.

A large and familiar room.

"The kitchens?" she gasped, staring around her at Egbert's old domain. As if on cue, the Kitchenmaster himself emerged from an antechamber, looking as sweaty and hassled as she remembered.

"I've packed as much as I can," he huffed, stuffing loaf-sized parcels into the cloth sack he was carrying as though to illustrate his point. "You'd better be right about her." He jabbed a fat finger at Freya, who was momentarily too horrified to respond; the parcels were wrapped in brown paper, but their contents were visibly wet, leaking dark, unspeakable fluids.

Gideon shoved her roughly away from him, then gestured with his knife towards the stairs, frowning a question at his apparent ally. Tables and other furniture had been haphazardly piled there, forming a barricade.

"No, none of them have tried to get in yet, thank God," babbled the chef, sounding close to panic. "Last I saw they were all still trying to break down the door of the Lords' tower. Wilfred and Okada are holed up in there; the other knights have surrendered already!"

She thought Gideon might be concerned to hear such news about his master, but the torturer barely batted an eyelid. "What's going on?" she stammered, finding her voice.

Egbert turned to her with fear and mistrust on his face. "The King sent some knights out to collect the food, and to speak with your angels. Those things slaughtered them with their bare hands, and stormed inside before we could shut the gates." *James*, she thought, stomach churning with dread. *What have you done?*

"Gideon thinks they'll let us go free if we've got you as a hostage," the chef continued, voice quavering with terror, threatening to ascend into the hysterical screech she remembered from every banquet when the demand had outstripped his cooking speed. "So we're about to make a break for it, and you're coming with us. Gideon, are you *sure* there aren't any more of those secret passages? One that could just lead us straight outside?"

She stared at the Kitchenmaster, incredulous. "You really did it, didn't you?" she sneered, unable to disguise her contempt. "I always thought you were a lowlife, Egbert, but I never thought you'd stoop to cooking your own people. Why didn't you *resist* him? Do something brave for once in your miserable—" Her words were cut off as Gideon struck her a cruel backhand blow across the face. She staggered backwards, but did not allow herself to fall. Her eyes met his, trying to stare shame and guilt into him, but she saw no remorse whatsoever in those slime-coloured depths.

"Open your mouth again and I'll gut you with my cleaver as soon as we're beyond the walls," ranted Egbert, but despite his imposing size, his words held no threat whatsoever. He was a frightened, weak man, bullied into unspeakable acts by a bogus king; but that was no excuse for what he'd allowed himself to become.

The charcutier to a cannibal tyrant.

Egbert hoisted the repulsive sack over his shoulder. "Anyway, enough of this — we need to go."

In a trice, Gideon darted across to her, driving her arm painfully up her spine once again. He pointed at her with the knife. *You'll have to do it. I'm busy watching this one.*

"For fuck's sake," Egbert spat, dropping the sack to the ground with a moist splat. Cursing and muttering, he began to dismantle the barricade that he and Gideon must have erected when they realised the castle had been breached. Then he stopped. For a moment, the cook stood stock still, face as white as his apron. Then she heard it: a muffled crashing sound from beyond the blockade.

The sound of something breaking through from the other side.

"Oh God, no," Egbert whimpered, staggering backwards and collapsing onto his bloated backside. "What should we do?" He jerked his head towards Gideon, as though the torturer somehow had the power to spirit them to safety. Gideon was behind her, so she couldn't see his scarred face, had no way of knowing what instruction he conveyed with a tilt of his head or a flash of his poisonous eyes.

Egbert seemed to understand, abandoning his appalling sack of provisions as he scrambled to his feet and wrenched a torch from a bracket on the wall. She felt herself spun towards the rear of the chamber, and at first thought Gideon was going to bundle her back into the tunnels through which they'd come. Then, when he changed direction and a familiar set of stone steps yawned ahead of them, leading downwards like an expectant gullet, she realised where she was being taken.

In his desperation, Gideon was fleeing towards the Pit.

Thirty four

"Good thinking," gabbled Egbert as they descended. "Hide down here while they search the kitchens, then make our escape later. Maybe we could even bury ourselves under the garbage if we need to ... it won't be easy, but you know what they say about survivors..."

Gideon released his grip on Freya, rounding on Egbert and thrusting him bodily against the wall. In a split second, his knife was poised millimetres from the cook's eyeball. Egbert froze; even the sweat beading his brow seemed momentarily suspended in place. Slowly, deliberately, Gideon raised his other hand, pressing a finger to his lips. Egbert nodded his understanding. The torturer studied him for a moment longer, as though weighing up whether the chef could be of any more use to him. Then he released his grip, and the Kitchenmaster sagged to his haunches, breathing a deep sigh of relief as he wiped the perspiration from his face with the back of a flabby arm.

Gideon didn't bother to take hold of her again; with the two of them blocking the narrow staircase, there was no way she could proceed but downwards. She turned and walked, desperately trying to figure out her next move. The sounds of distant crashing grew louder, then stopped abruptly, perhaps signalling that the angels had broken into the room above. Maybe she could call out to them, scream her whereabouts, and hope they saved her before Gideon's knife ended up in her neck.

She bit her lip and descended silently. For all she knew, James's foot soldiers were here to slaughter everyone in the Enclave.

Not a God. A thing. A thing they'd made, and given a name. People had created it, not the other way around.

More noises from the kitchen above, the sound of frenzied searching, of furniture being tossed aside as the room was ransacked. Gideon sped up, grabbing her once again and forcing her to match his pace. Egbert wheezed breathlessly as he followed behind. Their footsteps echoed as they ran, and Freya found herself unsure whether she was hearing the reflected sounds of their escape or the footfalls of their pursuers; either way, Gideon drove her faster, faster, until she thought she might slip and stumble headfirst down into the great reeking orifice, falling into the hole like some discarded, half-eaten fragment.

After what seemed an impossibly long descent, they reached the end of the staircase. The stench seemed to have taken on an even keener potency than she remembered, and she gagged as she imagined the offcuts that had been tossed into the Pit since her departure: human entrails, bladders, testicles, eyeballs. She looked at Egbert with renewed disgust, but the cook ignored her, seeming consumed by fear; his eyes swivelled in their sockets, jowls quivering as he muttered soundlessly to himself. He looked like he might be about to have a heart attack.

Gideon looked little better. The torturer was stock-still, listening intently, his body so tensed it seemed as though it might rupture. She joined him in trying to discern any sounds from above, but she heard nothing aside from the thunderous drumroll of her heartbeat.

Then, suddenly: footsteps, very fast, exploded down the stairs towards them.

Lightning-quick, Gideon reached for her — but this time she was a step ahead of him, already moving away, hurrying around the perimeter of the Pit. He scowled, baring his dirt-brown teeth, gesturing to Egbert to circle the opposite side. Then he followed her tentatively, perhaps not wanting to slip and fall into the unspeakable depths below.

Freya reached the midpoint between her two captors and stopped, staring down into the muck. Its stink was almost caustic, searing her eyes and clawing at her throat; it was all she could do not to vomit. Was she really considering jumping down into it? Was it worth it? The prospect of wading through the sludge might deter Gideon for a moment or two, but surely not the angels that were thundering down the stairs towards them. And even if some fluke of physics dislodged a clot of filth, and she was sucked down and away through a widening sinkhole, the only fate that awaited her was the agony of drowning amongst the sewage when she was disgorged into the ocean far below.

She glanced right, and saw Egbert edging towards her, his face cast a hellish crimson in the light of his flickering torch; to her left, Gideon was creeping along the wall like a spreading cancer. At her back was merciless stone; ahead of her was the Pit, and beyond it the stairwell, the sound of descending footsteps growing louder, closer. She stared, wondering how many angels would emerge from the gloom. What would they do? Would they know her? Did James communicate his instructions to those poor, enslaved souls in the same way he'd spoken to her, like some dreadful parasite squirming inside their brains?

She stared, and Gideon lunged for her, and she pivoted at the last moment and launched herself towards Egbert, knocking the fat man off balance with a desperate shoulder tackle. He shrieked, arms pinwheeling as he tottered on the rim of the effluence-choked abyss, the torch clattering to the ground as he clawed maniacally at the air. As he plummeted, wailing, into the slime, something reached the bottom of the staircase, bursting into the room with its deafening banshee scream, an inhuman battle cry like the sound of ten thousand dying soldiers.

Gideon had begun to make another flailing grab for her, but he froze in place before he could reach her, as momentarily transfixed as Freya. Facing them from the foot of the staircase, hoisting a sword as though he meant to use it to slice the world in half, was Errick.

***

Gideon managed to shake himself free of his stupor moments before Freya did, and succeeded in grabbing hold of her once again, his grip as firm as iron manacles. The stink of tobacco that suffused his skin and clothing was almost strong enough to block out the reek from the Pit itself. Once again she felt her arm bent into an excruciating angle, the torturer's blade pressed against her throat. She wondered if it was the same knife he'd used to flay Sir Thomas, and felt rage and nausea frothing in her stomach.

Gideon could not speak, but his terms were clear: *let me out of here or I gut this woman like a fresh carcass.* Egbert, meanwhile, was floundering in the festering trash below, screeching in horror as he tried to scramble across to the staircase. Freya ignored him; instead, she stared at Errick, whose eyes were fixed on hers, and dared to believe that he seemed to truly *see* her for the first time since his rescue.

"Errick!" she called, before Gideon clamped a rough hand across her mouth.

"Freya," the knight replied, and she knew then that he was restored to her, and felt tears of joy spring to her eyes. "Release her, miscreant," Errick continued, eyes iridescent with rage as he addressed Gideon, "and I'll let you go free."

She felt the shake of the torturer's head at her back, the coarse stubble of his chin snagging in her hair. *He still thinks he needs me to escape the angels,* she realised. She wondered what was happening above them, whether James's soldiers had succeeded in breaching the tower. Maybe Gideon's master was even now being torn limb from limb as his castle's defences crumbled.

295

"Release her, or you and this fat oaf will die," Errick snarled, pointing his sword at Egbert, who was cowering on the Pit's encircling stairs. The curved blade was slick with blood; if it was the same weapon Horace had once carried, then it was probably Errick's own. Egbert seemed terrified by the sight of the weapon aimed at his face, and staggered backwards, toppling back into the slurry with a squelch.

Gideon said nothing, of course; but neither did he release his grip on her, secured as tightly as one of his torture implements. For a long moment, the standoff seemed intractable. Then the knife moved from her neck to her chest, and she gasped in pain as Gideon drove it through the fabric of her robe and into the flesh just below her breast, drawing blood. She saw Errick's eyes blaze with fury, felt her blood boiling at the sight of its own wanton spillage. *How dare he? This sadist … this monster's underling…*

She bit down savagely on Gideon's fingers, wondering as she did so whether he was able to scream, feeling deeply satisfied when she heard that he was. Before he could retaliate, she pitched forwards, launching herself away from him and down into the Pit.

That was the only cue Errick needed. He tore around the perimeter of the hole, racing towards Gideon, whose dagger suddenly appeared woefully inadequate, a sapling alongside a great redwood. The torturer's eyes widened, the spectre of his imminent death reflected in their noxious green.

But Gideon was a man of tricks, and he still had another. As Errick advanced, Gideon lunged for the torch, still smouldering where it had fallen. Aiming it like a javelin, he hurled it down into the bog below. It landed with a splat, the flame immediately extinguished.

The chamber was plunged into total darkness.

***

Freya did not see Gideon dive into the Pit after her, but she heard the wet plop of his landing, inches from where she stood. She pulled away from him, stumbling through the quagmire, but he followed the sound, and she felt one of his flailing arms swipe against her shoulder. Another splash heralded Errick's arrival in the muck close by, the knight calling out to her in the darkness. "Freya, where are you?"

She sensed Gideon jerking away from her, scurrying towards the source of the sound. *No, Errick! You've given away your position!* The torturer moved as softly as a ghost, but could not entirely silence the vile sucking sounds his footfalls made in the slime. She felt the shifting of air as Errick scythed his sword about him. "Stay away, Freya!" the knight cried. "I don't want to hurt you by mistake!"

She heard more scampering footsteps, the treacherous whispers of a smaller blade moving rapidly through the air. She heard Errick's muted grunt of pain as Gideon's weapon danced its terrible jig across his flesh; the loss of sight seemed to suit the torturer more than it did his opponent. She heard the clang of steel on steel as the knight heaved his sword once again, beating his attacker away. Again came the knife, and again the sound of slicing air, slicing fabric, slicing skin. Another swing of the sword, this time cleaving nothing but the Pit's foul air.

Then a meatier, altogether more visceral sound. A sound that might have been a dagger sliding into an arm, a leg, a stomach. A heart.

"No!" she cried, throwing herself towards the unseen duel, not caring whether she was caught in its violence, knowing only that she had to do something to protect her friend. She heard a groan, the squelch of someone sinking to their knees in the muck, the barely perceptible footfalls of a predator circling its wounded victim.

She flung herself at the patch of blackness she thought contained Gideon, a shadow within a shadow. She felt herself collide with something, felt it driven into the mulch beneath her weight, wincing as her throat was immediately clamped in an iron grip.

Then the chamber was flooded with light.

Freya beheld Gideon sprawled beneath her, green eyes like twin pools of acid, frothing with hatred. She turned and saw Victor, suspended in Maxwell's arms at the foot of the staircase, the robot's eyes blazing illumination into the room. She watched Egbert, who had ascended the staircase in the darkness, stagger backwards in shock, wailing as he plummeted into the Pit for the third time in as many minutes.

She saw Errick kneeling at their side, the torturer's knife jutting from his flank. Blood oozed from the deep, dreadful wound, and his head had sagged forwards onto his chest, as though he had fallen asleep.

"Errick," she gasped, staring in horror at the motionless form of her friend. This couldn't be it, could not be the warrior's end; not here, half-submerged in this godforsaken sewer. *She would not allow it.* "Errick!"

Gideon tightened his hold on her neck, heaving her sideways off his chest and into the sludge. He rolled on top of her, pressing her down, lips peeled back into a snarl as venomous as his gaze; behind his crumbling teeth, the rotten stump of his tongue wriggled excitedly.

"Errick!" Victor echoed her cry of disbelief as Maxwell bore him towards the stairs. Their friend simply knelt, oblivious, and bled.

"I'm sorry," Freya whispered as her vision darkened. Gideon continued to choke her, his intention to keep her alive seemingly overcome by bloodlust.

James. This is the world you made for us.

Then, as though an electric current surged suddenly through his body, Errick lurched to his feet. His sword had fallen beside him; instead of picking it up, he reached across his body and yanked the dagger out of his abdomen, turning grimly towards them. Blood seeped from the wound in his side, and his chest and arms were criss-crossed with fresh lacerations. He looked like something from a nightmare, a monster that had assembled itself from the Pit's discarded offcuts.

The torturer had released his grip on Freya's throat, scrambling to his feet, but this time his speed was not enough. The knight fell upon him like a swooping dragon.

Gideon screamed for a second time, the last sound he would ever make. His cry was cut off as his own blade smashed its way through his ribcage and into his black heart.

***

Gideon crumpled into a sorry heap, like a bundle of tobacco-stained rags. Errick collapsed seconds later, whatever renewed vigour had flooded through him dissipating suddenly into the muck. But Maxwell was there to catch him as he sagged backwards, and together he and Freya helped the knight hobble across to the staircase, where they used torn strips of his robes to stem the flow of blood from the ugly hole Gideon's knife had made in his side.

"We need to get out of here," said Victor, who was resting at the bottom of the steps where Maxwell had left him. "That wound needs urgent attention." *Thanks to the Pit, it's probably riddled with infection too,* Freya reflected grimly.

"Come on, we need to get you up these stairs," she said with as much brightness as she could muster. The sharp intakes of breath Errick made with every faltering step told her how difficult the task would be for him. She had no idea how they would get him all the way back up to the kitchens.

Yes, you do. Just like how you came face to face with God: one step at a time.

Taking one arm around each of their shoulders, Freya and Maxwell managed to carry him up and out of the Pit, pausing to rest when they reached the top. She glanced downwards, frowning when she saw Victor waiting at the bottom of the steps.

"Aren't you coming?"

"He wrecked his arms yanking open the bars of the cage," Maxwell explained. "That's why we were late. Errick ran off after you, but I had to carry this one; he's heavy, for a man with no legs."

Victor looked up at her, light still streaming from his eyes, and her heart went out to him, to this loyal creature with his ravaged face and four destroyed limbs. Just like Errick, the robot had once again grievously damaged himself to save her.

She saw something move, and remembered Egbert. The chef skulked amongst the garbage, eyeing them furtively, as though trying to weigh up whether he could overpower such a weakened group. Freya felt rage coursing through her, like fire in her veins; the same fire that had scourged Asyla and sent a giant toppling to his doom. Before anyone could react, she hurtled back down the steps, dashing past Victor and out across the slime. It took her only a few seconds to find it, hidden amongst the detritus: Errick's sword, formerly Horace's. She snatched it from the filth and turned to point its blade at Egbert, whose eyes bulged as wide as two of his serving-plates.

"*You*," she snarled. "You will carry him. If you don't, I'll butcher you like you butchered your fellow castlefolk."

Egbert was almost a foot taller than her and twice as wide, but his expression told her he was in no doubt about the truth of her words. He shuffled meekly towards the stairs, stooping to pick up Victor in his flabby hands. Freya kept the sword aimed at his broad back, marching him up to join the others.

She found them staring into the face of an angel.

Thirty five

The creature stood at the bottom of the stairs, regarding them impassively. Freya realised she had never seen one of them this close-up before, and gasped at its size; it towered above them, taller and wider than the brawniest of the Enclave's knights, pristine armour gleaming in the light that streamed from Victor's eyes. Yet she knew, now, that beneath the splendour of those plates was nothing more than a prisoner, a soul tortured and lost in Raoul's terrible dungeon, condemned to bear the burden of its apparel for eternity.

Freya held her breath, wondering if the warrior intended to attack them. Egbert cowered backwards, whimpering at the sight of it, but Freya stood firm, pressing the sword into his spine. "Do not move an inch," she hissed. She glanced at Maxwell and saw that he was staring in awe at the new arrival from his seat on the rough stone floor. Errick's head was cradled in his lap, the knight's eyes now closed, his breathing ragged as he slept; she hoped he had succumbed merely to fatigue, and not to his dreadful injuries. At his side, Gideon's knife lay where he'd dropped it, a cruel reminder of the severity of her friend's wounds.

"Please," Freya called out, directing her words towards the angel. "This man will die if we don't get help. We need to get him upstairs."

For a moment, the sentinel was motionless, not even seeming to breathe. She wondered how much control the people trapped inside had over their actions; whether the suit was something like Victor, a machine with a mind of its own. Or perhaps they were merely vessels, jerked like marionettes to the opacities of James's will.

With a loud clanking sound — the sound of metal grinding against metal, the sound of worlds being ground slowly to dust — the angel moved forwards. Freya's breath caught in her throat as it advanced towards Errick and Maxwell. Fear writhed in her friend's face as the creature approached him, but he held his position bravely, keeping Errick as comfortable as he could.

Slowly, gently, the angel stooped towards the stricken knight. As effortlessly as though it was gathering fallen leaves, it scooped him up, placing him over one brutish shoulder. Then it turned, heading back towards the staircase.

"*March*," she commanded, prodding Egbert forward. "Maxwell, take Gideon's knife and follow behind us. If this tub of lard tries anything, stick it in his belly."

Maxwell looked visibly shocked by her pitiless words but did as he was bid, gingerly picking up the dagger as though it was something diseased. She couldn't see the chef's face, but all the colour seemed to have drained from the flesh of his arms and neck, his skin turning as grey as rotten meat.

The strange sextet ascended: the angel carrying Errick, Egbert carrying Victor, Freya and Maxwell behind. The angel's pace was deceptively fast, and she realised how exhausted she was, how every upward step felt like an ordeal. She wondered how many steps she'd taken since she first set foot outside the Enclave. *How many steps had brought her there in the first place, steps she could still scarcely remember? Steps entwined with Raoul's, and with the fate of a machine called James, and ... and with something else, something on the edge of her memory, still hidden in the mist.*

She saw Errick's blood seeping onto the angel's shoulder, smearing its white plates with crimson. "Hurry up!" she cried, and Egbert yelped as she poked the sword roughly between his shoulder blades.

After what felt like an eternity, they reached the kitchens. On the opposite side of the chamber, she saw the scattered remnants of the barricade through which Errick had clawed his way to rescue her. She wondered how he'd known where to find her. Perhaps he hadn't. She realised how lucky they were to be reunited, how overjoyed she was that his mind had been restored.

It would all be for nothing if he died.

The angel led them across the room, past Egbert's discarded sack, which had leaked a repulsive reddish puddle onto the floor. They reached the stairs that led up to the Great Hall, and again she felt the weight of memories crashing through her, of knights and Nobles summoning her to their tables, demanding more wine, or more beer, or an explanation for her scar.

After what she'd seen, after the magnificence of James's glass palace, the Hall did not seem particularly great anymore. She shuddered as they marched past tables that, in recent days, had doubtless borne platters of human flesh. The Enclave no longer felt like her home, but like a ghoulish imitation, like something irreparably violated.

The Hall was connected to the rest of the castle by many doors and corridors, like a vital organ that pulsated at the Enclave's centre. From here they could proceed to the servants' quarters, or to the grander chambers occupied by the Nobles, or perhaps to the conference room where the Lords had once squabbled and schemed. Instead, the angel navigated towards the courtyard. The final wooden door hung open, broken from its hinges, and she imagined the overwhelming power of the angels, how impossible it would be to resist them if their energies were turned towards destruction.

Following the creature, they stepped out into the daylight.

***

The sun hung high in the sky, watching them from behind wisps of cloud like some clandestine voyeur. The scene it illuminated was one of ruthless, efficient conquest.

In one corner of the courtyard, around a dozen captured knights were gathered, surrounded by a score of angels that had arranged themselves in an outward-facing, impenetrable circle. In the opposite corner, a similar number of the knights' dead comrades had been stacked, those ordered by Wilfred to attempt to halt the angels' progress, consigned to their doom by a cruel king. Freya felt sorrow and anger rise in her chest; their deaths had achieved nothing.

The door to the Lords' tower hung open, the monarch's last defences easily breached.

A crowd had gathered, large enough to be the entire remaining population of the Enclave, aside from those still languishing in the dungeon. They watched from the courtyard's perimeter with fear and fascination on their faces, their gazes torn between the arrival of Freya and the spectacle of their fallen king. Wilfred had been dragged to the centre of the square, forced to his knees by the angel that towered over him. Alongside him, Okada was similarly subjugated, a second angel holding the General in place with a single huge hand clamped onto his shoulder. The gallows cast its long shadow across the defeated men, its nooses twitching in the breeze as though hungry for fresh throats.

She stared around her, unsure what was about to happen. Then she realised that every angel, including the one carrying Errick, had turned to face her. They stared expectantly, a question in their frozen faces. Then, to her utter bewilderment, every one of them sank to one knee, moving in unison as though they were appendages of the same consciousness. The crowd gasped, and she heard whispers and mutterings rippling through it.

Then someone shouted, "Hail the Queen!" Before she could do anything, before she could find the words to deny this mistaken honour, the cry was taken up, echoing jubilantly from the lips of the assembled castlefolk like a solution to their woes.

"Hail the Queen!"

"No ... I don't..."

"Hail the Queen!" Their reply was undeniable, insistent.

"Please, I need ... I can't—"

"*Hail the Queen!*" The deafening chorus drowned out her pleas.

A shadow passed overhead, and she glanced upwards; there, amongst the distant clouds, a long and sinuous shape curved and wheeled in the sky. It might have been a trick of the light; or it might have been a dragon, impossibly vast and unfathomably powerful. As though responding to her gaze, words took shape in her head, as cold and cruel as newly formed ice.

"What will you do now, Queen Freya?"

She stared about her in desperation, searching the faces of the expectant congregation. "Where is the Ailmaster?" she cried. "Please! We have need of Frances' skills!" For a moment she thought she would be ignored, her entreaties lost in the cacophony of their exultation. But the cheers faded, and the crowd parted as Frances forced her way forwards, and Freya breathed a sigh of relief — at least Wilfred hadn't been stupid enough to kill and eat the castle's only doctor.

"This man is dying," Freya said, gesturing towards Errick, who was still slumped across the shoulder of the kneeling angel. "Please take him to the infirmary and..." *And bring him back to me.* "And see that his wounds are treated."

The Ailmaster was a slender, auburn-haired woman, her face kindly and freckled. Freya wondered if she would baulk at the idea of ministering to a plague carrier, but she merely nodded dumbly, looking half-unsure whether what was happening was real at all, or the meanderings of some strange dream.

"Follow us," Freya commanded, and Errick's angel rose to its feet. She turned towards the broken door at their backs, remembering the route to the infirmary, recalling the countless times she had cleaned its tiled floors and sweat-soaked beds.

"But what of your prisoners?" came the voice in her mind. *"The man that desecrated your home ... the warrior that fought for him ... the monster that carved and cooked your friends. The angels await your command, and your subjects demand justice."* The voice was

like a blade, maliciously twisted. *"Or you could just leave them here ... perhaps the people will try to take the law into their own hands, and the angels will be forced to suppress them. Your grand coronation will be marked with bloodshed."*

"I never asked for a coronation, you bastard," she hissed.

"Neither did I."

Freya froze in place, body and brain rent by indecision. *Errick ... all I want right now is to be by your side, to hold your hand.*

"You think me so monstrous, for how I used my power. I will be interested to see how you deal with even a sliver of it."

She turned to Frances. "Take him," she whispered and watched as the physician led the angel back into the castle, bearing her friend out of sight.

Swallowing her anxiety, Freya turned back towards the courtyard. The crowd had fallen silent, some of them dropping to their knees, mirroring the poses of the angels. Others still stood, scepticism and anticipation jostling for control over their expressions. She fixed her gaze on Egbert, who had lowered Victor to the ground, his arms not strong enough to carry the robot any longer.

"Go and kneel beside your king," she commanded, pointing with her sword at the humbled forms of Wilfred and Okada. A bloodthirsty cheer erupted from the congregation as Egbert trudged helplessly towards his masters, eyes darting wildly about in a renewed frenzy of terror. As he dropped obediently to his knees, a new chant began, spreading around the square like an uncontrolled blaze.

"Hang them! Hang them! Hang them!"

Freya looked grimly at the gallows. The breeze had dropped, and the three nooses hung in place as though standing to attention.

"Hang them! Hang them!"

Three nooses, three necks.

"Hang them! Hang them!"

Three men who required no trial to prove their culpability, or the severity of their crimes.

"Hang them!" shrilled the crowd.

"Hang them," echoed the voice that had invaded her brain.

"Silence!" Freya shouted, anger adding steel to her voice, compelling a respectful hush upon the baying mob. "Has Wilfred turned you all into monsters? Have you not seen more suffering than you can tolerate?"

The people shuffled awkwardly, eyes downcast. None dared defend themselves against her challenge.

"There will be no hangings. Not ever again. These men will be banished to the wastes, to wander and scavenge for survival while they reflect upon their evils."

The silence hung thickly, apart from the whistle of the rising wind. The nooses jerked, dancing their outrage.

Then a voice. "Yes! Let the plague take them!"

Freya closed her eyes, realising how much work was ahead of her.

"There is no plague," she replied. "And there is no God." Gasps at this, more murmurs and whispering. She raised her voice. "There is much I need to tell you all. But first, I want this obscenity torn down." She gestured towards the scaffold.

There was no reason for them to obey. She could have claimed God's blessing to command them, could have threatened them with the angels' wrath if they did not do her bidding. Could have bent the truth to suit her needs, just like every other despot.

"The angels will leave before sunset," came the voice in her mind. *"Do you really think you can control these fools without fear, without deceit?"*

I don't know, she thought, unsure whether James could detect the words. *I've trusted them with the truth — in turn, I will learn the truth about them.*

With a roar of approval, several people broke away from the crowd and sprinted towards the gallows. Others followed, and within minutes the structure had been smashed to pieces, the nooses ripped down and trampled underfoot like unwanted memories.

Thirty six

The dragon vanished from the sky, and James did not speak to Freya again.

She established a temporary headquarters in the Great Hall. From there she instructed the release of every prisoner, and that the food was brought in from the carts outside. The knights were asked, one by one, whether they wished to leave or remain; unanimously, they chose the latter.

She ordered that three of the now-empty wagons were loaded with the dead: one with the bones that Wilfred had heaped outside the gate, another with the bodies of those killed in the day's fighting, the last with the dreadful contents of Egbert's stores. Then she demanded that her three prisoners were brought before her. The trio traipsed dolefully into the chamber; stripped of his finery, Wilfred looked like the callous torturer she remembered, while without his armour Okada seemed diminished, dwarfed by the angel that stood guard over them. Egbert seemed broken and frightened, the colour still absent from his ashen flesh.

She allocated the first cart to Wilfred, Okada the second, and Egbert the third.

"These are the victims of your tyranny," she declared, feeling scoured of emotion. "Their bodies will not be entrusted to the angels. Instead, you will each bear your burden in a different direction, and bury them when you reach suitable soil, in line with the old traditions." Fragments of memory like this kept returning to her, of habits and customs long forgotten. "Then you will continue on your route until you are lost to the mist. You will be free, but not to return here. If you ever again seek to stain the Enclave with your presence, rest assured that you will have exhausted the limits of my mercy."

"Please, your grace!" begged Egbert, collapsing forwards onto his tear-streaked face. "They made me do it! I didn't want to ... I was only following orders!"

"Stop your snivelling," sneered Okada. "And be grateful that you aren't being roasted on your own skillet."

Wilfred said nothing. The torturer looked haunted, empty, drained like a cracked vessel. Like Frances, he seemed like someone inhabiting a dream.

Freya watched as they were led away to the courtyard, where their gruesome cargo awaited them.

The sun began to set as the people gathered on the battlements. They jeered as the three set out, pelting them with stones and insults, the more creative bringing scooped handfuls of filth from the Pit to hurl down at their chosen target. The sky blazed orange as the exiles trudged, the archers' arrows tracking them until they were out of range. A great cheer went up every time Egbert slipped and stumbled, and even Okada had to drop his wagon at one point when he became entangled in gorse thickets. Surprisingly, only Wilfred maintained a steadfast grip on his burden, hauling it with grim resignation, like a man yet to fully comprehend his fate.

When each had finally disappeared over three different horizons, the people constructed a bonfire in the square. On it they burnt the remains of the gallows, along with the throne Wilfred had installed in the Lord's tower, as well as his cloak and the other trappings of his brief and brutal rule. The torture chamber was raided next, its obscene instruments also tossed onto the blaze. The heat warmed the crowd in the dying sunlight. Some stayed to linger around the pyre, while others went back to the ramparts to watch the departure of the angels. As the creatures vanished into the swelling darkness, the onlookers prayed for their swift return, debating what their new queen had meant when she had said there was no God, and no plague, wondering whether their lives would ever be the same.

Maxwell and Victor oversaw all of this, the robot lashed to the Unskilled's chest by a makeshift harness Maxwell had constructed from some old belts.

"Do you think they'll come back?" Maxwell asked.

"Do you want them to?" the machine retorted.

Maxwell frowned. "But ... without them, what would we eat?"

"I used to live with someone who grew their own food."

"Ha! You must think I'm stupid."

"Not at all," replied Victor. "You seem very pleasant. In fact, I can think of many worse people to be attached to."

Maxwell laughed for what felt like the first time in an eternity.

Freya, meanwhile, missed all of this. After passing judgement on her prisoners, she hurried to the infirmary, where she sat at Errick's bedside, his withered hand clasped in hers. Frances had stitched his wounds and done everything else she could, but they didn't know whether he was going to recover. The knight's forehead burned with fever, while his hands and feet were deathly cold, a yellowish tinge making his skin look like old parchment.

"Please, Errick," Freya whispered, lifting his hand to her cheek. "I know you have suffered so much. But if I'm going to lead the Enclave, I need you beside me."

Errick's eyes moved beneath their lids, and she hoped his dreams showed him mercy.

***

The tournament rolled around again. It happened with a degree of regularity, although words like 'years' and 'anniversaries' had long since lost their meaning; the King simply decided that it was time, and his Royal Guard took up their staves and prepared to defend their livelihoods.

The knight knew he had competed many times before. He could tell by looking at the scabrous tissue that coated his palms; one scar for every time he had participated, so many that they had merged into a single mass of ruined flesh.

He had always reached the competition's final round, yet he had never won. Perhaps this would arouse suspicion, eventually. But other than the occasional suspicious glances of Phaedra, his perennial opponent, no-one seemed to mind. The Queen, certainly, seemed very happy to have him at her side.

He knew he had been happy too, once. There was a time when he'd wished for this cycle to go on forever. But now, as he stepped onto the platform, listening to the roar of the river's endless rage far beneath them, he felt a strange and urgent sensation, like something gnawing at his heart. The undeniable feeling that he was needed, desperately, somewhere else.

Opposite him stood Bellus, the brute who had upset the odds to vanquish Phaedra in the semi-finals. The monster was as cunning as he was strong, but Errick knew that he could defeat him, if he wanted to. This would not be required, of course; he looked at his queen, the beautiful Annalise, and knew that all he had to do was sustain the pretence of competition for a time, then pitch himself off the stage into defeat and blissful servitude.

And yet. The sensation still burned, clawing at his heart. *This is not your queen. Your true queen is somewhere else, and she needs you.*

He was so distracted that he almost missed Wolfram's signal, jerking out of his reverie as Bellus thundered towards him. He stepped smartly to one side, swinging his stave in a scything downward motion that struck his opponent in the shin, drawing a howl of pain from the giant as he staggered to a halt. *If I press the advantage now, I could drive him off the edge of the platform,* he thought; but then he glanced at Annalise once again, her eyes mesmerising and insistent, and he held back while Bellus recovered his composure.

Please, Errick. Please come back to me.

The feeling was almost like a voice, speaking to him, gentle but somehow audible above the tumult of the crowd, and the cacophony of the river below. A familiar voice, one that conjured feelings of immense, overwhelming love. He frowned, trying to focus as Bellus swung his own staff, blocking the blows easily but still staggered by their ferocity.

Please.

I need you.

His opponent's next move caught him by surprise, the big man drawing his stave backwards as though preparing for a huge arcing blow, but instead pitching the weapon like a javelin. Errick swatted it out of the air, but this left him vulnerable to Bellus's next attack, a vicious flying kick that caught Errick full in the chest. He grimaced as pain flared in his ribs, tumbling backwards towards the platform's edge.

This is as good a moment as any, he thought. *Your ribs might be broken, and your opponent has bested you convincingly. Just fall, and take your place at her side once again.*

But as he rolled over the precipice, he knew that this was not his fate. His arms flailed, the staff lost to the abyss, fingers clawing at the rim of the stage. They found purchase, digits screaming as they held him painfully suspended. It was then that he noticed that the netting was missing from the water below, and that the thundering river ran a deep, horrifying crimson.

Bellus loomed above him, untold evil in his triumphant smile.

"Let go, imbecile!" shrieked Annalise in a voice like shattering glass. "Let go, and stay with me forever! *I am your queen!*"

He clung, grimly, as Bellus raised a foot to stamp on his fingers.

Errick, please.

He jerked his hands outwards, the descending boot missing them, the blow so ferocious that it gouged a chunk out of the platform and sent it spinning into the broiling froth below. His wider grip made it harder to haul himself upwards, but adrenaline was coursing through him now, and he propelled himself over the edge of the stage, ploughing into Bellus like something clawing its way out of Hell.

"No!" roared the Queen, her voice like the sound of burning skin, like knives driven into innocent flesh. *No indeed,* his brain echoed. *You are* not *my queen.* He grappled with the man-monster, driving him back as he flung blow after blow into Bellus's ribs, his stomach, his jaw.

My queen is elsewhere, and she needs me.

Bellus swung a haymaker of his own, a colossal roundhouse punch that might have shattered Errick's skull. Errick ducked, avoiding the blow by millimetres, and then drove his knee mercilessly upwards into his opponent's unprotected groin. The giant gave a single, gurgling whimper, then sagged backwards. Errick watched as he disappeared through the hole at the centre of the stage.

The crowd roared their approval as Bellus fell. As one they rose to their feet, applauding, cheering, whooping.

All except Annalise. As the victor stared at her, breathing heavily, she shook her head in disgust. "You've failed me," she sneered. "I hereby banish you, traitor!"

But even as she spoke her proclamation, she began to fade, flickering like a candle flame. The phenomenon spread quickly to those nearby: the King, the monarchs' temporary bodyguards, the assembled nobles. Soon the entire audience had become a spectral, wraithlike memory of itself.

Deorsica, and the Great Well, and the hellish river at its base, dissipated like a dream. Soon Errick was alone, surrounded by only darkness.

He opened his eyes.

The first thing he saw was a very beautiful lady, whose face was bisected by a terrible scar. She looked very tired, but very happy.

The story of Freya, the Enclave, and the Scarred Earth will continue in Book Two.

About the author

Jon Richter lives in London, where he writes dark, gripping, and original thrillers in a variety of genres. His first novel, Deadly Burial, was published by HarperCollins, and he has since published six more thrillers and three horror anthologies. His novel, Rabbit Hole, was selected as the 2020 Book of the Year by bestselling international author Anita Waller. His books can be found at all good online retailers, and you can follow him on Twitter @RichterWrites. You can also find out more via Jon's website, www.jon-richter.com.

ROUNDFIRE
BOOKS

FICTION

Put simply, we publish great stories. Whether it's literary or
popular, a gentle tale or a pulsating thriller, the connecting theme
in all Roundfire fiction titles is that once you pick them up you
won't want to put them down.
If you have enjoyed this book, why not tell other readers by
posting a review on your preferred book site.

The Cause
Roderick Vincent
The second American Revolution will be a fire lit from
an internal spark.
Paperback: 978-1-78279-763-0 ebook: 978-1-78279-762-3

Don't Drink and Fly
The Story of Bernice O'Hanlon: Part One
Cathie Devitt
Bernice is a witch living in Glasgow. She loses her way in
her life and wanders off the beaten track looking for the garden
of enlightenment.
Paperback: 978-1-78279-016-7 ebook: 978-1-78279-015-0

Gag
Melissa Unger
One rainy afternoon in a Brooklyn diner, Peter Howland punctures
an egg with his fork. Repulsed, Peter pushes the plate away
and never eats again.
Paperback: 978-1-78279-564-3 ebook: 978-1-78279-563-6

The Master Yeshua
The Undiscovered Gospel of Joseph
Joyce Luck
Jesus is not who you think he is. The year is 75 CE. Joseph ben Jude
is frail and ailing, but he has a prophecy to fulfil …
Paperback: 978-1-78279-974-0 ebook: 978-1-78279-975-7

On the Far Side, There's a Boy
Paula Coston
Martine Haslett, a thirty-something 1980s woman, plays hard on the fringes of the London drag club scene until one night which prompts her to sign up to a charity. She writes to a young Sri Lankan boy, with consequences far and long.
Paperback: 978-1-78279-574-2 ebook: 978-1-78279-573-5

Tuareg
Alberto Vazquez-Figueroa
With over 5 million copies sold worldwide, *Tuareg* is a classic adventure story from best-selling author Alberto Vazquez-Figueroa, about honour, revenge and a clash of cultures.
Paperback: 978-1-84694-192-4

Readers of ebooks can buy or view any of these bestsellers by clicking on the live link in the title. Most titles are published in paperback and as an ebook. Paperbacks are available in traditional bookshops. Both print and ebook formats are available online.

Find more titles and sign up to our readers' newsletter at collectiveinkbooks.com

Follow us on Facebook at https://www.facebook.com/collectiveinkfiction
and Twitter at https://twitter.com/collectiveinkfiction